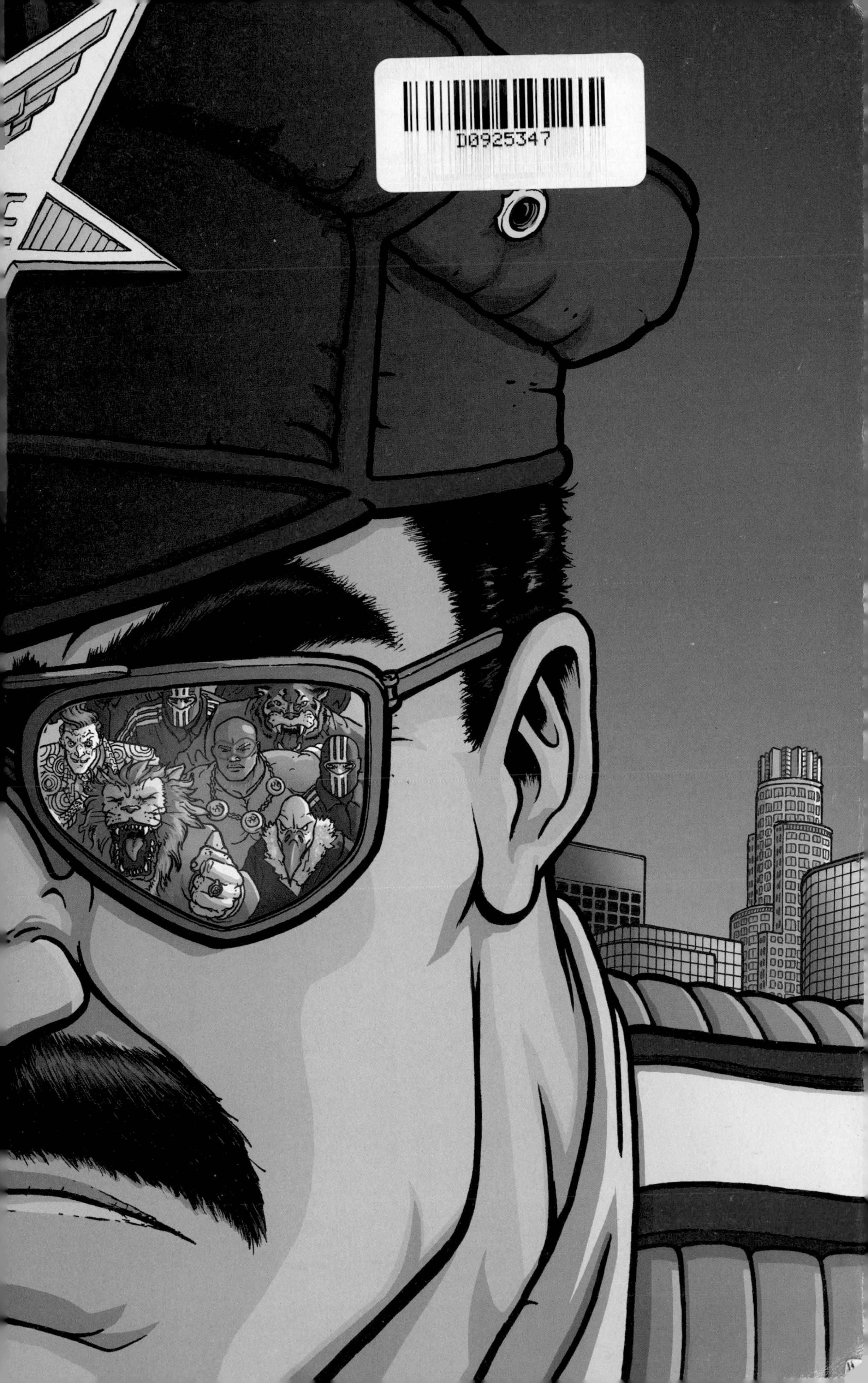

Think a
badge m
am the
chaos.
you. Yo
Besides

DOWNE starts up t

-- make

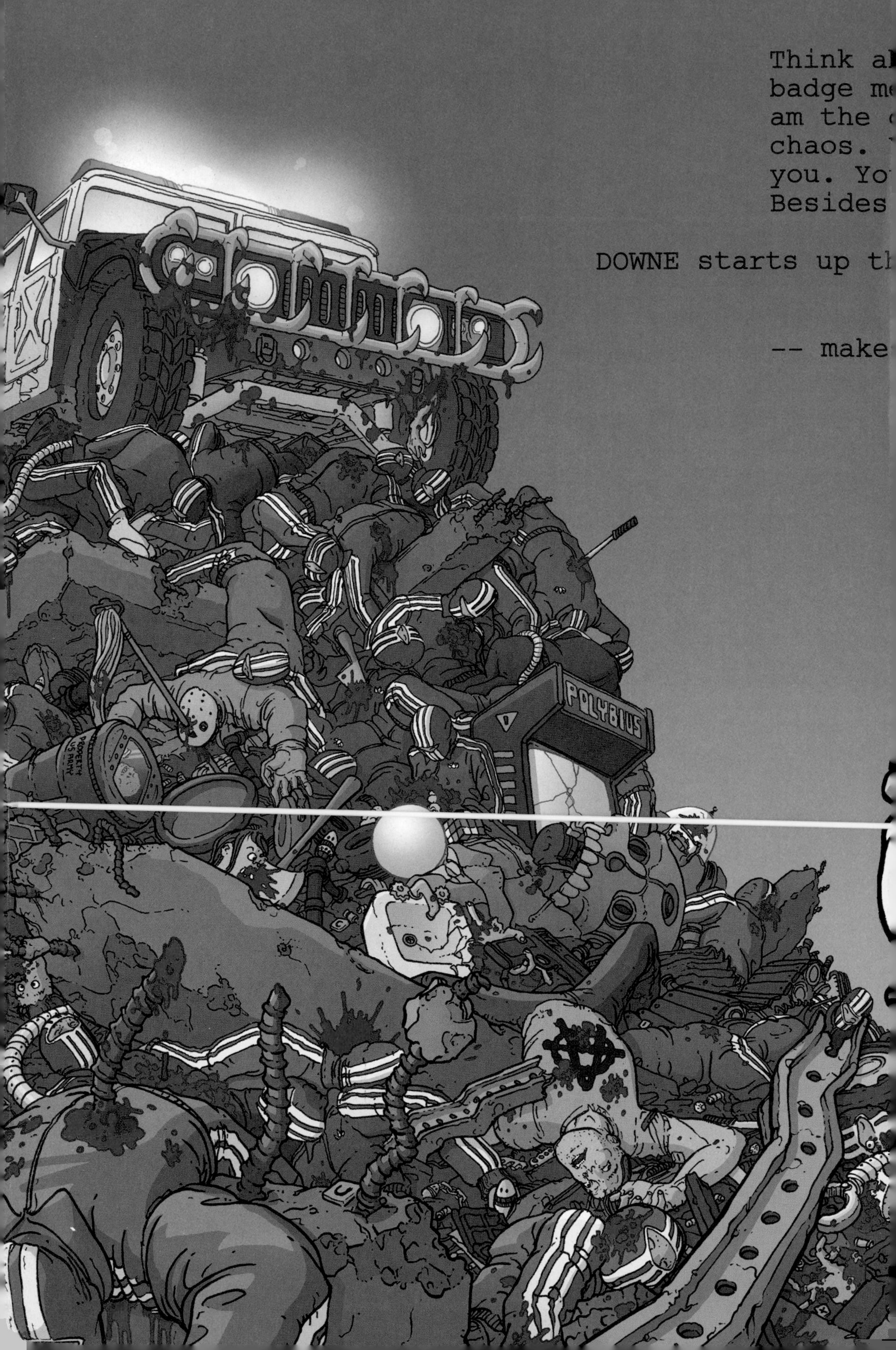

POLYBIUS

)WNE
it, shithead. This
something. It means I
 in a world filled with
e the chaos. All of
anged motherfuckers.
king your heads in --

airs. Smiles a bloody grin.

)WNE (CONT'D)
dick hard.

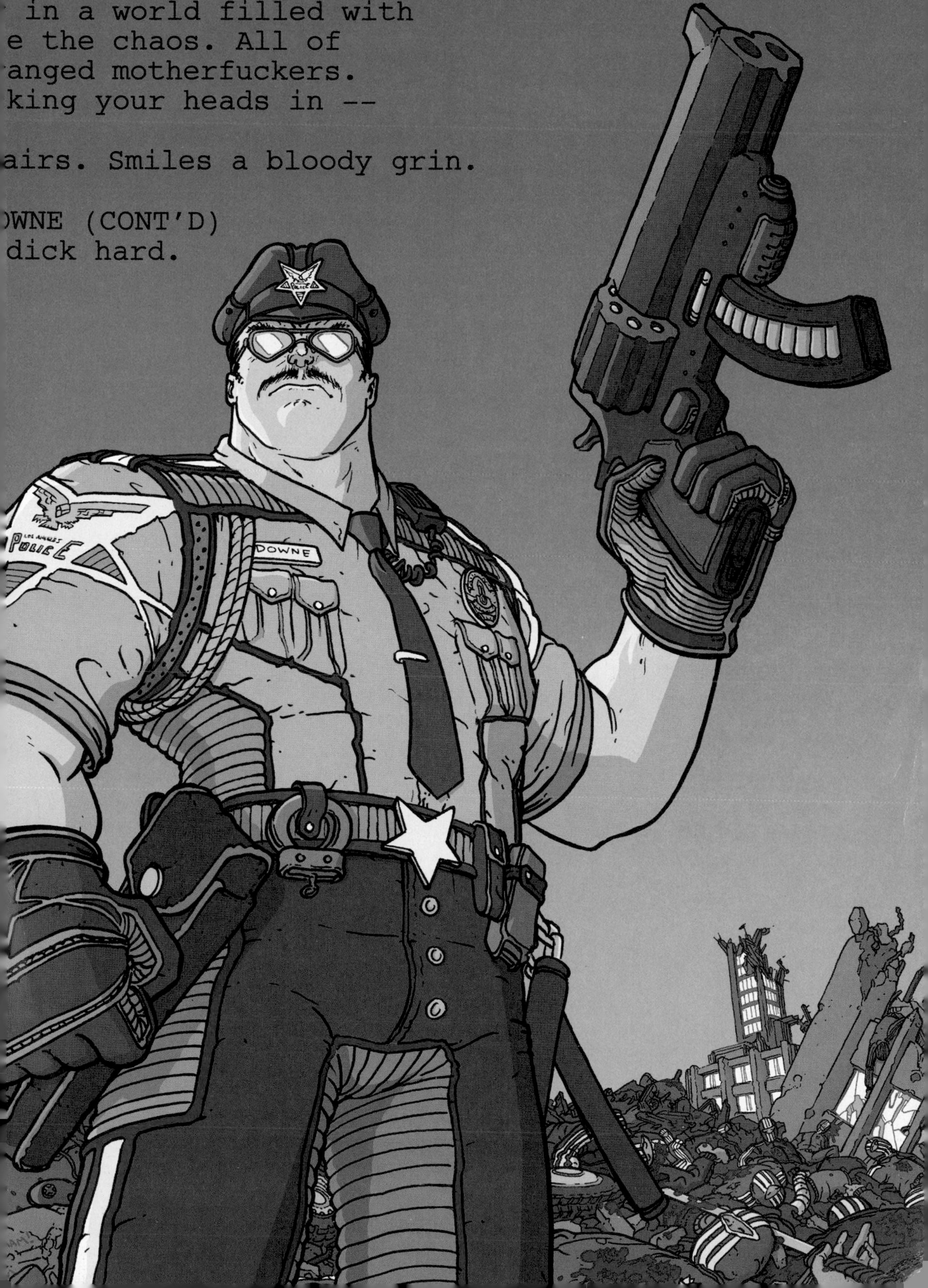
POLICE
DOWNE

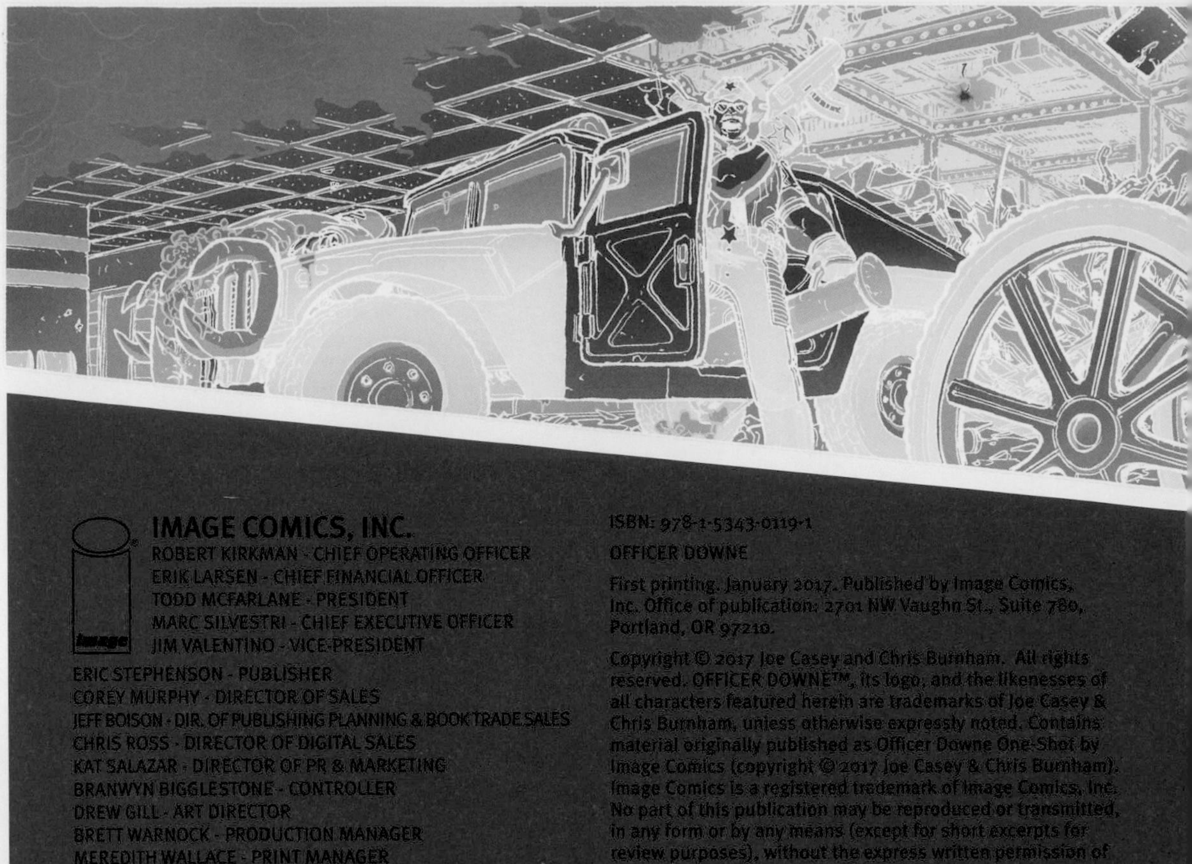


## IMAGE COMICS, INC.

ROBERT KIRKMAN - CHIEF OPERATING OFFICER
ERIK LARSEN - CHIEF FINANCIAL OFFICER
TODD MCFARLANE - PRESIDENT
MARC SILVESTRI - CHIEF EXECUTIVE OFFICER
JIM VALENTINO - VICE-PRESIDENT

ERIC STEPHENSON - PUBLISHER
COREY MURPHY - DIRECTOR OF SALES
JEFF BOISON - DIR. OF PUBLISHING PLANNING & BOOK TRADE SALES
CHRIS ROSS - DIRECTOR OF DIGITAL SALES
KAT SALAZAR - DIRECTOR OF PR & MARKETING
BRANWYN BIGGLESTONE - CONTROLLER
DREW GILL - ART DIRECTOR
BRETT WARNOCK - PRODUCTION MANAGER
MEREDITH WALLACE - PRINT MANAGER
BRIAH SKELLY - PUBLICIST
ALY HOFFMAN - CONVENTIONS & EVENT COORDINATOR
SASHA HEAD - SALES & MARKETING PRODUCTION DESIGNER
RANDY OKAMURA - DIGITAL PRODUCTION DESIGNER
DAVID BROTHERS - BRANDING MANAGER
MELISSA GIFFORD - CONTENT MANAGER
ERIKA SCHNATZ - PRODUCTION ARTIST
RYAN BREWER - PRODUCTION ARTIST
SHANNA MATUSZAK - PRODUCTION ARTIST
TRICIA RAMOS - PRODUCTION ARTIST
VINCENT KUKUA - PRODUCTION ARTIST
JEFF STANG - DIRECT MARKET SALES REPRESENTATIVE
EMILIO BAUTISTA - DIGITAL SALES ASSOCIATE
LEANNA CAUNTER - ACCOUNTING ASSISTANT
CHLOE RAMOS-PETERSON - LIBRARY MARKET SALES REPRESENTATIVE

IMAGECOMICS.COM

ISBN: 978-1-5343-0119-1

OFFICER DOWNE

First printing. January 2017. Published by Image Comics, Inc. Office of publication: 2701 NW Vaughn St., Suite 780, Portland, OR 97210.





Printed in the USA. For information regarding the CPSIA on this printed material call 203-595-3636 and provide the reference #RICH–719000.

For international licensing inquiries, write to: foreignlicensing@imagecomics.com


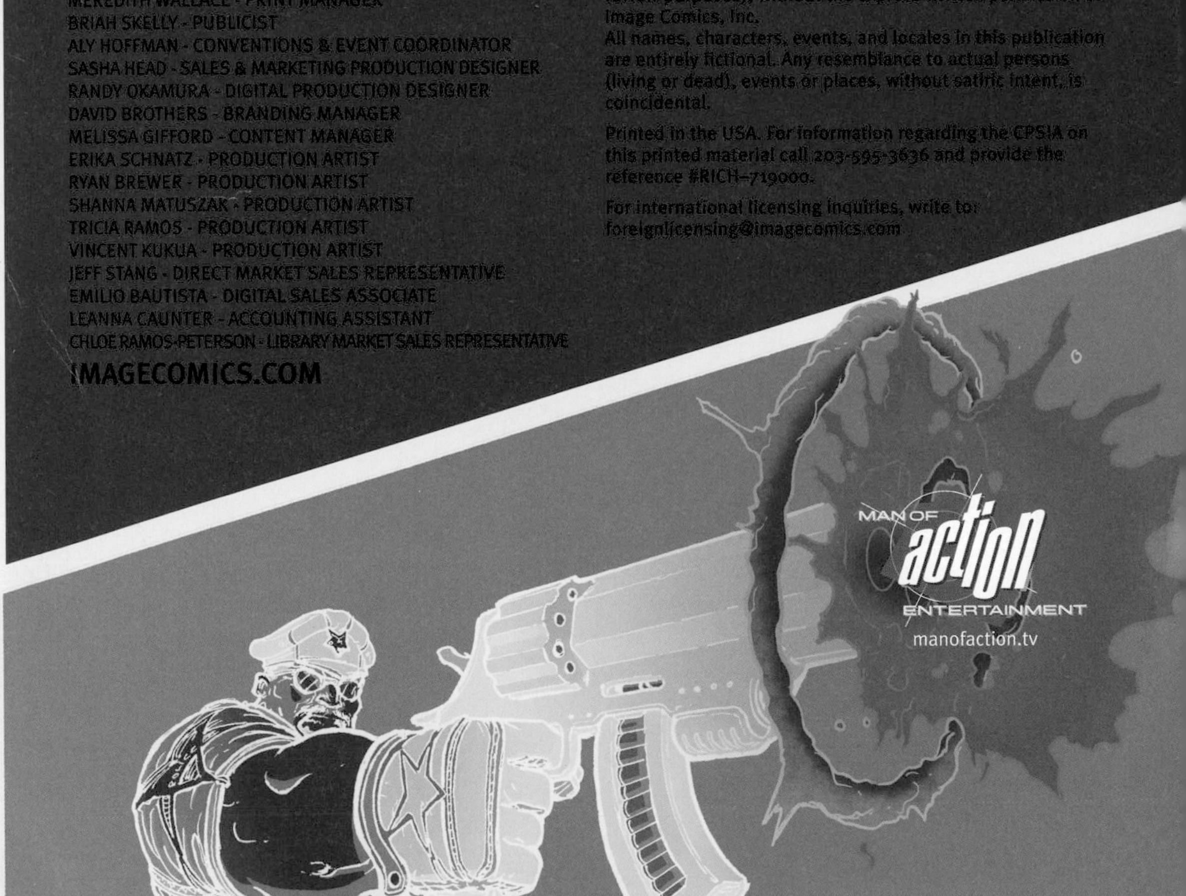

MAN OF action ENTERTAINMENT
manofaction.tv

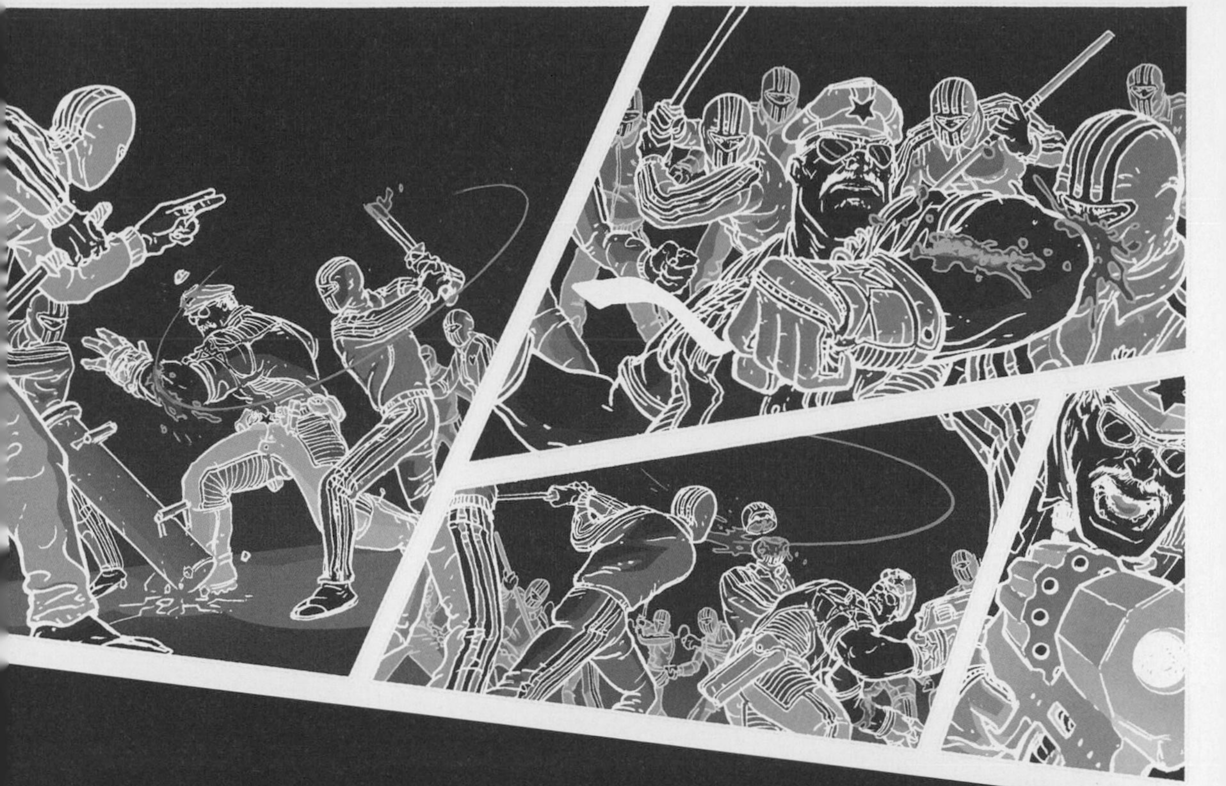

# OFFICER DOWNE

OFFICER DOWNE™ CREATED BY JOE CASEY & CHRIS BURNHAM

WRITER **JOE CASEY**
ARTIST **CHRIS BURNHAM**
COLOR **MARC LETZMANN**
LETTERS **RUS WOOTON**
LOGO & BOOK DESIGN **SONIA HARRIS**

SPECIAL THANKS TO MEADOW WILLIAMS



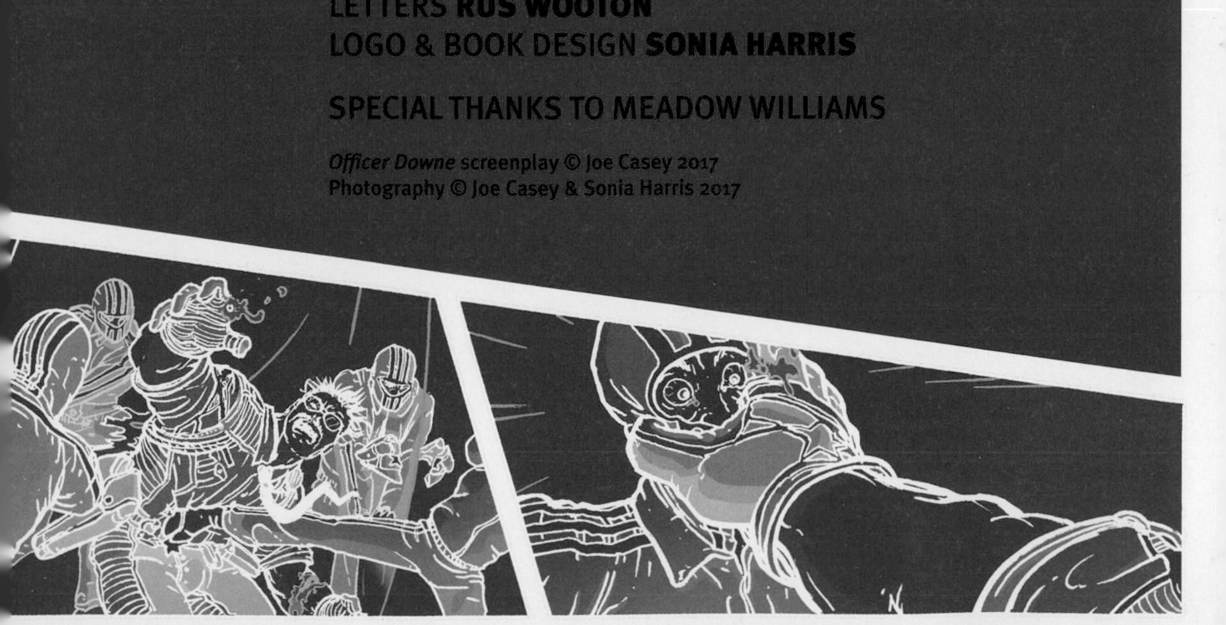

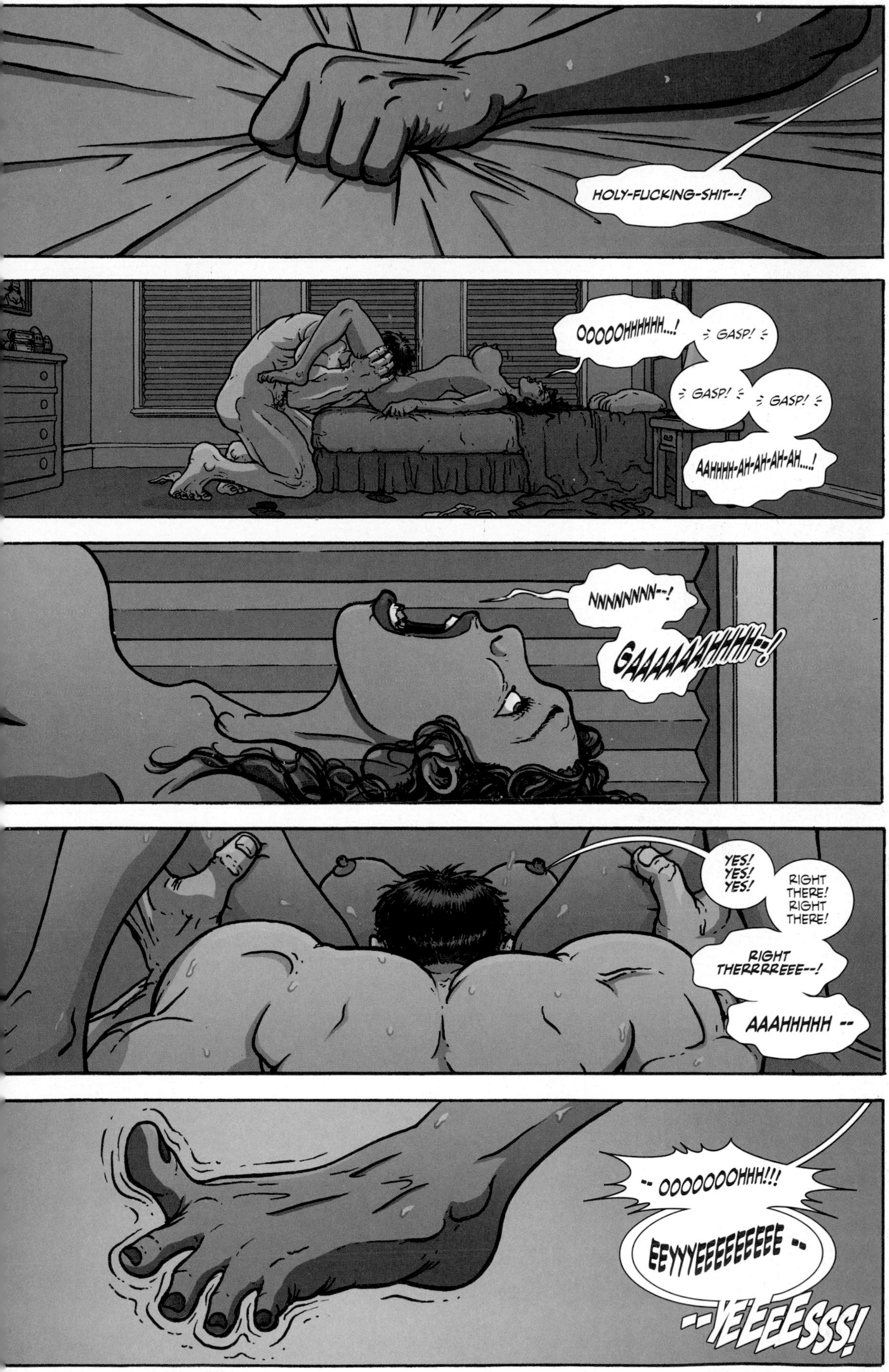
HOLY-FUCKING-SHIT--!
OOOOOHHHHHH...!
GASP!
GASP!
GASP!
AAHHHH-AH-AH-AH-AH...!
NNNNNNNN--!
GAAAAAAHHHH--!
YES! YES! YES!
RIGHT THERE! RIGHT THERE!
RIGHT THERRRREEE--!
AAAHHHHH --
-- OOOOOOOHHH!!!
EEYYYEEEEEEEE --
--YEEEESSS!

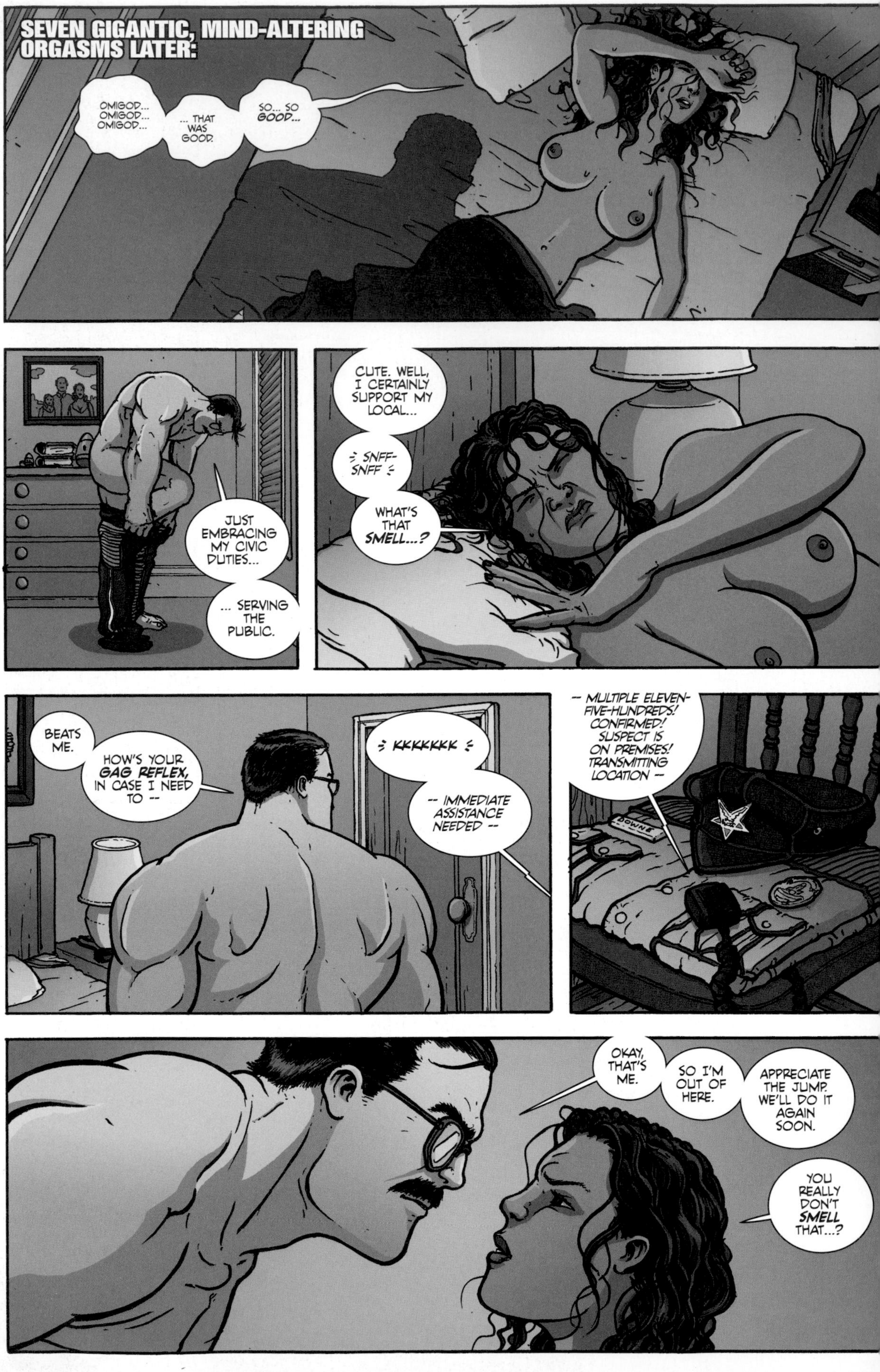
SEVEN GIGANTIC, MIND-ALTERING ORGASMS LATER:
OMIGOD... OMIGOD... OMIGOD...
... THAT WAS GOOD.
SO... SO GOOD...
JUST EMBRACING MY CIVIC DUTIES...
... SERVING THE PUBLIC.
CUTE. WELL, I CERTAINLY SUPPORT MY LOCAL...
SNFF-SNFF
WHAT'S THAT SMELL...?
BEATS ME.
HOW'S YOUR GAG REFLEX, IN CASE I NEED TO --
KKKKKKK
-- IMMEDIATE ASSISTANCE NEEDED --
-- MULTIPLE ELEVEN-FIVE-HUNDREDS! CONFIRMED! SUSPECT IS ON PREMISES! TRANSMITTING LOCATION --
DOWNE
OKAY, THAT'S ME.
SO I'M OUT OF HERE.
APPRECIATE THE JUMP. WE'LL DO IT AGAIN SOON.
YOU REALLY DON'T SMELL THAT...?

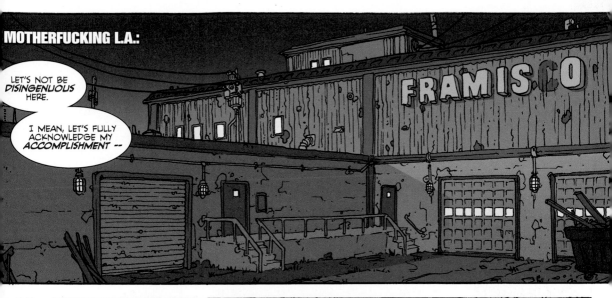

**MOTHERFUCKING L.A.:**

LET'S NOT BE *DISINGENUOUS* HERE.

I MEAN, LET'S FULLY ACKNOWLEDGE MY *ACCOMPLISHMENT* --

-- THIS SHIT IS *TOO GOOD!*

ONE TASTE OF THIS NEW FORMULA *SUPER-CRANK* AND THIS WHOLE *CITY'LL* BE SUCKING ME OFF, HUNGRY FOR MORE!

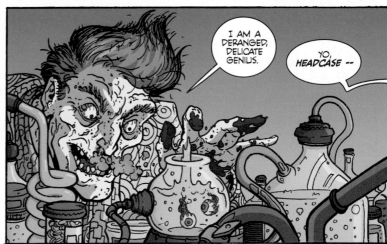

I AM A DERANGED, DELICATE GENIUS.

YO, *HEADCASE* --

-- YOU *HEAR* THAT? SOMETHING *OUTSIDE...*

YOU EXPECTING COMPANY OR WHAT?!

DON'T CALL ME THAT.

IT'S "HARRY", NOT --

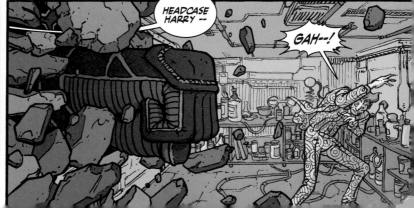

HEADCASE HARRY --

*GAH--!*

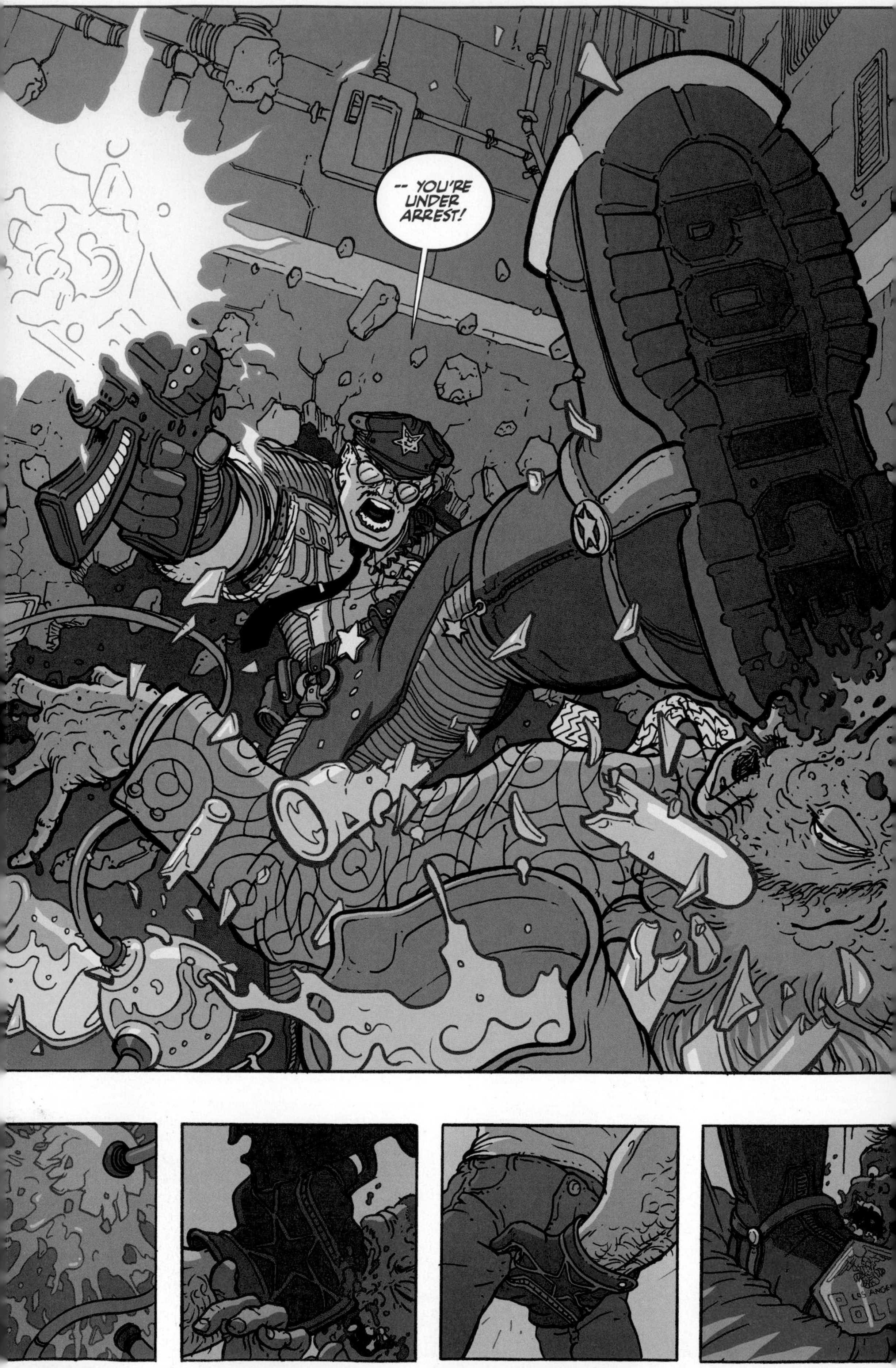
-- YOU'RE UNDER ARREST!

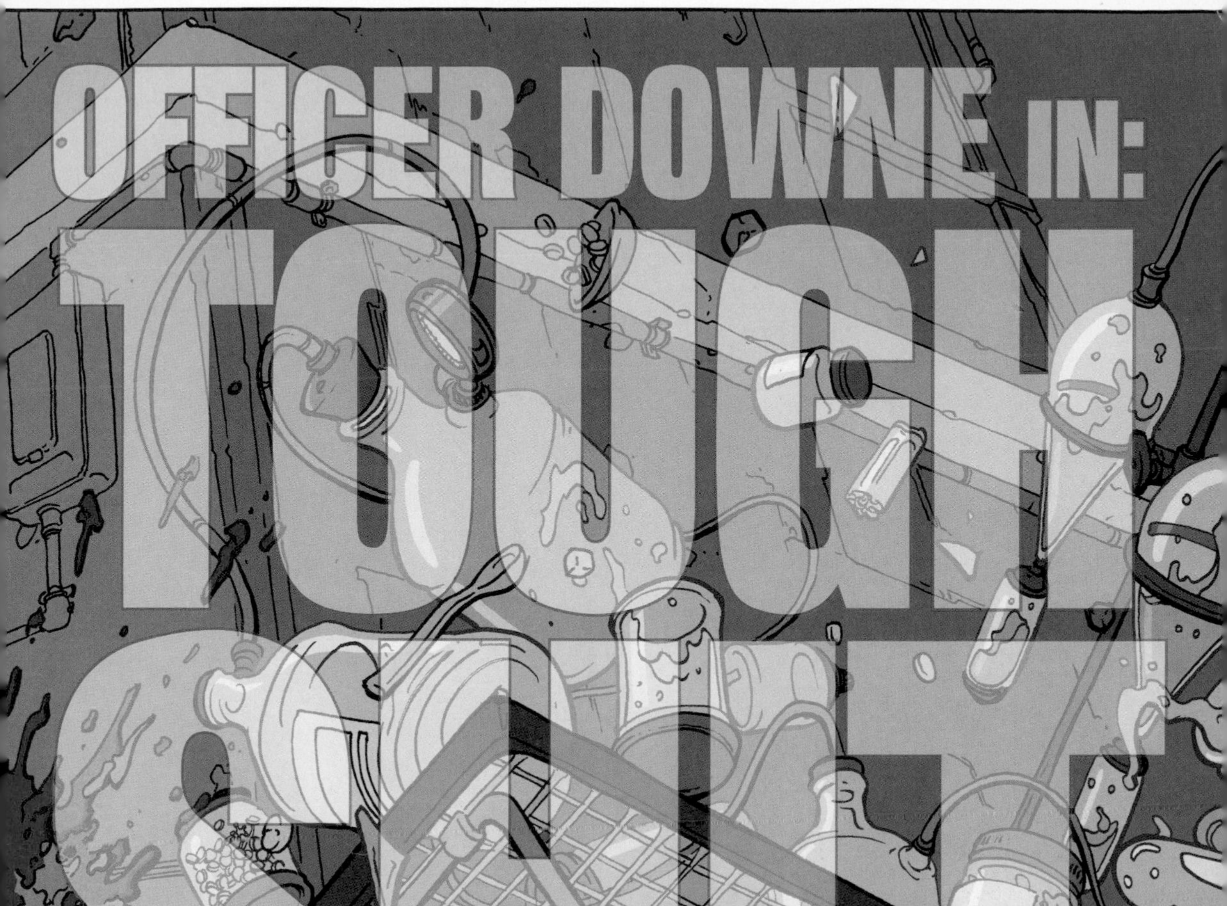
OFFICER DOWNE IN:
TOUGH SHIT
BY JOE CASEY AND CHRIS BURNHAM
WITH MARC LETZMANN: COLORS + RUS WOOTON: LETTERS

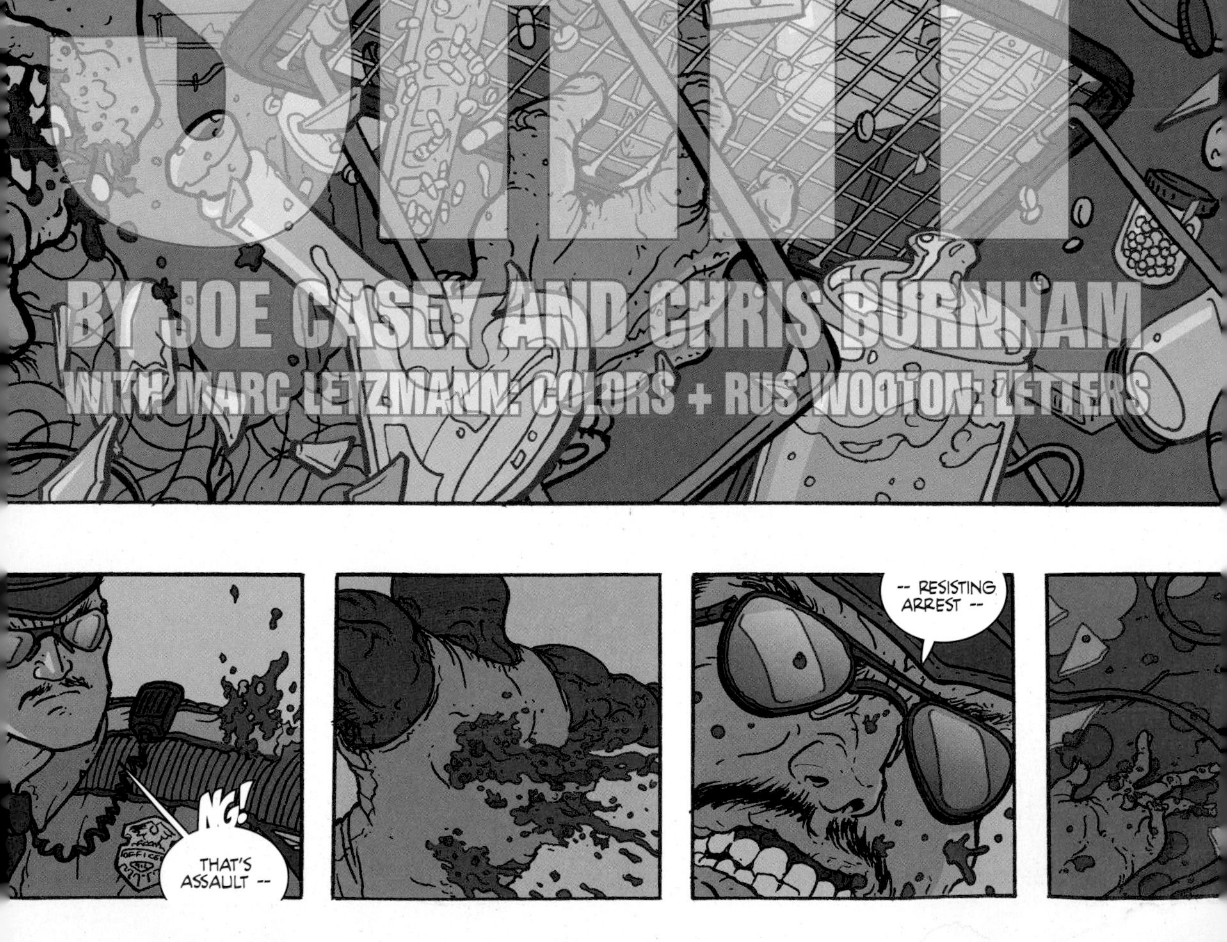
NG!
THAT'S ASSAULT --
-- RESISTING ARREST --

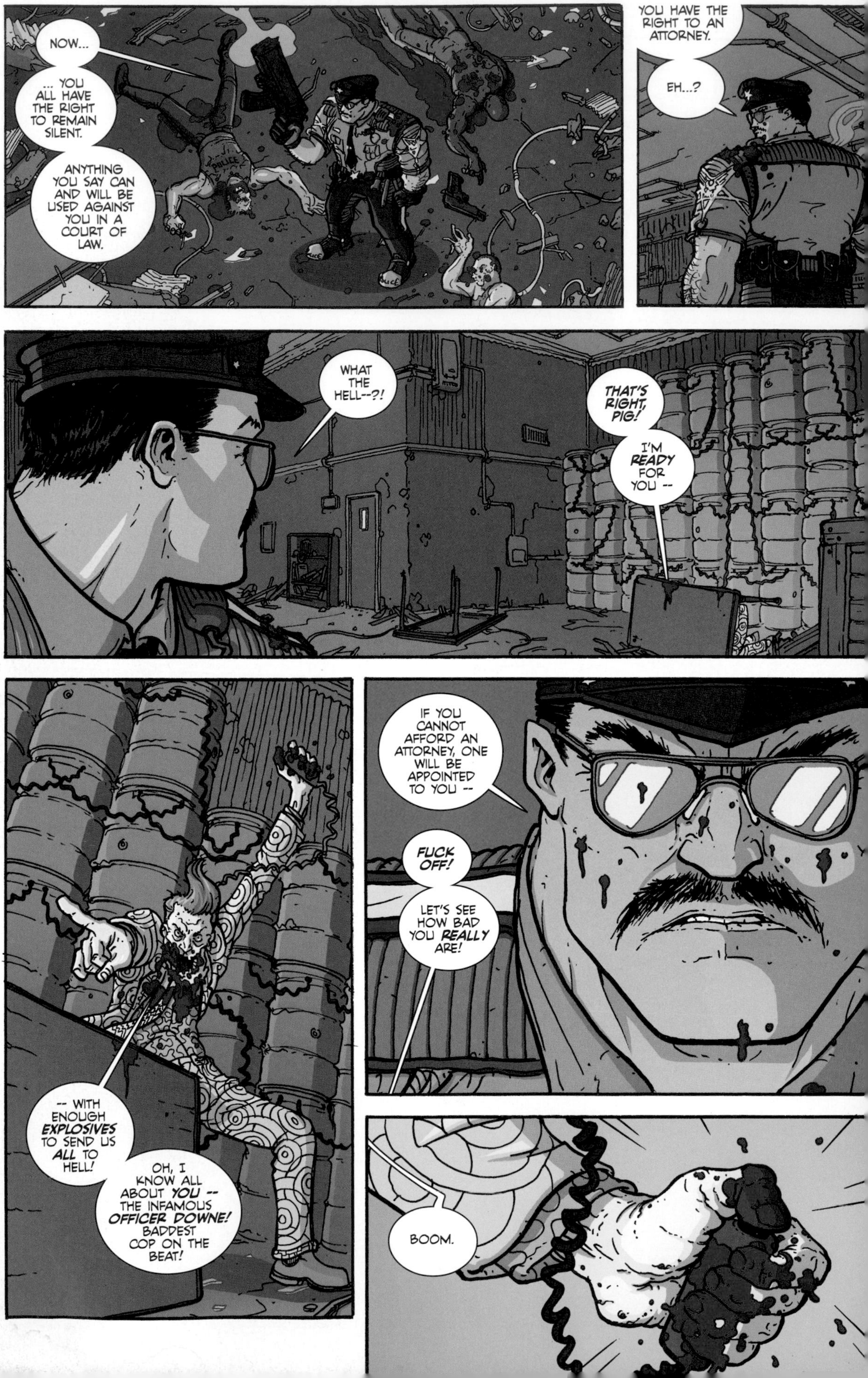
NOW...
... YOU ALL HAVE THE RIGHT TO REMAIN SILENT.
ANYTHING YOU SAY CAN AND WILL BE USED AGAINST YOU IN A COURT OF LAW.
POLICE
YOU HAVE THE RIGHT TO AN ATTORNEY.
EH...?
WHAT THE HELL--?!
THAT'S RIGHT, PIG!
I'M READY FOR YOU --
-- WITH ENOUGH EXPLOSIVES TO SEND US ALL TO HELL!
OH, I KNOW ALL ABOUT YOU -- THE INFAMOUS OFFICER DOWNE! BADDEST COP ON THE BEAT!
IF YOU CANNOT AFFORD AN ATTORNEY, ONE WILL BE APPOINTED TO YOU --
FUCK OFF!
LET'S SEE HOW BAD YOU REALLY ARE!
BOOM.

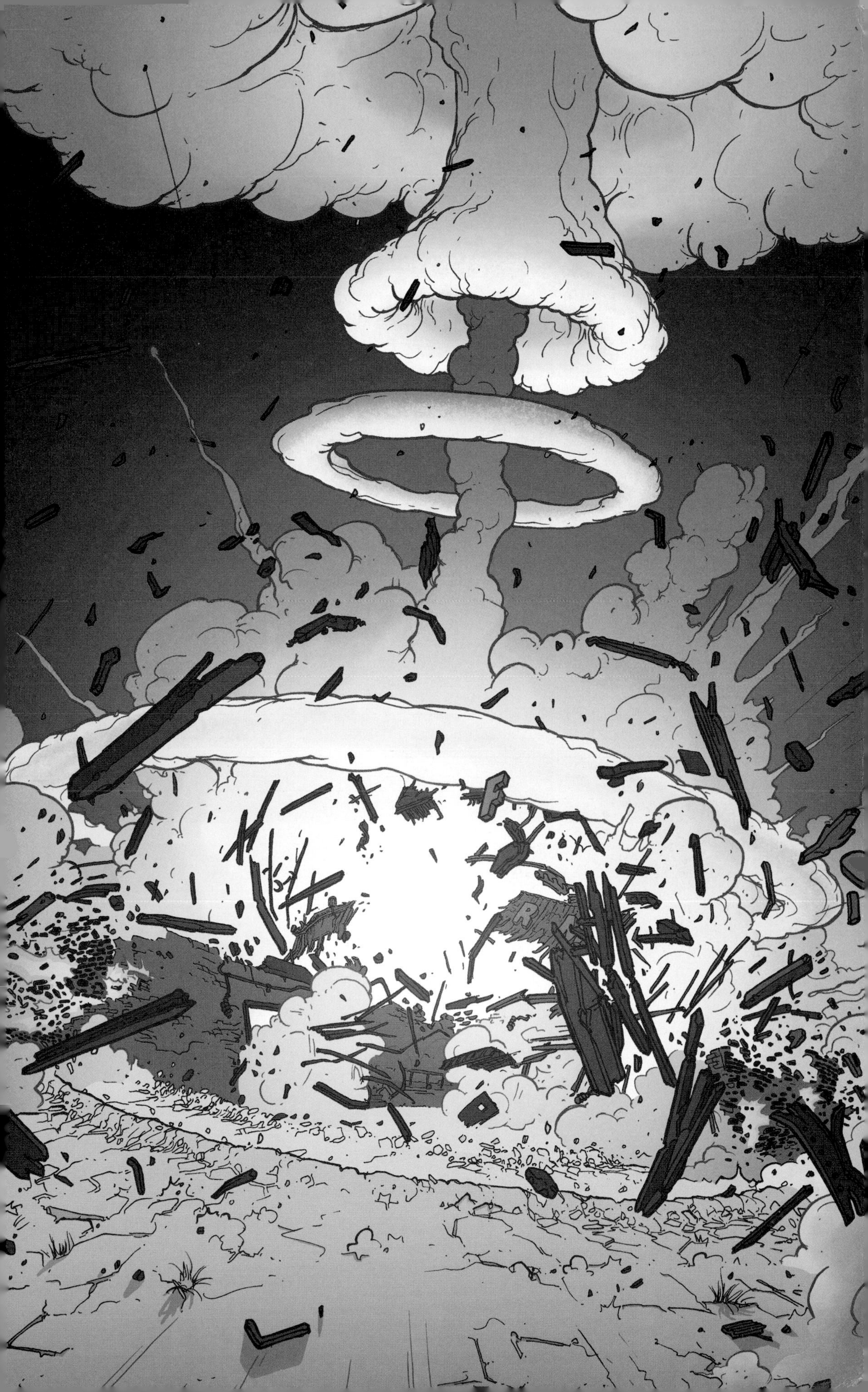

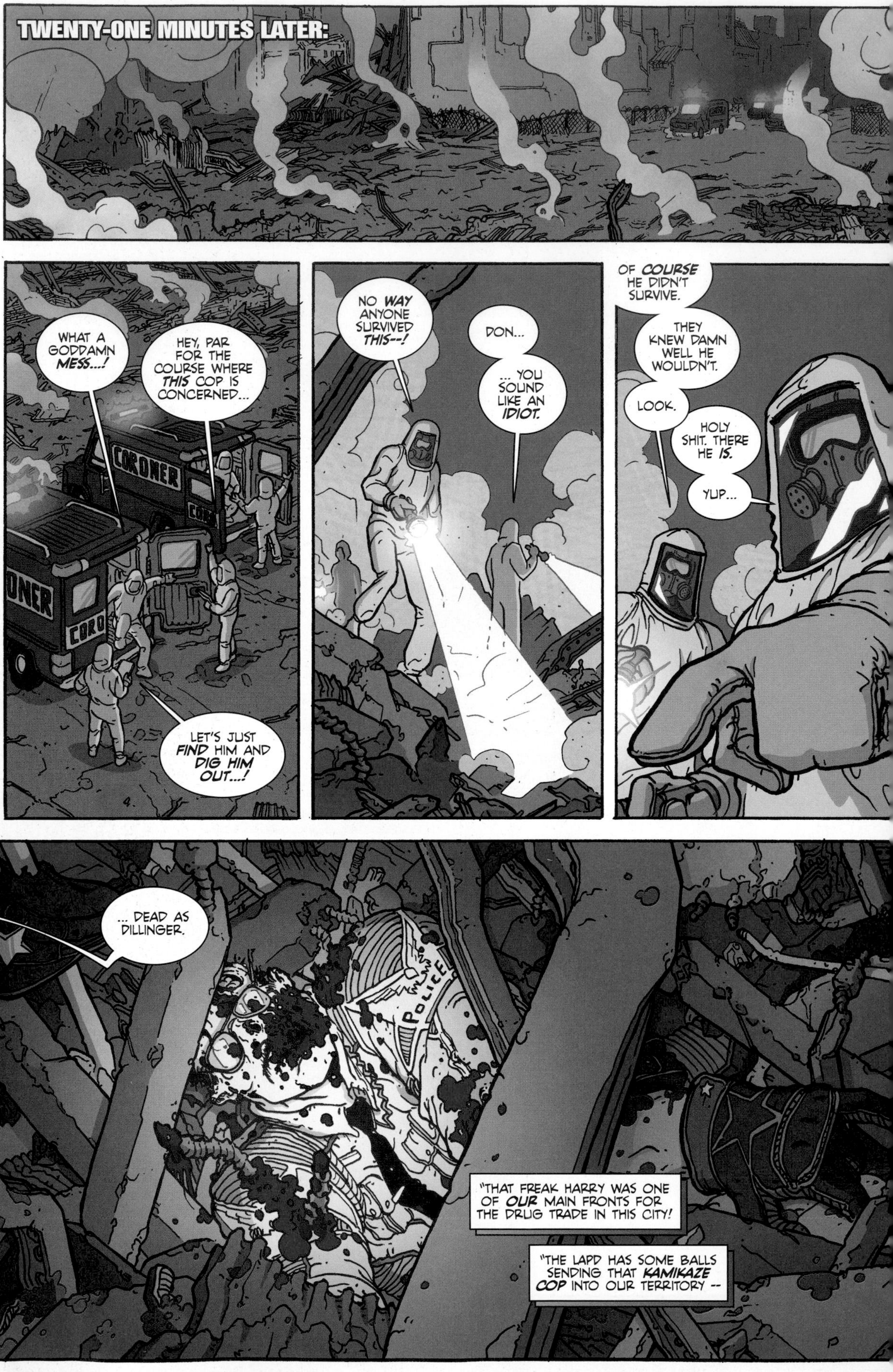
TWENTY-ONE MINUTES LATER:
WHAT A GODDAMN MESS...!
HEY, PAR FOR THE COURSE WHERE THIS COP IS CONCERNED...
CORONER
LET'S JUST FIND HIM AND DIG HIM OUT...!
NO WAY ANYONE SURVIVED THIS--!
DON...
... YOU SOUND LIKE AN IDIOT.
OF COURSE HE DIDN'T SURVIVE.
THEY KNEW DAMN WELL HE WOULDN'T.
LOOK.
HOLY SHIT. THERE HE IS.
YUP...
... DEAD AS DILLINGER.
POLICE
"THAT FREAK HARRY WAS ONE OF OUR MAIN FRONTS FOR THE DRUG TRADE IN THIS CITY!
"THE LAPD HAS SOME BALLS SENDING THAT KAMIKAZE COP INTO OUR TERRITORY --

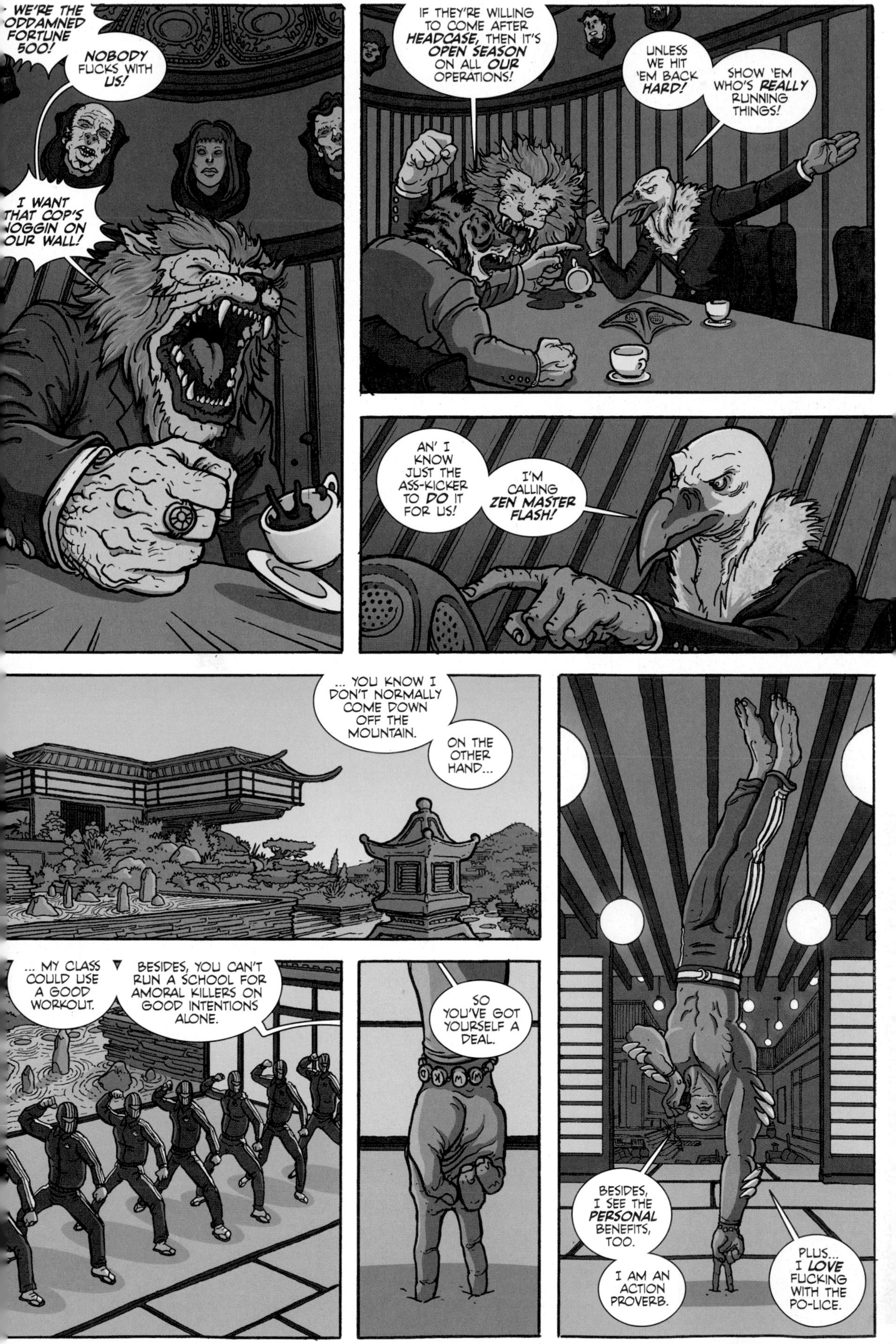
WE'RE THE ODDAMNED FORTUNE 500!
NOBODY FUCKS WITH US!
I WANT THAT COP'S NOGGIN ON OUR WALL!
IF THEY'RE WILLING TO COME AFTER HEADCASE, THEN IT'S OPEN SEASON ON ALL OUR OPERATIONS!
UNLESS WE HIT 'EM BACK HARD!
SHOW 'EM WHO'S REALLY RUNNING THINGS!
AN' I KNOW JUST THE ASS-KICKER TO DO IT FOR US!
I'M CALLING ZEN MASTER FLASH!
... YOU KNOW I DON'T NORMALLY COME DOWN OFF THE MOUNTAIN.
ON THE OTHER HAND...
... MY CLASS COULD USE A GOOD WORKOUT.
BESIDES, YOU CAN'T RUN A SCHOOL FOR AMORAL KILLERS ON GOOD INTENTIONS ALONE.
SO YOU'VE GOT YOURSELF A DEAL.
BESIDES, I SEE THE PERSONAL BENEFITS, TOO.
I AM AN ACTION PROVERB.
PLUS... I LOVE FUCKING WITH THE PO-LICE.

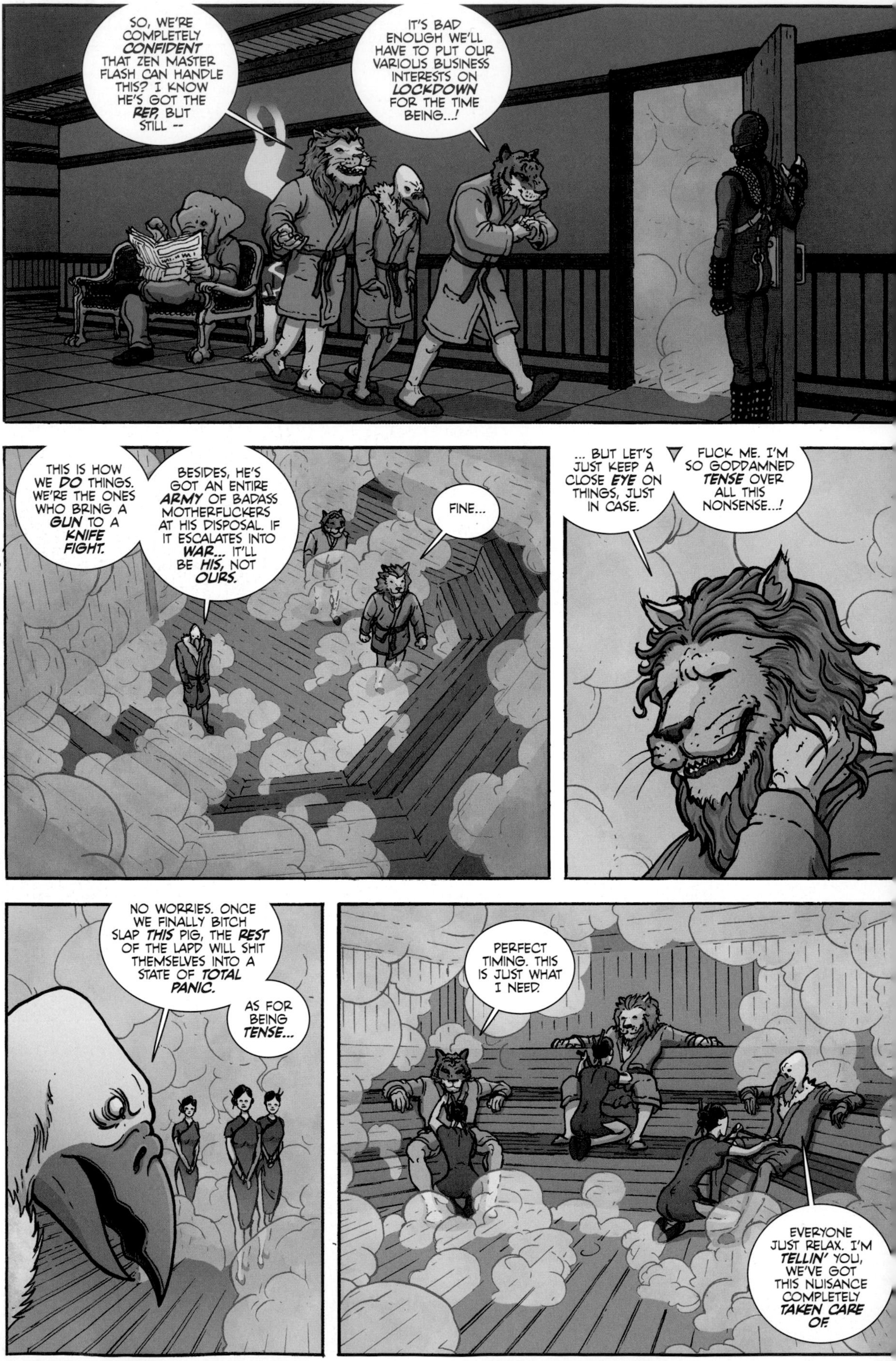
SO, WE'RE COMPLETELY CONFIDENT THAT ZEN MASTER FLASH CAN HANDLE THIS? I KNOW HE'S GOT THE REP, BUT STILL --
IT'S BAD ENOUGH WE'LL HAVE TO PUT OUR VARIOUS BUSINESS INTERESTS ON LOCKDOWN FOR THE TIME BEING...!
THIS IS HOW WE DO THINGS. WE'RE THE ONES WHO BRING A GUN TO A KNIFE FIGHT.
BESIDES, HE'S GOT AN ENTIRE ARMY OF BADASS MOTHERFUCKERS AT HIS DISPOSAL. IF IT ESCALATES INTO WAR... IT'LL BE HIS, NOT OURS.
FINE...
... BUT LET'S JUST KEEP A CLOSE EYE ON THINGS, JUST IN CASE.
FUCK ME. I'M SO GODDAMNED TENSE OVER ALL THIS NONSENSE...!
NO WORRIES. ONCE WE FINALLY BITCH SLAP THIS PIG, THE REST OF THE LAPD WILL SHIT THEMSELVES INTO A STATE OF TOTAL PANIC.
AS FOR BEING TENSE...
PERFECT TIMING. THIS IS JUST WHAT I NEED.
EVERYONE JUST RELAX. I'M TELLIN' YOU, WE'VE GOT THIS NUISANCE COMPLETELY TAKEN CARE OF.

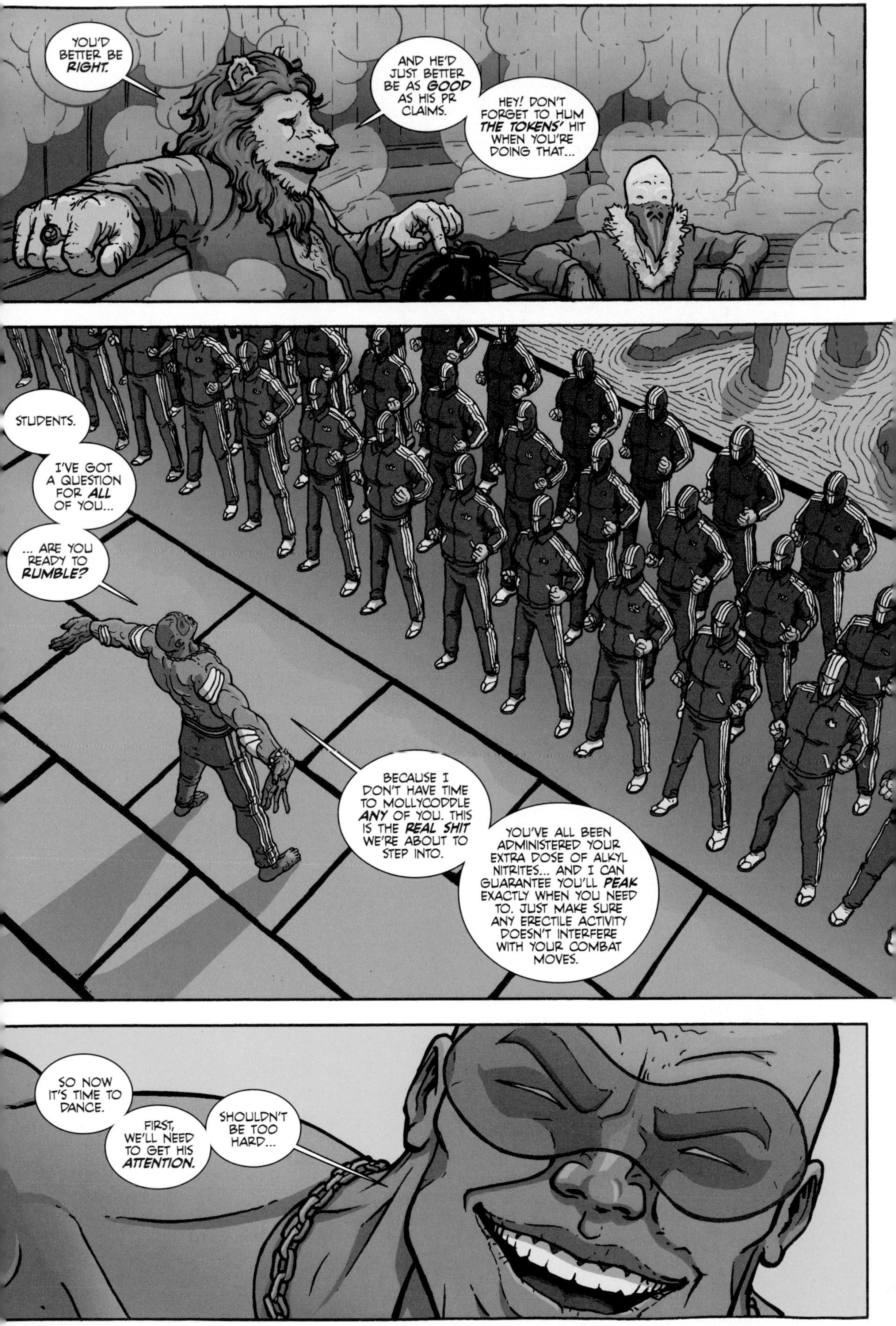
YOU'D BETTER BE RIGHT.
AND HE'D JUST BETTER BE AS GOOD AS HIS PR CLAIMS.
HEY! DON'T FORGET TO HUM THE TOKENS' HIT WHEN YOU'RE DOING THAT...
STUDENTS.
I'VE GOT A QUESTION FOR ALL OF YOU...
... ARE YOU READY TO RUMBLE?
BECAUSE I DON'T HAVE TIME TO MOLLYCODDLE ANY OF YOU. THIS IS THE REAL SHIT WE'RE ABOUT TO STEP INTO.
YOU'VE ALL BEEN ADMINISTERED YOUR EXTRA DOSE OF ALKYL NITRITES... AND I CAN GUARANTEE YOU'LL PEAK EXACTLY WHEN YOU NEED TO. JUST MAKE SURE ANY ERECTILE ACTIVITY DOESN'T INTERFERE WITH YOUR COMBAT MOVES.
SO NOW IT'S TIME TO DANCE.
FIRST, WE'LL NEED TO GET HIS ATTENTION.
SHOULDN'T BE TOO HARD...

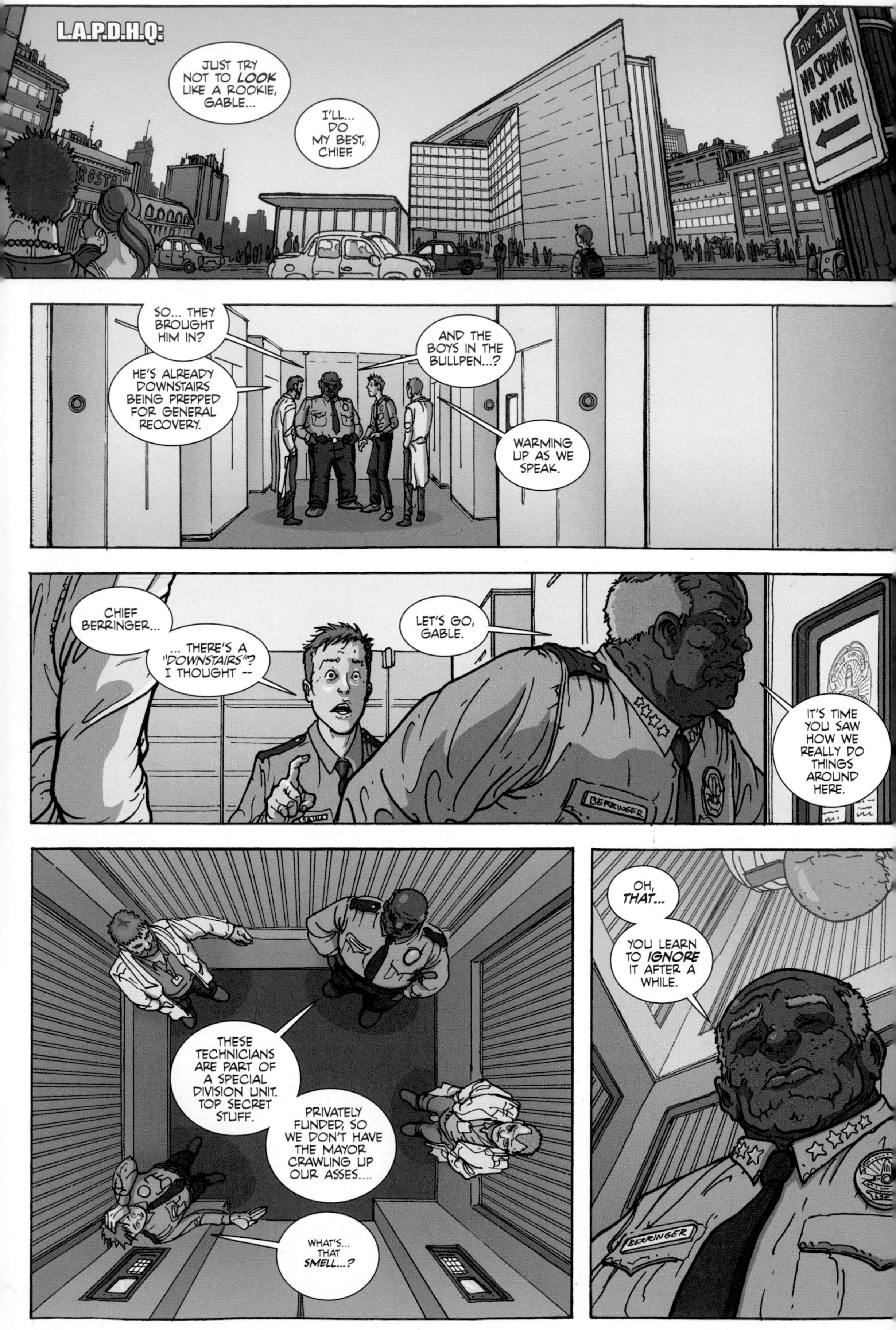
L.A.P.D.H.Q:
JUST TRY NOT TO LOOK LIKE A ROOKIE, GABLE...
I'LL... DO MY BEST, CHIEF.
TOW-AWAY NO STOPPING ANY TIME
SO... THEY BROUGHT HIM IN?
HE'S ALREADY DOWNSTAIRS BEING PREPPED FOR GENERAL RECOVERY.
AND THE BOYS IN THE BULLPEN...?
WARMING UP AS WE SPEAK.
CHIEF BERRINGER...
... THERE'S A "DOWNSTAIRS"? I THOUGHT --
LET'S GO, GABLE.
IT'S TIME YOU SAW HOW WE REALLY DO THINGS AROUND HERE.
BERRINGER
THESE TECHNICIANS ARE PART OF A SPECIAL DIVISION UNIT. TOP SECRET STUFF.
PRIVATELY FUNDED, SO WE DON'T HAVE THE MAYOR CRAWLING UP OUR ASSES....
WHAT'S... THAT SMELL...?
OH, THAT...
YOU LEARN TO IGNORE IT AFTER A WHILE.
BERRINGER

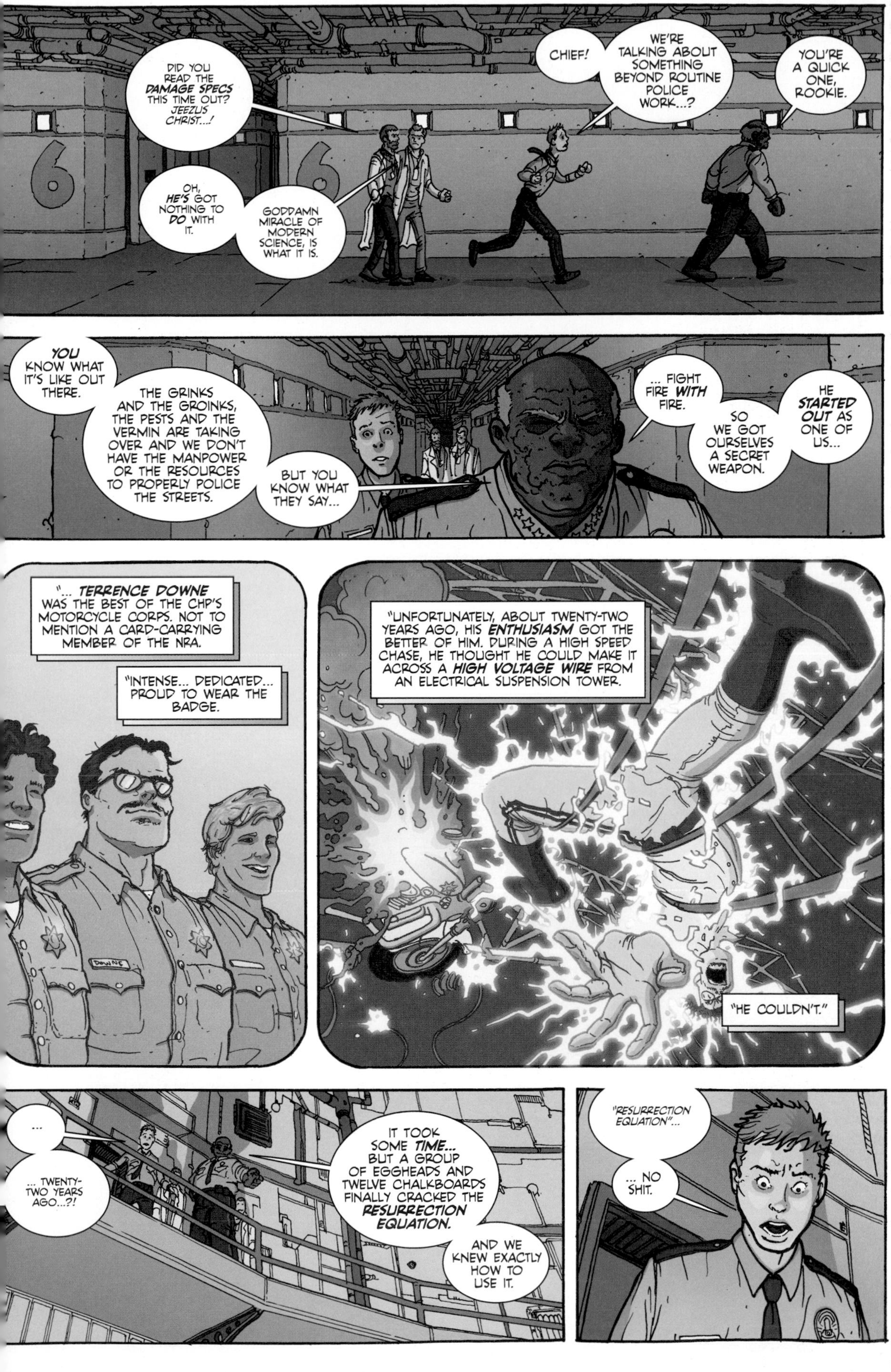
DID YOU READ THE DAMAGE SPECS THIS TIME OUT? JEEZUS CHRIST...!
OH, HE'S GOT NOTHING TO DO WITH IT.
GODDAMN MIRACLE OF MODERN SCIENCE, IS WHAT IT IS.
CHIEF!
WE'RE TALKING ABOUT SOMETHING BEYOND ROUTINE POLICE WORK...?
YOU'RE A QUICK ONE, ROOKIE.
YOU KNOW WHAT IT'S LIKE OUT THERE.
THE GRINKS AND THE GROINKS, THE PESTS AND THE VERMIN ARE TAKING OVER AND WE DON'T HAVE THE MANPOWER OR THE RESOURCES TO PROPERLY POLICE THE STREETS.
BUT YOU KNOW WHAT THEY SAY...
... FIGHT FIRE WITH FIRE.
SO WE GOT OURSELVES A SECRET WEAPON.
HE STARTED OUT AS ONE OF US...
"... TERRENCE DOWNE WAS THE BEST OF THE CHP'S MOTORCYCLE CORPS. NOT TO MENTION A CARD-CARRYING MEMBER OF THE NRA.
"INTENSE... DEDICATED... PROUD TO WEAR THE BADGE.
DOWNE
"UNFORTUNATELY, ABOUT TWENTY-TWO YEARS AGO, HIS ENTHUSIASM GOT THE BETTER OF HIM. DURING A HIGH SPEED CHASE, HE THOUGHT HE COULD MAKE IT ACROSS A HIGH VOLTAGE WIRE FROM AN ELECTRICAL SUSPENSION TOWER.
"HE COULDN'T."
...
... TWENTY-TWO YEARS AGO...?!
IT TOOK SOME TIME... BUT A GROUP OF EGGHEADS AND TWELVE CHALKBOARDS FINALLY CRACKED THE RESURRECTION EQUATION.
AND WE KNEW EXACTLY HOW TO USE IT.
"RESURRECTION EQUATION"...
... NO SHIT.

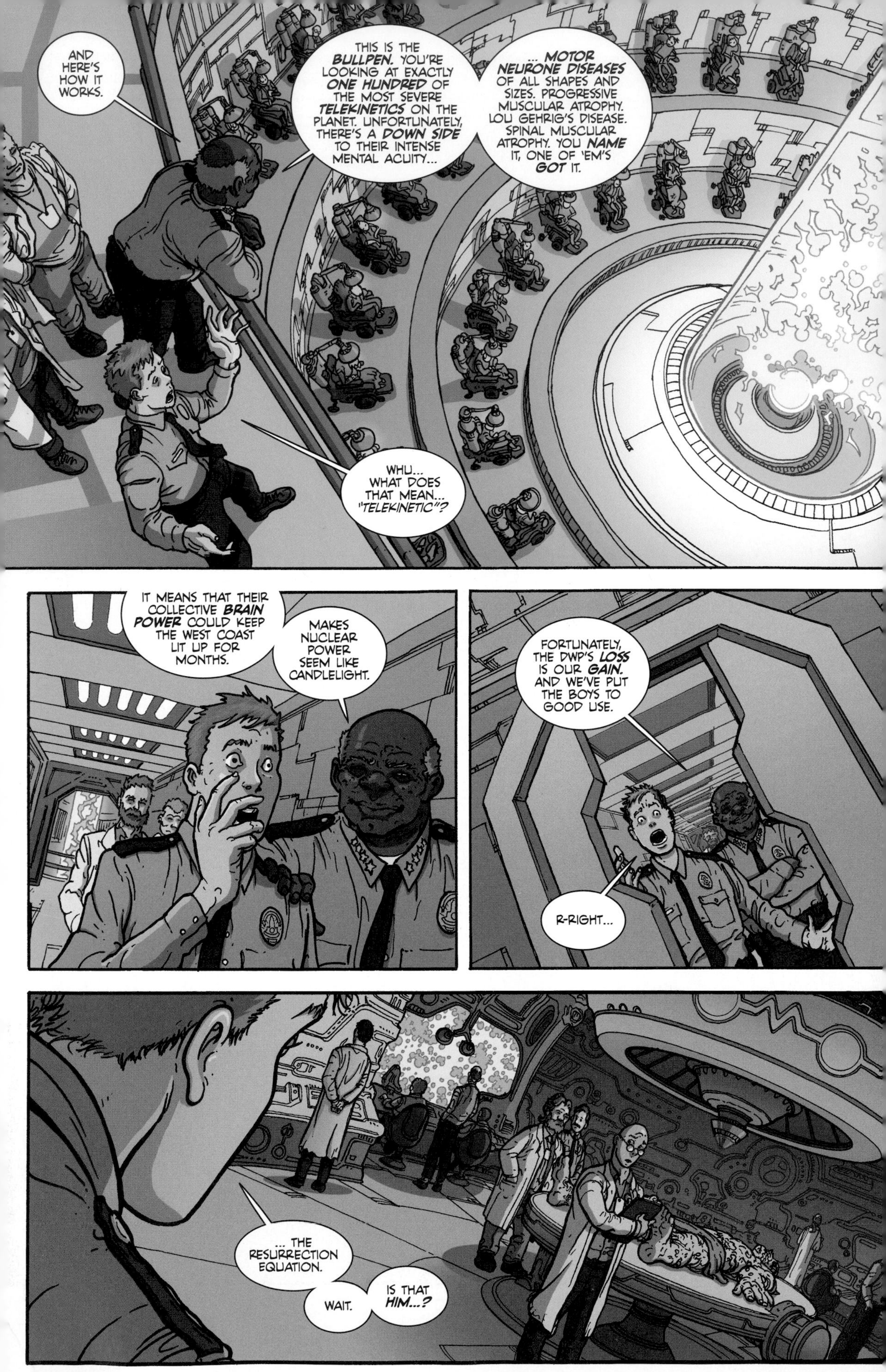
AND HERE'S HOW IT WORKS.
THIS IS THE BULLPEN. YOU'RE LOOKING AT EXACTLY ONE HUNDRED OF THE MOST SEVERE TELEKINETICS ON THE PLANET. UNFORTUNATELY, THERE'S A DOWN SIDE TO THEIR INTENSE MENTAL ACUITY...
... MOTOR NEURONE DISEASES OF ALL SHAPES AND SIZES. PROGRESSIVE MUSCULAR ATROPHY. LOU GEHRIG'S DISEASE. SPINAL MUSCULAR ATROPHY. YOU NAME IT, ONE OF 'EM'S GOT IT.
WHU... WHAT DOES THAT MEAN... "TELEKINETIC"?
IT MEANS THAT THEIR COLLECTIVE BRAIN POWER COULD KEEP THE WEST COAST LIT UP FOR MONTHS.
MAKES NUCLEAR POWER SEEM LIKE CANDLELIGHT.
FORTUNATELY, THE DWP'S LOSS IS OUR GAIN. AND WE'VE PUT THE BOYS TO GOOD USE.
R-RIGHT...
... THE RESURRECTION EQUATION.
WAIT.
IS THAT HIM...?

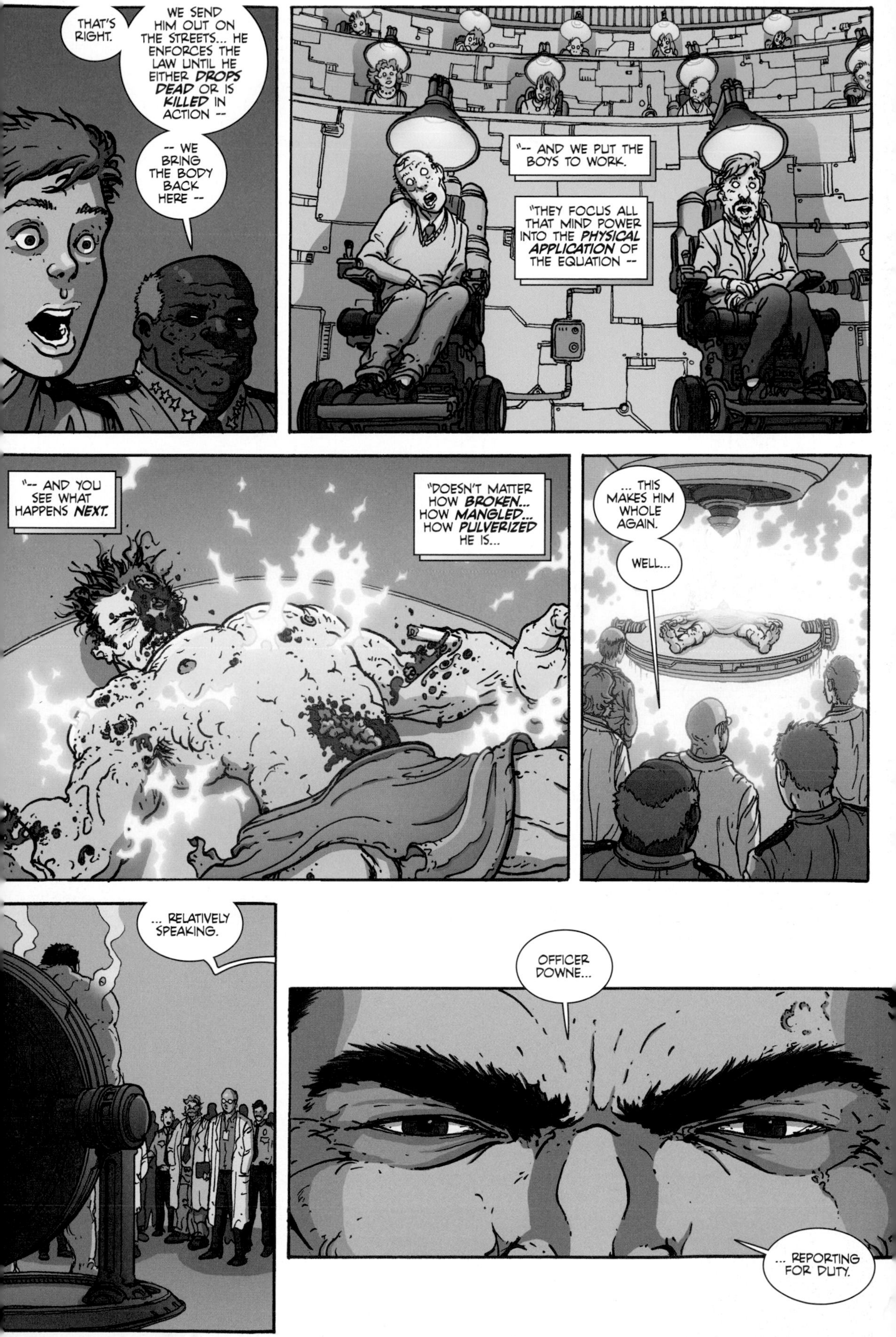
THAT'S RIGHT.
WE SEND HIM OUT ON THE STREETS... HE ENFORCES THE LAW UNTIL HE EITHER DROPS DEAD OR IS KILLED IN ACTION --
-- WE BRING THE BODY BACK HERE --
"-- AND WE PUT THE BOYS TO WORK.
"THEY FOCUS ALL THAT MIND POWER INTO THE PHYSICAL APPLICATION OF THE EQUATION --
"-- AND YOU SEE WHAT HAPPENS NEXT.
"DOESN'T MATTER HOW BROKEN... HOW MANGLED... HOW PULVERIZED HE IS...
... THIS MAKES HIM WHOLE AGAIN.
WELL...
... RELATIVELY SPEAKING.
OFFICER DOWNE...
... REPORTING FOR DUTY.

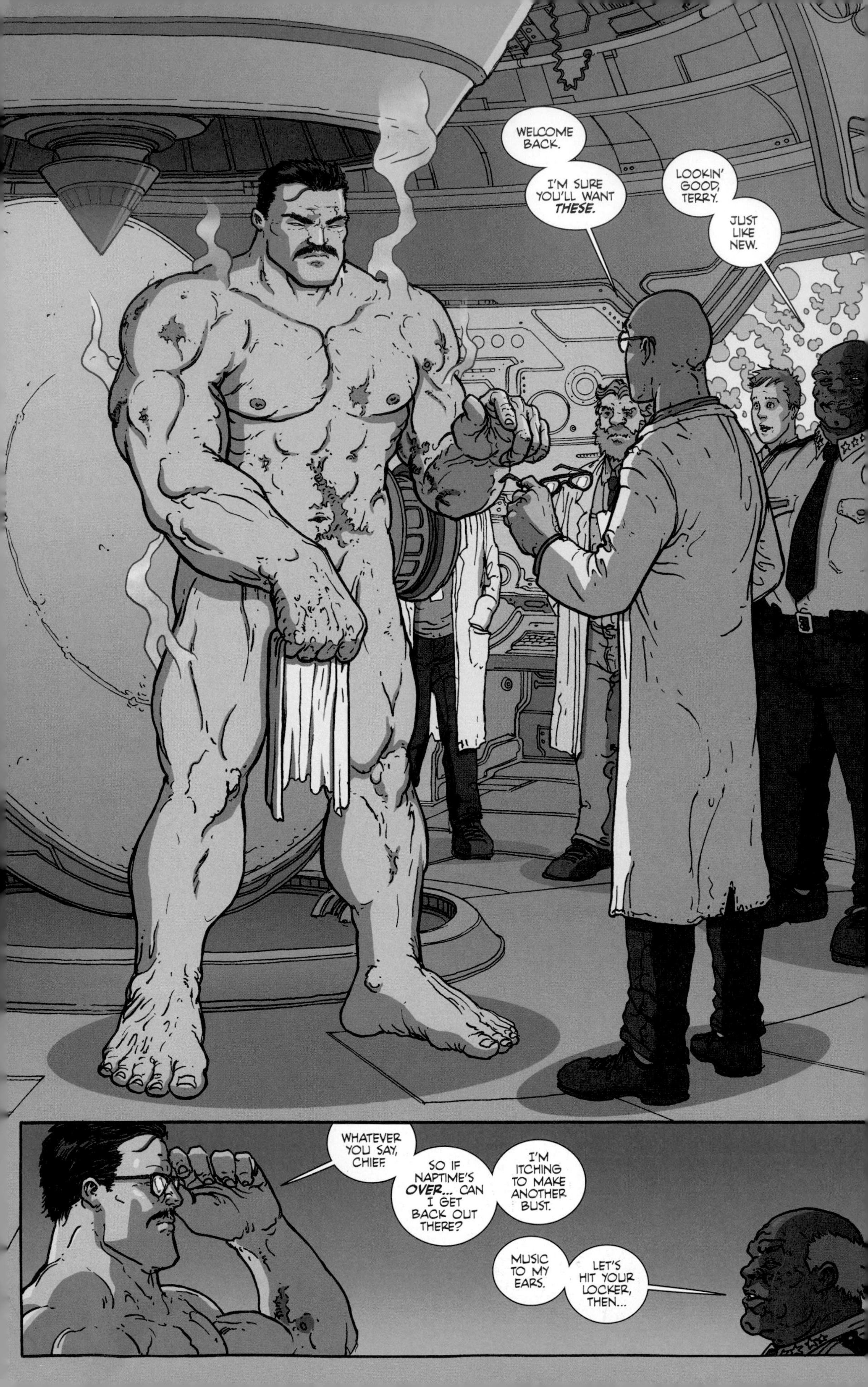
WELCOME BACK.
I'M SURE YOU'LL WANT *THESE.*
LOOKIN' GOOD, TERRY.
JUST LIKE NEW.
WHATEVER YOU SAY, CHIEF.
SO IF NAPTIME'S *OVER...* CAN I GET BACK OUT THERE?
I'M ITCHING TO MAKE ANOTHER BUST.
MUSIC TO MY EARS.
LET'S HIT YOUR LOCKER, THEN...

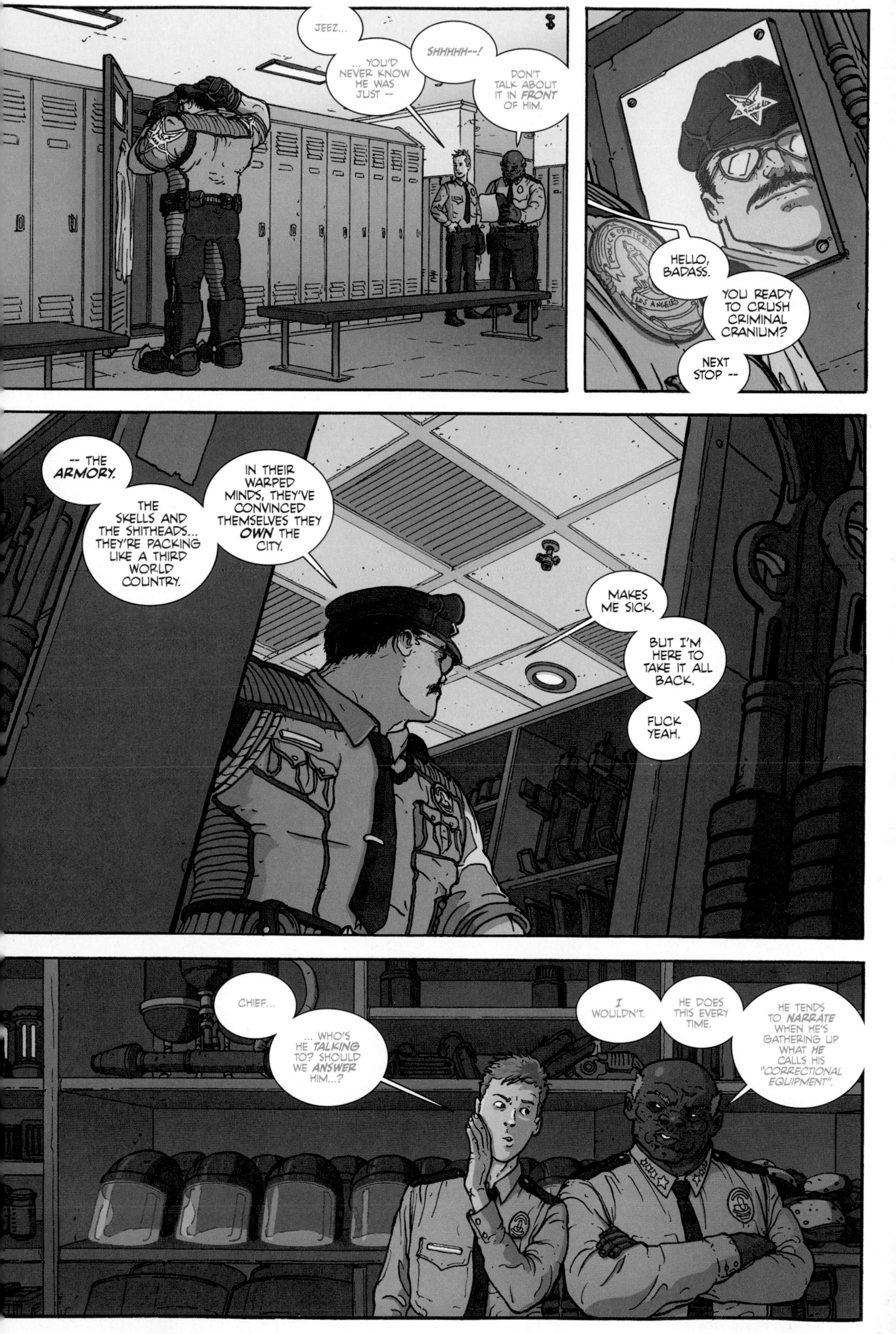
JEEZ...
... YOU'D NEVER KNOW HE WAS JUST --
SHHHHH--!
DON'T TALK ABOUT IT IN FRONT OF HIM.
HELLO, BADASS.
YOU READY TO CRUSH CRIMINAL CRANIUM?
NEXT STOP --
-- THE ARMORY.
THE SKELLS AND THE SHITHEADS... THEY'RE PACKING LIKE A THIRD WORLD COUNTRY.
IN THEIR WARPED MINDS, THEY'VE CONVINCED THEMSELVES THEY OWN THE CITY.
MAKES ME SICK.
BUT I'M HERE TO TAKE IT ALL BACK.
FUCK YEAH.
CHIEF...
... WHO'S HE TALKING TO? SHOULD WE ANSWER HIM...?
I WOULDN'T.
HE DOES THIS EVERY TIME.
HE TENDS TO NARRATE WHEN HE'S GATHERING UP WHAT HE CALLS HIS "CORRECTIONAL EQUIPMENT".

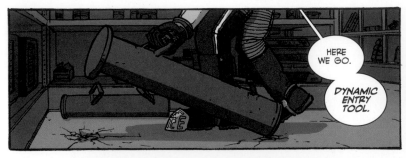

HERE WE GO.

DYNAMIC ENTRY TOOL.

... AND ALL THE *AMMO* IT CAN EAT.

.85 MAGNUM CUSTOMIZED.

THE *ANSWER MAN*...

SO... HE JUST PICKS UP RIGHT WHERE HE LEFT OFF...?

CHIEF. WHERE'S MY RIDE?

IT'S ALL HE *KNOWS*, GABLE.

HE'S THE PERFECT COP.

PARKED RIGHT WHERE IT *ALWAYS* IS.

NOW GET OUT THERE AND KICK SOME FUCKIN' ASS, DOWNE!

THERE'S A CITY FULL OF *PERPS* WAITIN' FOR YOU!

THERE SHE IS...

... *MOVING DEATH.*

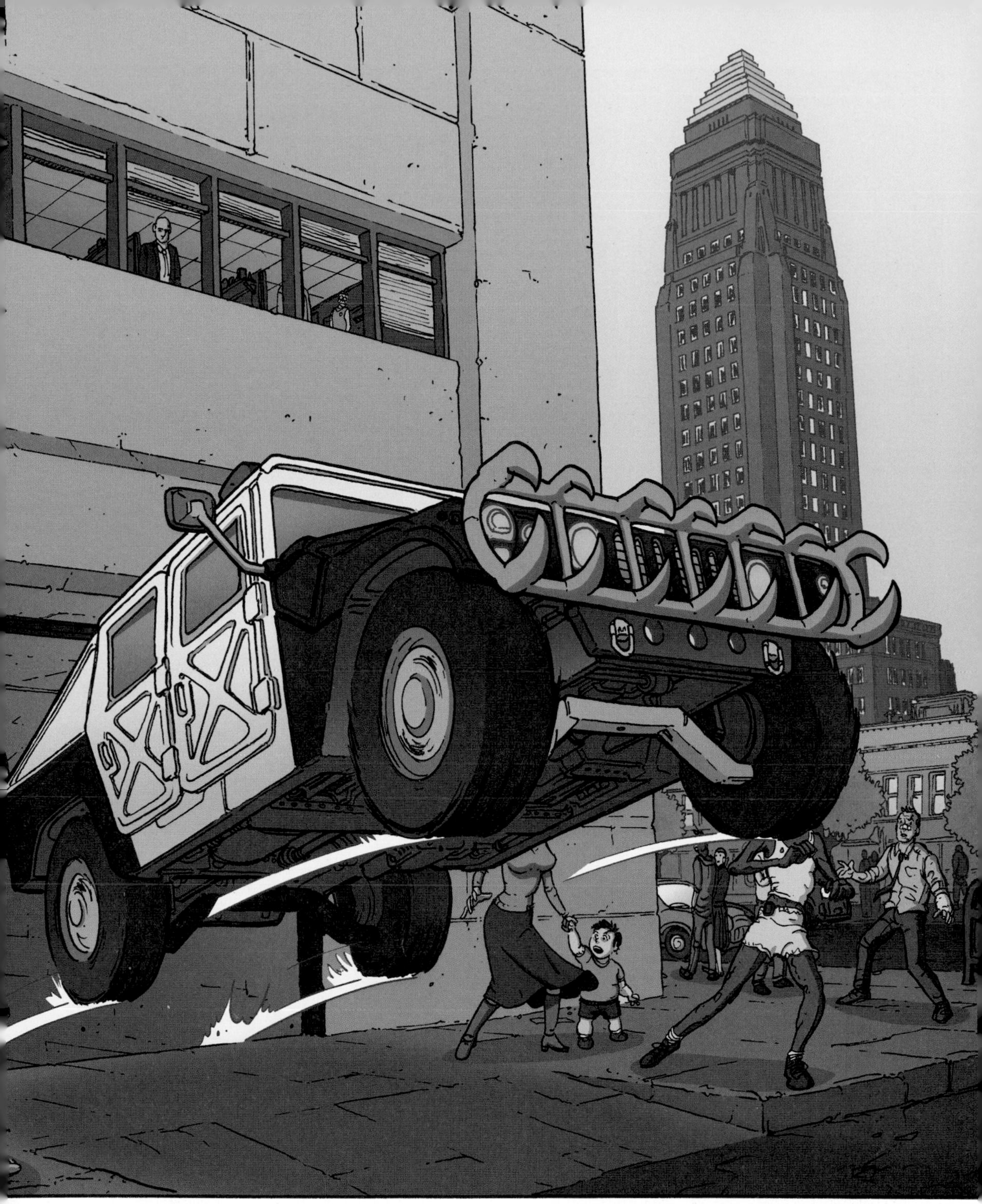

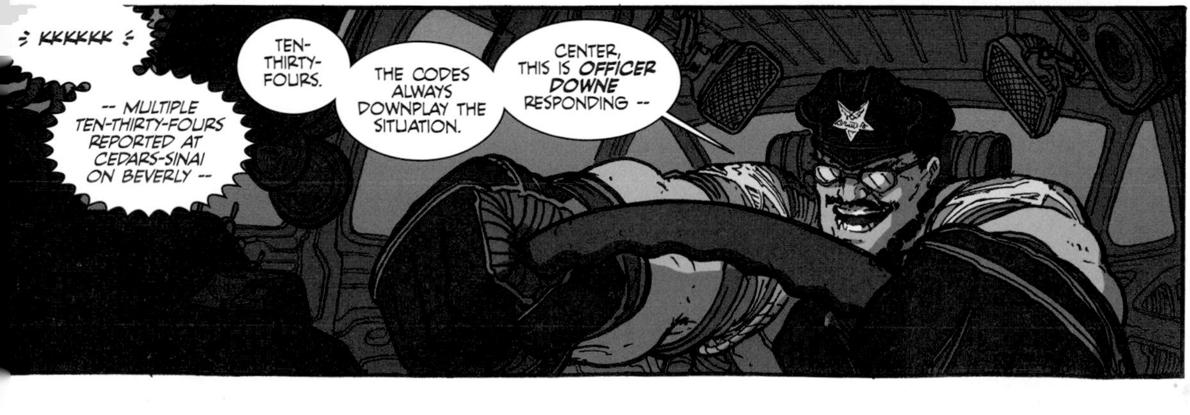

: KKKKKK :
-- MULTIPLE TEN-THIRTY-FOURS REPORTED AT CEDARS-SINAI ON BEVERLY --
TEN-THIRTY-FOURS.
THE CODES ALWAYS DOWNPLAY THE SITUATION.
CENTER, THIS IS OFFICER DOWNE RESPONDING --

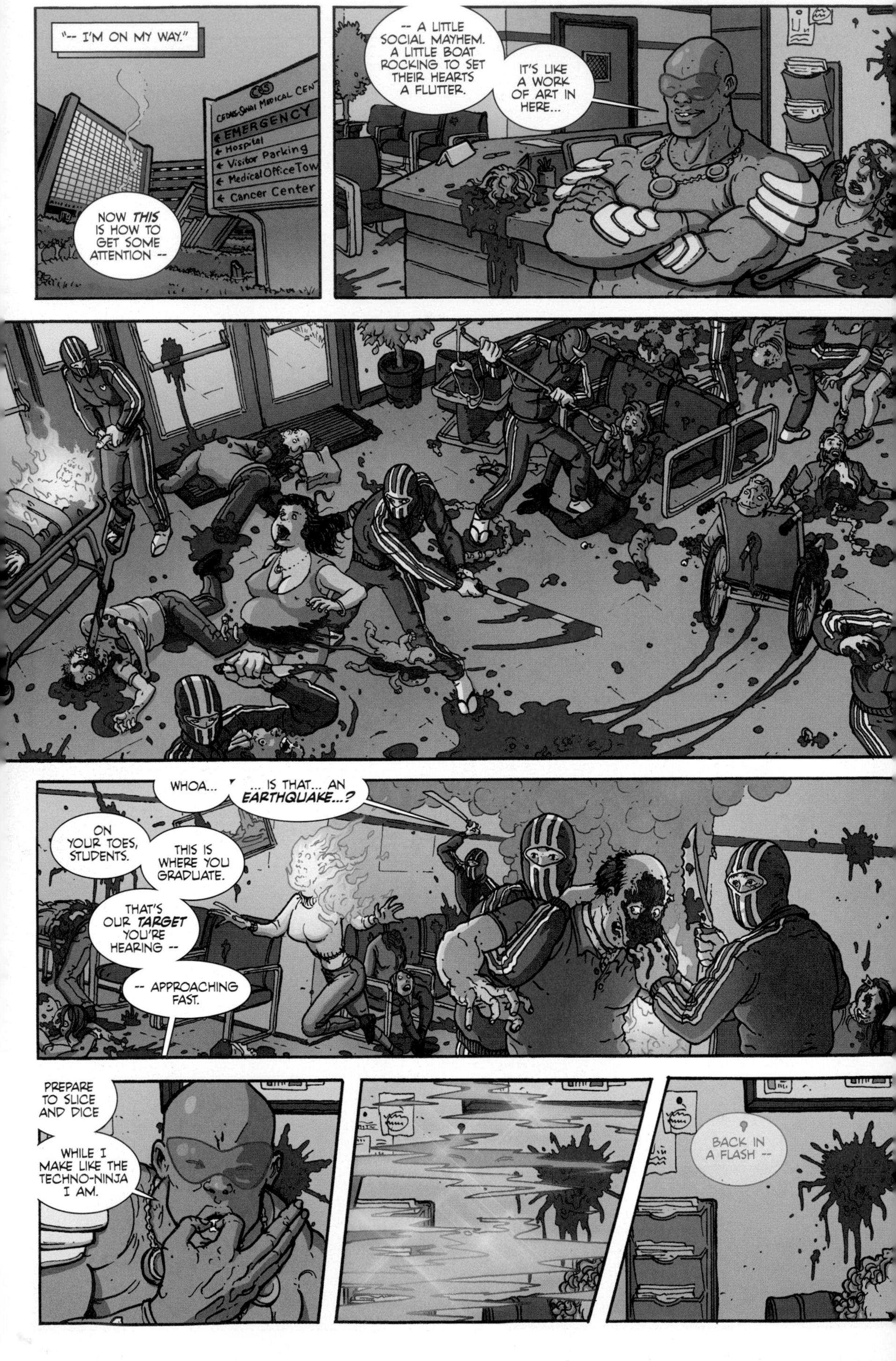
"-- I'M ON MY WAY."
CEDARS-SINAI MEDICAL CENT
EMERGENCY
Hospital
Visitor Parking
Medical Office Tow
Cancer Center
NOW THIS IS HOW TO GET SOME ATTENTION --
-- A LITTLE SOCIAL MAYHEM. A LITTLE BOAT ROCKING TO SET THEIR HEARTS A FLUTTER.
IT'S LIKE A WORK OF ART IN HERE...
WHOA...
... IS THAT... AN EARTHQUAKE...?
ON YOUR TOES, STUDENTS.
THIS IS WHERE YOU GRADUATE.
THAT'S OUR TARGET YOU'RE HEARING --
-- APPROACHING FAST.
PREPARE TO SLICE AND DICE
WHILE I MAKE LIKE THE TECHNO-NINJA I AM.
BACK IN A FLASH --

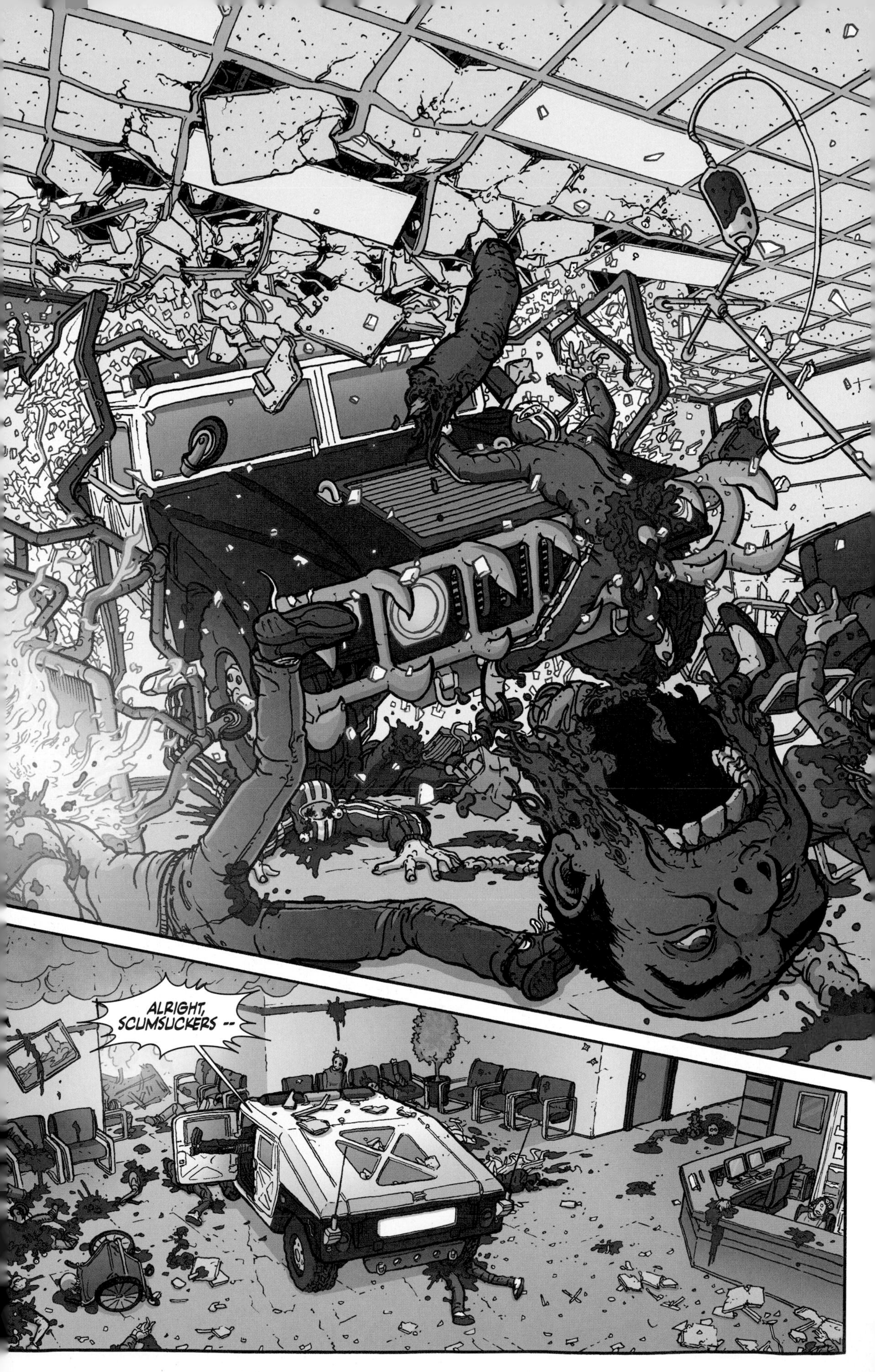
ALRIGHT, SCUMSUCKERS --

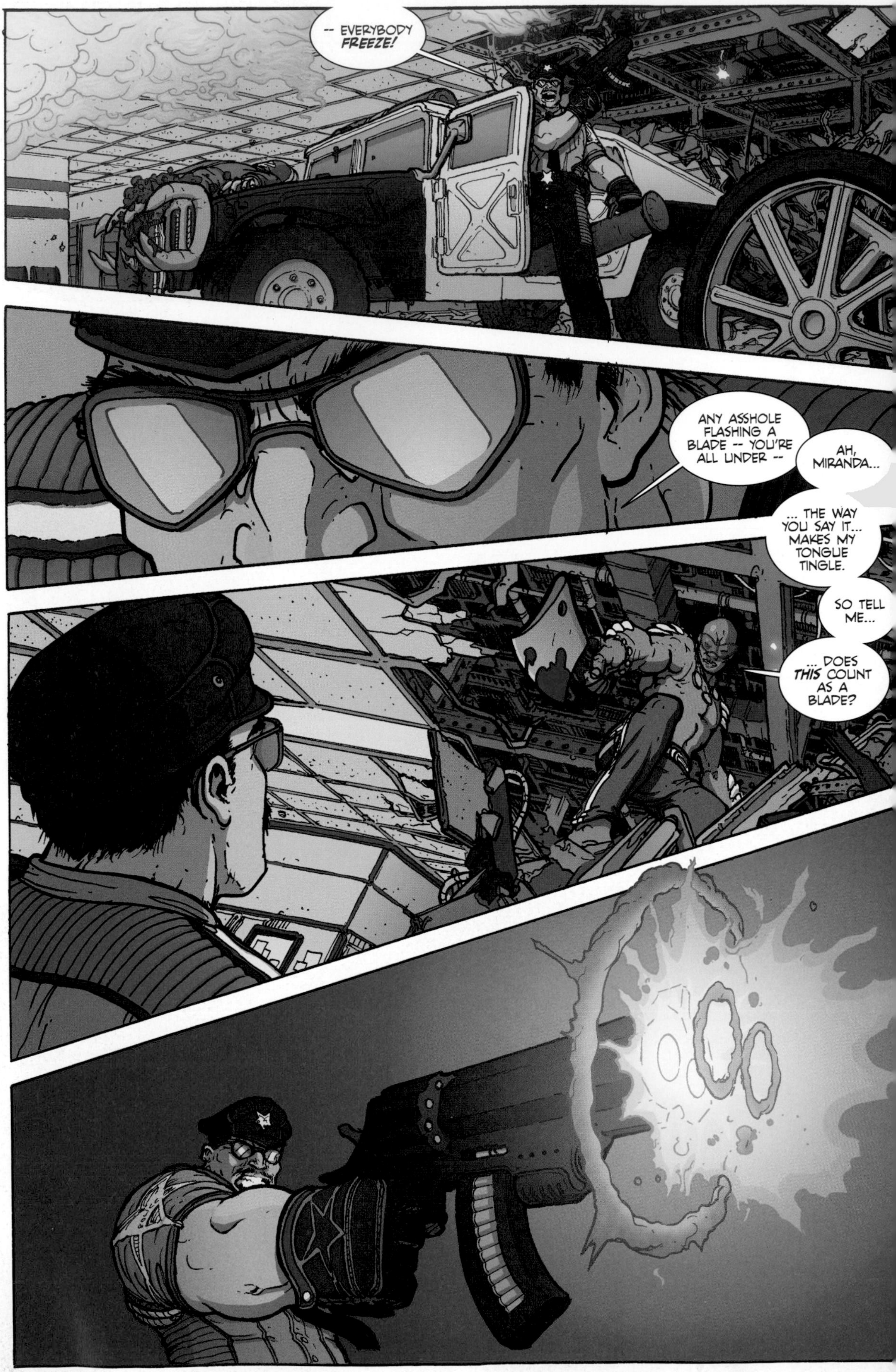
-- EVERYBODY FREEZE!
ANY ASSHOLE FLASHING A BLADE -- YOU'RE ALL UNDER --
AH, MIRANDA...
... THE WAY YOU SAY IT... MAKES MY TONGUE TINGLE.
SO TELL ME...
... DOES THIS COUNT AS A BLADE?

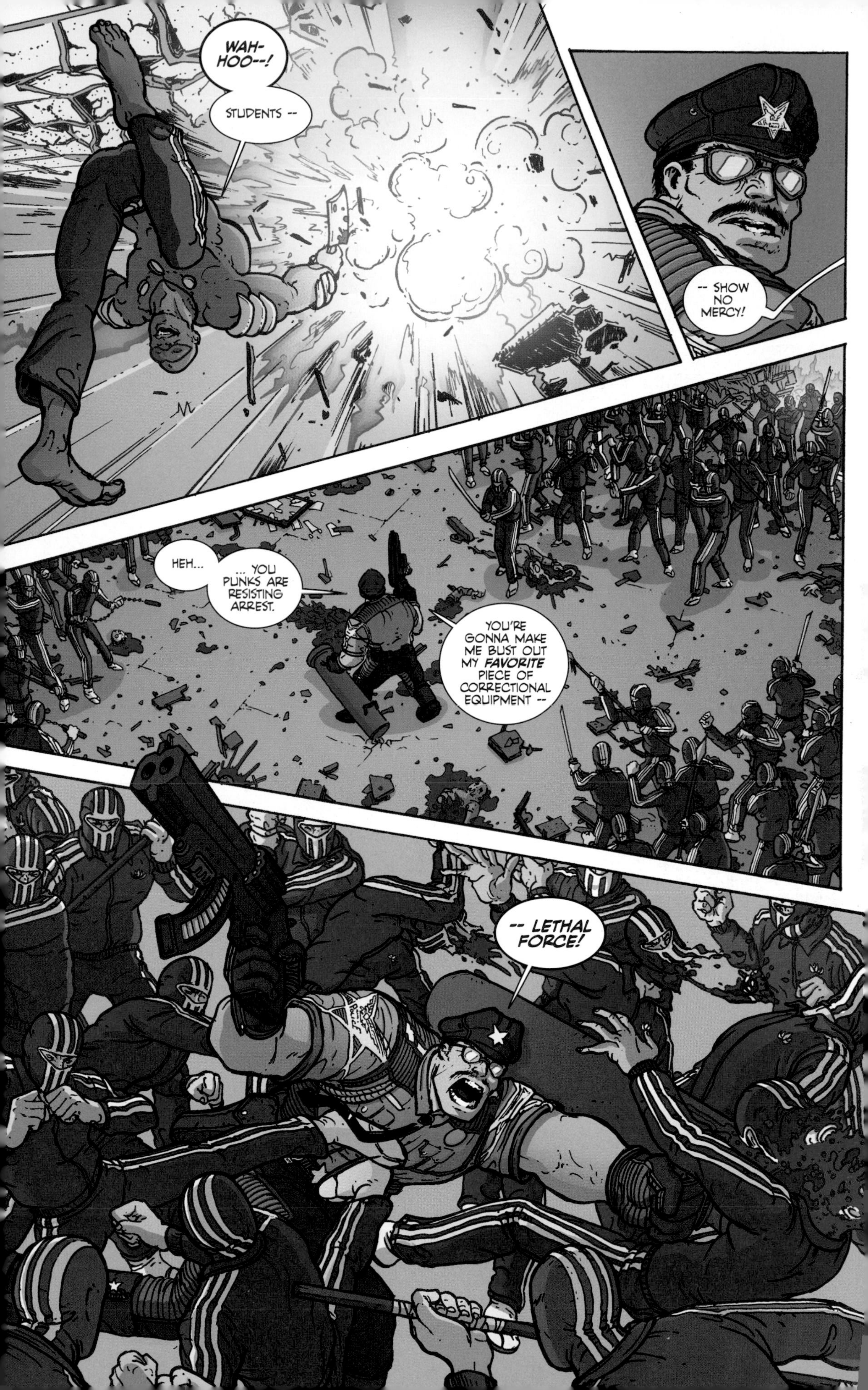
WAH-HOO--!
STUDENTS --
-- SHOW NO MERCY!
HEH...
... YOU PUNKS ARE RESISTING ARREST.
YOU'RE GONNA MAKE ME BUST OUT MY FAVORITE PIECE OF CORRECTIONAL EQUIPMENT --
-- LETHAL FORCE!

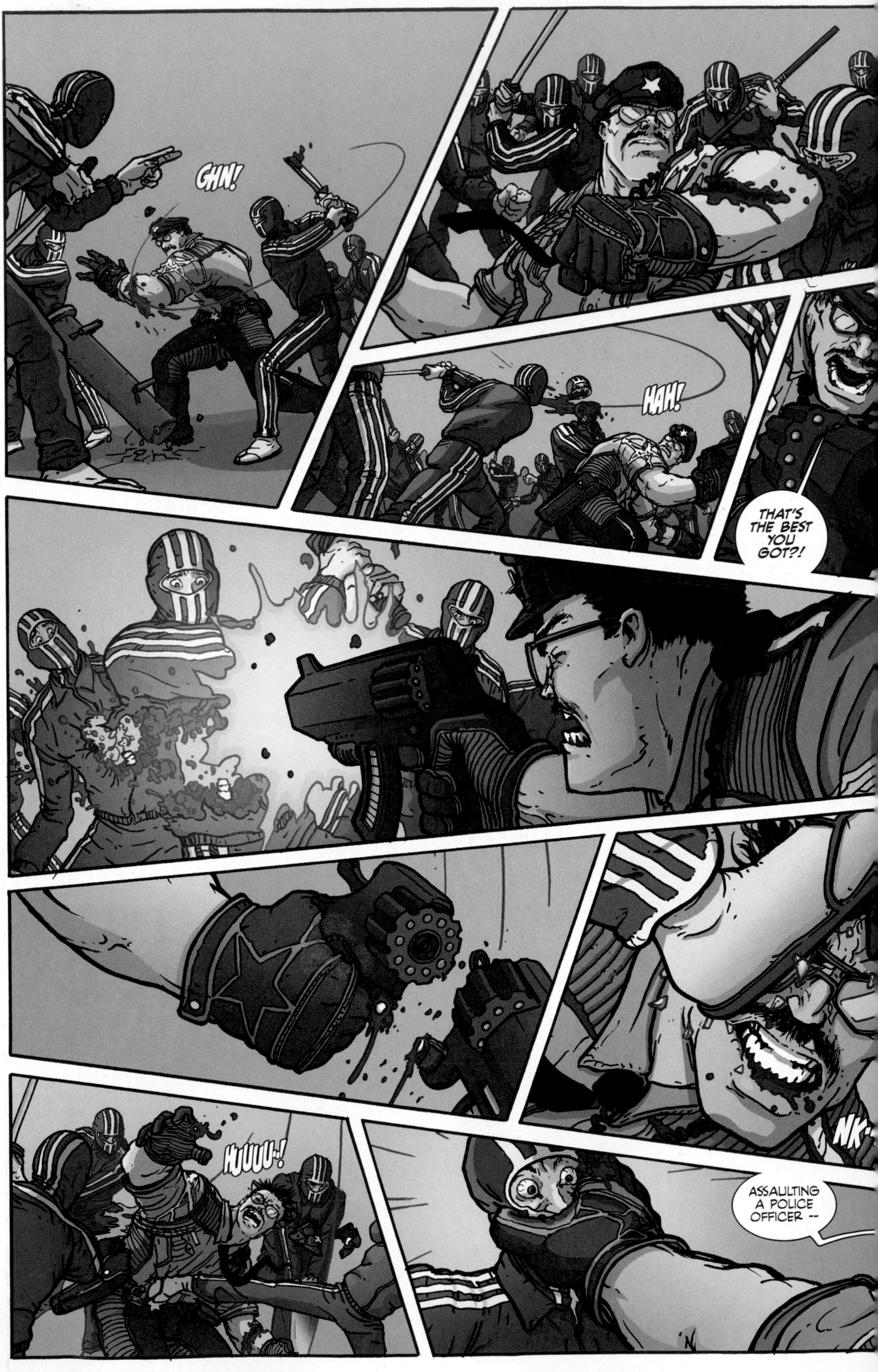
GHN!
HAH!
THAT'S THE BEST YOU GOT?!
HUUUU-!
ASSAULTING A POLICE OFFICER --

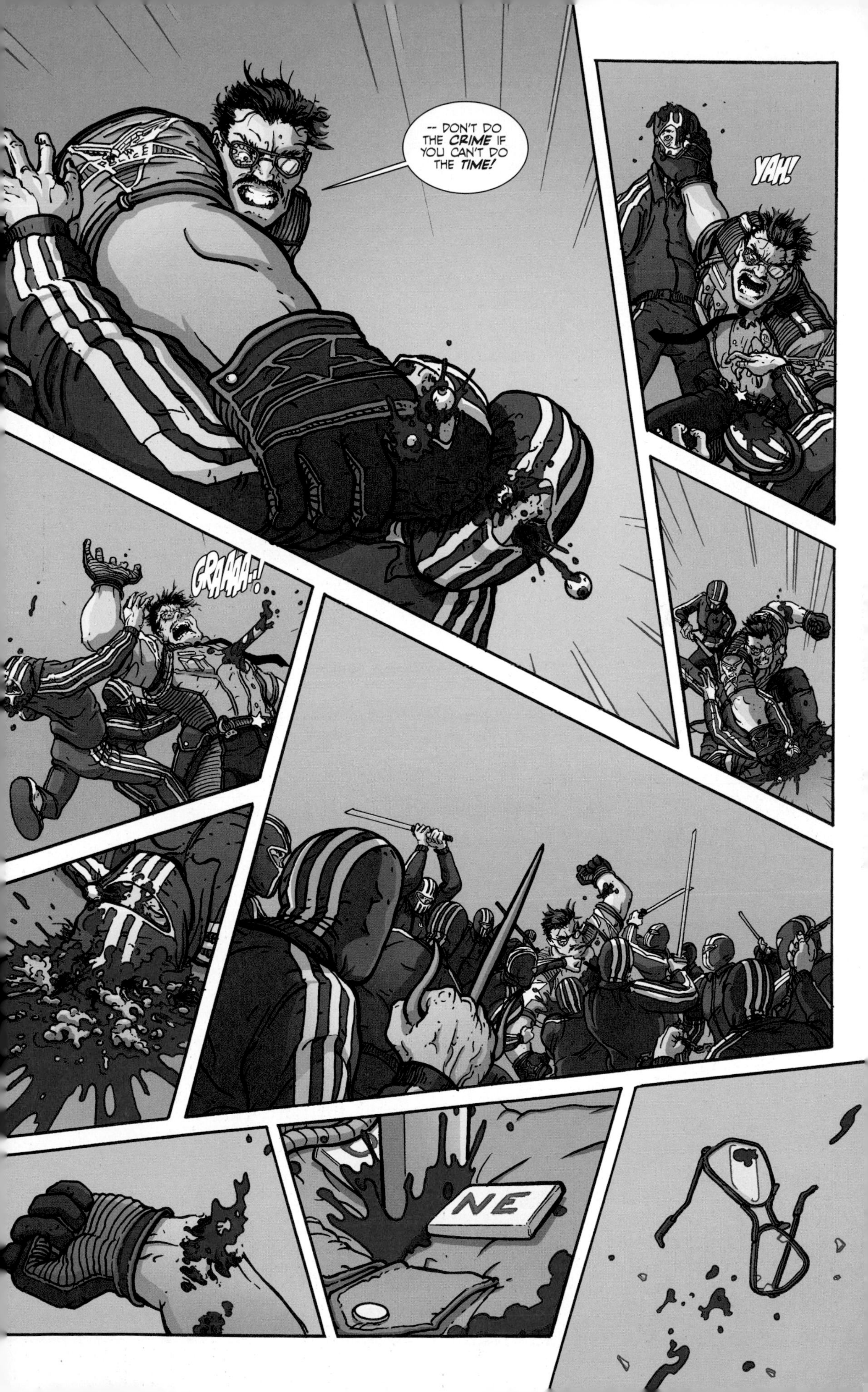

-- DON'T DO THE CRIME IF YOU CAN'T DO THE TIME!
YAH!
GRAAAA-!
NE

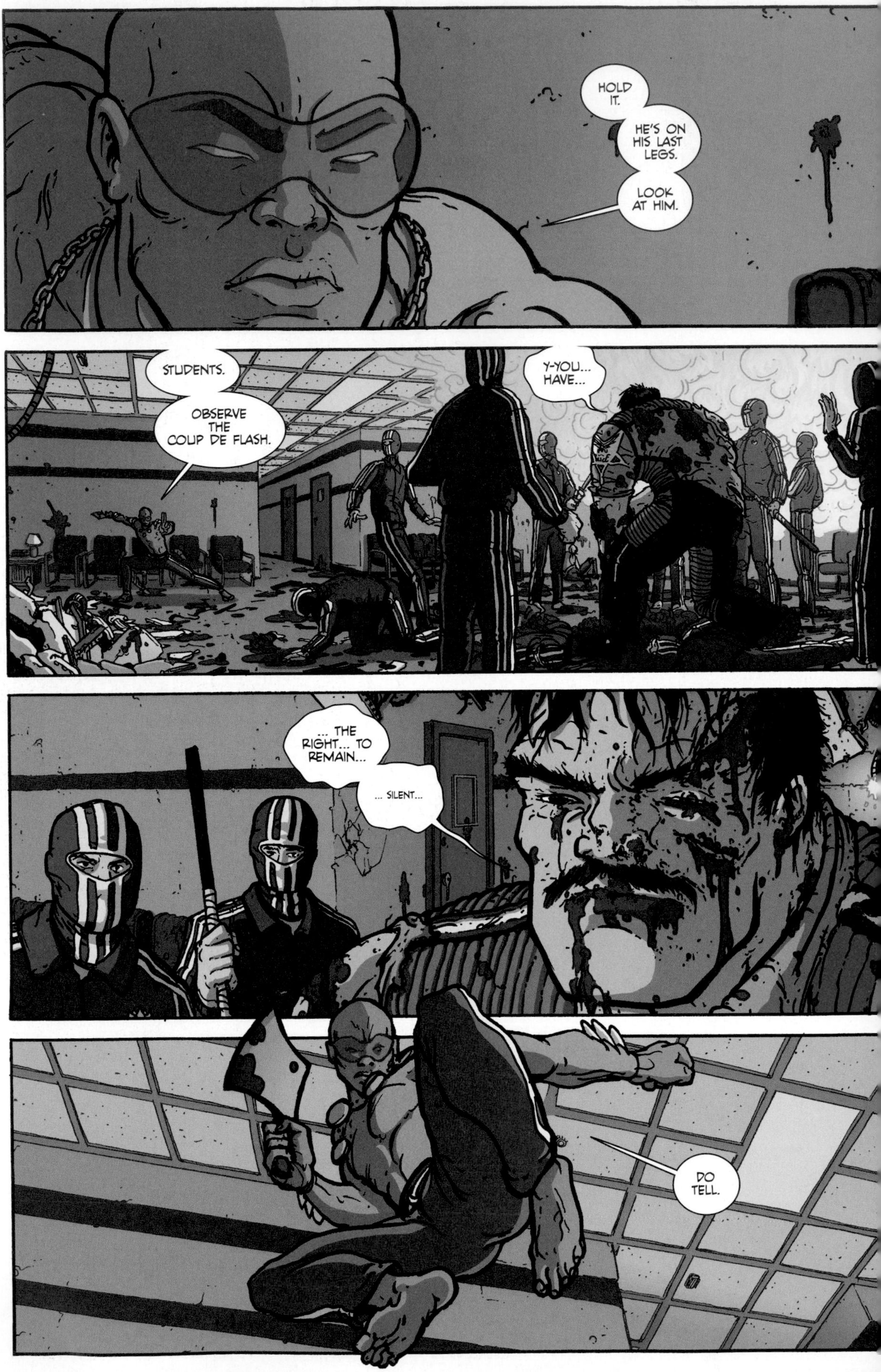
HOLD IT.
HE'S ON HIS LAST LEGS.
LOOK AT HIM.
STUDENTS.
OBSERVE THE COUP DE FLASH.
Y-YOU... HAVE...
... THE RIGHT... TO REMAIN...
... SILENT...
DO TELL.

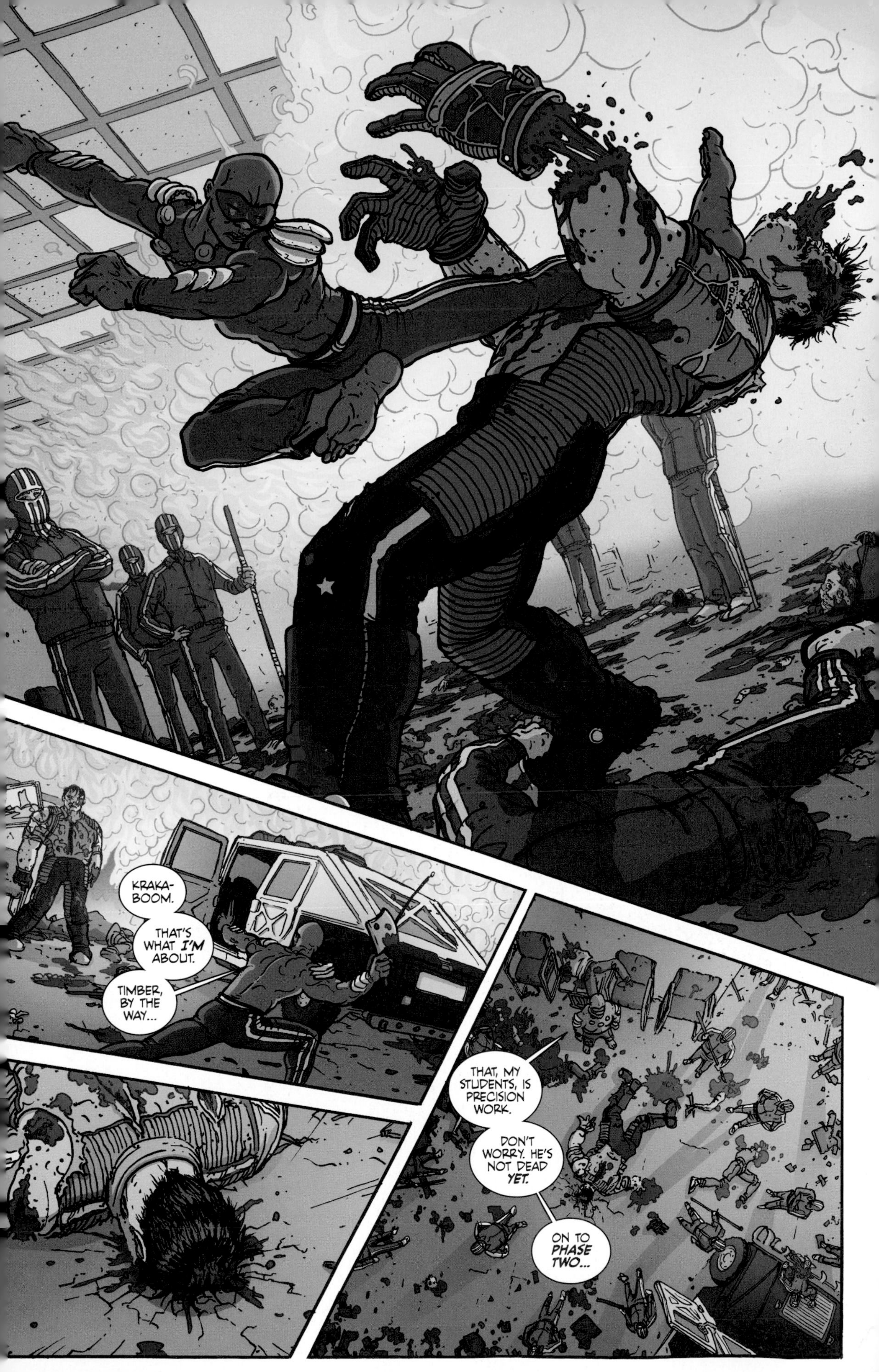
KRAKA-BOOM.
THAT'S WHAT *I'M* ABOUT.
TIMBER, BY THE WAY...
THAT, MY STUDENTS, IS PRECISION WORK.
DON'T WORRY. HE'S NOT DEAD *YET.*
ON TO *PHASE TWO...*

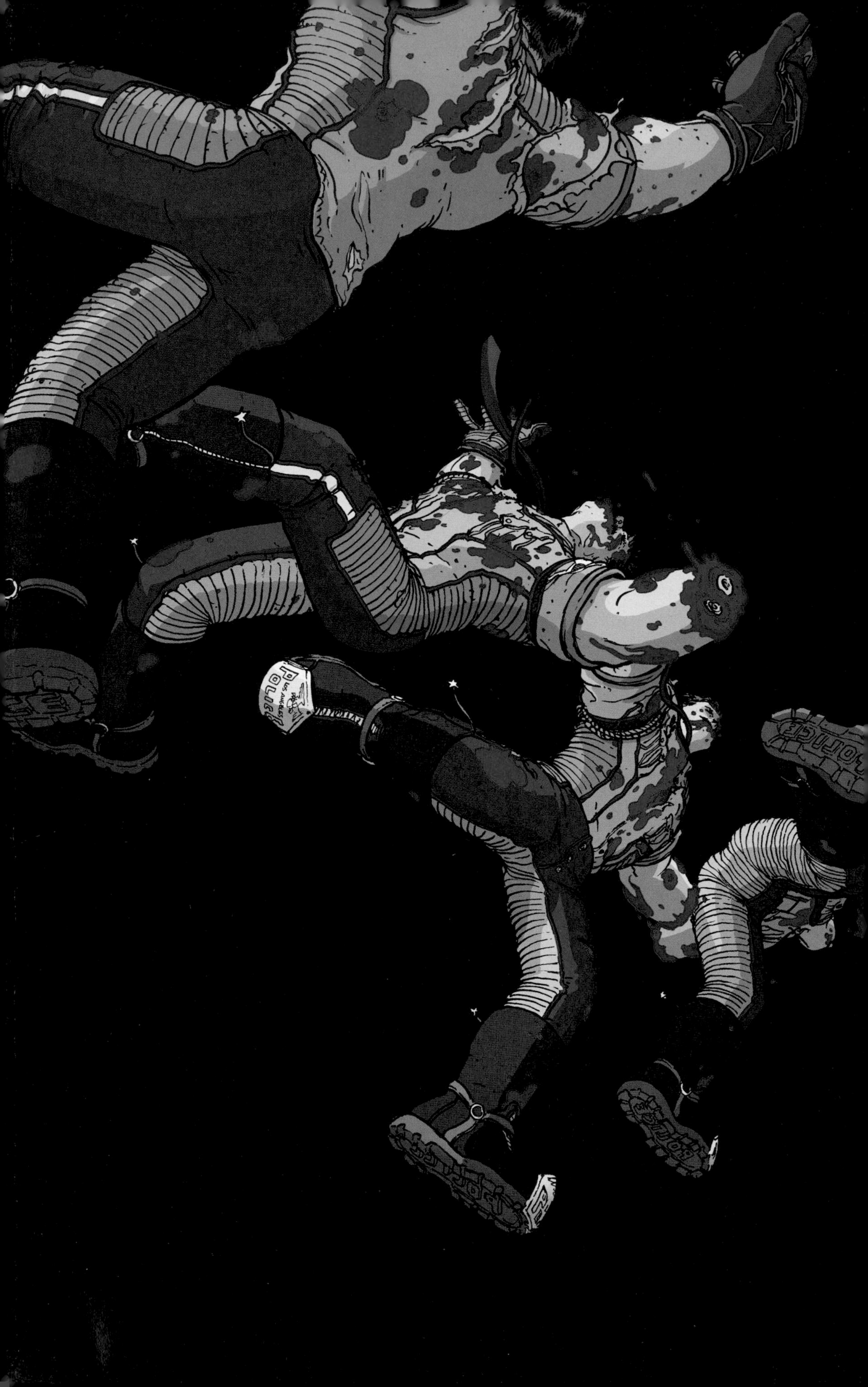

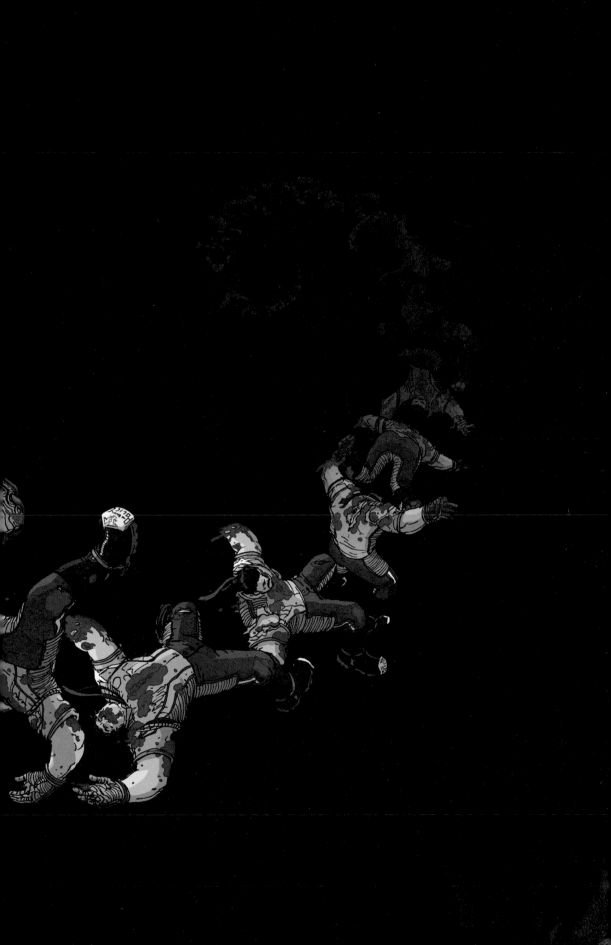

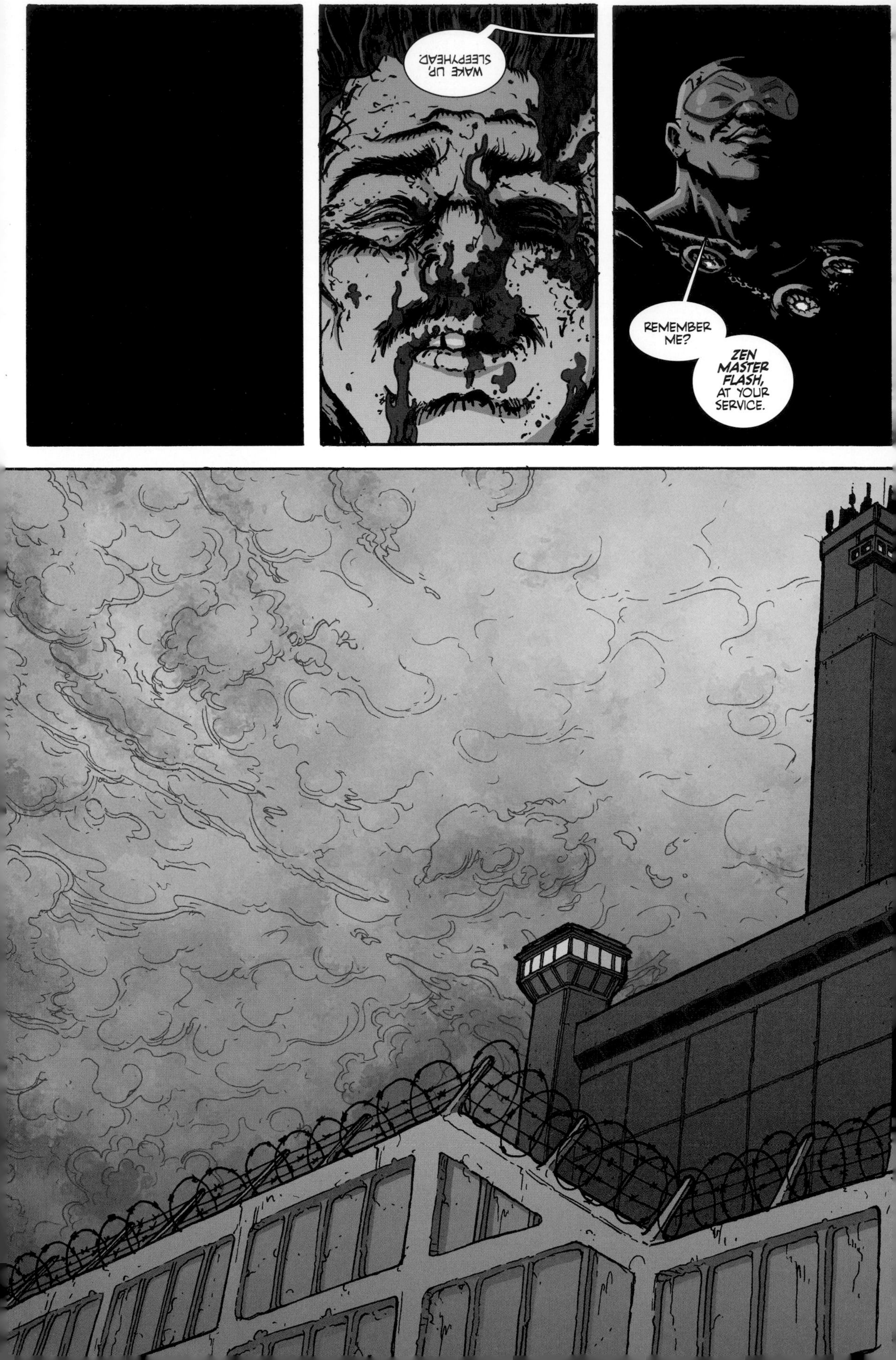
WAKE UP, SLEEPYHEAD.
REMEMBER ME?
ZEN MASTER FLASH, AT YOUR SERVICE.

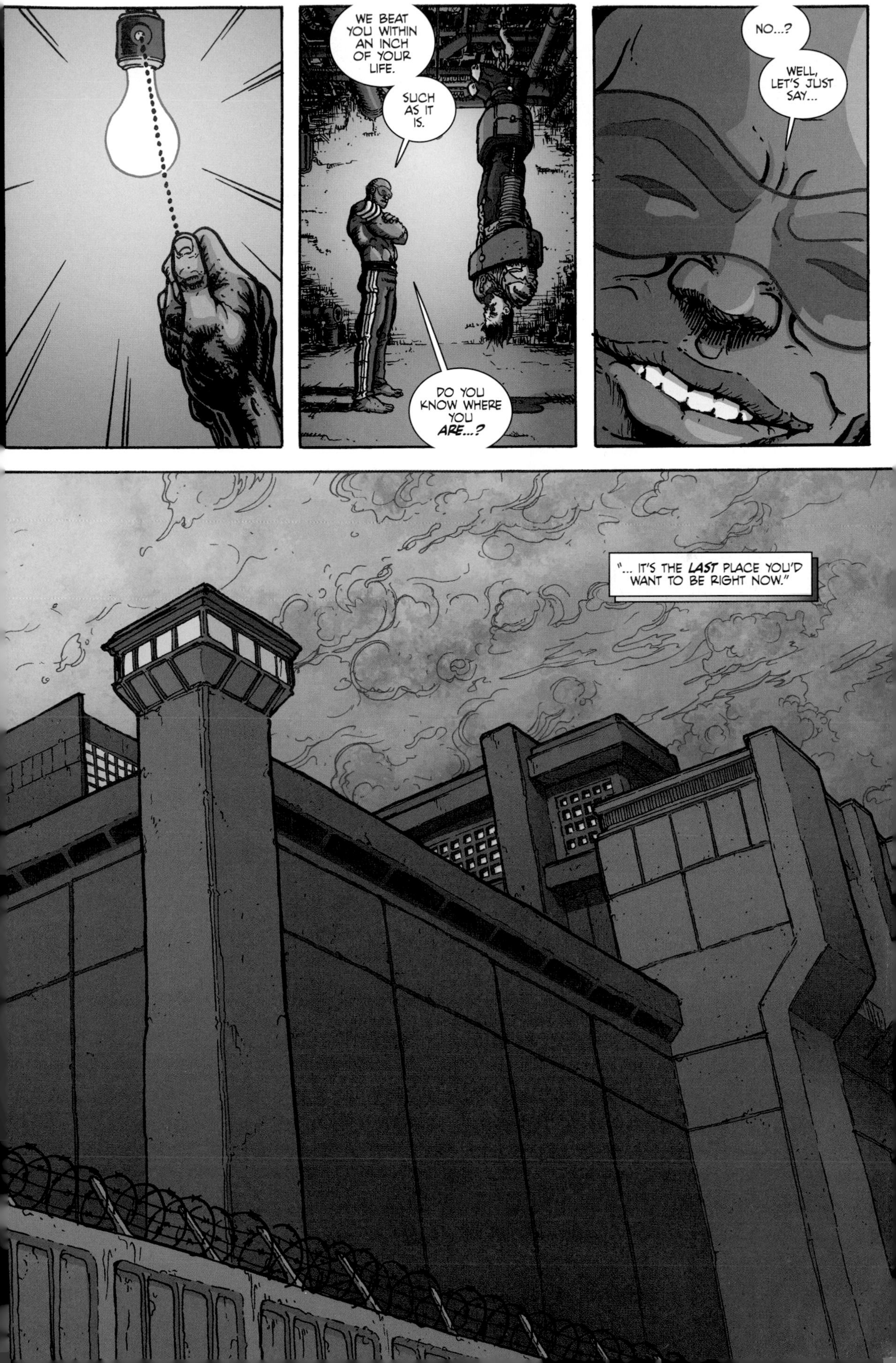
WE BEAT YOU WITHIN AN INCH OF YOUR LIFE.
SUCH AS IT IS.
DO YOU KNOW WHERE YOU *ARE...?*
NO...?
WELL, LET'S JUST SAY...
"... IT'S THE *LAST* PLACE YOU'D WANT TO BE RIGHT NOW."

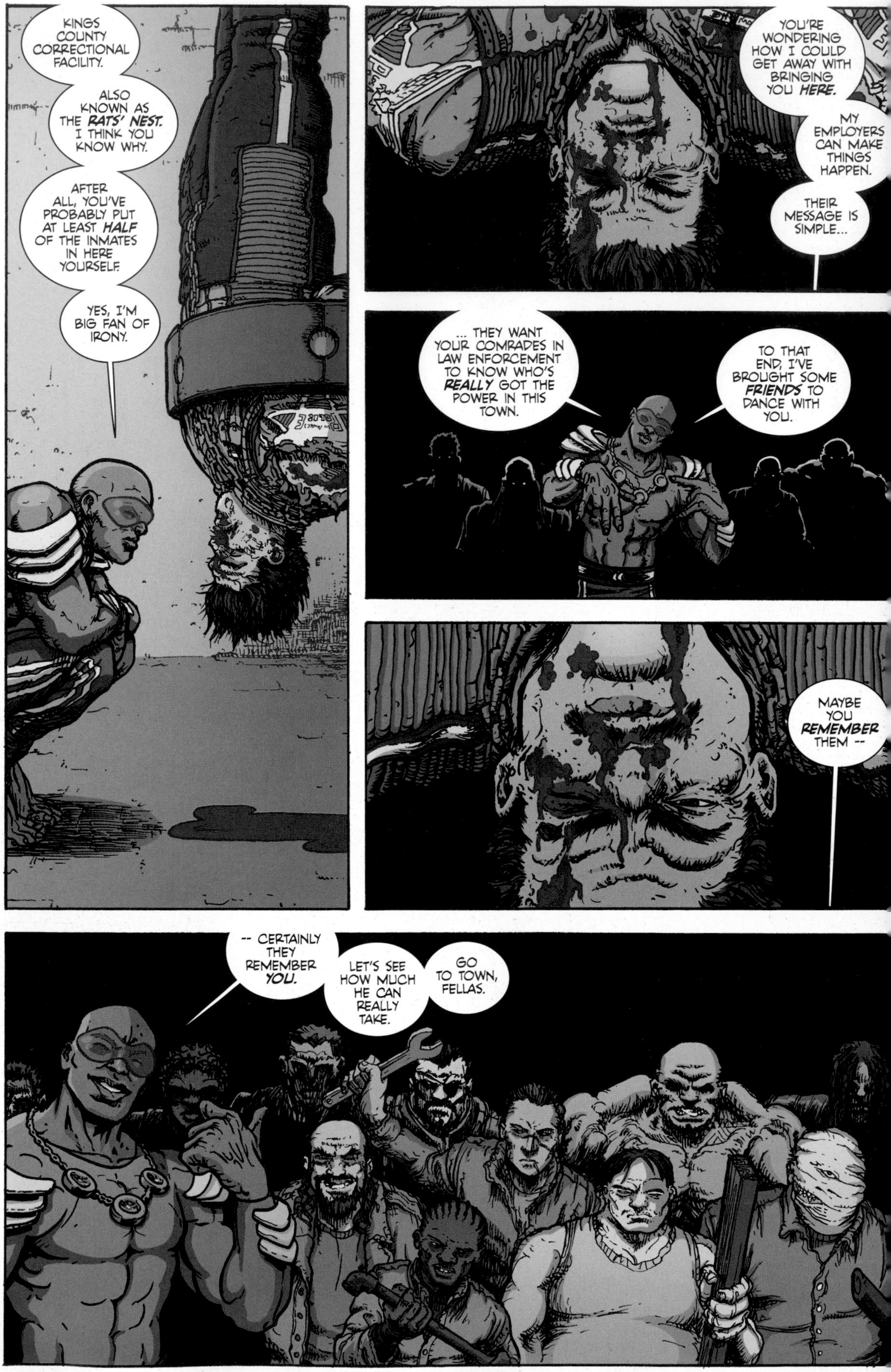
KINGS COUNTY CORRECTIONAL FACILITY.
ALSO KNOWN AS THE ***RATS' NEST.*** I THINK YOU KNOW WHY.
AFTER ALL, YOU'VE PROBABLY PUT AT LEAST ***HALF*** OF THE INMATES IN HERE YOURSELF.
YES, I'M BIG FAN OF IRONY.
YOU'RE WONDERING HOW I COULD GET AWAY WITH BRINGING YOU ***HERE.***
MY EMPLOYERS CAN MAKE THINGS HAPPEN.
THEIR MESSAGE IS SIMPLE...
... THEY WANT YOUR COMRADES IN LAW ENFORCEMENT TO KNOW WHO'S ***REALLY*** GOT THE POWER IN THIS TOWN.
TO THAT END, I'VE BROUGHT SOME ***FRIENDS*** TO DANCE WITH YOU.
MAYBE YOU ***REMEMBER*** THEM --
-- CERTAINLY THEY REMEMBER ***YOU.***
LET'S SEE HOW MUCH HE CAN REALLY TAKE.
GO TO TOWN, FELLAS.

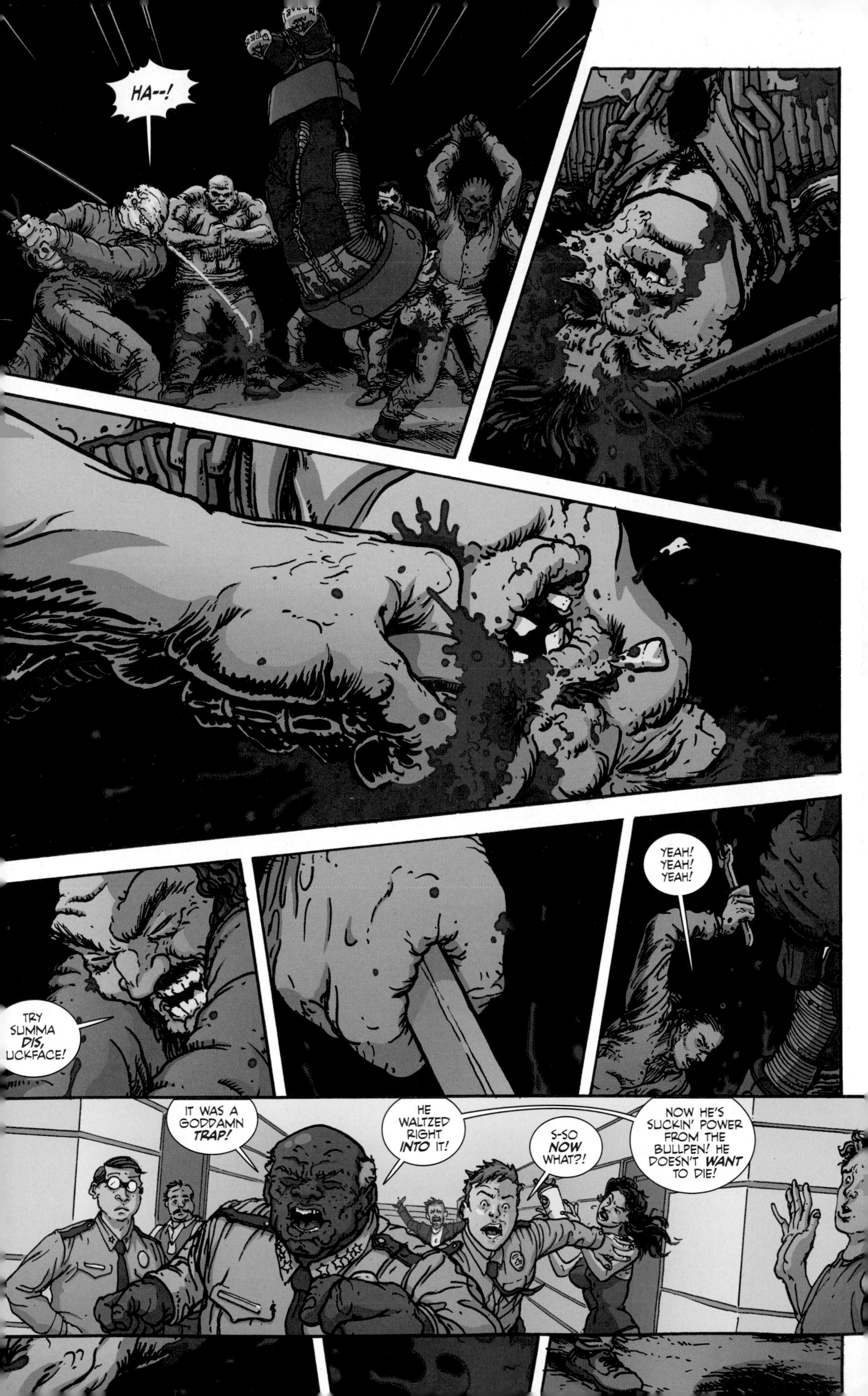
HA--!
TRY SUMMA DIS, UCKFACE!
YEAH! YEAH! YEAH!
IT WAS A GODDAMN TRAP!
HE WALTZED RIGHT INTO IT!
S-SO NOW WHAT?!
NOW HE'S SUCKIN' POWER FROM THE BULLPEN! HE DOESN'T WANT TO DIE!

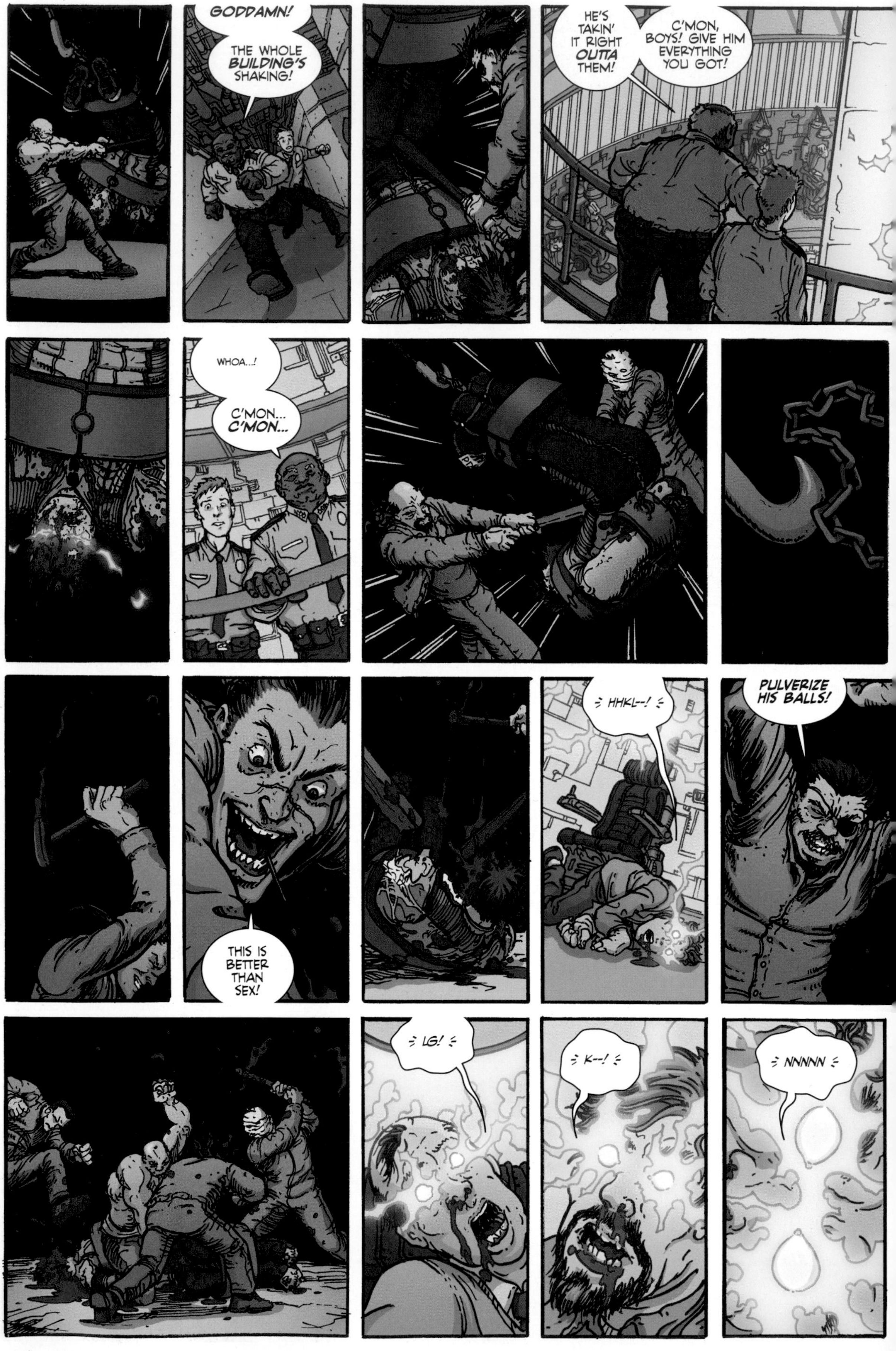
GODDAMN!
THE WHOLE BUILDING'S SHAKING!
HE'S TAKIN' IT RIGHT OUTTA THEM!
C'MON, BOYS! GIVE HIM EVERYTHING YOU GOT!
WHOA...!
C'MON... C'MON...
THIS IS BETTER THAN SEX!
HHKL--!
PULVERIZE HIS BALLS!
LG!
K--!
NNNNN

STILL BREATHING?

DAMN.

GK...!

KKKKKK...!

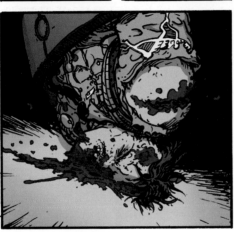

≈ URG--! ≈

FEEL THAT?!

BITCH!

RRRRRRR--

DAT'S WHAT I'M TALKIN' 'BOUT!

ANOTHER SHOT, RAMBLES!

...

CHIEF...

...WHAT'S HAPPENING TO THEM?

SON OF A BITCH.

THEY'VE NEVER BEEN PUSHED THIS FAR BEFORE...

THEY MIGHT'VE HIT THEIR LIMIT.

OKAY, BIG BOY.

AIN'T NO COMING BACK FROM THAT.

WHOA!

CHRIST ALMIGHTY.

MAYBE HE GOT WHAT HE NEEDED AFTER ALL...

FREEZE, ASSHOLES --

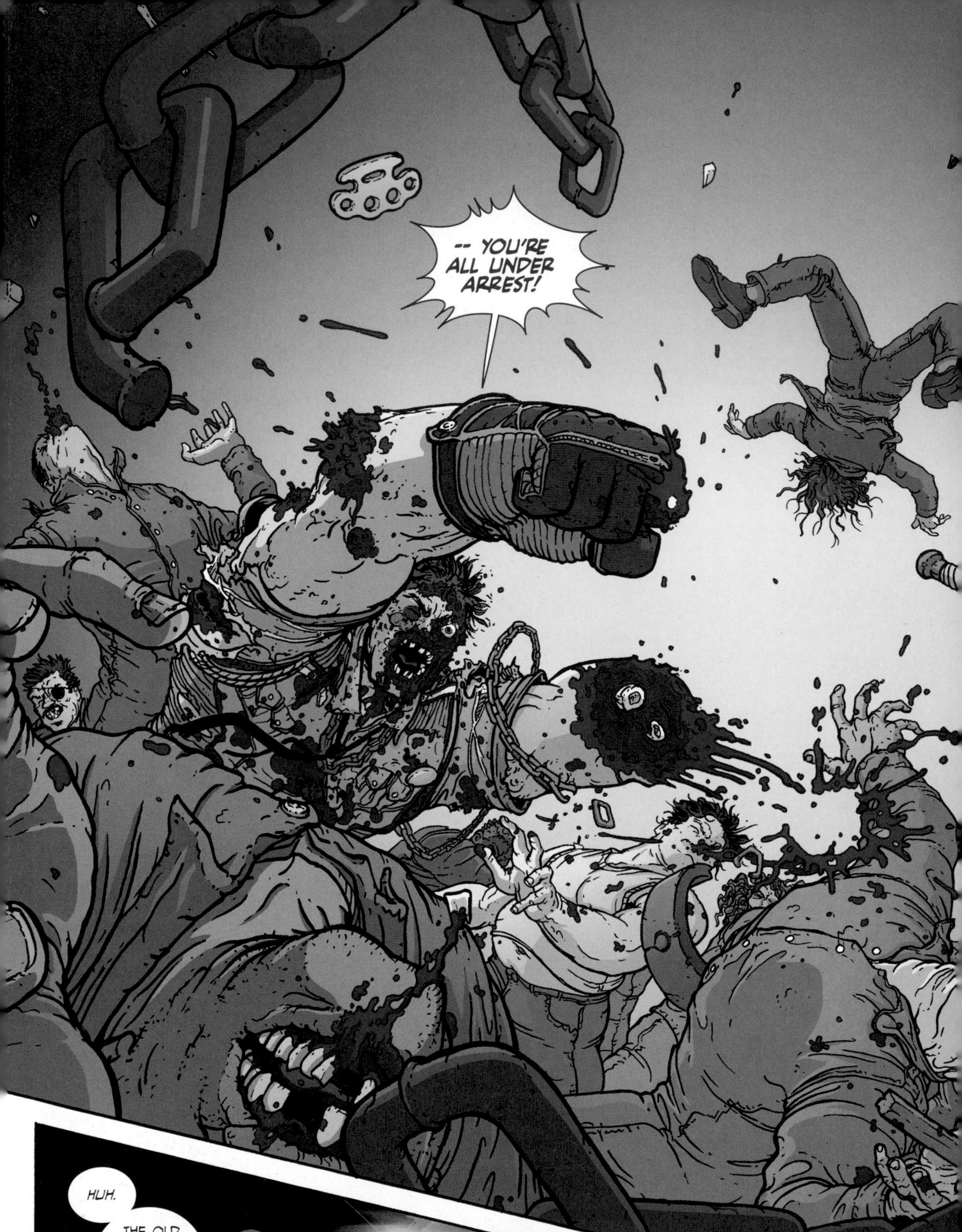
-- YOU'RE ALL UNDER ARREST!

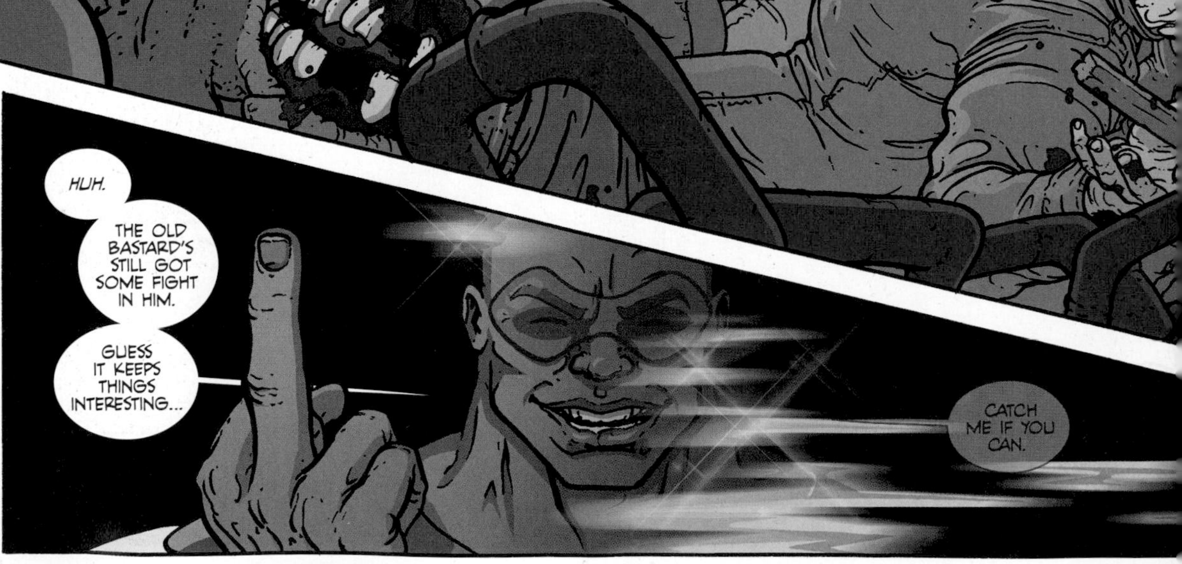
HUH.
THE OLD BASTARD'S STILL GOT SOME FIGHT IN HIM.
GUESS IT KEEPS THINGS INTERESTING...
CATCH ME IF YOU CAN.

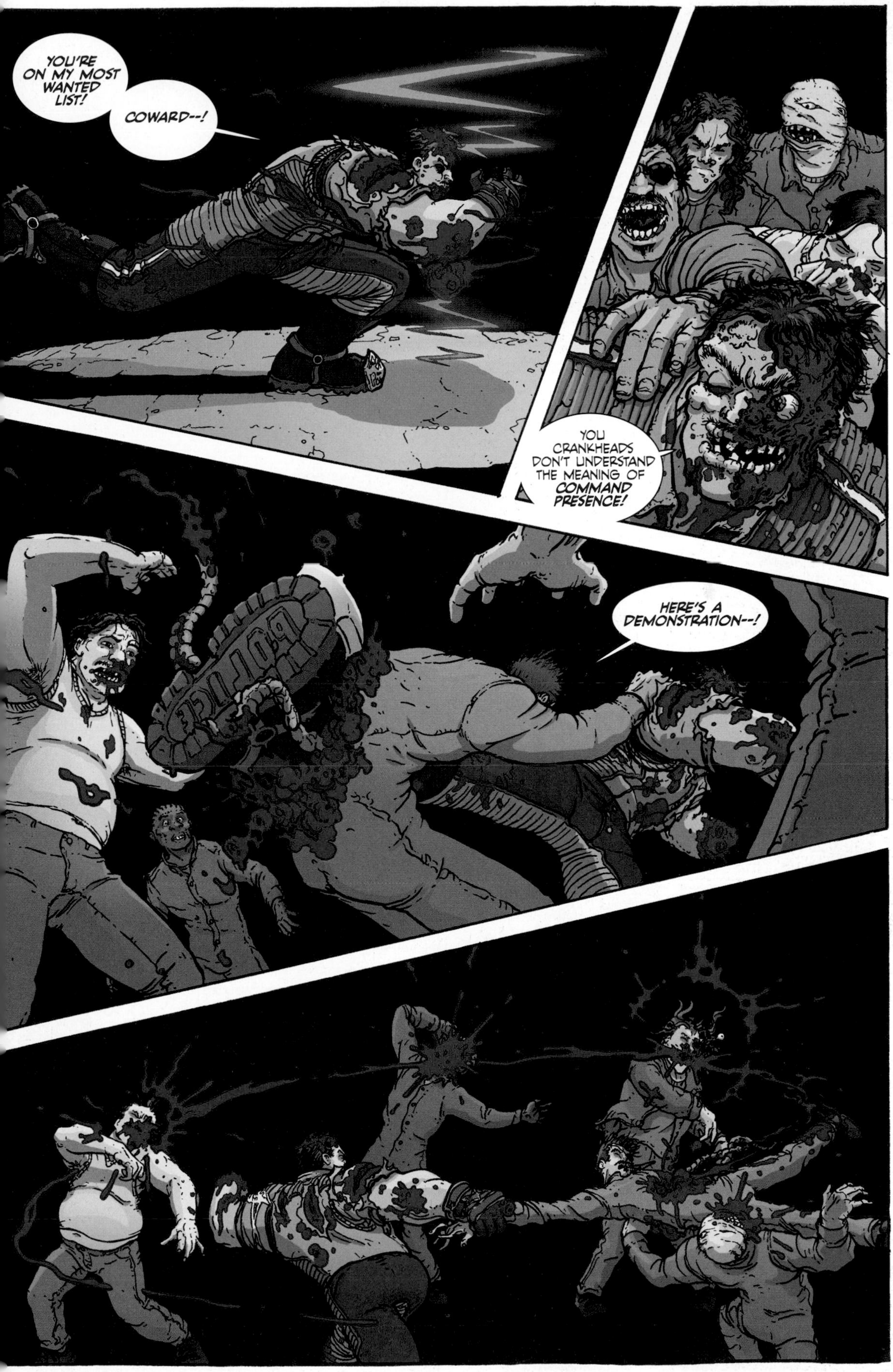
YOU'RE ON MY MOST WANTED LIST!
COWARD--!
YOU CRANKHEADS DON'T UNDERSTAND THE MEANING OF COMMAND PRESENCE!
POLICE
HERE'S A DEMONSTRATION--!

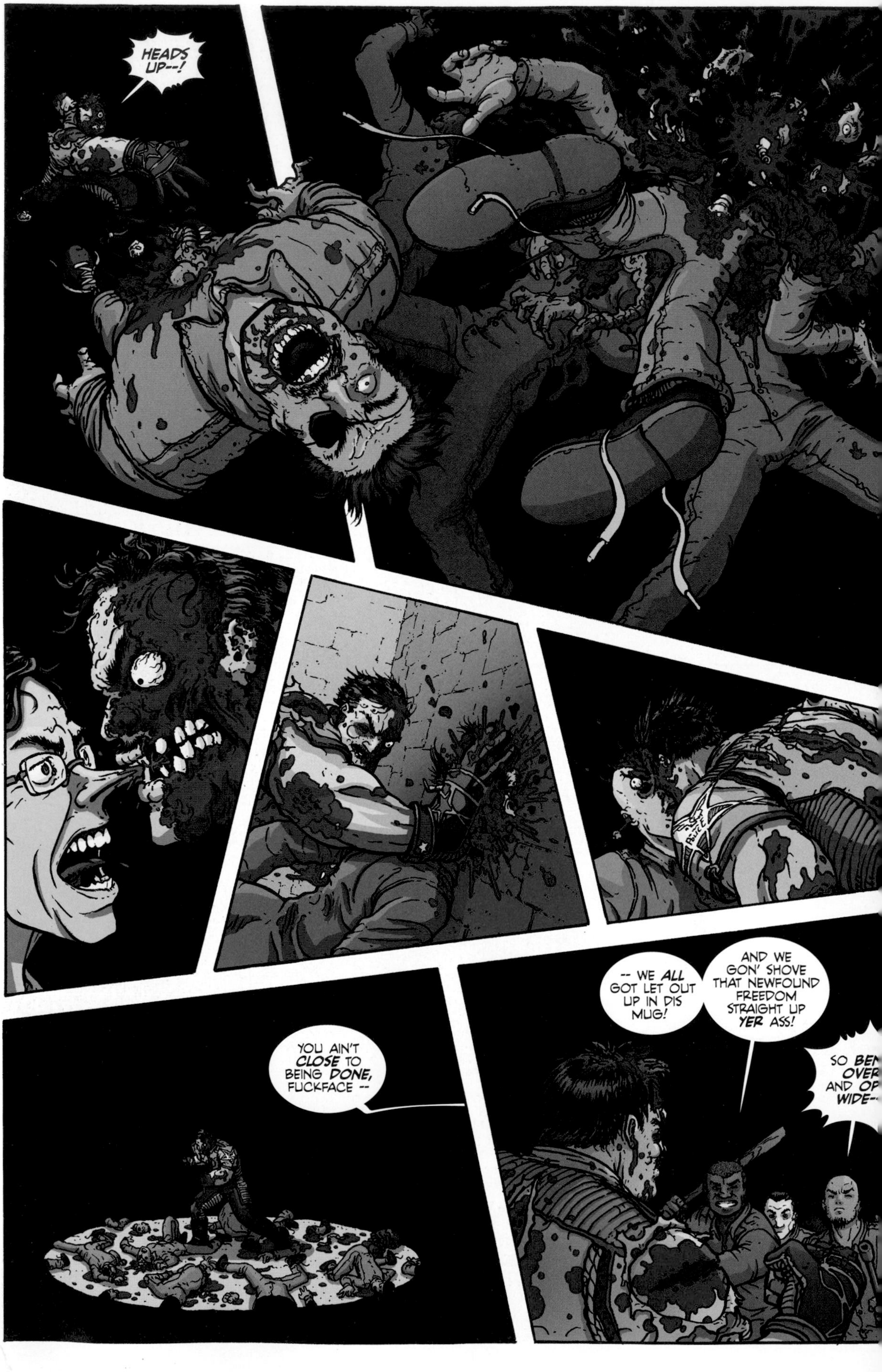
HEADS UP--!
YOU AIN'T CLOSE TO BEING DONE, FUCKFACE --
-- WE ALL GOT LET OUT UP IN DIS MUG!
AND WE GON' SHOVE THAT NEWFOUND FREEDOM STRAIGHT UP YER ASS!
SO BEN OVER AND OP WIDE--

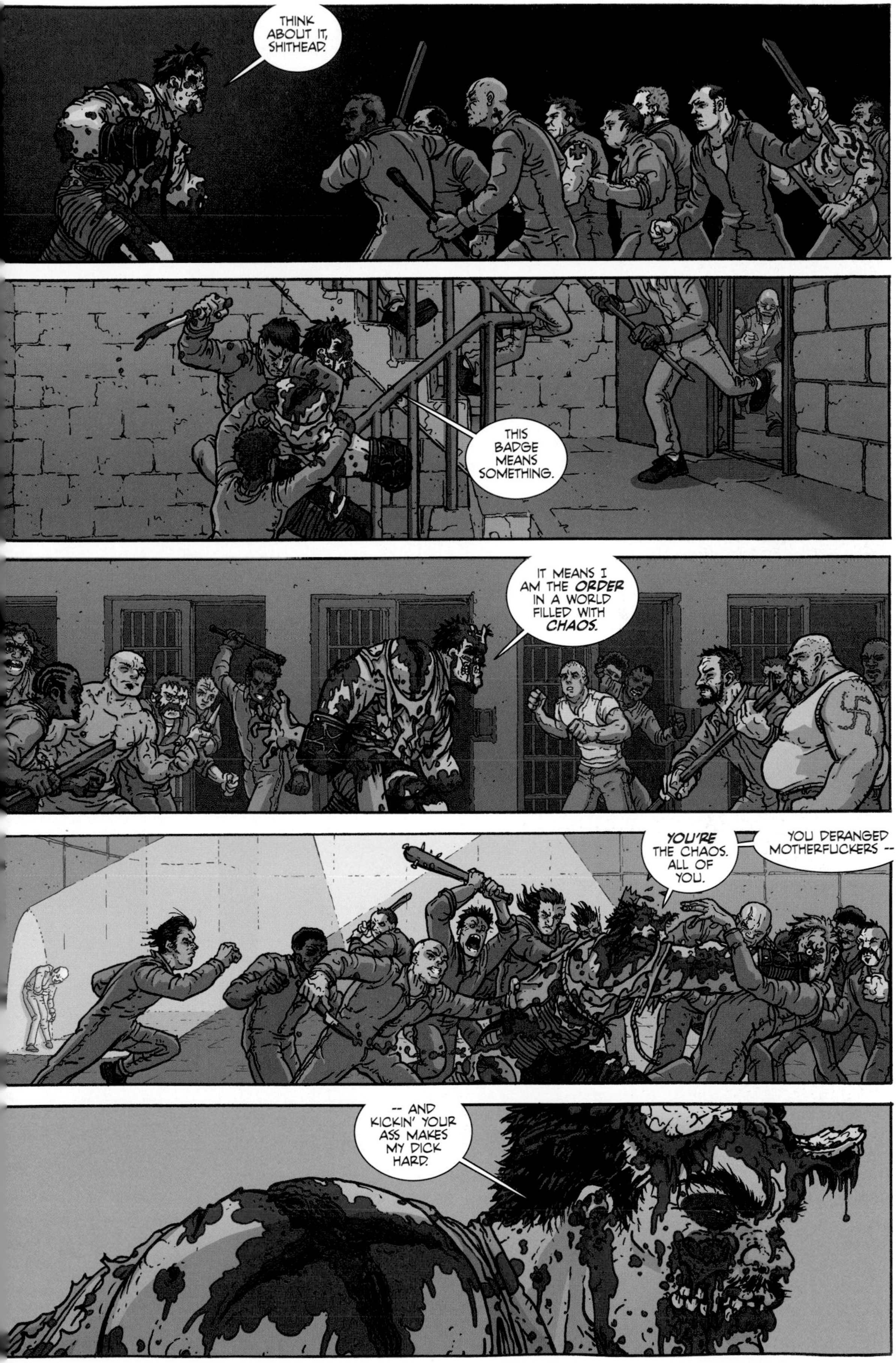
THINK ABOUT IT, SHITHEAD.
THIS BADGE MEANS SOMETHING.
IT MEANS I AM THE ORDER IN A WORLD FILLED WITH CHAOS.
YOU'RE THE CHAOS. ALL OF YOU.
YOU DERANGED MOTHERFUCKERS --
-- AND KICKIN' YOUR ASS MAKES MY DICK HARD.

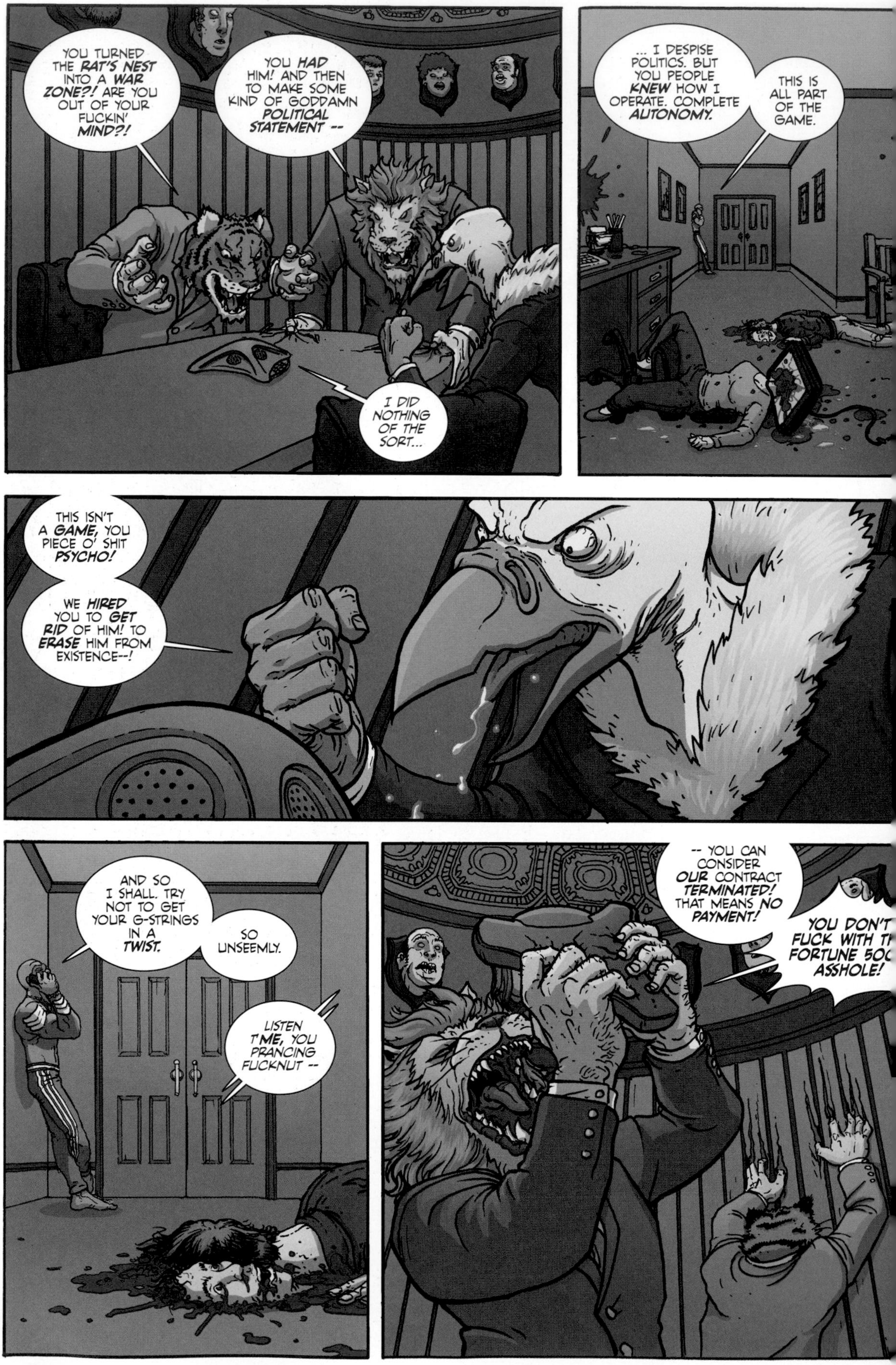
YOU TURNED THE RAT'S NEST INTO A WAR ZONE?! ARE YOU OUT OF YOUR FUCKIN' MIND?!
YOU HAD HIM! AND THEN TO MAKE SOME KIND OF GODDAMN POLITICAL STATEMENT --
I DID NOTHING OF THE SORT...
... I DESPISE POLITICS. BUT YOU PEOPLE KNEW HOW I OPERATE. COMPLETE AUTONOMY.
THIS IS ALL PART OF THE GAME.
THIS ISN'T A GAME, YOU PIECE O' SHIT PSYCHO!
WE HIRED YOU TO GET RID OF HIM! TO ERASE HIM FROM EXISTENCE--!
AND SO I SHALL. TRY NOT TO GET YOUR G-STRINGS IN A TWIST.
SO UNSEEMLY.
LISTEN T'ME, YOU PRANCING FUCKNUT --
-- YOU CAN CONSIDER OUR CONTRACT TERMINATED! THAT MEANS NO PAYMENT!
YOU DON'T
FUCK WITH T
FORTUNE 50
ASSHOLE!

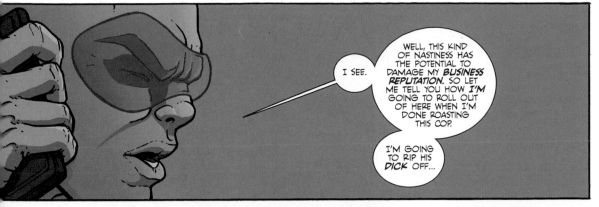

WELL, THIS KIND OF NASTINESS HAS THE POTENTIAL TO DAMAGE MY *BUSINESS REPUTATION.* SO LET ME TELL YOU HOW *I'M* GOING TO ROLL OUT OF HERE WHEN I'M DONE ROASTING THIS COP.

I SEE.

I'M GOING TO RIP HIS *DICK* OFF...

... AND THEN I'M GOING TO *FIND* YOU --

-- AND FUCK YOU TO *DEATH* WITH IT.

*ALL* OF YOU.

ENJOY THE REST OF YOUR EVENING. THIS IS ZEN MASTER FLASH SIGNING OFF...

OH SHIT.

UNPROFESSIONAL...!

FASHION NIGHTMARES...!

IT WOULD APPEAR THAT ESTABLISHING A *BEACHHEAD* IS IN ORDER...

THIS WHOLE THING...

... THIS IS *NOT* HOW IT WAS SUPPOSED TO GO...!

JESUS... THE U.S. ATTORNEY'S OFFICE IS GOING TO CRAWL RIGHT UP MY *ASS* FOR THIS... JUST LIKE THAT GRAND JURY INVESTIGATION...!

AND WHAT'RE *YOU* BLUBBERING ABOUT?

*ME?!* I'M BLUBBERING BECAUSE YOU *FUCKED* UP!

WHAT, ARE YOU *DEAF?!* CAN'T YOU HEAR WHAT'S HAPPENING OUT THERE?!

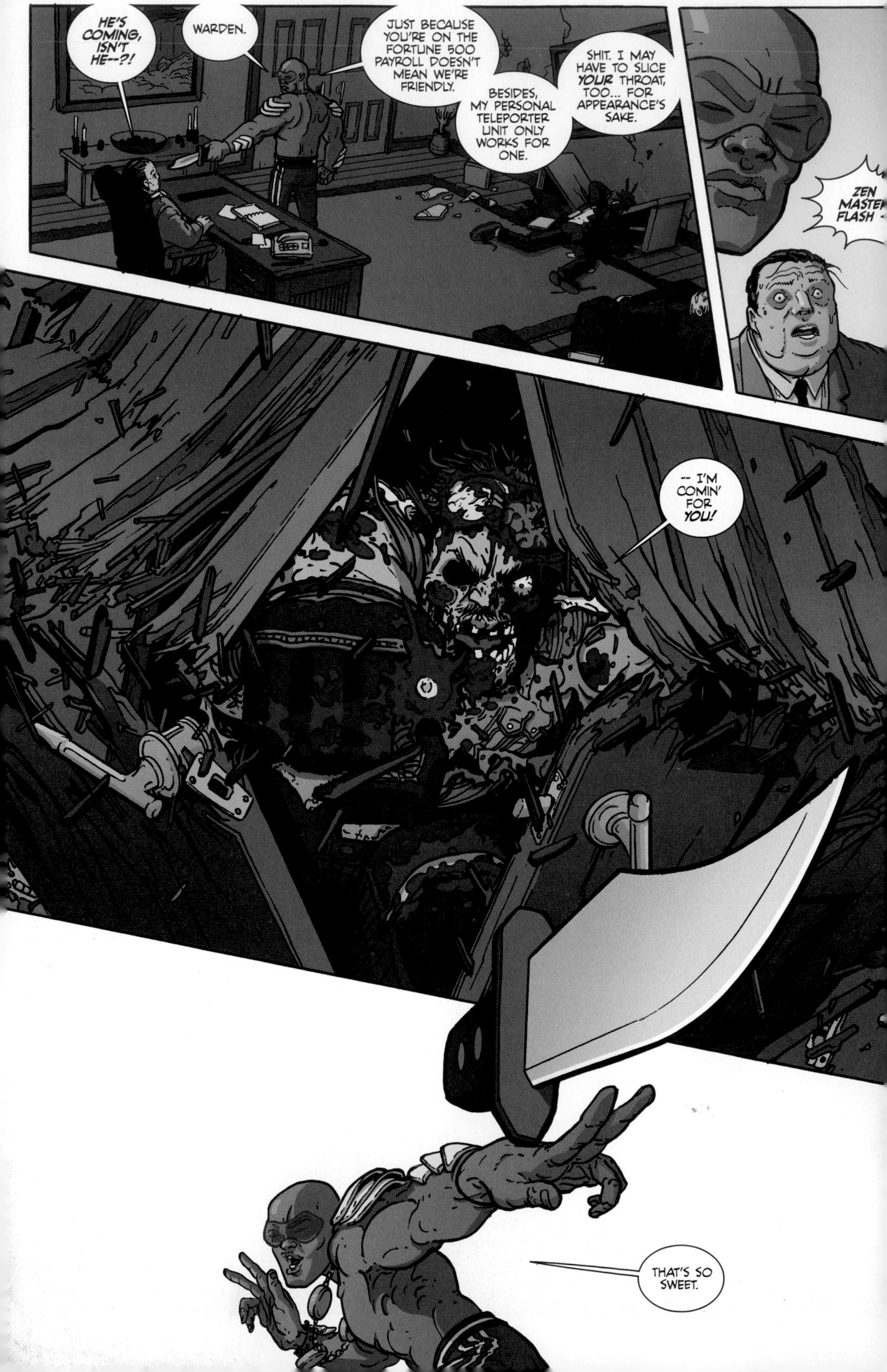
HE'S COMING, ISN'T HE--?!
WARDEN.
JUST BECAUSE YOU'RE ON THE FORTUNE 500 PAYROLL DOESN'T MEAN WE'RE FRIENDLY.
BESIDES, MY PERSONAL TELEPORTER UNIT ONLY WORKS FOR ONE.
SHIT. I MAY HAVE TO SLICE *YOUR* THROAT, TOO... FOR APPEARANCE'S SAKE.
-- I'M COMIN' FOR *YOU!*
THAT'S SO SWEET.

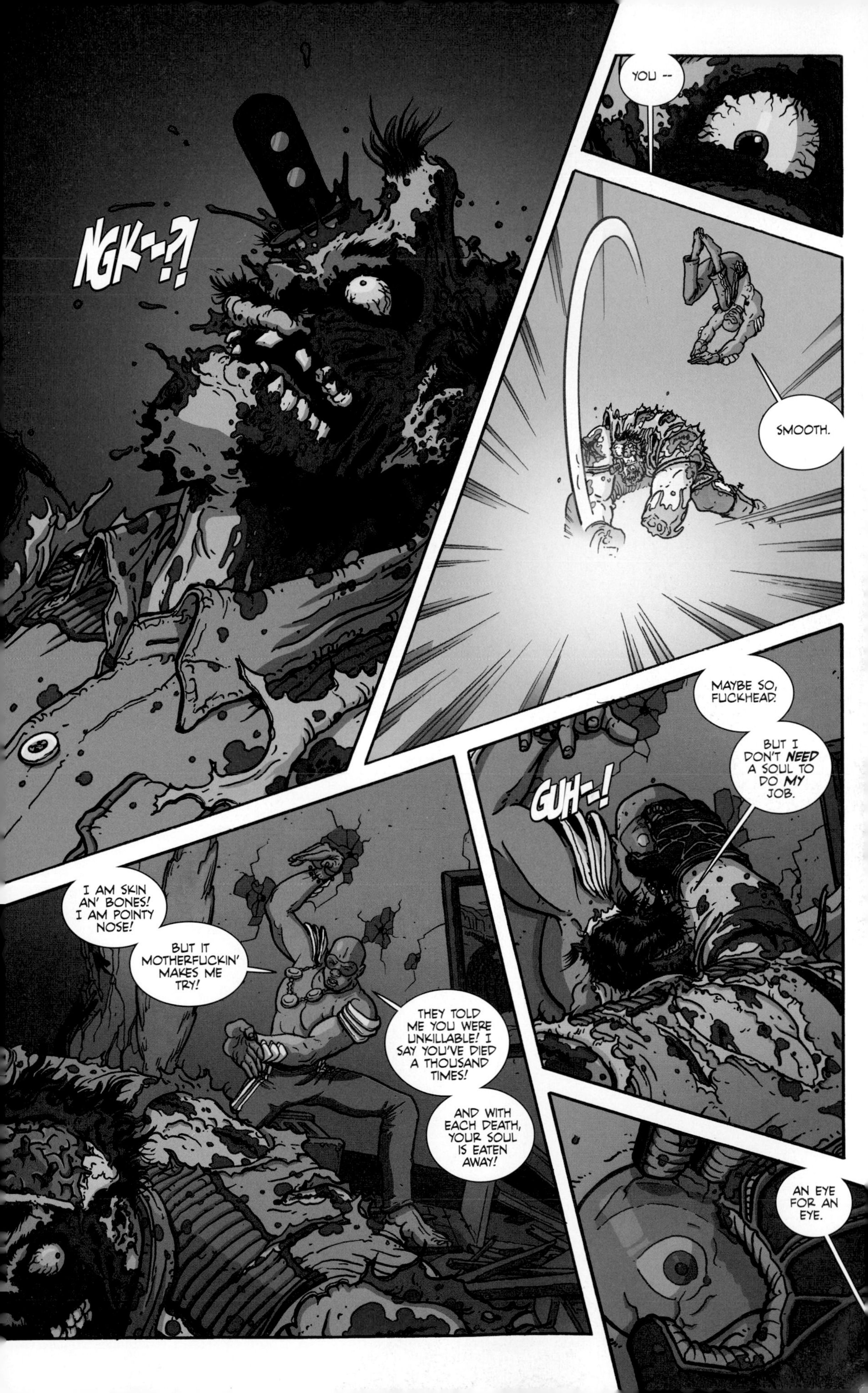
NGK--?!
YOU --
SMOOTH.
MAYBE SO, FUCKHEAD.
BUT I DON'T **NEED** A SOUL TO DO **MY** JOB.
GUH--!
I AM SKIN AN' BONES! I AM POINTY NOSE!
BUT IT MOTHERFUCKIN' MAKES ME TRY!
THEY TOLD ME YOU WERE UNKILLABLE! I SAY YOU'VE DIED A THOUSAND TIMES!
AND WITH EACH DEATH, YOUR SOUL IS EATEN AWAY!
AN EYE FOR AN EYE.

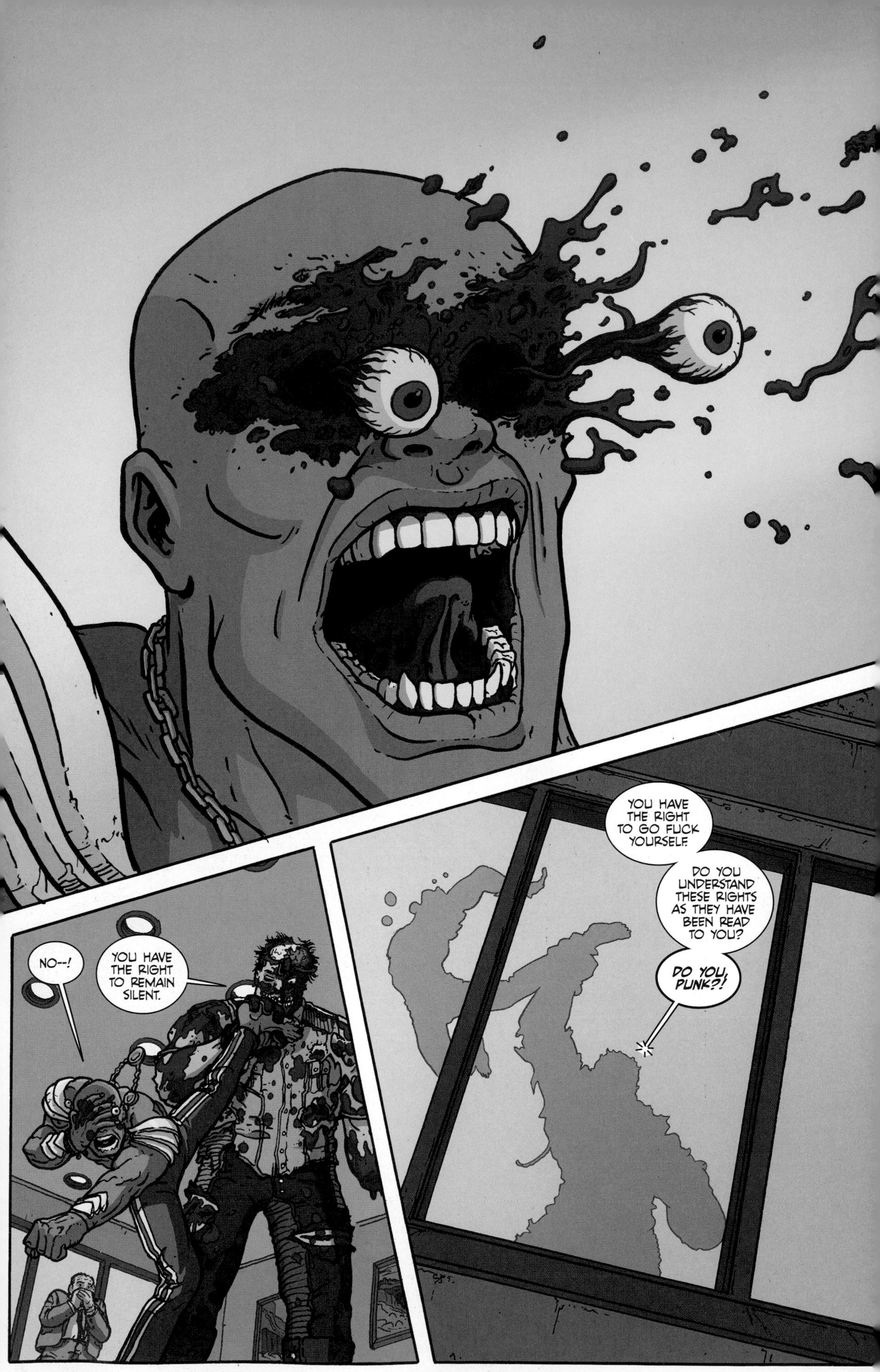
NO--!
YOU HAVE THE RIGHT TO REMAIN SILENT.
YOU HAVE THE RIGHT TO GO FUCK YOURSELF.
DO YOU UNDERSTAND THESE RIGHTS AS THEY HAVE BEEN READ TO YOU?
DO YOU, PUNK?!

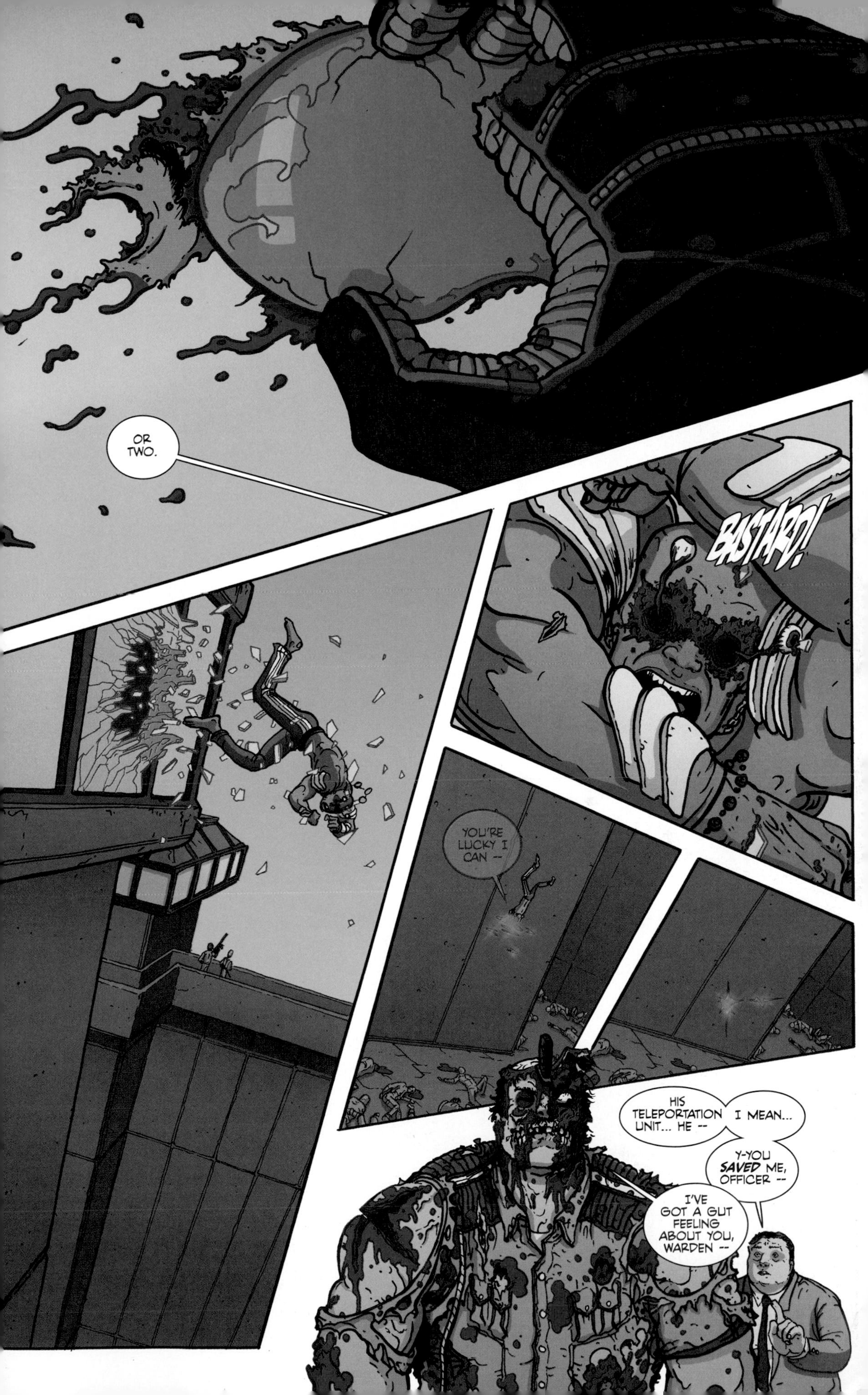
OR TWO.
BASTARD!
YOU'RE LUCKY I CAN --
HIS TELEPORTATION UNIT... HE --
I MEAN...
Y-YOU *SAVED* ME, OFFICER --
I'VE GOT A GUT FEELING ABOUT YOU, WARDEN --

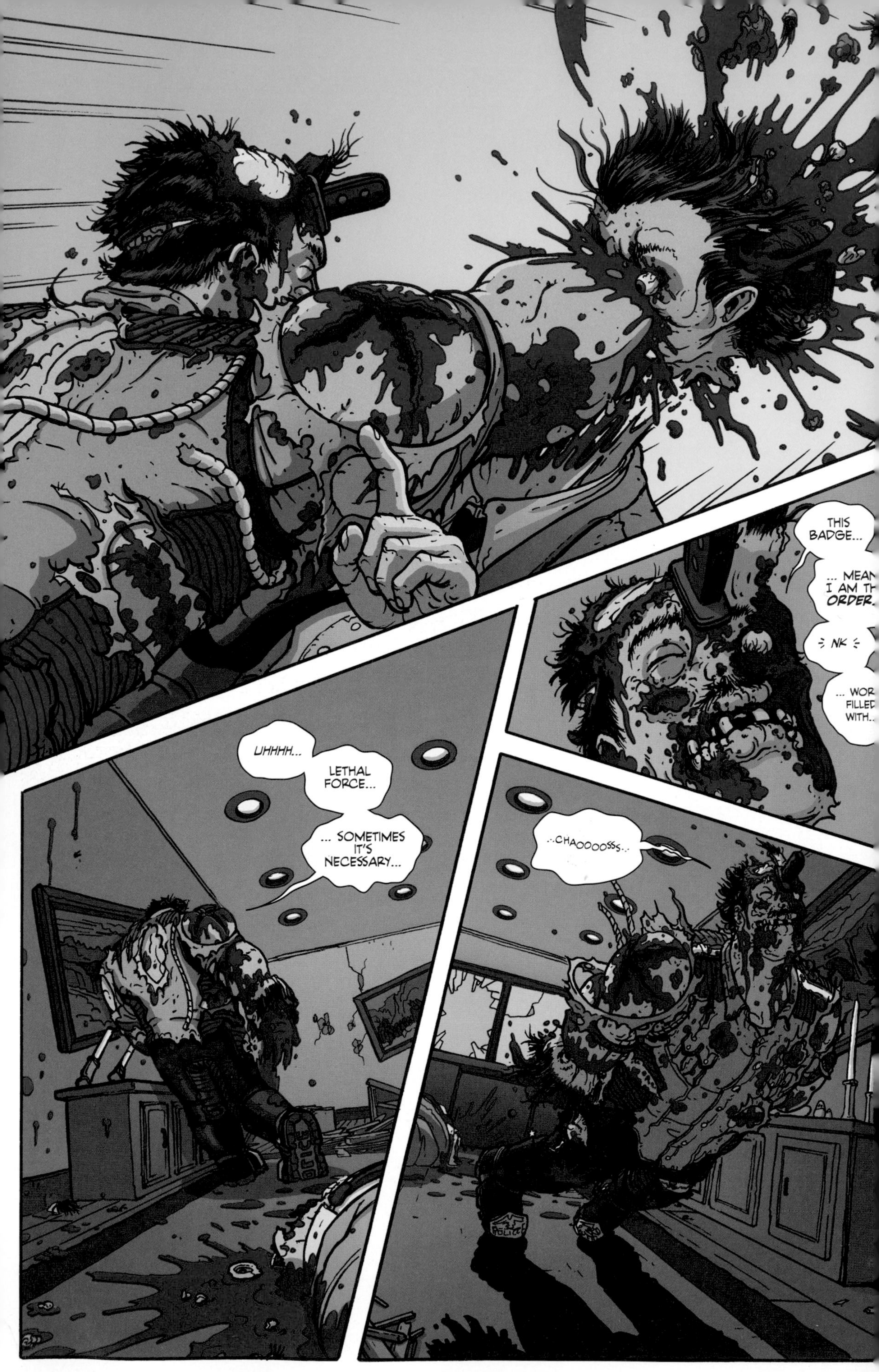
THIS BADGE...
... MEAN I AM TH ORDER.
NK
... WOR FILLED WITH...
UHHHH...
LETHAL FORCE...
... SOMETIMES IT'S NECESSARY...
..CHAOOOOSSS..

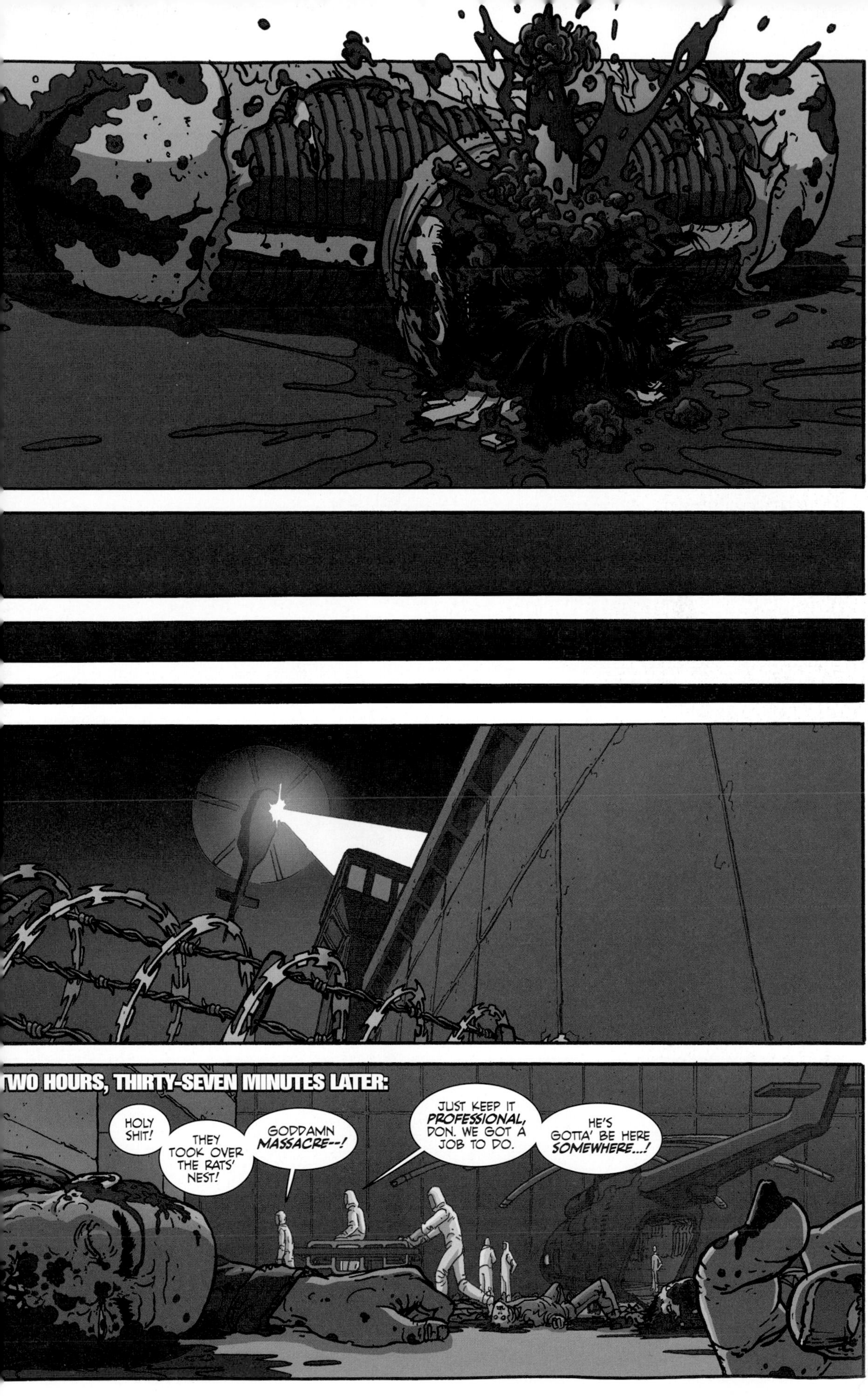
TWO HOURS, THIRTY-SEVEN MINUTES LATER:
HOLY SHIT!
THEY TOOK OVER THE RATS' NEST!
GODDAMN MASSACRE--!
JUST KEEP IT PROFESSIONAL, DON. WE GOT A JOB TO DO.
HE'S GOTTA' BE HERE SOMEWHERE...!

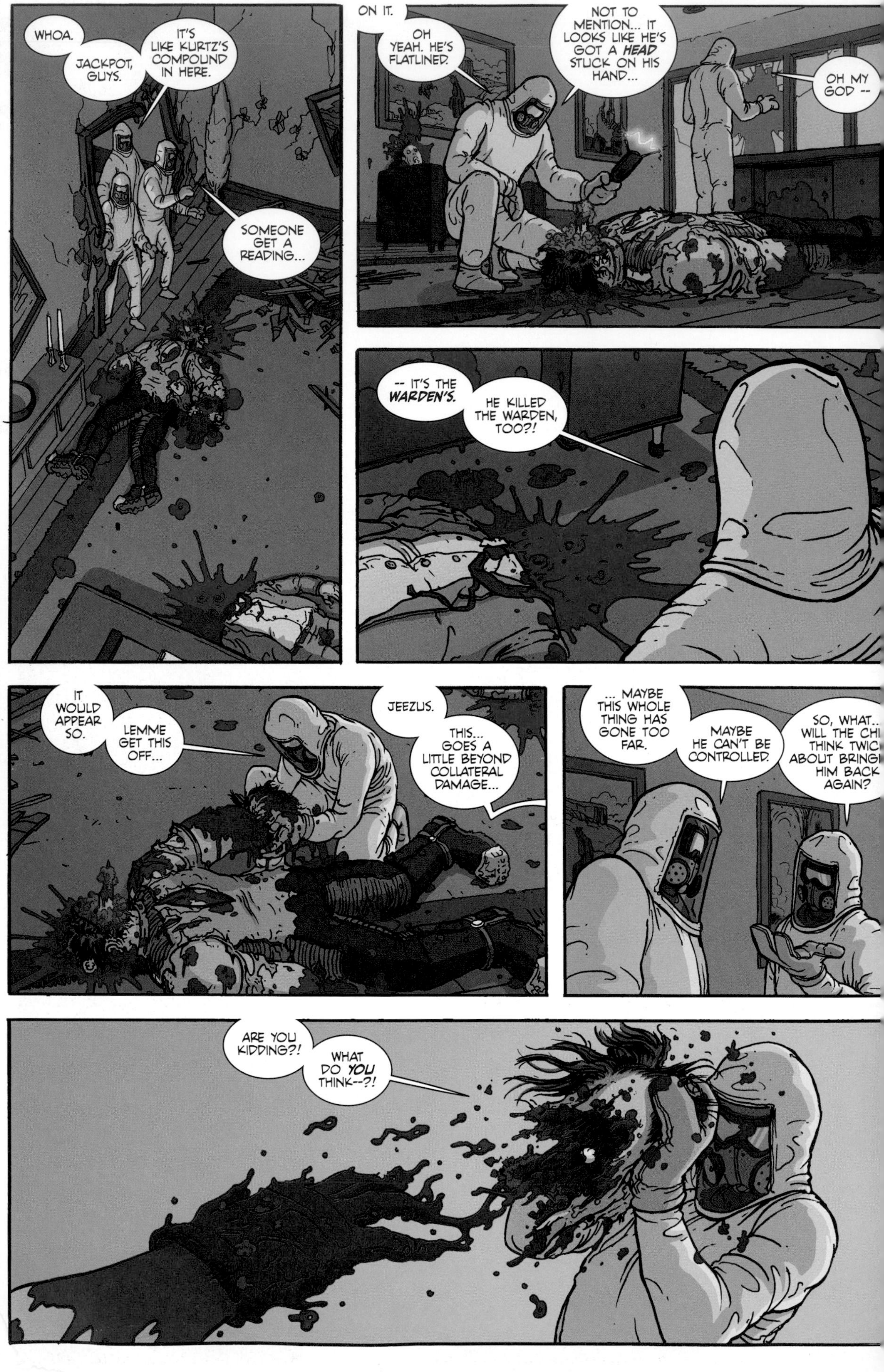
WHOA.
JACKPOT, GUYS.
IT'S LIKE KURTZ'S COMPOUND IN HERE.
SOMEONE GET A READING...
ON IT.
OH YEAH. HE'S FLATLINED.
NOT TO MENTION... IT LOOKS LIKE HE'S GOT A HEAD STUCK ON HIS HAND...
OH MY GOD --
-- IT'S THE WARDEN'S.
HE KILLED THE WARDEN, TOO?!
IT WOULD APPEAR SO.
LEMME GET THIS OFF...
JEEZUS.
THIS... GOES A LITTLE BEYOND COLLATERAL DAMAGE...
... MAYBE THIS WHOLE THING HAS GONE TOO FAR.
MAYBE HE CAN'T BE CONTROLLED.
SO, WHAT... WILL THE CHI THINK TWIC ABOUT BRINGI HIM BACK AGAIN?
ARE YOU KIDDING?!
WHAT DO YOU THINK--?!

...DO YOU SEE THE SHAPE HE IS IN?!

NO *WAY* HE'LL COME BACK FROM ALL THAT--!

CALM DOWN.

THE BOYS IN THE BULLPEN ARE BACK IN THE SADDLE.

JUST TAKES A WHILE...

... THE EXTENT OF THE DAMAGE... A LOT OF *REBUILDING* TO BE DONE...

HOW'S IT *GOING* OVER THERE, SIMMONS?

PRETTY GOOD, SIR.

SELF-REPAIR IS COMMENCING NICELY.

WE'RE AT ABOUT EIGHTY-THREE PERCENT...

THIS IS THE WORLD WE LIVE IN, ROOKIE. YEAH, IT'S A CORRUPT SYSTEM, ALL AROUND. NO SENSE IN DENYING IT.

DOWNE'S A *RARE* BREED. HE'S AN ABSOLUTE. HE DOESN'T WAVER. RIGHT OR WRONG...

... WE *NEED* HIM OUT THERE.

OKAY, THAT'S IT!

SHUT IT DOWN!

ALL SYSTEMS -- *OFF!*

OKAY...

... THIS WAS A ROUGH ONE.

MAYBE HIS MIND DIDN'T FULLY--

LOOKIN' GOOD, TERRY...

... JUST LIKE NEW.

HOPE YOU'RE NOT EXPECTING A *VACATION* OR ANYTHING.

YOUR JOB'S NOT DONE YET.

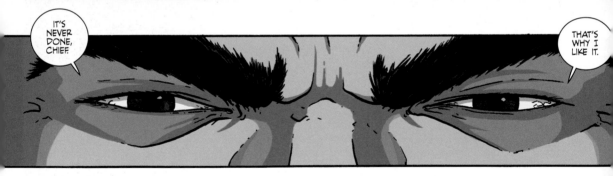

IT'S NEVER DONE, CHIEF.

THAT'S WHY I LIKE IT.

**THE MOTHERFUCKIN' 105:**

NOT A BAD HAUL, YO--!

COLLECTING IS THE NEW BLACK, NO DOUBT ABOUT IT.

NVR DED

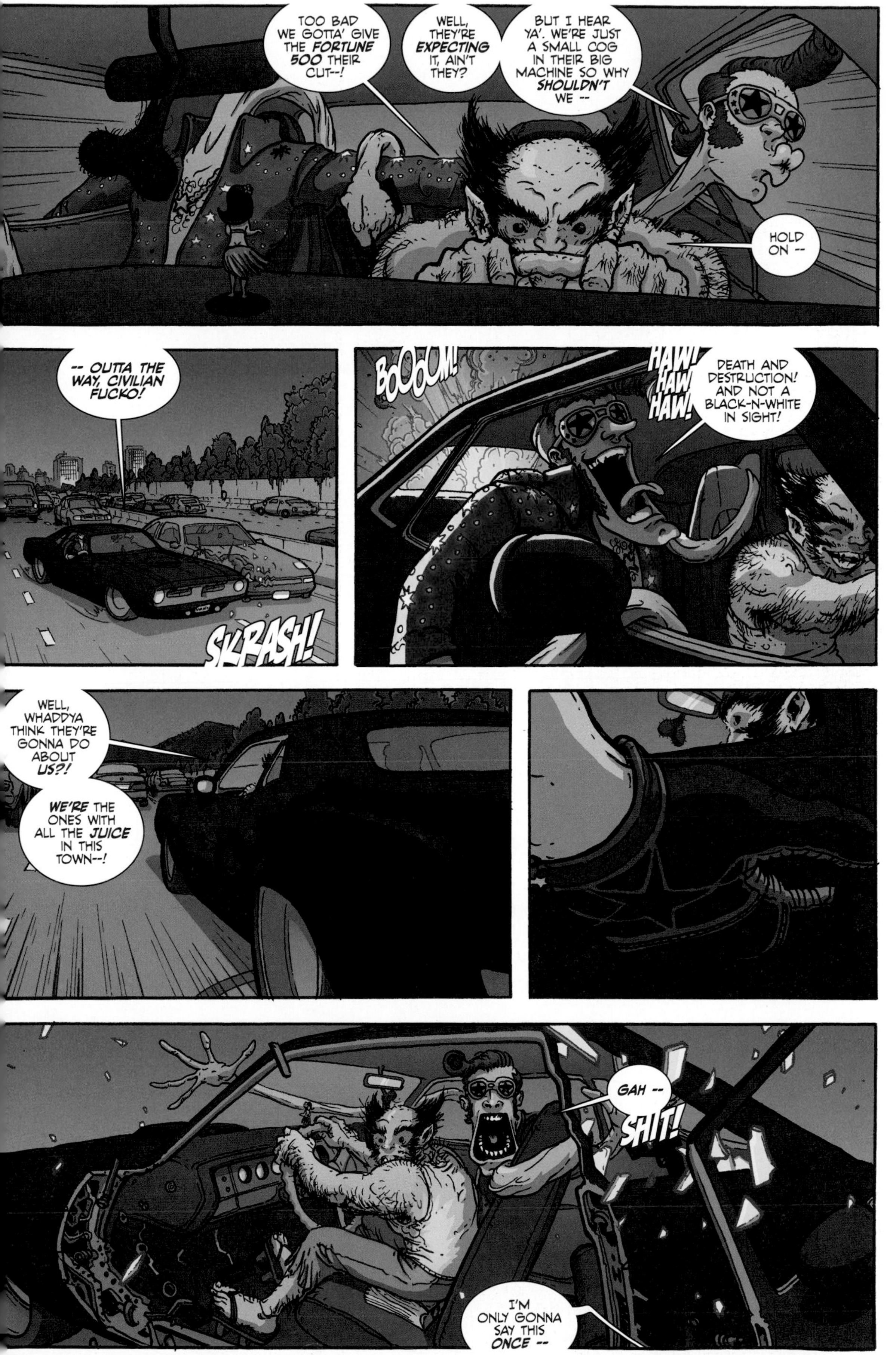
TOO BAD WE GOTTA' GIVE THE FORTUNE 500 THEIR CUT--!
WELL, THEY'RE EXPECTING IT, AIN'T THEY?
BUT I HEAR YA'. WE'RE JUST A SMALL COG IN THEIR BIG MACHINE SO WHY SHOULDN'T WE --
HOLD ON --
-- OUTTA THE WAY, CIVILIAN FUCKO!
SKRASH!
BOOOOM!
HAW! HAW! HAW!
DEATH AND DESTRUCTION! AND NOT A BLACK-N-WHITE IN SIGHT!
WELL, WHADDYA THINK THEY'RE GONNA DO ABOUT US?!
WE'RE THE ONES WITH ALL THE JUICE IN THIS TOWN--!
GAH --
SHIT!
I'M ONLY GONNA SAY THIS ONCE --

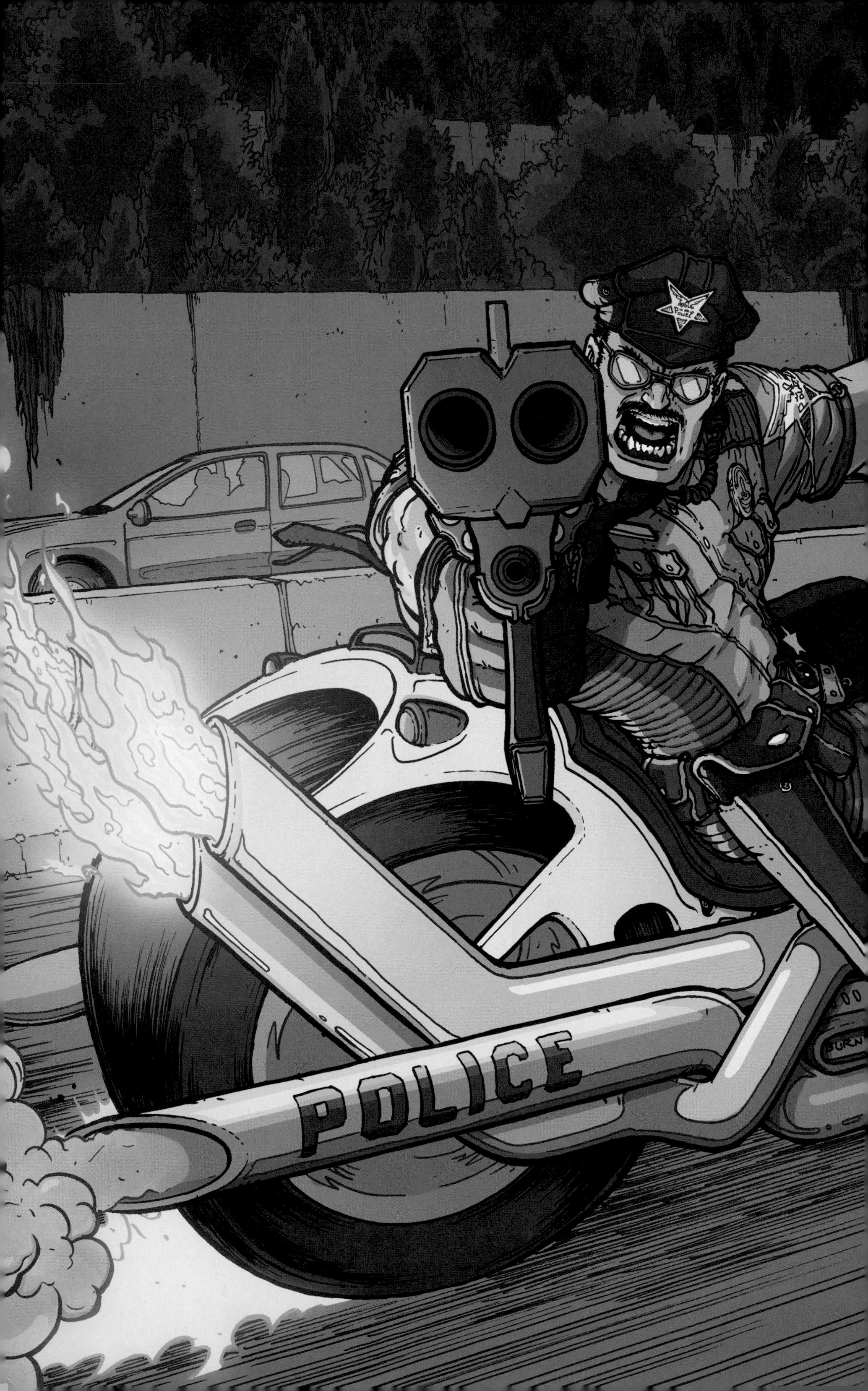
POLICE

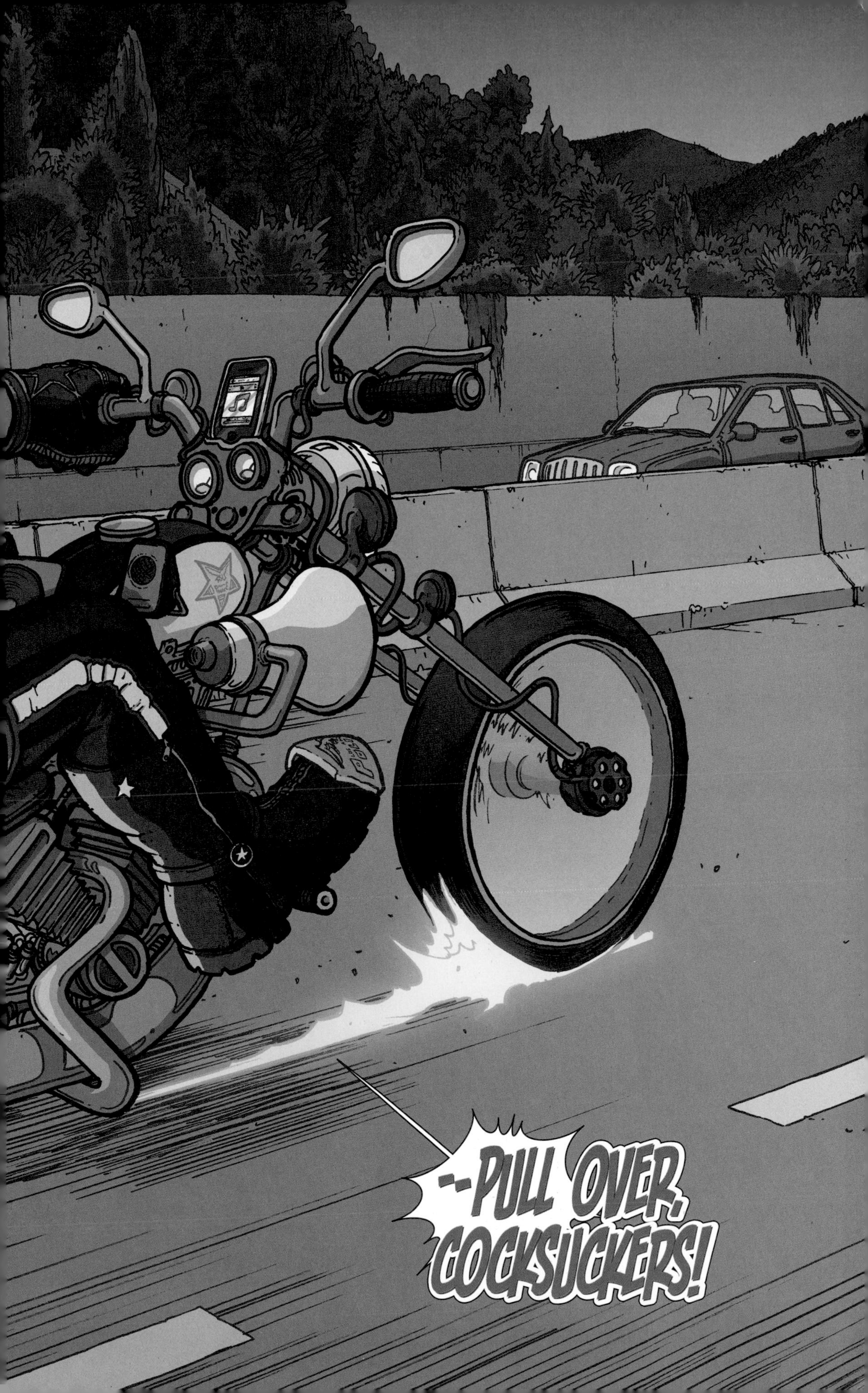
--PULL OVER, COCKSUCKERS!

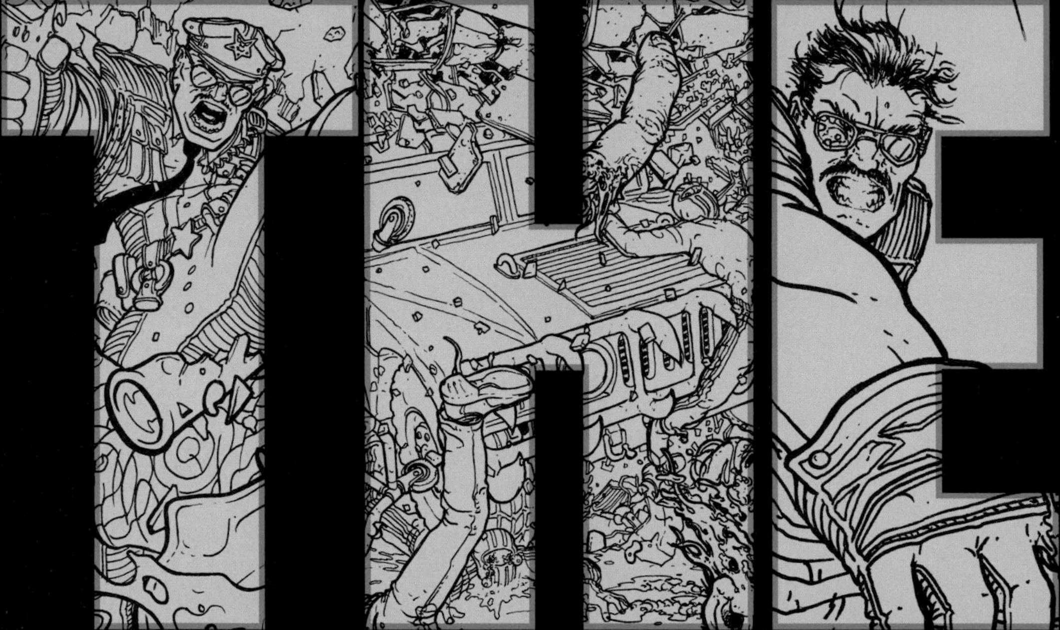
THE

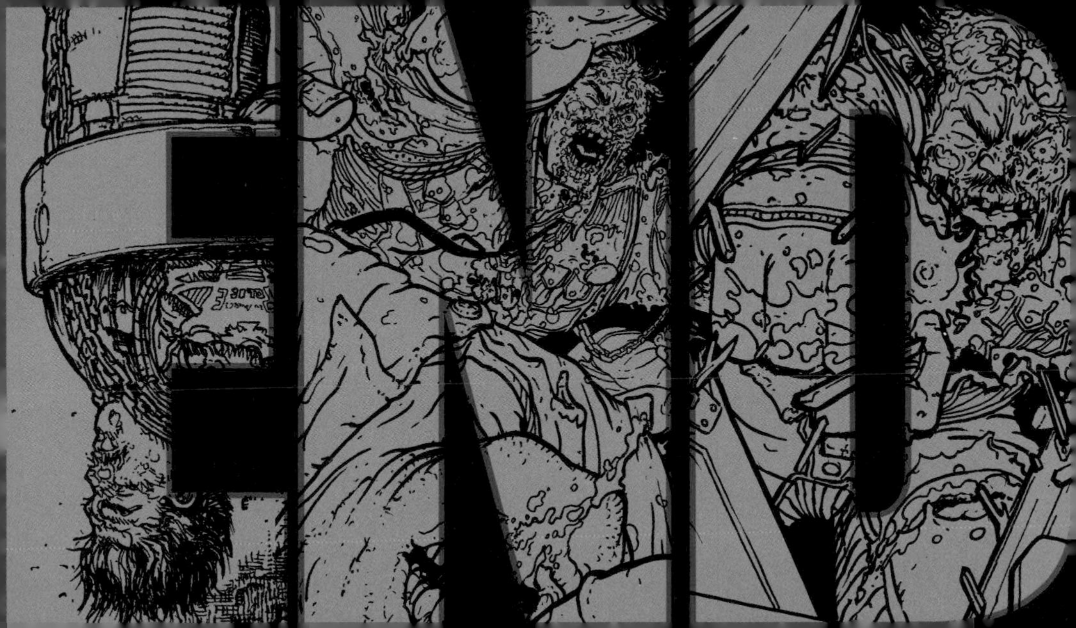
END

# FROM PRINT TO SCREEN (LIGHT MY WAY)

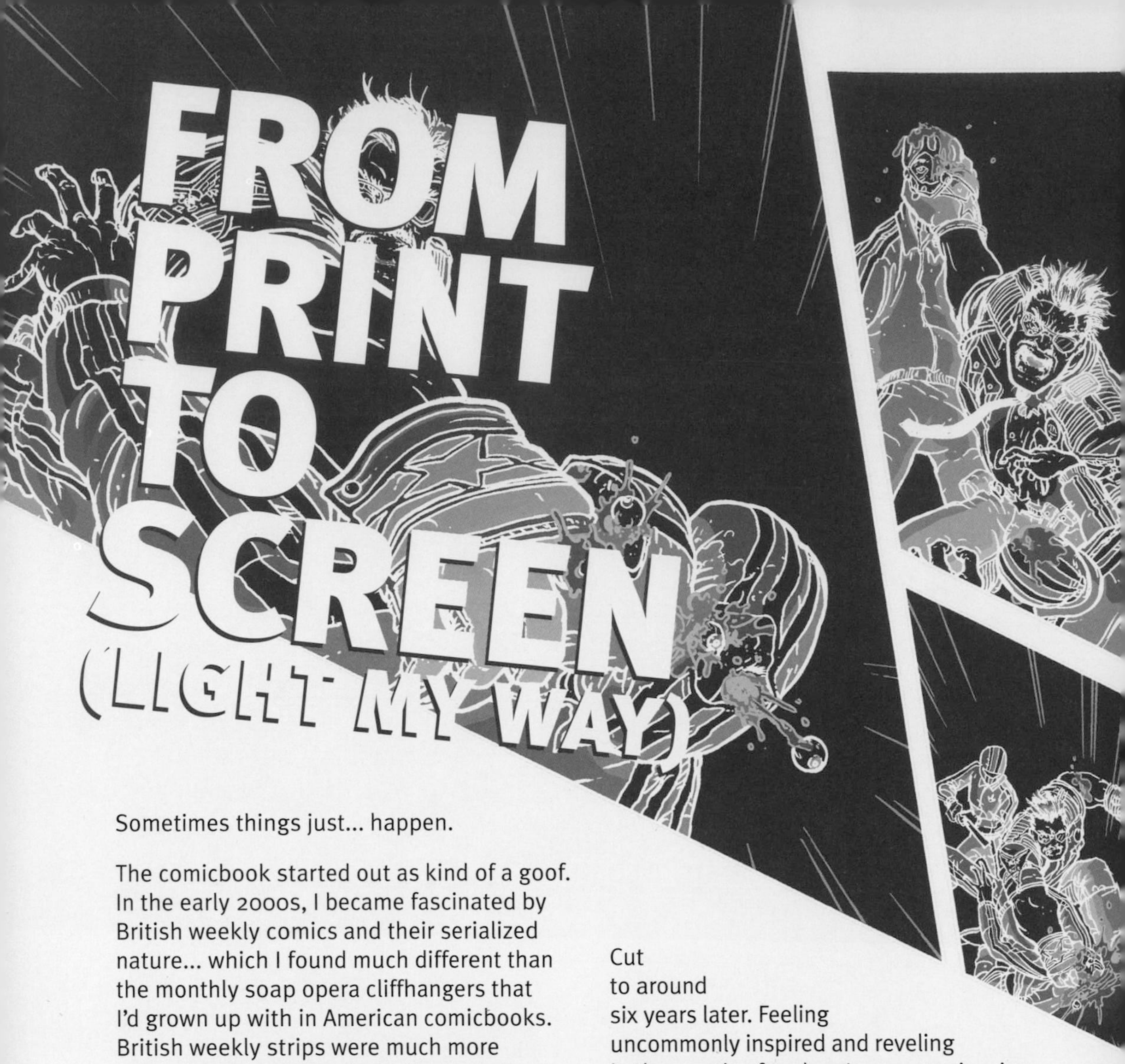

Sometimes things just... happen.

The comicbook started out as kind of a goof. In the early 2000s, I became fascinated by British weekly comics and their serialized nature... which I found much different than the monthly soap opera cliffhangers that I'd grown up with in American comicbooks. British weekly strips were much more sensationalized and adrenalized. Much more grindhouse in nature, heavy on the irony (something America has always had a little trouble with). When you're in the right mood for it, those comics can really hit the spot. From there, I came up with a bunch of half-baked ideas that were inspired by the vintage -- and by "vintage", I mean circa 1980–1994 -- strip concepts that seemed to just fall out of periodicals like *Deadline*, *Crisis*, *Toxic* and, of course, *2000AD*, where concept ruled over character.

*Officer Downe* was borne out of that private brainstorming-with-myself session. I wrote it up fairly quickly. It was all style and very little substance. Basically, everything was there... Officer Downe and his conceit, even the villains, the Fortune 500 and Zen Master Flash. But even though I discussed the idea with an editor at Dark Horse Comics, it never went anywhere and I moved on to other things.

Cut to around six years later. Feeling uncommonly inspired and reveling in the creative freedom I was experiencing in my relationship with Image Comics, I decided to dust off this idea and run it past my *Nixon's Pals* collaborator, Chris Burnham. I basically sent him the one sheet I'd typed up six years earlier. In record time, he was on board and we were off to the races. Again, it was something fairly low-impact... a one-shot comicbook where Burnham and I could have a few laughs indulging in a silly concept executed with over-the-top creative abandon. If you've just read this thing for the first time, you can probably attest to the fact that our self-indulgence certainly shines through.

Maybe three years after we published the initial volume, I got contacted out of the blue by producer Skip Williamson. He and *Crank* co-director, Mark Neveldine wanted to talk to me about *Officer Downe*. They wanted to make a movie out of it. They had picked up on the ironic, grindhouse nature of the thing.

They had a vague idea how to do it (which wasn't exactly how we ended up doing it, but we never lost the spirit of that initial concept) and I was into their vibe. I don't know what they were expecting in meeting me... they didn't have a clue about the whole Man Of Action Entertainment thing. They had no idea about *Ben 10* or anything else I'd done up until that point. Not that it mattered, but it did give me a little teeth in making my "demands" when it came to attempting a feature film adaptation of our little comicbook. I wanted to produce it with them, and I would write the screenplay. I even offered to write it on spec (translation: for free). Certainly, anything happening for free is too good to turn down. So we figured out the paperwork and I went on my merry way, firing up Final Draft and diving in.

Honestly, this wasn't my first time at the dance... so my expectations weren't especially high that this movie would ever get made. But I didn't let that stop me. I looked at it as an opportunity. Screenplays can be incredibly fun and easy to write. That is, if you've got a good grip on your story and characters. Which, in this case, I thought I did. I mean, I'd written the comicbook... who knew better than me how to tackle the material as a movie?

To say the *Officer Downe* comicbook is thin is only a slight exaggeration... although Burnham's work on it alone is worth hours of sitting and staring. The detail he put into it is staggering; every drawing tells its own story. Plot-wise? Well... what can I say? In a lot of ways, it was what I would call an "improv comicbook". Meaning, you have a basic idea and a loose framework and, from there, you basically make shit up as you go along and hope that it all works out in the end. It's a real tightrope walk, but for me, it's the only way I can get close in the *writing* of a comicbook to the feeling I can get *reading* one.

A good one, that is. Luckily, I've been doing this a long time and I've worked hard to amass the skills that I can call upon when I am improvising on the page.

Most of the time, it's worked out for me. It did in this case, anyway. I think the *Officer Downe* comicbook delivers exactly what you expect it should.

But this was going to be a feature film screenplay, and "thin" wasn't quite going to cut it. The first thing I did was a fairly straightforward and faithful adaptation of the material contained in the comicbook. Then I looked at what I had... which turned out to be just under an hour's worth of screen time. Even if I padded everything out with all the typical tricks that writers sometimes do to make something seem more substantial that is really is, it still wasn't enough to fill up the 90 to 100 minutes that lets you know you went to the fuckin' movies.

So that's when I remembered... the odds of this thing ever making it to production were so slim -- practically nonexistent -- that I might as well have fun writing the screenplay in the same way I had fun writing the original comicbook. In other words, I just dove in and winged it.

I added the Mother Supreme/gun-running nuns subplot. I beefed up Gable's role considerably. I tried to provide a little more depth to Downe's situation. I added more with the beat cops, fleshing out their motivations and why they might have a personal grudge against someone like Downe. I added a lot more action. I added more character interaction. I added more pathos to the relationship between Downe and the telekinetics in the Bullpen. I wrote with no budget in mind. I put things in just for the hell of it. In-jokes that only I might get.

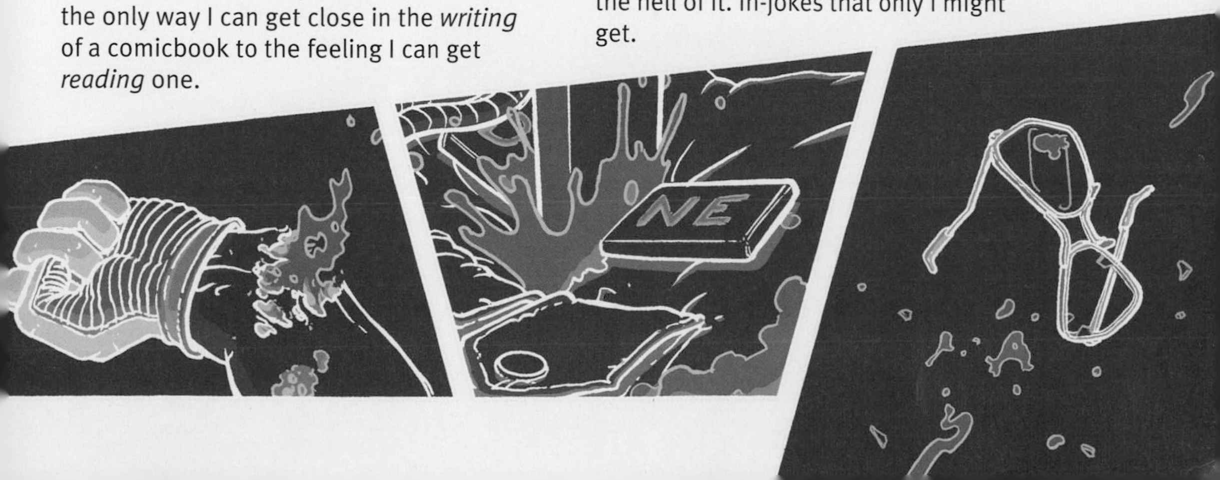
NE

Asides that were nods -- both obvious and not-so-obvious -- to things that had inspired me. For the most part, I just had a blast with it. After all, it's not like it was ever going to be *filmed*...!

Soon enough the script was done and Skip and Nev were happy with it. I kinda dug it, too. The lack of self-consciousness involved in writing the damn thing gave it a certain energy, a certain spark. At least, that's what I thought at the time. Once I was finished, aside from occasionally checking in with my fellow producers on any progress made, I didn't think too much about it.

And then, just about two years after I wrote the script, the weirdest thing happened... we actually found the money and suddenly the movie was going to get made.

At this point, as we careened headlong into actual production, budget *was* a real concern. I had to take a good, hard look at what I'd written. The fact was, there was only a certain amount of money we were given to make this thing, so there needed to be script revisions. Quite a few of them, actually. But that's *not* the script included here. For historical reasons... and because I'm lazy... the script reprinted here is the draft that went out to financiers, agents, actors, etc.

This was the script we had *before* the bell rang on pre-production. So if you've actually *seen* the finished film, you'll probably notice a few differences.

But as a lifelong process junkie myself, someone who occasionally reads screenplays for fun, I always appreciate seeing something in its "proto-form" as opposed to its polished, finished form. And, I do think, purely as a piece of screenwriting, this version reads much better than any strict transcript of the finished film would be.

I guess this is how I write movies when I don't give a fuck... and there's something kinda great about that. It certainly fits a movie like *Officer Downe*. And there's something pretty fucking great about *that*, too.

**Joe Casey**
**November 2016**

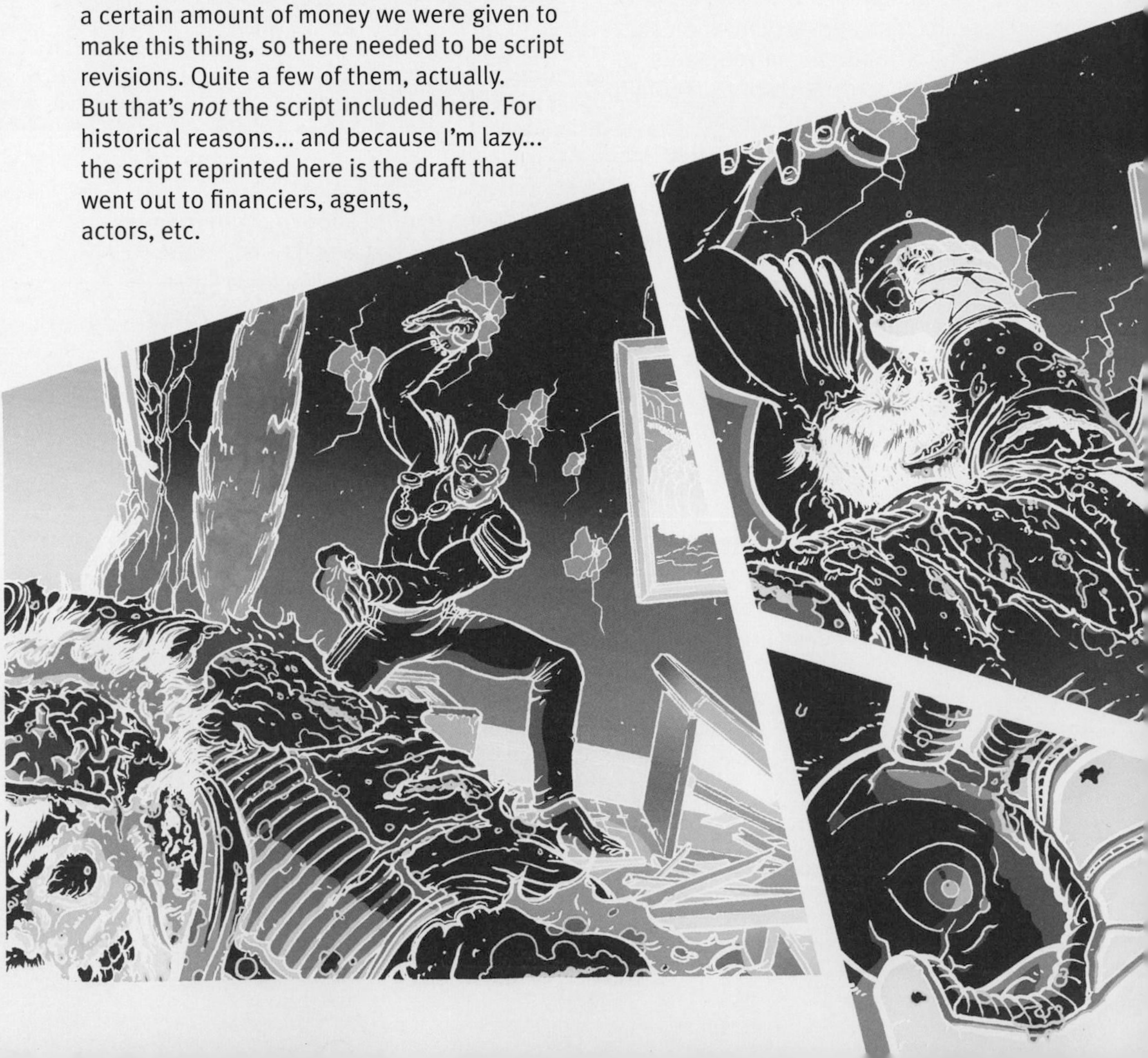

OFFICER DOWNE

written by

Joe Casey


based on the
graphic novel by
Joe Casey & Chris Burnham


FINAL DRAFT - 1.16.2105


Man Of Action Entertainment

INT. BEDROOM - NIGHT

A WOMAN'S HAND

Clutches the bedsheets. Her GRUNTS and MOANS cut through the silence of the room. The hand belongs to --

A NAKED WOMAN

Squirms across the bed. REVEAL a MAN'S HEAD buried between her legs.

(*The man's head belongs to our hero, OFFICER DOWNE*)

As DOWNE continues going down on her, the WOMAN wriggles and SHRIEKS her approval.

IN THE CORNER OF THE SCREEN: an ORGASM COUNTER graphic appears, along with NUMBERS that count upward with each moan and groan: 1... 2... 3... 4... and keep going up.

As things rise in intensity, DOWNE physically PICKS UP THE WOMAN -- always keeping his head in her crotch -- and they careen around the room. Her legs wrapped tight around his shoulders. They knock over furniture, bounce off the walls.

All the while, the WOMAN is loving it, achieving orgasm after orgasm.

The ORGASM COUNTER rises higher and higher: 9... 10... 11... 12...

DOWNE slams her down on the tip of the dresser. The WOMAN clutches the back of his head, pushing it deeper and deeper into her. Her GRUNTS of pleasure are getting bigger and louder.

The ORGASM COUNTER counts even higher: 17... 18... 19... 20...

On one of her ungodly, orgasmic SCREAMS we --

                                        SLAM CUT TO:


INT. BEDROOM - A FEW MINUTES LATER

The WOMAN is flat on her back, on her bed. Sweating, quivering and panting. The bedroom is trashed.

The ORGASM COUNTER (still supered in the corner of the screen) has stopped at 27.

                    WOMAN
                (breathless)
        Oh my God... oh my God... that
        was... oh my God...!

IN THE CORNER OF THE ROOM: DOWNE is pulling his underwear on.
Like nothing out of the ordinary happened here. He GRUNTS an
acknowledgement.

                    WOMAN (CONT'D)
                (still recovering)
        And you... didn't even... I mean,
        you just kept on... without... oh
        my God...!

Downe's POLICE UNIFORM is draped over a chair. He begins
pulling on his pants.

                    DOWNE
        Just doing my civic duty.

The WOMAN sits up in bed.

                    WOMAN
        Sure. Okay. Look, I get that we
        don't really know each other all
        that well, but --

The STATIC from Downe's POLICE RADIO interrupts:

                    VOICE OVER RADIO
        ... multiple eleven-five-hundreds.
        Confirmed. Suspect is on premises.
        Transmitting location.

DOWNE gets dressed much quicker.

                    DOWNE
        That's me. Back to work.
                (to the Woman)
        Thanks for the jump. Let's do it
        again sometime.


EXT. WAREHOUSE - NIGHT

A nondescript, rundown warehouse. Seemingly abandoned. But
there are lights on inside.

TITLE SUPER: MOTHERFUCKING L.A.

INT. WAREHOUSE - CONTINUOUS

HEADCASE HARRY lords over a table full of beakers, Bunsen
burners and copper wire coils. His fully-armed, beefy
HENCHMEN mill around.

> HARRY
> Super-crank. That's what I'm
> calling it. Got a nice ring to it,
> don'tcha think? This city loves its
> street drugs. Well, this is the
> mother of them all and they'll pay
> through the nose for it.
> (to his henchmen)
> You guys want a free taste? Well,
> FORGET IT!

One of the HENCHMEN suddenly feels something. A slight TREMOR
in the ground.

> HENCHMAN
> Anyone else feel that?

> HARRY
> Feel what?

Suddenly, the TREMORS increase. A RUMBLING sound grows
louder. The table starts to shake. Everything on it begins to
rattle. HARRY panics.

> HARRY (CONT'D)
> No! This is delicate work!

> HENCHMAN
> Yo, Headcase! We'd better split!

> HARRY
> Don't call me that! The name is
> "Harry", not --

Suddenly, the wall behind Harry EXPLODES inward! Through the
smoke, a FIGURE emerges --

> DOWNE
> Headcase Harry --

-- it's OFFICER DOWNE in full uniform. He OPENS FIRE with his
.85 MAGNUM (nicknamed, "THE ANSWER MAN") and KICKS HARRY in
the face, knocking him backward, sending him crashing through
his drug table, destroying it.

> DOWNE (CONT'D)
> -- you're under arrest!

The HENCHMEN RETURN FIRE. A spray of BULLETS impact across
Downe's body. Tiny explosions of blood. Downe is driven
backwards, but he does not fall.

                    DOWNE (CONT'D)
          Right. That's assault --

He LEAPS into the midst of the HENCHMEN and starts grabbing,
punching, shooting.

                    DOWNE (CONT'D)
          -- and resisting arrest!

In seconds, the henchmen lay dead on the floor around DOWNE.

                    DOWNE (CONT'D)
          You have the right to remain
          silent. Anything you say can and
          will be used against you in a court
          of law --

                    HARRY (O.S.)
          Fuck you!

HARRY emerges from behind a large wall of BARRELS. All of
them wired together. In his hand, a REMOTE DETONATOR.

                    DOWNE
          You have the right to an attorney.

                    HARRY
          You can take Miranda Rights and
          shove 'em up your ass, pig! I know
          who you are! That was my life's
          work you just trashed!

DOWNE walks calmly toward a panicked HARRY.

                    DOWNE
          If you cannot afford an attorney,
          one will be appointed to you --

                    HARRY
          Shut up!
              (holds up detonator)
          See this?! You know what this is?!

DOWNE stops. A moment of hesitation. Then he continues
walking toward HARRY.

                    HARRY (CONT'D)
          No! Stay back!

DOWNE keeps walking. HARRY is on the verge of crying. He
steadies himself.

                    HARRY (CONT'D)
          Fine.

He holds up the DETONATOR. Closes his eyes.

                    HARRY (CONT'D)
          Boom.

HARRY presses a button on the detonator.


EXT. WAREHOUSE - CONTINUOUS

The entire warehouse EXPLODES in a horrific, billowing ball
of fire!

From within the explosion, the TITLE flies out at us:

                    "OFFICER DOWNE"

                                        DISSOLVE TO:


EXT. WAREHOUSE - MINUTES LATER

The warehouse is completely demolished. Nothing but
smoldering rubble. A few random fires still burning.

Through the haze, several POLICE VANS approach. Their SIRENS
cutting through the haze.

They SCREECH to a halt. Several MEN in hooded, HAZMAT-STYLE
JUMPSUITS exit the vans. They carry flashlights and portable
scanners. Immediately, they fan out through the rubble.

                    HAZMAT #1
          Unbelievable. What a mess.

                    HAZMAT #2
          Just keep looking. Any scanner
          activity?

                    HAZMAT #1
          Not yet.
              (re: the rubble)
          Holy Christ. No way anyone survived
          this!

                    HAZMAT #2
          Don. I know you're new on this
          detail, but don't be an idiot.
              (MORE)

                    HAZMAT #2 (CONT'D)
          Of course he didn't survive. They
          knew he wouldn't.

Don (HAZMAT #1) suddenly stops. His foot hitting something
under the rubble.

                    HAZMAT #1
          Hold on. A little help here...!

Several other HAZMAT GUYS rush over. They all lift a large
piece of charred aluminum siding, REVEALING --

-- OFFICER DOWNE. Broken. Bloody. Burnt. Dead.

                    HAZMAT #1 (CONT'D)
          Well, there he is.
               (to the others)
          Okay, let's get him loaded up and
          back to the precinct.

                                        CUT TO:


INT. GABLE'S APARTMENT - BEDROOM - EARLY MORNING

GABLE picks himself up out of bed. Stumbles into the
bathroom.


INT. GABLE'S APARTMENT - BATHROOM - CONTINUOUS

GABLE splashes water on his face to wake up. Stares at
himself in the mirror. Gives himself a quick pep talk.

                    GABLE
          You're LAPD. You're one of the good
          guys... You're in the brotherhood.

More water to face.

                    GABLE (CONT'D)
          I'm a cop. I'm a cop. I'm a cop.

This seems to perk him right up.

                    GABLE (CONT'D)
          That's right.


EXT. LAPD HQ - DAY

The monolithic LAPD BUILDING stands set against the morning
sky.

INT. LAPD HQ - HALLWAY - DAY

GABLE (now in uniform) enters the crowded hall. An older
POLICE SERGEANT sees him and calls out to him:

                    POLICE SERGEANT
          Officer Gable!

GABLE spins around when he hears his name.

                    GABLE
          Yes?

The POLICE SERGEANT pushes through the crowded hallway to get
to GABLE.

                    POLICE SERGEANT
          Gable!

                    GABLE
          Good morning, Sergeant.

                    POLICE SERGEANT
          Go to my office. There's someone in
          there who wants to talk to you.

                    GABLE
          Should I check in before --

                    POLICE SERGEANT
          Now.

                    GABLE
          Yes sir.


INT. POLICE SERGEANT'S OFFICE - A FEW MINUTES LATER

GABLE enters.

Sitting behind the Sergeant's desk, CHIEF BERRINGER sits,
flipping through a file folder.

                    GABLE
          I was told that... well, did you
          want to see me?

CHIEF BERRINGER speaks without looking up from her folder.

                    CHIEF BERRINGER
          Officer Gable.

She finally looks up and sees GABLE. Fresh faced and eager.

                  CHIEF BERRINGER (CONT'D)
Come on in. Close the door behind
you.

GABLE does as instructed.

                  CHIEF BERRINGER (CONT'D)
Interesting psyche profile. You
like being a cop, don't you? I
mean, you take it seriously...

                  GABLE
As a heart attack.

                  CHIEF BERRINGER
We've been keeping a pretty close
eye on you --

                  GABLE
You have?

                  CHIEF BERRINGER
-- and, for the record, there were
one or two individuals in this
department who thought it was
premature for me to have this
conversation with you. Clearly, I
didn't listen to them. I went with
my gut on this one... so here you
are.

                  GABLE
Chief Berringer... am I in trouble?

BERRINGER smiles.

                  CHIEF BERRINGER
Depends on how you look at it.

                  GABLE
I don't understand.

                  CHIEF BERRINGER
You understand how bad it is out
there? While you're chasing
jaywalkers across Santa Monica
Boulevard and making your chicken
shit collars, some real heavy shit
is going down right now and you
have no idea, do you?

GABLE is confused.

                         CHIEF BERRINGER (CONT'D)
          Have you ever heard of the Fortune
          500?

                         GABLE
          The what?

                                                       CUT TO:


INT. FORTUNE 500 COMPOUND - HALLWAY - DAWN

A lone AIDE (wearing something akin to a bellboy uniform)
walks down the hall. Stops at a door. Steadies himself. Takes
a deep breath. Then opens the door and enters.


INT. FORTUNE 500 COMPOUND - MAIN OFFICE - CONTINUOUS

The AIDE enters the cavernous office. On the wall overhead, a
row of DECAPITATED HEADS looks down with their lifeless
stares.

The AIDE approaches the CONFERENCE TABLE. Sitting around it
are MISTER VULTURE, MISTER LION and MISTER TIGER (men
sporting the animal heads of their namesakes).

For a moment, the AIDE stands, silent. Until...

                         LION
          Well? Speak.

                         FORTUNE 500 AIDE
          Harry's operation has been
          compromised.

                         VULTURE
          "Compromised"?

                         FORTUNE 500 AIDE
          The LAPD sent their... beast.

                         VULTURE
          They've got balls sending that
          kamikaze cop into our territory.

                         TIGER
          Their overconfidence is annoying.

                         LION
          Goddammit! Nobody fucks with the
          Fortune 500! I want that cop's head
          on our wall!
                         (MORE)

                    LION (CONT'D)
                (to the AIDE)
        Get the fuck out of here!

The AIDE spins on his heels and runs full speed out of the
office.

                    TIGER
        Let's face it, gents, Headcase was
        their opening salvo. I'm betting
        they think it's open season on all
        our operations.

                    LION
        We gotta hit back. Hard.

                    VULTURE
        This has gone beyond the concept of
        deterrence. But let's not be
        despondent. On the contrary, let us
        rejoice! We have access to the
        ultimate WMD. A supreme ass-kicker
        par excellence.

                    LION
        What are you talking about?

MISTER VULTURE presses a button on the tabletop speaker
phone.

                    VULTURE
        Get me Zen Master Flash.

                                        CUT TO:


EXT. ZEN MASTER FLASH HQ - DAY

A peaceful, Asian-themed compound built into the side of the
Hollywood Hills.

                    ZEN MASTER FLASH (V.O.)
        You know I don't normally come down
        off the mountain...

NOTE ABOUT ZEN MASTER FLASH: *The character speaks in fluent
Mandarin, but we hear an OVERDUBBED VOICE in English (just
like a bad kung fu movie from the 70's). And it'll be this
way for the whole fuckin' movie.*


INT. ZEN MASTER FLASH DOJO - CONTINUOUS

On a pair of FINGERS

Pressed into the mat from above.

REVEAL: ZEN MASTER FLASH doing a one-armed handstand --
balancing on his two fingers -- as he talks on the phone. We
never see his eyes through his New Wave VISOR.

                    ZEN MASTER FLASH
          ... on the other hand, my latest
          class could use a good workout. You
          can't run a school for amoral
          killers without taking a few field
          trips. So you've got yourselves a
          deal.


INT. FORTUNE 500 COMPOUND - HALLWAY - DAY

MISTERS LION, TIGER and VULTURE, all wearing robes, move down
the hallway together.

                    LION
          So... you're sure this crazy fuck
          has the goods to take this on?

                    TIGER
          He's got a rep, no doubt about it.

                    VULTURE
          It's more than that. He's the best.
          We're bringing our gun to a knife
          fight.


INT. FORTUNE 500 COMPOUND - STEAM ROOM - CONTINUOUS

The three MISTERS enter the steam room (already full of
steam). They disrobe and get comfortable.

                    VULTURE
          Not to mention, he's got a ready-
          made army of bad-ass motherfuckers
          at his disposal. Think about it.
          Even if this escalates into a war,
          it'll be his, not ours. That's good
          business.

                    LION
          Fine. I still want his head.

Three beautiful Asian CONCUBINES enter from a side door. Each
of them kneels in front of a MISTER.

                    VULTURE
          I'm telling you, once we finally
          butcher this pig, the rest of them
          will shit themselves into a state
          of total panic. It'll be glorious.

The CONCUBINES all place their heads in the MISTERS' laps.  A
burst of steam punches of out from the pipes.

                                        CUT TO:


INT. LAPD HQ HALLWAY - DAY

POLICE CHIEF BERRINGER and GABLE enter the hallway.

                    CHIEF BERRINGER
          The Fortune 500 run the top tier of
          organized crime in this city.
          Almost every freak on the streets
          is connected to them in some way,
          shape or form, either working
          directly for them or as subsidiary
          fronts where the money flows right
          back into their pockets. Money from
          drugs, from illegal firearms, from
          protection rackets... you name it,
          if it's illegal, they're deep up in
          it. These animals are a force of
          nature. And how are you supposed
          fight that?

Before Gable can answer, they meet up with two LAB TECHS at a
set of ELEVATOR DOORS.

                    CHIEF BERRINGER (CONT'D)
          Everyone ready?
               (to Gable)
          Try not to look like a rookie.

                    GABLE
          Yes, ma'am.

                    CHIEF BERRINGER
          And cut the "ma'am" shit.

                    GABLE
          Yes, sir.

BERRINGER turns to the LAB TECHS.

                    CHIEF BERRINGER
          Well...?

                    LAB TECH #1
          They brought him in a few hours
          ago. He's downstairs, being prepped
          for general recovery.

                    CHIEF BERRINGER
          Okay, then. Let's go.

They move down the hallway.

                    GABLE
               (nervous)
          Chief Berringer --

CHIEF BERRINGER and the LAB TECHS enter the ELEVATOR. GABLE
stays out in the hall. They all turn and watch him.

                    CHIEF BERRINGER
               (firm)
          Courage, son.

GABLE enters the elevator.


INT. ELEVATOR - CONTINUOUS

Lilting muzak plays as they ride down to the sub-levels.

                    CHIEF BERRINGER
          These technicians are part of a
          special division. Top secret. A lot
          of private funding involved, which
          keeps the mayor and the city
          council off our ass.

                    GABLE
          Ummm... does anyone else smell
          that?

                    CHIEF BERRINGER
          Oh, that. Yeah, you learn to ignore
          that after a while.

The elevator PINGS. The doors open.


INT. SUB-LEVEL HALLWAY - CONTINUOUS

Everyone exits the elevator and continues down the dimly-lit
hallway.

The two LAB TECHS hang back as BERRINGER and GABLE walk ahead
of them. LAB TECH #1 checks his Ipad.

                    LAB TECH #1
Check it out. Got the damage specs
in.
      (reading)
Jeezus Christ...!

                    LAB TECH #2
Well, let's not evoke religion now!
Although that would be the name to
say, wouldn't it?

                    LAB TECH #1
I would laugh, if I didn't think we
were going to hell...!

                    LAB TECH #2
No doubt.

Now BERRINGER is outpacing GABLE, who hurries to catch up.

                    GABLE
Chief! Hold up! Are we talking
about --

                    CHIEF BERRINGER
I think you know exactly what we're
talking about. The rumors you've
been hearing -- they're all true.

                    GABLE
Rumors? I, um, haven't heard any
rumors...

                    CHIEF BERRINGER
Sure. In any case, it's no secret
what's going on out there. The
grinks and the groinks, the pests
and the vermin are taking over. We
don't have the manpower or the
resources to properly police the
streets. But you know what they
say...

They stop at a large VAULT DOOR. BERRINGER presses her hand
against a flat plate. It LIGHTS UP when it ID's her palm
print.

                    GABLE
They say... ?

                    CHIEF BERRINGER
Fight fire with fire. So we got
ourselves a secret weapon.

INT. RESURRECTION LAB - CONTINUOUS

A naked OFFICER DOWNE is laid out flat on a circular slab.

CHIEF BERRINGER, GABLE and the LAB TECH enter.

                    GABLE
          Holy shit.

GABLE walks over to the slab. Looks down at the broken,
beaten, bloody corpse of Officer Downe.

                    GABLE (CONT'D)
          Is he dead?

                    CHIEF BERRINGER
          What to you think? Of course he is.

                    GABLE
          But...

The Chief pulls Gable aside.

                    CHIEF BERRINGER
          Stand over here.

The LAB TECHS arrive at their control consoles.

                    LAB TECH #1
          Ready?

                    LAB TECH #2
          All systems go.

                    LAB TECH #1
          Then fire her up.

GABLE watches. Confused.

                    GABLE
          Chief...

                    CHIEF BERRINGER
          Hold on. Watch this.

On the TECHNICIANS, as switches are thrown. Buttons are
pushed.

A low HUM rises in the room. The machinery surrounding the
circular slab begins to activate. Sections light up and jets
of steam HISS out of various sections.

The circular slab -- with Officer Downe's body lying on it --
begins to ROTATE. The ceiling lights dim.

                    LAB TECH #2
          Opening channels A, B and C for
          immediate upload.

                    LAB TECH #1
               Initiate.

Several large power cells descend from the ceiling. They
hover in a geometric arrangement over the circular slab. They
GLOW and CRACKLE with weird energy.

GABLE and CHIEF BERRINGER shield their eyes, as the glow gets
so intense, it engulfs Officer Downe's body.

For a few moments, we can't see it at all. But something is
happening...

                    LAB TECH #2
               That's it! That's it!

More buttons pushed. The light, the crackling energy, the
noise... it all starts to dissipate and fade away.

The circular slab is obscured by SMOKE. As it rises off the
slab, it REVEALS a fully-healed OFFICER DOWNE.

The LAB TECHS are manning their control consoles, reading
their screens.

                    LAB TECH #1
               Hypothalamic levels are
               stabilizing. Cardiac activity,
               normal. Oxygen intake...
               circulatory systems... everything's
               back on line.

One of the LAB TECHS steps over to the slab, holding a pair
of SUNGLASSES.

OFFICER DOWNE stirs. Then SPASMS. Everyone in the room is
STARTLED by the sudden movement.

A weary GROAN from Downe's mouth is followed by him pulling
himself upright, sitting on the edge of the slab like he's
just woken up from a long sleep.

The LAB TECH holds out the sunglasses. After a moment, Downe
notices that he's there. Reaches out and takes the
sunglasses.

CHIEF BERRINGER steps up, beaming.

                    CHIEF BERRINGER
          There you go, Gable. Goddamn
          miracle of modern science.  Doesn't
          matter how broken, how mangled, how
          completely pulverized he gets out
          there. What happens in here makes
          him whole again.

DOWNE puts on his sunglasses. Turns his head as his NECK
CRACKS, then looks around the room with a blank stare.

                    CHIEF BERRINGER (CONT'D)
          Well, relatively speaking.

                    DOWNE
          Officer Downe, reporting for duty.

                    CHIEF BERRINGER
          Well done, everybody.
               (to Downe)
          How you feeling, Terry? Ready to
          get back out there?

DOWNE takes a deep breath. Then heads for the door. Still
naked.

CHIEF BERRINGER motions for GABLE to follow.


INT. LOCKER ROOM - A FEW MINUTES LATER

OFFICER DOWNE stands in front of his open locker, buttoning
up his uniform shirt. He's fully dressed.

CHIEF BERRINGER and GABLE stand at the opposite end of the
lockers, watching.

                    GABLE
               (whisper)
          Chief! Does he even know that he
          was --

                    CHIEF BERRINGER
               (whisper)
          Best not to dig to deep into the
          details. Technically, this is still
          an experiment. Just let him do his
          thing.

DOWNE checks himself out in the MIRROR hanging inside his
locker door.

                    DOWNE
              (to his own reflection)
         Look at you. You ready to crush
         some criminal cranium?

                    GABLE
              (whisper)
         He's talking to himself --

                    CHIEF BERRINGER
              (whisper)
         Shhhh!

DOWNE slams the locker shut. Quickly exits the locker room.

                    GABLE
              (whisper)
         Where's he going?

                    CHIEF BERRINGER
              (whisper)
         The armory.

CHIEF BERRINGER follows Downe out. GABLE is left completely
confused.


INT. ARMORY - CONTINUOUS

OFFICER DOWNE regards the shelves filled with weaponry. CHIEF
BERRINGER and GABLE watch from across the room.

                    DOWNE
         The skells and the shitheads...
         they're packing like a Third World
         country. They've convinced
         themselves they own this city.
         Makes me sick.

                    CHIEF BERRINGER
         So what are we doing about it,
         Terry?

                    DOWNE
         Taking it all back.

DOWNE heads deeper into the armory.

                    GABLE
              (whisper)
         What's he doing?

                    CHIEF BERRINGER
                 (whisper)
          Gathering up what he calls his
          "correctional equipment"...

DOWNE finds something.

                    DOWNE
          Here we go.

He pulls out a hand-held BATTERING RAM.

TITLE SUPER: <u>Dynamic</u> <u>Entry</u> <u>Tool</u>.

He pulls out a huge HANDGUN.

TITLE SUPER: <u>.85</u> <u>Magnum</u> <u>Customized</u>.

A second later, another TITLE SUPER underneath: <u>AKA</u> <u>"The</u>
<u>Answer</u> <u>Man."</u>

He steps over to several CRATES of ammo.

                    DOWNE (CONT'D)
          And all the ammo it can eat.

GABLE watches in slack-jawed disbelief.

                    DOWNE (CONT'D)
          Alright. Down to the motor pool.

DOWNE exits the armory. After a beat:

                    GABLE
          So, he just picks up right where he
          left off?

                    CHIEF BERRINGER
          It's all he knows. He's the perfect
          cop.

                    GABLE
          I just can't believe it. I mean...
          how?!

                    CHIEF BERRINGER
          What do you mean, how?

                    GABLE
          I mean, how?! What kind of
          technology can actually take a man
          who's clinically dead and --

                    CHIEF BERRINGER
          Rookie, you were vetted pretty
          extensively for this detail.
          Psychological testing profile
          suggested you were adequately
          equipped to deal with these
          particular circumstances without
          struggling with any of the moral
          implications involved. It's exactly
          why you've been brought inside. Now
          you need to tell me right here,
          right now... are you focused?

A beat.

                    GABLE
          Yes, sir.

                    CHIEF BERRINGER
          Then let's go.


INT. MOTOR POOL - CONTINUOUS

DOWNE stands alone, scanning the motor pool full of police
vehicles. Cars, jeeps, motorcycles, paddy wagons, etc.

CHIEF BERRINGER and GABLE enter.

                    DOWNE
          Chief. Where's my ride?

                    CHIEF BERRINGER
          Parked right where it always is.

In the corner of the parking lot -- a tricked out, armor-
plated HUMMER, painted in LAPD black & white.

TITLE SUPER: Moving Death.

                    CHIEF BERRINGER (CONT'D)
          This town is infected, Terry!  I
          need you to clean it up! I need you
          to show them what's what.

DOWNE runs his hand across the hood of the Hummer, like a
long lost friend.

                    DOWNE
          I will show them the law.

DOWNE climbs into the truck. Guns the engine. Peels out.

CHIEF BERRINGER turns to GABLE.

                    CHIEF BERRINGER
          Okay, rookie. You're on.

                    GABLE
          For what?

                    CHIEF BERRINGER
          One thing we learned this last
          round... we need to do a better job
          backing him up in the field.

                    GABLE
          What do you mean?

                    CHIEF BERRINGER
          I mean, forget about picking
          daisies in West La. As of today,
          right now, I'm putting you on this
          detail. His back up detail. A
          special unit that'll stay close,
          but remain unseen, alongside
          Officers Fritch, Carter, and Hanzo.

                    GABLE
          I'm sorry, sir... I don't follow.

                    CHIEF BERRINGER
          He'd never call in for support.
          Point of fact, he won't even know
          you're there. I'd imagine he'd be
          pretty pissed off if he knew. But
          you'll be there, all the same.

                    GABLE
          In case of what? No offense, Chief,
          but he doesn't even --

                    CHIEF BERRINGER
          You'll know what to do when the
          time comes.

A small group of UNIFORMED COPS enters the motor pool. Heads
for their cars.

CHIEF BERRINGER leads GABLE in the same direction.

                    GABLE
          You said he'd be pissed off if he
          knew?

                    CHIEF BERRINGER
          Did I say that?

                         GABLE
            Yes sir, I believe you did.

CHIEF BERRINGER opens the passenger's side door of the
nearest POLICE CAR for GABLE to get in.

                    CHIEF BERRINGER
            In that case, don't piss him off.

BERRINGER pushes GABLE into the car and shuts the door before
he can respond. It speeds off.

                                        CUT TO:


INT. ZEN MASTER FLASH DOJO - DAY

ZEN MASTER FLASH addresses a room full of STUDENTS. They all
dress alike (track suits and masks). They stand in formation.

                    ZEN MASTER FLASH
            Assembled students. I've got a
            question I'd like to pose to all of
            you.
                 (pause)
            Are you ready to rumble?

The STUDENTS remain silent. Their allegiance is obvious in
their cold, hard stares.

                    ZEN MASTER FLASH (CONT'D)
            Because I have neither the time nor
            the inclination to mollycoddle any
            of you. As far as I'm concerned,
            you're good to go. You've all been
            administered your extra does of
            alkyl nitrites, and our chemists
            have assured me that you'll peak
            exactly when you need to. Just make
            sure any erectile activity doesn't
            interfere with your combat moves.

ZEN MASTER FLASH walks along the first line of STUDENTS.

Suddenly, he stops. In a heartbeat, Zen LASHES OUT with a
single-fisted HEAD STRIKE, which the STUDENT BLOCKS.

For a moment, they are all locked in this stance, unmoving.
Then, very slowly and gracefully, they simultaneously lower
their arms.

Zen continues his speech as though nothing happened.

                    ZEN MASTER FLASH (CONT'D)
          So now it's time to dance. First
          things first. We'll need to get his
          attention. Shouldn't be too
          difficult. Our target tends to get
          involved in some serious shit.


EXT. GUARDIAN ANGEL CONVENT - NIGHT

A large, monolithic building in Inglewood, CA.


INT. GUARDIAN ANGEL CONVENT - HALLWAY - CONTINUOUS

Two NUNS walk together down the hallway. They wear full-on
habits (head piece, collar and dress).

At the other end of the hallway, a MAN waits. Dressed more
like a street hustler. The NUNS reach him. One of them is
SISTER BLISTER.

                    SISTER BLISTER
          She will see you now.

                    MAN
          About fuckin' time.

                    SISTER BLISTER
          Please watch your language.
          Remember where you are.

                    MAN
          Yeah... where exactly are we? This
          place --

                    SISTER BLISTER
          This is a house of divine truth.
          And I sense the stench of deception
          all over you.

The NUNS lead the MAN back down the hallway.


INT. GUARDIAN ANGEL CONVENT - OFFICE - CONTINUOUS

The NUNS and the MAN enter a dark office. A metal TABLE sits
in the middle of the room, underneath a harsh spotlight.

Opposite the Man, another NUN (wearing a much more ornate
habit) steps forward to the table. This is MOTHER SUPREME.

                    MAN
          You're Mother Supreme?

                    MOTHER SUPREME
          Indeed I am. Welcome to the
          Guardian Angel Covenant. You have
          come to do business?

The MAN puts out his hand to shake.

                         MAN
          I'm Dominic. I've come to
          negotiate.

Mother Supreme looks at the outstretched hand. Doesn't shake
it.

                    MOTHER SUPREME
          Negotiate? On who's behalf?

                       DOMINIC
          My boss felt like there might be
          some wiggle room when it came to
          price.

                    MOTHER SUPREME
          Is that so?

                       DOMINIC
          Hey, don't kill the messenger,
          alright? He wants what you're
          selling. He'd just hoped that,
          instead of a long-term payment plan
          at your price, we'd pay our price
          all in one, lump sum. Fuckin' sweet
          deal, if you ask me.

                    MOTHER SUPREME
          You are crude like your boss.

                       DOMINIC
          Hey, I'm just trying to be friendly
          here --

                    MOTHER SUPREME
             (interrupting)
          Do not speak again.

                       DOMINIC
          Oh, come on.

                    MOTHER SUPREME
          Another broken down street mongrel
          trying to walk tall.

                    DOMINIC
          Y'know, this is no way to do
          business. I was told you'd be
          amenable.

                    MOTHER SUPREME
          Who told you that?

                    DOMINIC
          Who do you think?

                    MOTHER SUPREME
          Your boss. Yes.
               (pause)
          Your boss has no balls.

This stops Dominic in his shoes. *Did he hear her correctly?*

                    DOMINIC
          Excuse me?

                    MOTHER SUPREME
          Your boss has no balls.

Dominic looks around, suddenly nervous. Shit just got very
creepy in here.

                    DOMINIC
          Ummm... are you allowed to talk
          like that?

                    MOTHER SUPREME
          He sends you here with no real
          knowledge of what you are dealing
          with. Do you even know what we do
          here? Do you even know what
          merchandise you have been sent to
          negotiate over?

                    DOMINIC
          I... wasn't given that information.

                    MOTHER SUPREME
          Of course you weren't. If you had
          been, you never would've come. Yet,
          here you are... trying to earn your
          stripes within an organization
          that's only distinguishing
          characteristic is that it's not the
          Fortune 500. And now you must pay
          the price.

Dominic tries to stay cool. After all, he's in a room full of
nuns...

                    DOMINIC
          Look... you don't wanna fuck with
          me, sister. You don't want me or my
          boss making trouble up in here.

Suddenly, the sound of a DOOR LOCKING. Dominic spins around --

-- the two NUNS that brought him in stand together, blocking
the only way out.

                    DOMINIC (CONT'D)
          What is this...?

He turns back to MOTHER SUPREME, who is pulling out a GOLD-
PLATED .45 from inside her robe. She aims it at Dominic.

                    MOTHER SUPREME
          This is what we sell.

                    DOMINIC
          You... you're gonna shoot me?! A
          goddamn nun?! You're gonna fuckin'
          shoot me?!

                    MOTHER SUPREME
          Of course not.

DOMINIC unclenches for a moment. Allows himself to exhale.

And then, he hears the CLIK-CLAK of weapons coming from
behind him. He turns back to the TWO NUNS --

                    MOTHER SUPREME (CONT'D)
          They are.

-- who pull out M-16'S from inside their robes.

They OPEN FIRE on DOMINIC. His body literally explodes from
MULTIPLE GUN SHOTS. He is blown half-way across the room.
Collapses in a bloody heap.

                    MOTHER SUPREME (CONT'D)
          That should send the appropriate
          message as to how we "negotiate".
               (to the nuns)
          Take him down to the morgue.


EXT. GUARDIAN ANGEL CONVENT - NIGHT

The convent remains quiet and still. We move DOWN THE BLOCK
and into a DARK ALLEYWAY, where several POLICE CARS are
parked in the shadows (mostly hidden from view).

GABLE and a few other uniformed POLICE OFFICERS -- named
FRITCH, CARTER and HANZO -- also stay tucked in the shadows,
with an eye on the convent down the street.

>                    GABLE
>               (whisper)
>          Gun-running nuns? You gotta be
>          kidding me.

>                    FRITCH
>               (whisper)
>          I wish I was, rook. These bitches
>          are hard-core.

>                    CARTER
>               (whisper)
>          Five months we've been building our
>          case...

>                    FRITCH
>               (whisper)
>          Don't start.

>                    CARTER
>               (whisper)
>          Well, pardon me, but I'm pissed
>          off. Our own detectives work with
>          the ATF to nail this shit down and
>          suddenly Supercop gets to swoop in
>          and make the bust? It's bullshit.

>                    HANZO
>               (whisper)
>          You wanna be the first to go in
>          there? You know what's in there.

>                    CARTER
>               (whisper)
>          C'mon, Hanzo, you armor up and you
>          knock that shit down. Easy-peasy.

>                    FRITCH
>               (whisper)
>          Easy-peasy, is it? I'll be glad to
>          explain that to your wife and two
>          daughters.

>                    CARTER
>               (whisper)
>          Hey, fuck you. They know exactly
>          what I signed up for.

                    FRITCH
               (whisper)
          Right, sure. Tough guy. Wanna go in
          there, all Martin Riggs, and show
          'em what's what?

                    HANZO
               (whisper)
          All who?

                    FRITCH
               (whisper)
          Martin Riggs, Mel Gibson, Lethal
          Weapon.

                    HANZO
               (whisper)
          Oh, right.

FRITCH and CARTER shake their heads in frustration.

                    GABLE
               (whisper)
          So when do we go in?

                    CARTER
               (whisper, to the others)
          Is he fucking shitting me?

                    HANZO
               (whisper)
          Ha.

                    FRITCH
               (whisper)
          We don't go in. Not until it's
          done.

                    GABLE
               (whisper)
          Until what's done?

                    HANZO
               (whisper)
          Until he's done.


INT. GUARDIAN ANGEL CONVENT - HALLWAY

The two NUNS are pushing a STRETCHER down the hall. Dominic's
CORPSE is under a sheet on the stretcher.

They reach the end of the hallway and a heavy-set DOOR. They
pull it open and enter --

INT. GUARDIAN ANGEL CONVENT - MORGUE

-- a full-on MORGUE with three rows of refrigerated container doors set into one wall. A few of them are open, with CORPSES covered with SHEETS laid out on the long drawer platforms.

The NUNS roll the stretcher next to one of the (empty) container doors, when suddenly --

-- one of the CORPSES POPS UP! It pulls off the sheet, revealing that it's OFFICER DOWNE! He points his .85 Mag at the nuns and BARKS:

                    DOWNE
          You're under arrest!

The NUNS don't even flinch -- they simply pull out their M-16's and aim them at Downe!

Downe OPENS FIRE!

                                        CUT TO:


INT. GUARDIAN ANGEL CONVENT - OFFICE

MOTHER SUPREME hears the GUNFIRE. She quickly slams her hand down on a SPEAKERPHONE.

                    MOTHER SUPREME
          Blessed are those who speak with
          thunder! Scramble! Scramble!


INT. GUARDIAN ANGEL CONVENT - HALLWAY

The hallway leading to the morgue suddenly fills with more NUNS, each one packing a weapon. They quickly get into formation, locked and loaded and aiming for the closed morgue door.

For a moment -- silence. And then --

-- the door EXPLODES. The nuns take cover from the debris ricocheting all around the hallway walls. By the time they get their bearings --

-- OFFICER DOWNE emerges from the smoke, FIRING his .85 MAG! He bellows over his own gunfire:

                    DOWNE
          You have the right to remain
          silent!

The NUNS return fire! DOWNE is sprayed down one arm by multiple IMPACT WOUNDS! He switches gun hands and dives for cover down a connecting hallway!

EXT. GUARDIAN ANGEL CONVENT - ALLEYWAY - CONTINUOUS

Everyone REACTS to the muffled sounds of EXPLOSIONS and GUNFIRE coming from inside the convent structure.

GABLE tenses, but the other cops recover quickly and go back to standing around.

                    GABLE
          Well?

                    CARTER
          Well, what?

                    GABLE
          We go in, right?

                    FRITCH
          Sorry, rook. Not yet.

                    HANZO
          We've got our orders. When things
          calm down, then we go in. For now,
          we just sit back and enjoy the
          fireworks.

                    GABLE
          But what if he needs us?

The other cops CHUCKLE. Gallows laughter.

                    CARTER
          Yeah, right.

GABLE unholsters his weapon. He's ready to go. The other COPS step forward.

                    CARTER (CONT'D)
          Whoa, cowboy. Don't even think
          about it. Just holster that heater
          and cool your jets.

                    GABLE
          You said you were pissed off! Is
          this detail what you signed up
          for?! Aren't we all cops here?

The COPS tense up. This kid's got some balls. GABLE sees that he's offended them. Unsure how to respond.

                         FRITCH
             What are you trying to say, rook?

                         GABLE
               Nothing.

More muffled GUNFIRE from the convent breaks the tension.


INT. GUARDIAN ANGEL CONVENT - HALLWAY - CONTINUOUS

OFFICER DOWNE is in the middle of a full-on SHOOT OUT with
the NUNS. They're making their way down the hallway, spraying
bullets everywhere, chewing up everything in their path.

DOWNE KICKS DOWN A DOOR and leaps through it. The DOOR FRAME
is destroyed by GUNFIRE behind him.


INT. GUARDIAN ANGEL CONVENT - ANOTHER ROOM - CONTINUOUS

The NUNS races through the smoldering door frame.

Suddenly, from the side, DOWNE slides on his back, past the
feet of the first NUN. As he passes her, he shoves his .85
MAG up her frock and FIRES, blowing the top of her head off
from underneath!

The other NUNS OPEN FIRE -- but DOWNE is already gone. They
spray their ammo all over the room.

DOWNE is crouched in a small alcove, reloading his gun. A
shower of debris all around him as the room is shot to hell.
He's only got one way out --

-- he charges out into the center of the room, BLASTING at
the NUNS, who dive for cover.

Some of them return fire, and DOWNE is nailed several times
by gunfire. He then aims his .85 Mag at the ALCOVE he was
just taking cover in, FIRES MULTIPLE ROUNDS into the back
wall, then charges back and SMASHES THROUGH the wall (which
was already partially destroyed by the gun blasts).


INT. GUARDIAN ANGEL CONVENT - MAIN HALL - CONTINUOUS

DOWNE picks himself up quickly off the ground.

He's in the main worship hall of the convent. A dais, a
podium, stained glass decoration, rows of pews, etc.

Several DOORS BURST OPEN, and more NUNS come rushing in,
armed to the teeth.

DOWNE tosses a FLASH BOMB. It DETONATES! He uses the moment to OPEN FIRE, mowing down as many NUNS as he can.

Some of them find cover and return fire. DOWNE takes a couple of shots before finding cover among the pews.


INT. GUARDIAN ANGEL CONVENT - ANOTHER HALLWAY - CONTINUOUS

MOTHER SUPREME enters the hallway, joined by FOUR NUNS (including SISTER BLISTER) carrying huge rifles. They surround her and escort her down the hall.

The sounds of GUNFIRE can be heard in another part of the convent.

                    MOTHER SUPREME
          Our house has been defiled. Now let
          us find the perpetrators -- whoever
          they may be -- and finish this.


EXT. GUARDIAN ANGEL CONVENT - ALLEYWAY - CONTINUOUS

FRITCH sits in the front seat of his car, on the radio. He has to speak over the COMBAT NOISES coming from down the street.

                    FRITCH
          Roger that. We're holding position
          here. But we need some backup to
          form a perimeter, keep the
          civilians out...

                    RADIO VOICE (V.O.)
          Copy that. Back up units on route.

FRITCH steps out of the car. CARTER and HANZO are waiting for him.

                    FRITCH
          Okay, we're good. Soon as shit
          calms down we can secure the area.

                    CARTER
          And the stiff Techs can fish
          Frankenstein out of the wreckage.
          What a bunch of fuckin' bullshit.

HANZO notices something...

                    HANZO
          Hey -- where's the rookie?!

Gable has disappeared. The cops panic.

                    FRITCH
   Fuck.

                                      CUT TO:

INT. GUARDIAN ANGEL CONVENT - HALLWAY - CONTINUOUS

GABLE pushes his way through a side door. Gun drawn. Heavy
smoke hangs in the air. The walls are like swiss cheese.

He's nervous as hell, pointing his gun at any noise that he
hears.

Suddenly, more GUNFIRE can be heard deeper within the
convent. GABLE races toward the noise.

INT. GUARDIAN ANGEL CONVENT - MAIN HALL - CONTINUOUS

DOWNE is tearing through the attacking NUNS. Shooting,
punching, kicking. Taking punishment as much as he doles it
out.

Suddenly, a break in the action -- MOTHER SUPREME is now in
the main hall, with her own cadre of armed NUNS.

                  MOTHER SUPREME
        You have besmirched the sanctity of
        this blessed soil. And, for that,
        you shall receive righteous
        punishment.

But DOWNE doesn't back down. He opens fire! The NUNS open
fire!

Pews are cut to pieces all around Downe. He falls over,
riddled with bullets.

Most of the nuns go down from his return fire. The only ones
left... are MOTHER SUPREME herself, and the final NUN --
SISTER BLISTER, of course -- who are still armed.

They move in to finish off the fallen DOWNE when GABLE bursts
in, gun drawn.

                    GABLE
       Freeze! LAPD!

SISTER BLISTER spins around. OPENS FIRE on GABLE, who dives
for cover.

And then -- CLICK-CLICK-CLICK-CLICK-CLICK-CLICK --

-- Sister Blister's out of ammo. She quickly tosses her empty gun down --

-- GABLE emerges from his cover, gun still drawn --

-- but SISTER BLISTER pulls out another gun from her frock. Aims it at Gable. Now it's a standoff. GABLE vs. SISTER BLISTER and the unarmed MOTHER SUPREME.

                    MOTHER SUPREME
          You seem troubled, young man. We
          can help you here.

                    GABLE
          Sorry, lady. I'm an Atheist. Now
          drop your weapons.

                    MOTHER SUPREME
          With all due respect... I cannot
          take seriously one who has
          abandoned his beliefs in a higher
          power.

                    GABLE
          I'm LAPD. That is my higher power.

                    SISTER BLISTER
          Shall I put one between his eyes,
          Mother?

                    MOTHER SUPREME
          Patience, Sister. Perhaps this one
          will come to his senses.

                    GABLE
          Drop the weapon! Don't make me --

Suddenly, a nearly-dead DOWNE emerges from a pile of debris and SHOOTS SISTER BLISTER dead --

-- then pops off a shot to kill MOTHER SUPREME, but only gets her in the arm before GABLE rushes in and slaps the cuffs on her.

                    GABLE (CONT'D)
          Stay down!
               (to Downe)
          Hold it --

DOWNE now picks himself up fully from the debris he was buried. Like something out of a monster movie.

He looks like hell -- bloody from head to toe, broken bones sticking out, etc.

                    GABLE (CONT'D)
          Holy shit...!

Downe takes a few stumbling steps forward, aims his gun at Mother Supreme to finish her off.

But GABLE gets in front of her, protecting her.

                    GABLE (CONT'D)
          Take it easy, okay? She's in
          custody now. Let's just do things
          by the book...

For a moment, it seems like DOWNE might take both of them out. He's clearly pissed.

He reaches out. Is he going for Gable? Even Gable doesn't know. But we'll never know for sure --

-- because DOWNE keels over, face-first and hits the ground.

GABLE rushes over to the body. MOTHER SUPERIOR is on her knees, still cuffed.

                    MOTHER SUPREME
          You will all be judged!

                    GABLE
          Shut the fuck up!

GABLE kneels next to DOWNE'S BODY. He struggles to turn him over onto his back. He checks his pulse. Downe is dead.

Gable is clearly struck by what he's just witnessed.

An eerie quiet hangs in the room. And then --

-- FRITCH, CARTER and HANZO bust in. Pissed off.

                    FRITCH
          Are you fucking kidding me, rook?!
          This is gonna be your ass!

CARTER barks into his walkie talkie.

                    CARTER
          We're inside. Requesting immediate
          back up.
              (to Gable)
          Is he dead?

GABLE doesn't respond. He's still staring at Downe's body.

                    CARTER (CONT'D)
          Rook! Is he fucking dead or what?!

More silence from GABLE. But his face says it all...


INT. LAPD HQ - CHIEF BERRINGER'S OFFICE - DAY

GABLE sits in a chair. Nervous and uncomfortable.

BERRINGER paces around him, enraged.

                    CHIEF BERRINGER
          Looks I had you pegged all wrong!
          You couldn't keep your dick in your
          pants, son!

                    GABLE
          Chief --

                    CHIEF BERRINGER
          When I talk, that means you don't
          talk! I gave you explicit
          instructions on how to comport
          yourself on this detail -- and
          that's because I made a judgment
          call on you. Looks like it was the
          wrong one!

BERRINGER plops down in her own chair, behind her desk.

                    CHIEF BERRINGER (CONT'D)
          I had a long talk with Carter and
          Fritch and even Hanzo. Those three
          never seem to agree on anything --
          except where you're concerned.

A beat.

Another beat.

GABLE looks up at BERRINGER. Waits.

BERRINGER'S eyebrows raise.

                    GABLE
          Sorry... is this the part where I
          talk?

                    CHIEF BERRINGER
          I have one nerve left, Gable --

                    GABLE
          What did they say?

                    CHIEF BERRINGER
          They said you were a chatty little
          fuck. Said you tried to be a hero.

                    GABLE
          You asked me to be back up. I'm a
          cop. And I backed him up. We
          should've gone in earlier.

                    CHIEF BERRINGER
          Didn't we talk about this in the
          motor pool? I believe we did. That
          cowboy stunt in the convent
          could've been your ass.
               (pause)
          He almost went for you, didn't he?

GABLE is conspicuously silent.

                    CHIEF BERRINGER (CONT'D)
          You should've listened. I'll bet
          you pissed yourself.

More awkward silence.

                    CHIEF BERRINGER (CONT'D)
          Well, in any case, I've got a
          problem. You're on the inside now.
          I can either put you back on the
          outside -- which could put the
          whole program at risk -- or I can
          give you one last chance to get
          your head out of your ass and help
          us make a difference in this city!

Suddenly, the LIGHTS in the office FLICKER and momentarily
DIM. Both of them notice.

                    GABLE
          That's him?


BERRINGER nods and stands up. Now she's looming over GABLE.

                    CHIEF BERRINGER
          So, you know what I need from you
          now? We're clear on that?

                    GABLE
          I think so...

                    CHIEF BERRINGER
          Do your job, be a shadow, and maybe
          you'll learn a little something
          along the way. You may not
          understand what we're doing here...
          but right now, that's not my
          problem. And, you know what, it's
          not yours either.

                                        CUT TO:


INT. LAPD HQ - LOCKER ROOM - DAY

GABLE shuffles through his locker. After a beat, he looks
over at DOWNE'S LOCKER.

Steps over and, after a moment's hesitation, OPENS the
locker. Looks inside.

Several identical UNIFORMS hang on hangers. GABLE'S HAND
moves across the uniforms, until it reaches an EMPTY HANGER.

Suddenly, a HIDDEN DOOR (in an otherwise nondescript wall)
OPENS -- GABLE is startled by the sound and SLAMS Downe's
locker door shut -- and a hi-tech, jumpsuited LAB TECH
emerges.

When he sees GABLE standing in the locker room, he seems a
bit nervous. GABLE averts his gaze.

After a beat, the LAB TECH continues on and exits the locker
room. GABLE watches him leave.

Then he turns to look at the WALL -- the spot where the
HIDDEN DOOR is located. He walks over to it.

He takes another moment. Steadies himself. Then places a hand
on the wall. The DOOR OPENS. Gable slips inside.


INT. HALLWAY - CONTINUOUS

GABLE moves down the hallway. Cautiously. Carefully. There
are several DOORS set into the walls.

One of them OPENS (with a pressurized HISSING sound), and
another LAB TECH emerges (differently dressed than anything
we've seen before).

The Lab Tech is gone before the door can fully close. At the
last minute, GABLE slips inside.

The door CLOSES behind him with a pressurized KA-THUNK.

INT. LAPD HQ - THE BULLPEN - CONTINUOUS

GABLE emerges into a huge, circular LAB. It's like a big
silo, with higher levels circling the walls. Several
TECHNICIANS are buzzing around, manning computer consoles,
etc.

In the center of the room, a configuration of ONE HUNDRED
PEOPLE, all in hi-tech WHEELCHAIRS, all hooked up to a
central machine.

Each one of them looks slightly emaciated, comatose, glassy
eyed. As though they were in some sort of mass trance.

The lab hums with power and energy. GABLE is dumbfounded...
this is underneath the LAPD building?!

A younger TECHNICIAN approaches. Very friendly.

                    BULLPEN TECH
          Amazing, huh?

                    GABLE
          Ummm, yeah.

                    BULLPEN TECH
          I've been down here for six months,
          and I'm still in awe. I mean, it's
          the Bullpen, right?

                    GABLE
          The Bullpen. Right. I'm... Officer
          Gable. I'm on Downe's field detail.

                    BULLPEN TECH
          Oh, of course. Well, as long as
          you've got clearance.

GABLE nods, letting the lie stand.

                    GABLE
          So... what are they? I mean --

                    BULLPEN TECH
          Nobody told you? Each of them
          suffer from some kind of motor
          neuron disease. Progressive
          muscular atrophy, Lou Gehrig's
          disease, spinal muscular atrophy,
          some stuff they haven't named yet.
          Pretty amazing stuff, actually.

                    GABLE
          I don't get it.

                    BULLPEN TECH
Oh, sorry. Well, for whatever
reason -- I sure as hell couldn't
tell you why, and I spend most of
my time with them -- they all
possess telekinetic abilities on a
level that we can't even measure. I
don't know if it's a side effect of
their conditions or what.

                    GABLE
Telekinetic...?

                    BULLPEN TECH
The amount of energy this group
creates, you can't imagine. It's
enough to --

                    GABLE
To bring someone back from the
dead.

                    BULLPEN TECH
Exactly. We call it the
"Resurrection Equation." We harness
their energy, channel it up to the
recovery bay where it regenerates
and resuscitates him each and every
time.

                    GABLE
That's... unbelievable.

                    BULLPEN TECH
Yeah. Cool, huh?

                    GABLE
How did they pick Downe?

                    BULLPEN TECH
Oh, this is a great story. Terrence
Downe. Metro division from back in
the day. Intense guy. Fanatical.

                    GABLE
Fanatical about what?

                    BULLPEN TECH
About being a cop. His freeway
pursuits were legendary. He never
let anyone get away. Then again...
his enthusiasm ended up costing
him.

                    GABLE
          What do you mean?

                    BULLPEN TECH
          He had... well, I guess you could
          call it an accident.

                                        SMASH CUT TO:


EXT. ELECTRICAL PLANT - NIGHT - FLASHBACK

A moment of spectacular violence: OFFICER DOWNE (back when he
was alive), smashes his MOTORCYCLE through a high railing (a
curve on a hill that overlooks the plant).

He separates from his bike and falls into the POWER LINES
below. A massive surge of ELECTRICITY explodes through the
wires -- and through DOWNE'S BODY!

                                        SMASH CUT BACK
                                                TO:


INT. BULLPEN - RESUMING

GABLE flinches from his own perception of the event.

                    BULLPEN TECH
          The circumstances under which he
          passed away left his body in a
          state that turned out to be perfect
          for this particular experiment.

GABLE'S head is spinning.

                    GABLE
          How long ago was it?

                    BULLPEN TECH
          Was what?

                    GABLE
          His accident.

                    BULLPEN TECH
          Closing in on twenty years, I
          think.

                    GABLE
          Twenty years?!

                         BULLPEN TECH
                    Hey, this stuff doesn't happen
                    overnight. What's the matter?

          GABLE steadies himself against a nearby console.

                         GABLE
                    I don't know... I mean, it's
                    just...

                         BULLPEN TECH
                    Are you okay?

                         GABLE
                    I'm... fine. It's amazing what
                    science can do, I guess.

                         BULLPEN TECH
                    Bet your ass. This is the cutting
                    edge of technology, right here.

                         GABLE
                    There's got to be a down side to
                    this, right?

                         BULLPEN TECH
                    Down side? I'm not sure what you're
                    getting at.

          GABLE steps over to the ONE HUNDRED.

                         GABLE
                    Well, have you ever lost one of
                    them to... this process?

                         BULLPEN TECH
                    One or two since I've been here. A
                    few from before my time. Nature of
                    the beast, I guess.

                         GABLE
                    Nature of the beast?! These poor
                    souls sit down here and are forced
                    to give their --

                         BULLPEN TECH
                    Whoa, whoa, whoa -- what're you
                    talking about? No one's forcing
                    anyone.

                         GABLE
                    What do you mean?

                    BULLPEN TECH
          These people are volunteers. Every
          last one of them.

                    GABLE
          So... they know?

                    BULLPEN TECH
          Of course they know. This gives
          them a purpose. You can see it in
          their eyes.

                    GABLE
          See what?

                    BULLPEN TECH
          Pride. Pride in what they're doing.
          In what they're contributing to.

                    GABLE
          You gotta be kidding me. Does Downe
          even know about them?

The BULLPEN TECH is about to respond -- but then his
expression changes. GABLE notices it... *there's something
behind him.*

GABLE turns around --

-- it's OFFICER DOWNE. He stands motionless. Expressionless.
Not a scratch on him. No sign of the hell he went through in
the convent.

The BULLPEN TECH shrinks away. DOWNE turns to the ONE
HUNDRED. Steps over to them.

And then, he kneels -- reverently -- in front of the NEAREST
ONE. Takes off his sunglasses to look into his eyes. A moment
between them, even as their expressions remain unchanged.

DOWNE stands back up. Begins walking through the ONE HUNDRED,
between their chairs, occasionally pausing to regard specific
individuals. Sometimes he even places a gentle hand on their
shoulders. Simple gestures that give a sense of the
connection between Downe and these people (even though they
have no response at all).

GABLE watches him. Trying to process what he's seeing.

Finally, DOWNE steps away from the ONE HUNDRED. Notices that
GABLE is still watching him.

                    DOWNE
          You wanna stop staring at me?

GABLE snaps out of his trance. Steps over to DOWNE.

>           GABLE
>      Hey, Downe... listen...

No response. GABLE takes a step closer.

>           GABLE (CONT'D)
>      No hard feelings. I mean, what
>      happened before... no hard
>      feelings.

DOWNE ignores him.

>           GABLE (CONT'D)
>      But I just... want you to know... I
>      was trying to help. That's all.

>           DOWNE
>      The fuck are you talking about?

>           GABLE
>      What am I...? I was the one who...
>      I mean, I was in the convent. I,
>      um, made the arrest...

DOWNE finally turns. A slow burn on GABLE, who takes a step back.

DOWNE stares him down. Their eyes are locked. And just before GABLE pisses himself --

-- DOWNE puts on his sunglasses.

A moment later, DOWNE spins on his heels and walks out.

GABLE allows himself to breathe again. The BULLPEN TECH steps over.

>           BULLPEN TECH
>      Intense guy.

>           GABLE
>      No shit.


EXT. LAPD HQ - NIGHT

GABLE'S CAR (his civilian car, not a police car) is parked across the street.

GABLE is sitting in the front seat, watching police HQ. Specifically, the PARKING GARAGE ENTRANCE.

Suddenly, DOWNE'S HUMMER pulls out of the garage. Heads down the street.

GABLE starts up his car and follows at a safe distance.


EXT. VARIOUS LA STREETS - CONTINUOUS

DOWNE'S HUMMER moves through traffic at a steady pace (in other words, he's not chasing anyone).

GABLE'S CAR is following close behind.

IN GABLE'S CAR

Gable's making sure the hummer doesn't get away from him.


EXT. APARTMENT BUILDING - NIGHT

DOWNE'S HUMMER stops at the curb in front of a modest downtown apartment building.

GABLE'S CAR parks on the opposite side of the street, about a block away.

IN GABLE'S CAR

GABLE shuts off the car. Stays low in his seat as he watches--

DOWNE

He gets out of his Hummer and heads into the building.

As soon as he's inside, GABLE exits his car. Cautiously crosses the street and heads into the ALLEY next to the building.


EXT. ALLEYWAY - CONTINUOUS

GABLE finds the FIRE ESCAPE. Pulls down the ladder and begins climbing.

As he makes his way up the fire escape, he takes a quick peek into every LIT WINDOW.

Finally, on the EIGHTH FLOOR, he sees DOWNE'S PANTS and SHIRT plop down across the back of the chair just inside the nearest window. The surprise impact causes GABLE to FLINCH. He makes sure he's in the shadows... and gets comfortable.

He can hear a bit of CONVERSATION coming from inside the apartment. Mostly a WOMAN'S VOICE, but a few bits of DOWNE'S VOICE as well...

... and then the SEX NOISES begin.

At first, GABLE listens more closely. *Is he hearing what he thinks he's hearing?*

Yes he is.

GABLE'S not quite sure how to react. Should he leave? Should he wait it out? Does this make him a pervert?

The SEX NOISES are getting more intense (mainly the FEMALE noises).

IN THE CORNER OF THE SCREEN: the ORGASM COUNTER graphic re-appears. The NUMBERS begin counting upward with each female moan and groan: 1... 2... 3... 4... and keep going.

We do several TIME JUMP CUTS in a row --

GABLE is confused. The ORGASM COUNTER still counting: 12... 13... 14...

GABLE is in complete disbelief. The ORGASM COUNTER still counting: 29... 30... 31...

GABLE is nodding off. The ORGASM COUNTER still counting: 45... 46... 47...

GABLE is asleep. The ORGASM COUNTER has stopped at 69.

A passing CAR down on the street wakes him up with a start. He panics. Gets his bearings and checks in the window --

-- Downe's UNIFORM is gone.

GABLE scurries down the fire escape. Runs out into the street. Downe's HUMMER is gone, too.

                    GABLE
            (out of breath)
        Shit.


INT. FORTUNE 500 COMPOUND - MAIN OFFICE

The MISTERS -- LION, TIGER and VULTURE -- sit at their main conference table, playing the board game, "Risk"...

... except this is *their* version of "Risk", which doesn't involve the nations of the world but instead the LA underworld. It's the way they monitor their empire... by playing it as a board game.

                    TIGER
          How many territories can one boss
          occupy? Let's find out!

MISTER TIGER rolls the dice.

                    TIGER (CONT'D)
          Smashing! I'm rolling into the West
          Side, gentlemen!

                    LION
          Y'know, this is all well and good,
          fucking fun and games, but we
          haven't talked about Mother Supreme
          yet.

                    VULTURE
          She got busted. Her entire
          operation is godless. Good for us.
          Less competition.

                    LION
          Except -- you've got the same intel
          I do. It was that cock-munching
          super-cop that took her down. So
          he's still out there. What the fuck
          is up with Zen Master Flash?!

                    TIGER
          He is taking his sweet time. And on
          our dime...!

                    VULTURE
          And worth every one of those dimes.
          You know his reputation. If he
          hasn't moved yet, that just means
          that what he's got planned... is
          going to be rather... nasty.


EXT. BAR - NIGHT

The Rusty Nail Lounge in downtown LA.


INT. RUSTY NAIL LOUNGE - NIGHT

GABLE (in his civilian clothes) enters.

This is a Cop bar, so naturally it's filled with COPS. Uniformed. Plain clothes. You name it, they come here to drink and unwind.

GABLE nervously approaches the end of the bar. He gestures for the BARTENDER (a beefy, older ex-cop), who completely ignores him. Gable's shoulders slump. He knows it was a mistake to come here.

He tries again.

                    GABLE
          'Scuse me.

This time, the BARTENDER notices.

                    BARTENDER
          Yeah...?

                    GABLE
          Jack and Coke.

                    BARTENDER
          You LAPD? 'Cause that's who we like
          to serve here.

GABLE brings out his BADGE.

                    BARTENDER (CONT'D)
          Good enough. Jack and Coke, coming
          up.

The BARTENDER fixes the drink. GABLE looks around the bar. Everyone else in here is having a great time.

His Jack and Coke is set in front of him. He takes a big gulp from it right away.

                    BARTENDER (CONT'D)
          Whoa. Slow down, cowboy. We make
          'em strong.

                    GABLE
          Good. I need it.

                    BARTENDER
          You look pretty young to be looking
          so fucked off.

                    GABLE
          Let's just say... it's been a
          strange couple of days.

The BARTENDER raises his own drink to toast.

                    BARTENDER
          Well, then... here's to a boring
          night.

GABLE raises his own glass to acknowledge the toast, then
takes another big swallow.

                    GABLE
          I'm gonna need another one of
          these. And maybe another after
          that.

                    BARTENDER
          Just gimme the high sign.

The BARTENDER walks away. GABLE takes another look around the
room. The booze is already starting to affect him.

ACROSS THE ROOM:

FRITCH, CARTER and HANZO (also in their civvies) are sitting
together. They've already got their drink on, big time.
Suddenly, they notice Gable at the bar.

                    FRITCH
          Well, well, well... lookie what we
          have here!

                    CARTER
          It's Officer Integrity! Officer
          Ethics! Officer Dipshit!

GABLE shrinks away, but the trio is already on their feet,
moving toward him.

                    CARTER (CONT'D)
          Everyone! Listen up! We've got a
          hero in our midst -- this kid's
          angling to be Super-cop's partner!
          Right by his side! Through thick
          and thin! The Robin to his Batman!
          The Lois Lane to his Superman!

The other cops LAUGH and HOLLER their drunken approval.

GABLE finds his resolve. Turns to face the trio, who now
surround him.

                    HANZO
          Got any ass left, rook? Or did
          Berringer chew it all off?

                    GABLE
          Look, I don't want to get into it.
          Not here.

                    FRITCH
          Well, if not here, then where?

                    CARTER
          Never mind that. You got some
          balls. I mean, for fuck's sake, you
          think you actually belong in here?

                    GABLE
          I'm a cop, just like you.
               (pause)
          Just like Downe.

                    FRITCH
          Bullshit.

                    CARTER
          You think anyone in here is
          anything like that freak?

                    GABLE
          You're drunk.

                    CARTER
          Not drunk enough to keep me from
          kicking your skinny ass.

For a moment, they stare each other down. Is it going to
escalate into violence?

Suddenly, the BARTENDER slams his hand down on the bar. Gets
everyone's attention. The whole bar does quiet.

                    BARTENDER
          All of you fuckers stand down! This
          is ri-goddamn-diculous! You're all
          cops up in here! The assholes are
          out there! Save this shit for them!

He brings out a WOODEN AXE HANDLE.

                    BARTENDER (CONT'D)
          The next guy who gets in anyone's
          face gets this horse cock upside
          their head! My mother gave this to
          me and she taught me how to use it!
          Anyone?!

FRITCH, CARTER and HANZO look at each other. Taking in the
Bartender's words. GABLE watches them, ready for anything.

Suddenly, FRITCH softens a little.

                    FRITCH
          Fuck.

He turns to the others.

                    FRITCH (CONT'D)
          Hard to argue with that logic,
          innit? Not the bit about the horse
          cock...

CARTER and HANZO exchange looks.

                    HANZO
          Ah, buy the rook a drink.

GABLE is confused, but relieved.


EXT. DOWNTOWN LA STREETS - NIGHT

MOVING DEATH rolls down the street. It's a particularly seedy
part of downtown.


INT. MOVING DEATH (MOVING) - CONTINUOUS

DOWNE behind the wheel. Eyeballing the streets like Travis-
fucking-Bickle.

Suddenly, he sees something in the rear view mirror.

DOWNE'S POV:

A MAN crossing the street -- not at a crosswalk!


EXT. DOWNTOWN LA STREET - CONTINUOUS

MOVING DEATH'S brakes squeal! The truck SPINS AROUND hard in
the middle of the street! It speeds off back the way it came.

ON THE SIDEWALK

The MAN has reached the other side of the street. He nearly
shits himself with a SPOTLIGHT hits him. He freezes in his
tracks at the sound of DOWNE'S VOICE:

                    DOWNE (V.O.)
                  (over loudspeaker)
          You! Jaywalking is subject to a
          fine of up to one hundred dollars!

The MAN turns to face his accuser. MOVING DEATH is parked just a few feet away from him, its SPOTLIGHTS aimed in his eyes.

> MAN
> Who, me?

> DOWNE (V.O.)
> (over loudspeaker)
> That's right! You!

> MAN
> What... you're serious?

The DRIVER'S DOOR to Moving Death OPENS. DOWNE steps out, NIGHT STICK in hand. He slowly walks to the front of the vehicle, into the glare of the headlights.

DOWNE gets right in the MAN'S face, bearing down on him.

> DOWNE
> Malcontent!

The MAN is starting to sweat now.

> DOWNE (CONT'D)
> Anarchist!

DOWNE places the end of his NIGHT STICK underneath the MAN'S CHIN, pushing his head up. Putting him on his tip-toes.

> DOWNE (CONT'D)
> I should take your head off right
> here and now. Maybe then you'll
> think twice before jaywalking in my
> city!

TEARS start running down the MAN'S cheeks. He's trying not to openly whimper... and failing.

From DOWNE: no reaction... no reaction... no reaction...

... and then...

... a facial TWITCH... slight, but it happens...

... then DOWNE blinks...

... he removes the NIGHT STICK from the MAN'S chin. The MAN collapses to his knees. DOWNE looms over him.

> DOWNE (CONT'D)
> Don't be an asshole.

DOWNE walks back to Moving Death. Gets in. The engine ROARS.
Moving Death speeds away.

The MAN is left alone. Tries to catch his breath. Looks
around frantically.

                    MAN
          Did anyone get that on video?!


INT. RUSTY NAIL LOUNGE - NIGHT

CARTER, FRITCH, HANZO and GABLE sit together at a table.
Empty glasses litter the table top.

GABLE'S pretty tipsy at this point. The other three are even
more bleary eyed, but still pushing ahead. The alcohol has
greased the tension.

                    CARTER
          Another round!

                    GABLE
          Seriously? Jeezus Christ...

                    HANZO
          Iron livers here, Gable. Get used
          to it.

                    FRITCH
          Come on, rook! You said it yourself
          -- you're a cop! You gotta start
          drinking like one.

                    GABLE
          So... Downe ever been in here?

                    CARTER
          Are you kidding? Not a chance in
          hell. He don't fraternize.

                    HANZO
          Not with anyone.

A SERVER places another round of shots on the table. All four
cops reach for them. FRITCH raises his glass to toast.

                    FRITCH
          To busting Gable's cherry...

The rest of them raise their glasses in response.

                    HANZO
        To the cop shows that get it
        right...

                    CARTER
        To my girlfriend's bald eagle. The
        best thing I ever tasted...

GABLE holds his glass up. The rest of them wait for his
toast.

                    GABLE
        To all our brothers in uniform
        that've fallen in the line of
        duty...

A beat.

Then everyone knocks back their drink. GABLE winces as he
swallows.

                    GABLE (CONT'D)
        Goddamn!

                    FRITCH
        That's the way to do it!

                    CARTER
        That's some rocket fuel, boy!

                    GABLE
        So... you guys wanna tell me the
        real reason you don't like Downe?

                    FRITCH
        What do you mean?

                    CARTER
        Don't play stupid, Fritch...

                    FRITCH
        Hey, I know you're pissed off. I'm
        pissed off. What're you gonna do
        about it now?

                    GABLE
        I don't get it...

                    CARTER
        You think we wanted this detail?
        Back up for that freak?! Fuck that
        son of a bitch!

                         HANZO
              You think you could do what he
              does? You want that?

                         CARTER
              I'm not saying that...

                         HANZO
              Well, that's part of the deal,
              okay? We've seen what happens. We
              know it happens. Look, I'd take a
              bullet in the line of duty. I'd lay
              my fucking life down. That's what
              it's all about. But I'd only have
              to do it once, y'know? That fact
              makes it bearable...

                         FRITCH
              Man's got a point, Carter.

                         CARTER
              You can't say that. You don't know
              how he does it. None of us do.
                   (to Gable)
              Do you?

     GABLE hesitates.

                         CARTER (CONT'D)
              Hold on...

                         FRITCH
              You know something we don't, rook?

                         GABLE
                   (beat)
              What the hell would I know?

     All three of them eyeball GABLE. And then HANZO breaks the
     tension:

                         HANZO
              C'mon, they're not gonna tell this
              fetus anything!

                         CARTER
              I guess not. It's all fucking
              Franken-science anyway.

                    GABLE
        Well... I don't know about that.
        You're talking about someone made
        out of dead body parts, from
        different corpses. I don't think
        that Downe --

                    CARTER
              (interrupting)
        Whatever. I still say we got Boris
        Karloff with a badge and that is
        some fucked up shit...!

                    HANZO
        Who?

                    CARTER
        Boris Karloff? Frankenstein? From
        the movie...!

                    HANZO
        That was De Niro.

CARTER and FRITCH exchange incredulous looks.

                    FRITCH
        Come on...!

                    CARTER
        Travis Bickle played Frankenstein?!

                    GABLE
        Y'know, I think that's right...

                    CARTER
        That is the most bizarre fucking
        thing I've ever heard!
              (to Hanzo)
        Bullshit!

                    HANZO
        What do you want from me? That's
        the Frankenstein movie I saw!
        Robert De Niro as Frankenstein!

                    GABLE
        You mean Frankenstein's monster.

                    CARTER
        What did you say, rook?

                    GABLE
        Well, people always call the
        monster, "Frankenstein".
              (MORE)

                    GABLE (CONT'D)
          Technically, he's Frankenstein's
          monster, created by Dr.
          Frankenstein.

                    HANZO
          Whatever, it was a great movie.

CARTER and FRITCH wince. GABLE smiles and drinks.

                    CARTER
          Oh my fucking God! For the last
          time, Hanzo... watch a real goddamn
          movie for once in your miserable
          life...!

As their drunken conversation/argument continues, we MOVE
AWAY from their table. We move through the room, moving
amongst the off-duty cops drinking and hanging out...

... until we land ON AN EMPTY TABLE.

A single POLICE WALKIE TALKIE is on. We push in super close.
And then, above the din of the bar, WE HEAR:

                    POLICE RADIO VOICE
          Multiple ten-thirty-fours reported
          at Cedars-Sinai at Beverly and San
          Vicente. All units respond.


EXT. DOWNTOWN LA STREETS - NIGHT

MOVING DEATH tears ass down the street. Other cars get the
fuck out of the way!


INT. MOVING DEATH (MOVING) - CONTINUOUS

OFFICER DOWNE drives. A VOICE crackles over the radio:

                    POLICE RADIO VOICE
          Multiple ten-thirty-fours reported
          at Cedars-Sinai at Beverly and San
          Vicente. All units respond.

Downe picks up the radio mike.

                    DOWNE
          Center, this is Officer Downe
          responding. I'm on my way.

INT. CEDARS-SINAI HOSPITAL ER - NIGHT

The place is a horror show. Dead bodies everywhere. Patients.
Doctors. Nurses.

ZEN MASTER FLASH walks confidently through the mayhem. His
STUDENTS stand at attention, their jumpsuits covered head to
toe in their victims' blood.

                    ZEN MASTER FLASH
              Well done, students. Like sending
              up the brightest flare to passing
              rescue ships...

ZEN MASTER FLASH pauses. He hears the ENGINE SOUND of a
vehicle approaching outside.

He holds up a finger to silence his students, then turns to
them:

                    ZEN MASTER FLASH (CONT'D)
              Now -- this is where you graduate.
              That's our target you're hearing
              and he's coming fast. Prepare to
              slice and dice. I'll be back in a
              flash --

He TELEPORTS away. The STUDENTS look at each other, confused.
The ENGINE SOUNDS are getting louder. They scatter --

-- as MOVING DEATH CRASHES into the ER, through the glass
entryway. Shattered glass and broken metal flies everywhere.

The vehicle slams to a halt, and DOWNE bursts out the
driver's side door, .85 Mag in one hand, his "Dynamic Entry
Tool" in the other.

                    DOWNE
              Alright, scumsuckers! Everybody
              freeze!

In the haze and dust hanging in the air, the STUDENTS are
nowhere to be seen.

                    DOWNE (CONT'D)
              Any asshole I see flashing a blade--

Suddenly, a voice from above:

                    ZEN MASTER FLASH
              No Miranda?

ZEN MASTER FLASH is perched in the exposed rafters of the
ceiling. Holding a butcher's hand axe.

          ZEN MASTER FLASH (CONT'D)
    I was hoping to hear you say it.
    Anyway, does this count as a blade?

DOWNE FIRES! ZEN leaps out of the way as the round EXPLODES
in the ceiling, further destroying it.

ZEN does and impossible flip and lands gracefully on top of
MOVING DEATH.

          ZEN MASTER FLASH (CONT'D)
    Students! Show no mercy!

Suddenly, from every direction, his STUDENTS emerge. All of
them carrying weapons -- swords, clubs, knives -- and
surround Downe.


INT. BAR - CONTINUOUS

AT GABLE'S TABLE

GABLE, CARTER, FRITCH and HANZO are still drinking and
talking.

GABLE is a lot looser now. He holds up his drink to toast.

          GABLE
    Another toast. To being a cop.

The others bring up their glasses.

          FRITCH
    Are you gonna make a toast to
    anything else? Every one is about
    being a cop...!

          GABLE
    Well, what's better than that?!

They clink their glasses and down their drinks.

          GABLE (CONT'D)
    C'mon, it's a goddamn glorious
    thing. And, hey, Downe... he's
    right there with us.
      (off their looks)
    I mean, isn't he...?

          CARTER
    Why do you give a fuck about this
    guy anyway? It's not enough that
    you get to clean out his litter box
    with the rest of us?

                    GABLE
          I dunno... I don't like that part
          of it any more than you do.

                    HANZO
          Obviously.

                    GABLE
          But I sure as hell don't blame
          Downe. At least, I don't think I
          do...

                    FRITCH
               (sarcastic)
          Oh yeah, I'm sure he's just an
          innocent victim in all of this.

                    CARTER
          Meanwhile, good cops -- the ones
          we're toasting to -- are out there
          on the beat every single day,
          risking their shit against God-
          knows-what and when they eat it,
          they don't come back!

                    HANZO
          You're an angry drunk.

                    CARTER
               (indignant)
          I know I am!

                    FRITCH
          You want the horse cock, don'tcha?

ON THE OTHER SIDE OF THE ROOM

One of the other COPS in the bar -- a little wobbly on his
feet -- steps over and picks up the WALKIE TALKIE. And HE
HEARS:

                    POLICE RADIO VOICE
          Multiple ten-thirty-fours reported
          at Cedars-Sinai at Beverly and San
          Vicente. All units respond.

                    COP
          Oh shit.

AT GABLE'S TABLE

All four of them stop and listen to the COP across the room,
calling out to everyone:

                          COP (CONT'D)
                Anyone who can stand -- get to
                Cedars! It's a fucking massacre
                over there!

The four cops look at each other. Should they go?

                          FRITCH
                Fuck it. Let's go be cops.
                     (to Gable)
                You comin', rook?

GABLE stands. A little uneasy on his feet.

                          GABLE
                You bet your ass I am.


INT. CEDARS-SINAI HOSPITAL ER - CONTINUOUS

Picking up right where we left off, DOWNE is surrounded by
weapon-carrying STUDENTS.

                          DOWNE
                You punks are resisting arrest.
                You're gonna make me bust out my
                favorite piece of correctional
                equipment --

DOWNE dives into the fray.

                          DOWNE (CONT'D)
                -- lethal force!

The STUDENTS swarm all over Downe, trying to take him to the
ground or cut him into pieces.

But Downe is a blur of action, firing his .85 Mag and bashing
their brains in with his battering ram!

The STUDENTS slice at him with their edged weapons. A
hurricane of steel! Some of them connect, tearing through
flesh and drawing blood!

One STUDENT gets in close, swings his blade. Downe ducks out
of the way, and ANOTHER STUDENT'S HEAD is cleaved clean off
from the blow.

                          DOWNE (CONT'D)
                That's the best you can do?!

He OPENS FIRE once again with his .85 Mag, mowing down and
entire row of STUDENTS, blasting huge holes through their
midsections.

Another STUDENT leaps in from the side, wielding a samurai sword.

He slices downward, cutting through the BARREL of Downe's .85 Mag.

Several more STUDENTS take the opportunity to move in and connect with a flurry of martial arts attacks. Downe is knocked around like a rag doll.

For a moment, we think he's had it. But with sudden, lightning speed, he reaches out and GRABS one of the STUDENTS by the face!

                    DOWNE (CONT'D)
          Assaulting a police officer --

Downe takes that STUDENT -- by the face -- and SLAMS his head into ANOTHER STUDENT. Both of their heads smash to pulp in an EXPLOSION OF BLOOD!

                    DOWNE (CONT'D)
          -- don't do the crime if you can't
          do the time!

Suddenly, a SWORD BLADE erupts out of Downe's shoulder, from behind.

DOWNE turns quickly -- so quickly that it wrenches the blade's handle out of the STUDENT'S hands.

DOWNE reaches back and grabs the hilt of the sword. Pulls it out. Lashes out and lops off the head of the STUDENT, which goes flying straight up into the air.

Downe CATCHES the head, then throws it like a cannonball into a group of oncoming STUDENTS. It knocks them down like bowling pins.

Across the room, ZEN MASTER FLASH grabs a METAL BED PAN and hurls it -- frisbee-style -- across the room.

DOWNE hears it coming, whistling through the air. He turns just in time -- and we go to SLO MO for this moment -- for it to SLAM square into his face. His sunglasses SHATTER into a thousand pieces from the impact.

We go back to NORMAL SPEED --

DOWNE staggers. It's just enough time for a mini-swarm of STUDENTS to move in, hacking and kicking and punching. One of the STUDENTS is hacking away at one of Downe's WRISTS with a butcher knife, nearly cutting through it!

At this point, it's too much for Downe to fight back. He is pummeled and pounded into submission. But, throughout the beating, he stays on his feet.

ZEN MASTER FLASH steps up. Gestures to his STUDENTS.

                    ZEN MASTER FLASH
          Hold it. Look at him.

DOWNE is out on his feet. One hand is barely hanging off his arm by a few threads of bloody flesh.

ZEN MASTER FLASH paces around him, just out of arm's reach.

                    ZEN MASTER FLASH (CONT'D)
          All this fuss over you. I'm not
          quite as impressed as I thought I'd
          be. Guess I need to lower my
          expectations.

DOWNE weakly tries to grab for him. It's the arm with the hand almost cut off, so it just dangles precariously from his wrist...!

                    DOWNE
          You have... the right...

ZEN MASTER FLASH steps a little closer.

                    ZEN MASTER FLASH
          What's that...?

                    DOWNE
          ... to remain...

Closer still.

                    ZEN MASTER FLASH
          Come again...?

                    DOWNE
          ... silent.

ZEN MASTER FLASH assesses DOWNE. He's out on his feet.

ZEN MASTER FLASH gestures for his STUDENTS to make a path. He walks down the length of the ER lobby.

                    ZEN MASTER FLASH
          Ah... do tell. Students, observe
          the coup de Flash.

He steadies himself. Takes a deep breath.

Then he gets a running start -- launches himself in the air
and NAILS DOWNE in the face with a brutal FLYING KICK that
sends DOWNE to the ground. His nearly-severed HAND is finally
torn loose in the impact and flies off his arm!

ZEN MASTER FLASH poses flamboyantly over his fallen opponent.

> ZEN MASTER FLASH (CONT'D)
> Kraka-Boom, motherfucker. That's
> what I'm about.
> (pause)
> Timber, by the way.

He turns to his STUDENTS and smiles.

> ZEN MASTER FLASH (CONT'D)
> That, students, is what precision
> work looks like. But don't worry,
> he's not dead. Not quite yet,
> anyway. So, on to Phase Two...

> CUT TO:

INT. FORTUNE 500 COMPOUND - MAIN OFFICE - LATER

A CORK pops out of a CHAMPAGNE BOTTLE. The MISTERS LION,
TIGER and VULTURE are celebrating.

> VULTURE
> What'd I tell you?! I toldja he'd
> get the big bastard!

> LION
> I hope he burned him like a witch!

> TIGER
> Like a bitch!

> VULTURE
> I'm sure we'll get the deets any
> minute now! One of our lieutenants
> is in direct contact.

> LION
> This is a righteous fucking
> victory!

> TIGER
> Let's see the LAPD come back from
> *this* one! Who runs this city?!

The trio CLINKS their glasses together. And then --

-- a KNOCK on the door.

                    VULTURE
          Here we go. Right on cue.
               (calling out)
          Get your ass in here!

Their AIDE enters. MISTER LION sits down, puts his feet up on
the conference table.

                    LION
          Talk slow. I want to enjoy this.

                    TIGER
          I wanna hear some key words.
          Eviscerated. Disemboweled.
          Beheaded. Castrated.
               (to the Lieutenant)
          Go on.

                    FORTUNE 500 AIDE
          Well, sirs... I wish I could use
          any of those words. How about...
          kidnapped?

The MISTERS are confused.

                    VULTURE
          What the fuck are you talking
          about?

                    FORTUNE 500 AIDE
          Apparently, Zen Master Flash
          subdued Downe and transported him
          to another location. By all
          accounts... he's still alive.

MISTERS LION and TIGER explode with rage.

                    LION
          What?!

                    VULTURE
          You're shitting me.

                    LION
          What, does he think he's gonna get
          ransom money outta the LAPD?!

                    TIGER
          That wasn't the deal we made! That
          motherfucker --

                    VULTURE
          Okay, okay, calm down. Let's not
          jump to conclusions --

                    LION
          Oh, come on! We hired him to
          eliminate this freak, to burn him
          off the face of the Earth--!

                    VULTURE
          And I'm sure he will! Just put your
          peckers in park and let's find out
          exactly what the fuck he's up to!


INT. CEDARS-SINAI HOSPITAL ER - LATER STILL

The entire ER is a wrecked bloodbath. BODIES strewn
everywhere. Doctors. Nurses. Patients. Zen's students.

Moving Death remains crashed and immobile.

Several UNIFORMED COPS -- including the civilian-attired
GABLE, FRITCH, CARTER and HANZO -- rush in, guns drawn.

                    HANZO
          Holy Christ!

                    CARTER
          Goddamn. Fuckin' bloodbath in here!

                    FRITCH
          Check for survivors!

GABLE (barely able to hide his drunken state) sees the
crashed MOVING DEATH.

                    GABLE
          Downe got here first!

He scrambles over piles of debris and bodies to get to MOVING
DEATH. He looks in the driver's side. The cab's empty. GABLE
pops back out.

                    GABLE (CONT'D)
          Anyone find his body?!

                    FRITCH
          Who gives a shit? Look at this
          place!

GABLE stumbles awkwardly through the room. We can see the
concern on his face. *Where is Downe?!*

And then --

-- he sees DOWNE'S SEVERED HAND lying on the ground, amidst the other dead bodies. He picks it up.


INT. KINGS COUNTY CORRECTIONAL FACILITY - BASEMENT - NIGHT

Blackness. Nothingness.

And then, the sound of water dripping. Drip... drip... drip...

And finally, a VOICE:

                    ZEN MASTER FLASH (V.O.)
          Wake up, sleepyhead.

Suddenly, the darkness fades away, revealing an UPSIDE-DOWN ZEN MASTER FLASH looking right into camera. Smiling.

                    ZEN MASTER FLASH
          Remember me? Zen Master Flash, at
          your service.

Now we see what's going on in here. We're in a dark, shadowy sub-basement. Pipes and duct work line the ceiling.

DOWNE hangs upside-down in the middle of the room, by a chain that wraps around his body, keeping his legs and arms bound.

ZEN MASTER FLASH is kneeling down, so he can get right in Downe's face.

                    ZEN MASTER FLASH (CONT'D)
          How're you feeling there? You know,
          we beat you within an inch of your
          life. Such as it is.

He reaches out. Pushes at the edge of Downe's body so it slowly rotates on its own.

ZEN MASTER FLASH stands. Begins to pace around the slowly rotating Downe.

                    ZEN MASTER FLASH (CONT'D)
          You don't know where you are, do
          you? Well, let me give you a little
          hint... it's the last place on
          Earth where you'd want to be right
          now.

He steps over to a concrete wall. Runs his fingers across it. Gives it a friendly knock.

THE KNOCK ECHOES and grows LOUDER and we ZOOM OUT TO REVEAL:

EXT. KINGS COUNTY CORRECTIONAL FACILITY - NIGHT

The place is pure concrete. No windows. Monolithic. Scary as hell.

INT. KINGS COUNTY CORRECTIONAL FACILITY - BASEMENT - RESUME

                    ZEN MASTER FLASH
          That's right. Kings County
          Correctional Facility. Also known
          as the "Rats' Nest". And I think
          you know why. After all, I'm sure
          you've personally placed a healthy
          number of inmates in here. What can
          I say? I'm a big fan of irony.

He steps back over to DOWNE.

                    ZEN MASTER FLASH (CONT'D)
          Now, I'm sure you're wondering to
          yourself, how could I possibly get
          away with bringing you here, of all
          places? Well, let's just say that
          the folks who hired me are the kind
          of people who hold a certain
          influence. They might not have the
          vision, but they certainly have the
          resources. And, by association, so
          do I.

He leans down to get closer to DOWNE'S FACE.

                    ZEN MASTER FLASH (CONT'D)
          So how fucked do you feel right
          now?

INT. LAPD HQ - BATHROOM SHOWER

GABLE stands underneath the cold water, trying to catch his breath (and sober up).

A FEW MINUTES LATER

GABLE stands at the bathroom sink counter. Watches himself in the mirror. Searches his own reflection for some kind of affirmation.

ON THE COUNTER: DOWNE'S SEVERED HAND wrapped in a towel. Gable peeks inside the towel, but closes it up quickly.

He looks back in the mirror.

                    GABLE
              (to himself)
         What the fuck are you doing?

                    CARTER (O.S.)
         Good question.

GABLE spins around, startled by the voice. CARTER is walking
in, holding a thick FILE FOLDER.

                    GABLE
         Jeezus...!

                    CARTER
         No, just me.

                    GABLE
         Come to rub it in?

                    CARTER
         What do you mean?

                    GABLE
         I mean, the "freak" is finally
         gone. Missing in action. Probably
         chopped up into little pieces and
         scattered all over L.A. He'll end
         up in the Toro rolls at Matsuhisa.
         Something else for you to drink to.
              (re: the severed hand)
         This is all that's left. You want
         it as a souvenir?

                    CARTER
         So that's it, then? He's gone and,
         what, you turn in your badge, too?
         Is that the kind of cop you are?

                    GABLE
         I don't know what kind of cop I am
         anymore. I really don't. And what's
         it matter anyway? We blew it! We
         were his back up and we blew it!
              (completely defeated)
         Besides, when it gets out what my
         blood-alcohol level was when I'm
         showing up at a crime scene...!
         Well, that's it for me.

                    CARTER
              (sarcastic)
         Awww, lemme get you a tissue...

GABLE turns on CARTER. Gets right in his face.

             GABLE
       You wanna go now? Because I don't
       think I've got anything left to
       lose.

             CARTER
       Give me a fucking break, rook. No
       one gives a shit if you knocked a
       few back tonight. You really think
       you're done, fine... but don't
       blame it on that.

             GABLE
       Being a cop is all I have!

CARTER hesitates.

             CARTER
       No wonder you like him so much.

             GABLE
       What are you talking about?

             CARTER
       Never mind. Brought you a little
       gift.

He places the FILE FOLDER on the counter top. GABLE picks it
up.

             GABLE
       What is it?

             CARTER
       Personnel file. Dating back to the
       late 70's. Terrence Downe.

             GABLE
       What?!

             CARTER
       Take a look.

GABLE picks up the file. Starts flipping through it.

             GABLE
       Where the hell'd you get this?

                    CARTER
          Hey, you're the rookie. When you've
          been around as long as I have,
          you'll figure out how to lift a
          piece of evidence when you need to.

                    GABLE
               (reading)
          This is from when he was...

                    CARTER
          Alive? Yeah. You think you've got a
          one-track mind? This motherfucker
          was King Cop from day one. No
          family. No attachments. Nothing but
          the job.

                    GABLE
          The accident that put him in the
          program...

                    CARTER
               (finishing his sentence)
          ... just seems like a fait
          accompli. I think if you're
          wondering if he's being exploited
          or any of that bullshit... well, I
          think that file tells the whole
          story.

CARTER heads for the exit.

                    CARTER (CONT'D)
          We all read it, by the way. If it
          makes a difference, we hate him a
          little less now.

CARTER pauses, just before he leaves. GABLE is still pouring
through the file.

                    CARTER (CONT'D)
          Man up, wouldja?


INT. KINGS COUNTY CORRECTIONAL FACILITY - BASEMENT - RESUME

ZEN reaches out and gives DOWNE a gentle PUSH, who swings
like a pendulum on the chain.

                    ZEN MASTER FLASH
          You know, having you here, in my
          clutches, so to speak, I've decided
          to use you to send a little
          message.
               (MORE)

> ZEN MASTER FLASH (CONT'D)
> Mainly to your comrades in law
> enforcement. You see, the most
> annoying thing about cops... is
> that they think they're in charge.
> They think they have power. The
> arrogance...! They need to be shown
> who has the real power. They need
> to know who swings the biggest
> dick.

ZEN MASTER FLASH stops Downe's swing. Uses his hands to turn
him around so he can face the EMPTY SHADOWS of one end of the
basement.

> ZEN MASTER FLASH (CONT'D)
> Of course, visionary that I am, I
> realized the most entertaining
> thing to do now would be to bring
> down some friends to dance with
> you. Maybe you remember them --

From out of the SHADOWS, a large group of INMATES. Dressed in
their orange jumpsuits (some of them customized). These are
bad ass motherfuckers. Uber-steroid freaks. Big and beefy.
Like a pack of hungry wolves.

> ZEN MASTER FLASH (CONT'D)
> -- certainly they remember you.

ZEN steps over and addresses the INMATES.

> ZEN MASTER FLASH (CONT'D)
> So, all you rats of the Rats'
> Nest... let's find out just how
> much damage he can take.

ZEN MASTER FLASH turns his back, and the INMATES practically
explode across the room!

They swarm all over DOWNE and tear his body down from his
hanging position and begin to beat the shit out of him!

Like wild animals, they tear at his flesh, they pound him
with their boots, they ROAR and HOWL their approval at every
vicious blow. The blood-lust has taken hold!


INT. LAPD HQ LOCKER ROOM SHOWER - RESUMING

GABLE is still reading Downe's FILE.

IN THE FILE: We see old ID PHOTOS of OFFICER DOWNE (pre-
death). Several letters of commendation. Typed evaluations on
yellowing pages.

A few NEWSPAPER CLIPPINGS with the headlines: "ROOKIE COP SAVES HUNDREDS", "MEDAL OF VALOR AWARDED TO LA POLICEMAN" and "POLICE OFFICER GIVES LIFE IN THE LINE OF DUTY".

GABLE can't get through it fast enough. Each new page gets him more pumped up. His own commitment and determination being renewed right before our fucking eyes!

Finally, he slams the file shut. Checks his look in the mirror one more time. Now it's a whole different Gable:

> GABLE
> You're LAPD. You're in the
> motherfucking brotherhood now.
> You're a cop.
> (pause)
> That's right.


INT. LAPD HQ HALLWAY - CONTINUOUS

GABLE bursts through a doorway, heading down the hall. He's carrying Downe's SEVERED HAND, still wrapped up in the bloody towel.

He is met by an angry CHIEF BERRINGER, coming from the opposite end.

> CHIEF BERRINGER
> Goddammit, Gable! You show up at a
> fresh crime scene after floating
> all night at the Rusty Nail with
> those jerkoffs in your detail?!

> GABLE
> Are we going after Downe?!

> CHIEF BERRINGER
> Going after him?! Are you out of
> your fucking mind?!

> GABLE
> Listen to me, Chief! You can't give
> up on him!

> CHIEF BERRINGER
> Downe ain't your problem, is it?
> It's nobody's problem. It's over.

GABLE pulls out Downe's bloody, gloved HAND.

> GABLE
> You see this?! It's not over!

GABLE moves past CHIEF BERRINGER and heads off down the hall.

> CHIEF BERRINGER
> Where're you going?!

INT. LAPD HQ - LOCKER ROOM - CONTINUOUS

GABLE rushes in. Heads for the "secret door". CHIEF BERRINGER is right behind him. Sees where he's going.

> CHIEF BERRINGER
> Stop right there, rook!

> GABLE
> Chief --

> CHIEF BERRINGER
> Don't fuck around, Gable. This is beyond you. Maybe beyond all of us. Obviously, he walked into a goddamn trap! It was only a matter of time before --

> GABLE
> (interrupting)
> Before what? Before the department cuts Downe loose because it's not cost effective to track him down?!

> CHIEF BERRINGER
> Don't get political on me, you little shit!

> GABLE
> So you don't want to go after him? You'd rather find the next test subject?

> CHIEF BERRINGER
> What did you say?!

> GABLE
> Chief, I know about the Bullpen!

> CHIEF BERRINGER
> The what?

> GABLE
> The Bullpen! The one hundred Telekinetics!

CHIEF BERRINGER goes ballistic!

                    CHIEF BERRINGER
          What the fuck do you know about
          that?!

                    GABLE
          Enough to know that, if they're
          what's been juicing him up -- if
          they've got that connection with
          him, however it works -- then maybe
          we can use them to find him and
          help him!

                    CHIEF BERRINGER
          Bullshit...!

GABLE heads into the SECRET DOORWAY. CHIEF BERRINGER is right
behind him, pissed.

                    CHIEF BERRINGER (CONT'D)
          Hey--!


INT. BULLPEN - A FEW MINUTES LATER

GABLE bursts in. CHIEF BERRINGER is right on his heels,
yelling at him. The BULLPEN TECHS are startled at their
entrance.

                    CHIEF BERRINGER
          This is your ass, Gable! Count on
          it!

                    GABLE
          I don't care. We gotta try!

                    CHIEF BERRINGER
          You don't even know what they do!

The BULLPEN TECH from the earlier scene rushes up, nervous.

                    BULLPEN TECH
          Ummm... what's happening here?
              (recognizes Berringer)
          Chief Berringer...

                    CHIEF BERRINGER
          Don't ask.
              (to Gable)
          Gable!

GABLE stops. Turns and faces the Chief. Determined.

                    GABLE
          I'm betting they can track him or
          they can help him! Either way, it's
          worth a shot.

                    CHIEF BERRINGER
          That's not how it works! If he's
          gone, he's gone! They can't bring
          him back unless the body's
          upstairs!

                    GABLE
               (to the Bullpen Tech)
          Is that true?

                    BULLPEN TECH
          Are we... talking about a long
          distance revival?

                    GABLE
          Yes we are.

                    BULLPEN TECH
          Well, I have no idea... it's never
          been attempted before... I'm not
          sure why we'd even --

                    GABLE
               (interrupting)
          But you're saying it's not
          impossible.

                    CHIEF BERRINGER
          Gable! I'm telling you for the last
          time -- you get your ass up out of
          here right-fucking-now!

                    GABLE
          He's still a cop, Chief.
               (pause)
          Isn't he...?

A silence hangs in the air.

Finally, CHIEF BERRINGER turns to the BULLPEN TECH.

                    CHIEF BERRINGER
          Fine. Fire 'em up.
               (off the Bullpen Tech's
                hesitation)
          Do it!

The BULLPEN TECH rushes off to join the other TECHS, who
quickly get to work at their stations.

CHIEF BERRINGER turns to GABLE.

                    CHIEF BERRINGER (CONT'D)
          If this doesn't work...

GABLE steps over to the ONE HUNDRED. They all wear blank
stares. Are they even aware...?

                    GABLE
          You all know Terry Downe. He's the
          recipient of your... talents...
          your abilities. One good cop knee-
          deep in the shit every day, no
          matter what the cost.
               (Gable pauses)
          And it's cost him a lot. He's out
          there somewhere and he needs your
          help. All of you. And even though
          he might be beyond repair... you
          have to try. You have to give it
          everything you've got!

GABLE searches their faces for any sign of acknowledgement.
So far, nothing.

                    CHIEF BERRINGER
          Gable...

GABLE senses something. Suddenly, the ONE HUNDRED spark to
life. Their eyes LIGHT UP with psycho-kinetic activity. The
machinery around them starts to GLOW. A low HUM rumbles
through the room.

                    GABLE
          Here we go.


INT. KINGS COUNTY CORRECTIONAL FACILITY - BASEMENT -
CONTINUOUS

The INMATES tear him down from his hanging position. They get
him on the ground, tearing into him. The pounding never
stops.

Finally, one of the INMATES gestures for everyone to take a
break.

                    INMATE #1
          Hold on! Hold on! Wait a second,
          assholes! I wanna see if he's still
          breathing...

The INMATES spread out. OFFICER DOWNE is sprawled out on the floor, face down in multiple pools of blood. From the sidelines. ZEN MASTER FLASH steps up.

                    ZEN MASTER FLASH
          Go ahead then. Turn him over.

A pair of INMATES reach in and turn DOWNE over, onto his back. He sputters and spits blood, gasping for breath.

                    ZEN MASTER FLASH (CONT'D)
          Still breathing. Damn.

This inspires a RIOTOUS YELL of approval from the INMATES, who are thrilled to keep inflicting pain on the fallen DOWNE. They start back in. Pounding. Hacking. Biting. Kicking. Smashing.


INT. LAPD HQ - THE BULLPEN - CONTINUOUS

The ONE HUNDRED are fully active.

The BULLPEN TECHS man their machines. But they look worried.

                    BULLPEN TECH
          Reading a static particle build
          up... a lot of telekinetic energy
          being generated -- but with nowhere
          to go!

                    GABLE
          What?!

                    BULLPEN TECH
          Bypassing local receptors...

GABLE gets closer to the ONE HUNDRED. But it's getting tougher to get in close proximity to them.

                    GABLE
          Come on! You can do it! Push it!

The whole room starts to SHAKE.


INT. KINGS COUNTY CORRECTIONAL FACILITY - BASEMENT - CONTINUOUS

The INMATES are still having their way with DOWNE.

Finally, a VOICE from the shadows stops them:

                    MOTHER SUPREME (O.S.)
          Stop.

MOTHER SUPREME steps forward, emerging from the shadows.
She's wearing her own version of the prison jumpsuit (it's
orange, but it's in the form of a nun's frock).

ZEN MASTER FLASH is still off to the side, watching. He
smiles

                    ZEN MASTER FLASH
          Beautiful.

The INMATES separate, parting like the Red Sea, and allow her
to get close to DOWNE. He's flat on his back.

She places her BOOT HEEL on his throat.

                    MOTHER SUPREME
          You have been judged as unworthy.
          You have been judged as unclean.
          This is the price you pay for your
          lack of belief.

DOWNE struggles under her boot, but it's no use. He's too
weak. She presses down harder.


INT. LAPD HQ - THE BULLPEN - CONTINUOUS

Amidst the shaking and quaking of the room -- some of the ONE
HUNDRED are overloading! One of them KEELS OVER in his chair.
Bleeding from the eyes.

GABLE and CHIEF BERRINGER look on in shock and horror.

                    GABLE
          Oh shit...!

                    CHIEF BERRINGER
          What's happening?!

The BULLPEN TECHS frantically monitor their consoles.

                    BULLPEN TECH
          We lost one! And more right on the
          brink!

                    CHIEF BERRINGER
          Hold on--!

                    BULLPEN TECH
          Organic circuits are overloading!
          They can't take the feedback!

                    CHIEF BERRINGER
          Shut it down!

                    GABLE
          No--!

                    CHIEF BERRINGER
          Gable! You want to be responsible
          for losing them, too?!

This stops GABLE in his tracks.

The entire mechanism -- the ONE HUNDRED -- power down. The
whole lot of them goes dark. An eerie silence hangs in the
room.

                    GABLE
          Dammit...


INT. KINGS COUNTY CORRECTIONAL FACILITY - BASEMENT -
CONTINUOUS

The INMATES are HOWLING for blood now. MOTHER SUPREME is
still on top of DOWNE, yelling down at him over the inmates'
cacophonous noise.

                    MOTHER SUPREME
          Mine is a vengeful god. She speaks
          through me. She tells me that you
          resist the afterlife. You resist
          the everlasting glory.

DOWNE weakly COUGHS out a sputter of blood.


INT. LAPD HQ - THE BULLPEN - CONTINUOUS

GABLE, CHIEF BERRINGER and the BULLPEN TECHS stand around in
awkward silence.

GABLE finally accepts the inevitable.

                    GABLE
          I guess that's it --

But before he can finish the sentence, the room SPUTTERS back
to life! The eyes of the ONE HUNDRED suddenly LIGHT BACK UP,
at full power.

The BULLPEN TECHS scramble to their consoles.

                    BULLPEN TECH
          Oh my God!

                         CHIEF BERRINGER
                What's happening?!

                         GABLE
                Don't you see, Chief?! They're
                doing it on their own! They're not
                giving up...

The GLOW around the ONE HUNDRED gets even more intense.
Suddenly, several of them FLAIL ABOUT and COLLAPSE out of
their chairs!

The BULLPEN TECHS can't get close enough to help them. The
ENERGY the remaining ONE HUNDRED is throwing off is too much.

Some of the COMPUTER EQUIPMENT and other TECH start to SPARK
and SHORT OUT. The BULLPEN TECH'S try to maintain their
stations. Some of them get nailed with the shorting
electricity.

GABLE and CHIEF BERRINGER can only stand and watch *and hope
that it's working...!*


INT. KINGS COUNTY CORRECTIONAL FACILITY - BASEMENT -
CONTINUOUS

DOWNE struggles under MOTHER SUPREME'S boot, but it's no use.
He's too weak.

                         MOTHER SUPREME
                This time you will join the
                endless, blackest night. The
                eternal sleep. Your final penance.

ON DOWNE

His eyes rolling back in his head.

INSIDE HIS MIND --

-- a swimming cauldron of energy! He experiences VISIONS --
quick FLASHES of the various FACES of the ONE HUNDRED! Their
EYES GLOW with their own internal energy! They pass in and
out of his mind, piling on top of each other and then fading
away in quick succession --

BACK IN THE BASEMENT

MOTHER SUPREME presses down even harder on DOWNE with her
boot.

                    MOTHER SUPREME (CONT'D)
          Your days of cheating death --
          cheating nature -- have come to a
          vainglorious end.


INT. LAPD HQ - THE BULLPEN - CONTINUOUS

The BULLPEN TECHS are struggling at their consoles. The ONE
HUNDRED -- the ones that are still active, that is -- are
practically vibrating in their seats.

Another one of them FALLS OUT of their chair. Collapses on
the floor, bleeding from every orifice.

Everyone has to YELL over the RUMBLING and the ACTIVE
MECHANISM.

                    BULLPEN TECH
          Oh my God...!

                    CHIEF BERRINGER
          What is it?!

                    BULLPEN TECH
          Looks like... their power's being
          sucked out of them! No idea how!

GABLE and CHIEF BERRINGER exchange frantic looks.

                    GABLE
          That means --

Suddenly, one of the ONE HUNDRED bursts into psycho-kinetic
flame!

                    CHIEF BERRINGER
          Goddammit--!

                    BULLPEN TECH
          They can't do this much longer!
          They're burning out right in front
          of us!

And just at the moment where we think all is lost --


INT. KINGS COUNTY CORRECTIONAL FACILITY - BASEMENT -
CONTINUOUS

-- something in DOWNE'S EYES changes. They suddenly find
focus. The fire reignites. His expression changes.

Only ZEN MASTER FLASH notices.

                    ZEN MASTER FLASH
          Huh.


INT. LAPD HQ - THE BULLPEN - CONTINUOUS

Suddenly, everything SHUTS DOWN again. The room goes dark.

                    CHIEF BERRINGER
          Oh shit.


INT. KINGS COUNTY CORRECTIONAL FACILITY - BASEMENT -
CONTINUOUS

Just as MOTHER SUPREME is going to bear down and snap his
neck, DOWNE reaches up. GRABS her ankle (with his one good
hand) -- TEARS HER LEG OFF HER BODY!

MOTHER SUPREME falls down, screaming bloody murder and
bleeding out from her hip.

                    MOTHER SUPREME
          Goddamn mother-cunting beast-
          fucker!

DOWNE quickly springs to his feet. For the moment, he's super-
charged. Turns on the still shocked INMATES.

                    DOWNE
          You're not supposed to be out of
          your cells, are you?

Still holding the leg, he dives into the nearest group of
INMATES and beats the shot of them with the LEG!

He then turns on ZEN MASTER FLASH, who stands in a meditation
pose.

                    ZEN MASTER FLASH
          Still got some fight left in you?
          Guess it keeps things interesting.
          Catch me if you can.

And with that, ZEN TELEPORTS away. DOWNE leaps for him --

                    DOWNE
          You're on my most wanted list!

-- and passes right through the wisp of teleportation energy
left over.

DOWNE turns and faces off against the rest of the INMATES,
who have recovered from their shock and are ready to rumble!

                    DOWNE (CONT'D)
         You crankheads don't understand the
         meaning of command presence! Here's
         a demonstration--!

Now it's DOWNE vs. the INMATES. An explosive burst of
violence! He fights his way through them. Uses the bloody leg
as a club, a battering ram, a bludgeon. Whatever it takes to
cut a swatch through the swarming INMATES!

DOWNE takes more punishment, but nothing slows him down. He
takes out each and every INMATE with brutal efficiency,
leaving a floor littered with bloody, broken bodies.

He finally DROPS the leg. Takes a quick look back at the
basement filled with bodies. Then exits into the --


INT. KINGS COUNTY CORRECTIONAL FACILITY - STAIRWELL -
CONTINUOUS

DOWNE staggers into the stairwell. He looks up.

At the top of the stairs -- another throng of bloodthirsty
INMATES! They hold clubs and pipes and shivs of all sizes.

                    INMATE
         You think you're done, fuckface?!
         You ain't close to being done!
         We're all up outta dis mug! And we
         gon' shove our newfound freedom
         straight up yo' ass! So bend over
         wide!

                    DOWNE
         Think about it, shithead. This
         badge means something. It means I
         am the order in a world filled with
         chaos. You're the chaos. All of
         you. You deranged motherfuckers.
         Besides, kicking your heads in --

DOWNE starts up the stairs. Smiles a bloody grin.

                    DOWNE (CONT'D)
         -- makes my dick hard.

DOWNE and the INMATES crash into each other in the middle of
the stairwell! They're tearing and clawing at each other.

DOWNE is punching and stomping his way up the stairs, tossing
INMATES left and right. Slams their heads into the concrete
walls. Slams heads into each other. Scoops up the fallen
inmates' WEAPONS and uses them on the rest!

A cacophony of pure chaos! And for as much punishment and
damage that DOWNE is taking -- and he's taking quite a bit --
he fights on.

Finally, he reaches he top of the stairwell. The steps behind
him are completely covered with inmate bodies.


EXT. KINGS COUNTY CORRECTIONAL FACILITY - YARD - CONTINUOUS

DOWNE bursts out the door and stumbles out into the main yard
-- which is filled with THE REST OF THE INMATE POPULATION!

They come at him from all sides. DOWNE reverts to basic,
animal survival tactics -- and takes them all on at once! A
big-ass, climatic one-vs-a-multitude fight!

As he tears through the INMATES, he smashes his fist
completely through the sternum of a big, beefy INMATE --
erupting out the other side! He then uses the hulking body as
a battering ram to plow through the other INMATES, knocking
them every which way.

Finally, he breaks out of the throng of INMATES, but his
momentum with the INMATE/BATTERING RAM takes him across the
rest of the yard --

-- he CRASHES through a CHAIN-LINK FENCE and slams the dead
INMATE/BATTERING RAM face-first into the prison GENERATOR!

The generator EXPLODES from the impact. The inmate's body is
instantly FRIED and DOWNE is blown backwards by the
explosion.

The LIGHTS all around the prison FLICKER and then go dark!


INT. LAPD HQ - THE BULLPEN - CONTINUOUS

An eerie silence hangs in the darkened bullpen. Wisps of
smoke hang in the air.

GABLE and CHIEF BERRINGER look at each other. Then they RUSH
for the exit door.


INT. LAPD HQ HALLWAY - CONTINUOUS

GABLE and CHIEF BERRINGER haul ass down the hallway. The
lights are flickering on and off. GABLE is frantic!

                    GABLE
          Did it work?! Holy shit, it worked,
          right?!

                    CHIEF BERRINGER
          Shut the fuck up, Gable!

                    GABLE
          So now what?!

                    CHIEF BERRINGER
          You're asking me?!

They are met by another COP (the same one from the bar,
earlier), also frantic.

                    COP
          Chief!

                    CHIEF BERRINGER
          We need to mobilize all available --

                    COP
               (interrupting)
          So you heard?

                    CHIEF BERRINGER
          Wait -- heard what?!

                    COP
          King's County Prison! Reports of a
          massive riot! They've lost power!
          All hell is breaking loose out
          there!

CHIEF BERRINGER and GABLE share a look. *Of course...!*


EXT. KINGS COUNTY CORRECTIONAL FACILITY - THE YARD -
CONTINUOUS

DOWNE continues to take down the remaining INMATES still
willing to fight him. Every move is brutal -- painful --
bloody!

He looks like he's been through a war -- but keeps moving!
Keeps fighting! Keeps winning!


INT. FORTUNE 500 COMPOUND - MAIN OFFICE

The LION, TIGER and VULTURE are gathered around their meeting
table, staring down the SPEAKER PHONE on the table.

                    TIGER
          You wait this long to check in --
          and we're hearing that you turned
          the Rats' Nest into a war zone?!
          Are you out of your mind?!

                    LION
          You had him! What makes you think
          this was the time to make some kind
          of goddamn wacko political
          statement?!


INT. KINGS COUNTY CORRECTIONAL FACILITY - HALLWAY - NIGHT

ZEN MASTER FLASH talks on his cell phone. The lights are out
in here (as they are throughout the entire prison).

The sounds of EXPLOSIONS and other chaos can be heard in the
distance (coming from other parts of the prison). Zen remains
calm.

                    ZEN MASTER FLASH
          I did nothing of the sort,
          gentlemen. That is a completely
          uninformed assessment of my
          actions. I despise politics. But
          you were well aware how I operate.
          Complete and total autonomy. Your
          fatal flaw -- as with most sad
          bastards who have held onto power
          for far too long -- is that you
          lack vision. This is all part of
          the game.

WE CUT BACK AND FORTH BETWEEN THEM:

                    VULTURE
          This isn't a game, you piece of
          shit psycho! This is our business!
          We hired you to get rid of him! To
          erase him from existence!

                    ZEN MASTER FLASH
          And so I shall. Try not to get so
          emotionally involved. That's the
          first lesson of business.

                    LION
          Listen to me, you prancing fucknut--

LION picks up the speaker phone. Screams into it:

                    LION (CONT'D)
          -- you can consider our contract
          terminated! That means -- you can
          forget about your payment, asshole!
          That's what you get for fucking
          with the Fortune 500!

                    ZEN MASTER FLASH
          I see. Well, this brand of
          nastiness has the unfortunate
          potential to damage my professional
          reputation. So allow me to convey
          how I'm going to roll out of here
          when I'm done roasting this cop.

LION, TIGER and VULTURE get very quiet...

                    ZEN MASTER FLASH (CONT'D)
          I'm going to find the lot of you.
          No matter how far you think you can
          run, no matter how well you think
          you can hide, I will find you. At
          which point, the fate I have in
          store for you will have you begging
          for death.

ZEN MASTER FLASH smiles. He loves fucking with people.

                    ZEN MASTER FLASH (CONT'D)
          Enjoy the rest of your evening,
          gentlemen. This is Zen Master
          Flash, signing off.

The line goes dead. They look at each other.

                    VULTURE
          Oh shit.


INT. KINGS COUNTY CORRECTIONAL FACILITY - WARDEN'S OFFICE -
NIGHT

ZEN MASTER FLASH enters. Closes the door behind him. The
WARDEN is cowering behind his desk.

                    ZEN MASTER FLASH
          It would appear that establishing a
          beachhead is in order. This office
          may suffice.

                    WARDEN
          This whole thing... this is not how
          it was supposed to go! Jesus, the
          U.S.
                    (MORE)

                    WARDEN (CONT'D)
          Attorney's office is going to crawl
          right up my ass for this... just
          like that grand jury investigation!


                    ZEN MASTER FLASH
          What are you blubbering about?


                    WARDEN
          Me? What do you think I'm
          "blubbering" about?! Can't you hear
          what's happening out there?!

The sounds of VIOLENCE are getting closer.

                    ZEN MASTER FLASH
          Warden. Just because you're on the
          Fortune 500's payroll doesn't mean
          you and I are friendly. Point of
          fact, at the moment, that puts us
          on opposing sides...

ZEN pulls out a fresh BLADE to kill him. Suddenly, the DOOR
EXPLODES inward. OFFICER DOWNE enters. He looks like a
walking war.

                    DOWNE
          Zen Master Flash -- I'm coming for
          you!

                    ZEN MASTER FLASH
          That's so sweet.

DOWNE charges. ZEN MASTER FLASH acrobatically leaps out of
the way. Downe's momentum sends him CRASHING into the
Warden's desk, destroying it.

ZEN MASTER FLASH leaps in with a flurry of KUNG-FU KICKS.
DOWNE is sent careening across the room. He slams into the
far wall.

ZEN MASTER FLASH is on him in an instant, wielding his
BUTCHER'S AXE!

He goes for Downe's face, but Downe dodges the blow and the
axe blade buries itself into the wall behind him.

Downe is slumped against the wall -- too weak to stand? -- as
ZEN MASTER FLASH struggles to pull his blade out of the wall.

                    ZEN MASTER FLASH (CONT'D)
          They told me you were unkillable! I
          say you've died a thousand times!
          And with each death, your soul is
          eaten away!

DOWNE lunges up. Grabs ZEN MASTER FLASH by the throat!

> DOWNE
> Maybe so, fuckhead. But here's what
> I've learned. To do my job, I don't
> need a soul.

DOWNE grabs ZEN MASTER FLASH'S VISOR.

> DOWNE (CONT'D)
> An eye for an eye.

He PULLS. The VISOR tears off Zen's face in a small splatter
of blood --

-- both EYE BALLS are torn out of his eye sockets, too (more
connected to the visor than his head).

> DOWNE (CONT'D)
> Or two.

ZEN MASTER FLASH starts screaming like a bitch. Clutching at
his face, which is a bloody mess.

> ZEN MASTER FLASH
> No! You bastard!

DOWNE tosses away the blood-soaked visor. He's weak on his
feet, but still moving.

> DOWNE
> You have the right to remain
> silent.

He PICKS UP Zen Master Flash.

> DOWNE (CONT'D)
> You have the right to go fuck
> yourself.

He carries him across the room, toward the window.

> DOWNE (CONT'D)
> You have the right to lay down and
> die.

He stops at the window, still holding a squirming ZEN MASTER
FLASH over his head.

> DOWNE (CONT'D)
> Do you understand these rights as
> they have been read to you?

He THROWS ZEN MASTER FLASH out the window. The window glass
SHATTERS and Zen plummets to the ground (far below) amidst a
shower of glass.

But, before his body IMPACTS on the concrete yard below, he
TELEPORTS away. The shower of glass hits the ground.

UP AT THE WINDOW: DOWNE looks down at the yard. Frowns at
Zen's escape.

The WARDEN appears at his side. Quickly -- and nervously --
goes into his act:

                    WARDEN
          You... you saved me, Officer! He
          was a maniac! He was just about to
          kill me!

DOWNE turns to the WARDEN. Stares him down hard.

                    DOWNE
          Y'know, I've got a gut feeling
          about you, Warden.

                    WARDEN
          What... what do you mean...?

                    DOWNE
          I just don't think you're a victim
          here.

The terrified WARDEN scrambles to his desk. Opens a drawer.
Pulls out a HANDGUN.

Before he can fire, DOWNE shoves his (only) FIST through the
WARDEN'S FACE! It EXPLODES out the back of his head! With the
Warden's head stuck to his hand, he TEARS IT off his body.

The Warden's headless, lifeless body collapses to the floor.

In the silence of the aftermath, Downe's injuries finally
catch up to him. He's uneasy on his feet.

                    DOWNE (CONT'D)
          Lethal force... necessary...

He braces himself against the desk, preventing himself from
falling over.

                    DOWNE (CONT'D)
          ... this badge... means I am the
          order... in a world filled with
          chaos...

Downe falls face-first onto the floor. Dead.


EXT. KINGS COUNTY CORRECTIONAL FACILITY - THE YARD - NIGHT

A small fleet of POLICE HELICOPTERS descend onto the yard.
Spotlights shining down.

Heavily armed, body armored COPS file out of the copters,
fanning across the yard.

CHIEF BERRINGER and GABLE, also armored up, exit a copter and
head into the prison. They step over the numerous INMATE
BODIES scattered everywhere.

                    GABLE
          Jesus Christ...!


INT. KINGS COUNTY CORRECTIONAL FACILITY - CONTINUOUS

The COPS move through the prison, heading up stairs. CHIEF
BERRINGER and GABLE are among them.

They notice the BODIES and BLOOD STAINS everywhere -- all of
them are INMATES.

                    GABLE
              Chief--!

                    CHIEF BERRINGER
              Just keep moving. Follow the
              blood...


INT. WARDEN'S OFFICE - CONTINUOUS

The armored COPS burst in, guns ready.

All they find is the bloody aftermath. One of the COPS
motions for CHIEF BERRINGER to enter. GABLE slips in behind
him. Sees DOWNE face-down on the floor.

The HAZMAT SUITED GUYS file in. GABLE calls out to them:

                    GABLE
              Right there. C'mon--!

The HAZMAT SUITS gather around DOWNE'S BODY. With some
effort, they flip him over. They see the WARDEN'S HEAD still
wrapped around Downe's WRIST.

                    HAZMAT #1
              Holy hell. Look at this.

HAZMAT #1 grabs the WARDEN'S HEAD and PULLS... straining to get it off. Finally, it POPS off in a spray of blood and goo that narrowly misses GABLE and CHIEF BERRINGER.

                    CHIEF BERRINGER
          Goddammit! Will you assholes watch
          what you're doing?!

                    HAZMAT #1
          Sorry, Chief.

HAZMAT #2 kneels down. Checks Downe's vitals.

                    HAZMAT #2
          He's dead.

                    HAZMAT #1
               (sarcastic)
          No shit.

CHIEF BERRINGER steps in.

                    CHIEF BERRINGER
          Let's get him back to headquarters.

Everyone hesitates. Seeing Downe's corpse -- and how torn up he is -- it's hard to believe anything could bring him back. Suddenly, Gable steps up:

                    GABLE
          What are you waiting for?! MOVE IT!


INT. RESURRECTION LAB - DAY

DOWNE'S BODY is laid out on the slab. The various LAB TECHS are prepping him for the procedure.

One of them places his SEVERED HAND on the slab next to the stump of his arm.

GABLE and CHIEF BERRINGER watch from the sidelines.

                    GABLE
          Maybe we should let him be.

                    CHIEF BERRINGER
          What do you mean?

                    GABLE
          I mean, let him rest in peace.

                    CHIEF BERRINGER
          Rest in peace? What does that even
          mean? You're the one who convinced
          me to bring him back...!

GABLE turns away. He knows the Chief is right.

                    CHIEF BERRINGER (CONT'D)
          Something we all need to get used
          to... you, me, everyone in here.
          This is the world we live in. Is it
          fucked? Probably. And if that's the
          case, you know what a fucked up
          world needs most of all?

A beat.

                    GABLE
          A cop.

                    CHIEF BERRINGER
          That's right. But not just any cop.
          It needs a cop that never gives up.
          A cop that always comes back. And
          we got him. Now, right or wrong...
          we need him out there.

                    GABLE
          I just think... maybe after all
          this, he's finally done his duty.

                    CHIEF BERRINGER
          You think so, huh? You think it
          ever ends, rookie?

                    GABLE
          Chief? Don't call me rookie
          anymore. It's Officer Gable.

BERRINGER turns. Does a slow burn on GABLE.

And then...

                    CHIEF BERRINGER
          Very good.
               (to the techs)
          Light him up.

The lights in the room dim.

                    LAB TECH #1
          Accessing bullpen. Opening channels
          A, B and C for immediate upload.

                         LAB TECH #2
              Initiate.

The power cells descend from the ceiling, GLOWING and
CRACKLING with weird energy once again.

Everyone shields their eyes from the glow that envelops
Downe's body.

The procedure ends. DOWNE stirs. TECHNICIANS rush in to help
him up. One of the LAB TECHS approaches CHIEF BERRINGER.

                         LAB TECH #1
                    (whisper)
              That was a rough one, Chief. We
              can't be certain that his mind is
              still --

                         CHIEF BERRINGER
                    (interrupting)
              Lookin' good, Terry. Just like new.

CHIEF BERRINGER steps over to DOWNE, who pulls himself off
the slab. He is given a towel to cover his naughty bits. He
swats it away with his newly reattached hand.

                         DOWNE
              I need to see 'em. Right now.

                                             CUT TO:


INT. BULLPEN - A FEW MINUTES LATER

DOWNE -- now dressed -- quietly and calmly walks around the
perimeter of the ONE HUNDRED TELEKINETICS (or, what's left of
them).

He observes the ones who give him power, the ones who give
him life. They all seem to acknowledge his presence.

He stops in front of some of them, sharing a moment. No words
need to be spoken between them.

He silently acknowledges several EMPTY CHAIRS scattered among
the one hundred. The ones who sacrificed themselves. The
fallen.

GABLE and CHIEF BERRINGER watch from the sidelines.

And then... DOWNE slowly approaches GABLE. Looks him right in
the eye. GABLE looks right back, unflinching. DOWNE stares at
him.

                    DOWNE
          You get it now?

GABLE nods. DOWNE starts to walk off.

CHIEF BERRINGER steps up.

                    CHIEF BERRINGER
          Hope you're not expecting a
          vacation or anything. Your job's
          not done yet.

He hands DOWNE a new pair of SUNGLASSES.

                    DOWNE
          It's never done, Chief.

                                        CUT TO:


EXT. LA FREEWAY - DAY

A MUSTANG screams down the busy freeway.

TITLE SUPER: THE MOTHERFUCKING 105

INSIDE THE MUSTANG

Three freakish CROOKS are whooping it up, celebrating.

                    CROOK #1
          Awww, yeah, boy! Now that's a
          motherfuckin' haul!

                    CROOK #2
          Collecting is the new black, no
          doubt about it!

                    CROOK #1
          You think the Fortune 500 still
          gets a cut or what?

                    CROOK #2
          Are you shitting me? You think just
          cause they got their ears boxed
          that they ain't still running the
          show?

                    CROOK #1
          Yo, I hear they got a lot more than
          their ears boxed. They got their
          balls racked, hard! And that says
          what? It says it's the
          motherfuckin' Wild West up in here!
                    (MORE)

                    CROOK #1 (CONT'D)
          Every crook for himself! But I
          think they'll still fuck us up if
          we cross 'em!

                    CROOK #2
          Some pussy shit...!

                    CROOK #1
          Hey, fuck you, turtledove! You
          wanna high-tail it with your cut,
          you feel free!

                    CROOK #2
          I'm just sayin', might as well take
          advantage of the situation! We're
          the ones with all the juice in this
          town! Madness and mayhem as far as
          the eye can see -- and not a black-
          n-white in sight! It's fuckin'
          beautiful, man!

OUTSIDE THE CAR

A HAND grabs onto the driver's side door handle -- and then
TEARS THE DOOR RIGHT OFF THE CAR!

The CROOKS look over in horror --

-- as OFFICER DOWNE -- good as new and riding a bad-ass
police hog -- tosses the car door aside and pulls out his .85
MAG. Aims it at the crooks.

                    DOWNE
          PULL OVER, COCKSUCKERS! YOU'RE ALL
          UNDER ARREST!


               THE MOTHERFUCKING END

# THE GREAT SPACE COASTER (GET ONBOARD)

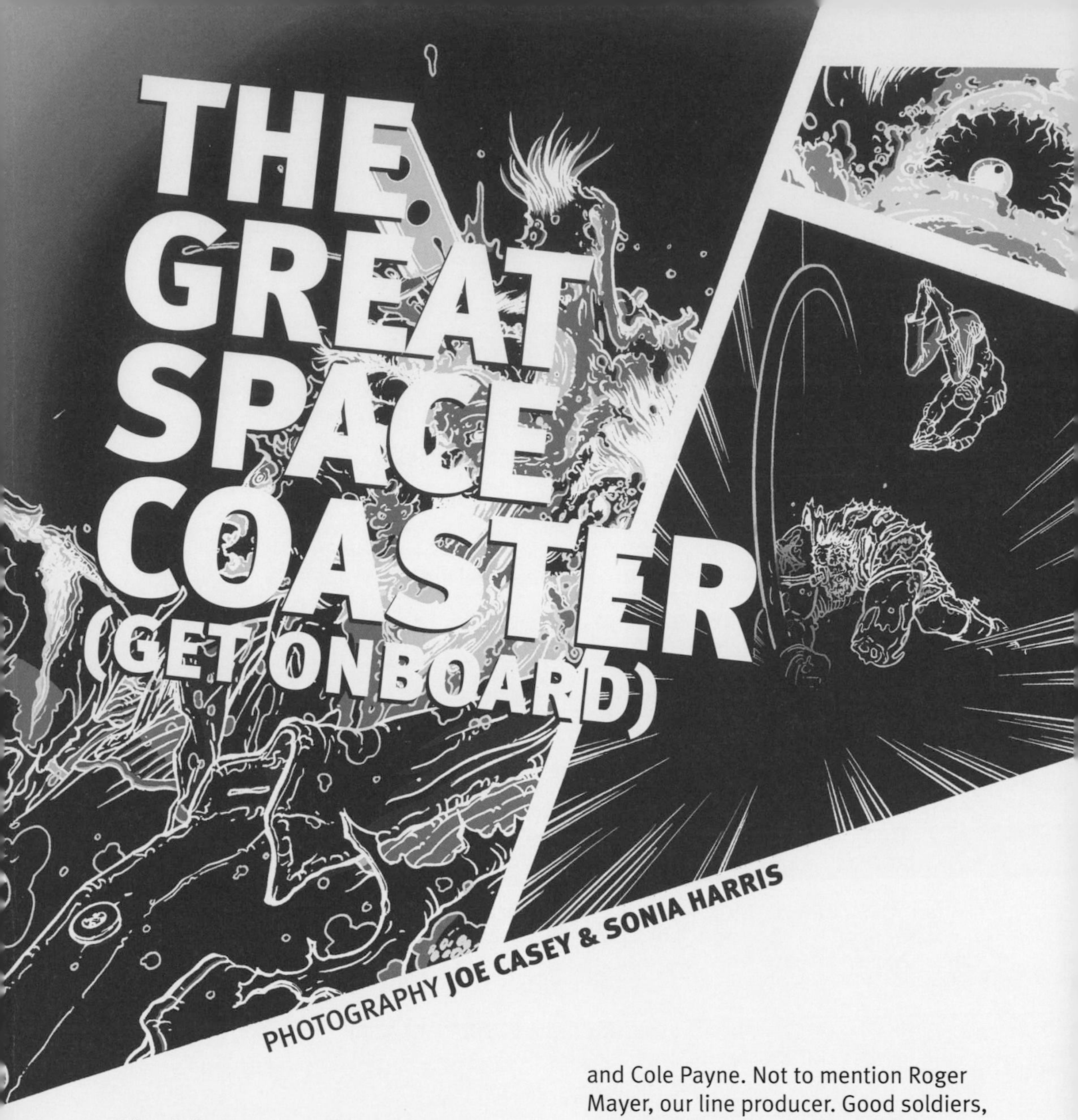

PHOTOGRAPHY **JOE CASEY & SONIA HARRIS**

What follows is something akin to a scrapbook...

Yeah, that's a decent enough name for it, I guess. I dunno. I've never been in this position before. As far as scrapbooks go, this is probably my first.

So I didn't just write the screenplay for *Officer Downe*... I was a bona fide producer on the film. That means I was on set every day of the shoot, pitching in when needed, making sure certain things stayed on the right track, reminding folks of details that might've otherwise been forgotten in the mad rush of production. This movie had four producers, actually... along with myself, there was Mark Neveldine, Skip Williamson and Cole Payne. Not to mention Roger Mayer, our line producer. Good soldiers, one and all. It takes a village, right...?

Making a film from the ground up can be a lot like a military incursion. It's a limited engagement. It's quickly constructing a small corporation, packed with personnel and equipment, putting the pedal to the medal, and then dismantling the entire thing when you're done. It's a large group of creative technicians coming together to achieve a common goal. There's a real transient mentality to the whole thing... deep down, everyone knows we're in a temporary situation. But while we're *in* it, it's the entire world. There really is nothing much else that exists until you cross that finish line (or, in this case, attend the wrap party).

I wasn't terribly diligent about documenting the proceedings. Mainly because I was too busy working. Also, I've never been great with taking pictures... of *anything*. It's just not my thing. What I recall happening most of all on set was seeing Clown or Nev take a phone pic of something... which would often remind me that *I* could do that, too. So I would.

And what follows is the basic result of those random impulses. A cornucopia of memories, scattered across several weeks in the spring of 2015. Each photo is its own slice of memory. Pay particular attention to co-creator Chris Burnham, who shows up as an extra. In the film, he's dead on the floor during the ER slaughter sequence. He was caked in stage blood for two days. Better him than me, but it's all part of the stew. I was more than happy to take a couple of snaps of my comicbook co-conspirator on the set of the film our work inspired.

Full disclosure: not all of these photos were taken by me. Graphic designer Sonia Harris spent some time on the *Officer Downe* set and she took some pictures. She was also at the LA Film Fest premiere and snapped a few photos there, as well. These are also included on the following pages.

Looking over this now, what strikes me most is how many moving parts are involved when it comes to making a film. A multitude, you might say. And, in some respects, the inherent success of a film -- at least during principal photography -- depends on all of those moving parts operating exactly as they should. And, on *Officer Downe*... for the most part, they did. It's a strange feeling to watch an end credits crawl and realize that you know most of the names listed personally. Even if these relationships were only fleeting alliances... foxhole mentalities colliding... friendships of coincidence and convenience... they all still mean something to me. They all made valuable contributions. Hell, we made a fuckin' movie together.

Hopefully by now, you've all seen it.

Joe Casey
November 2016

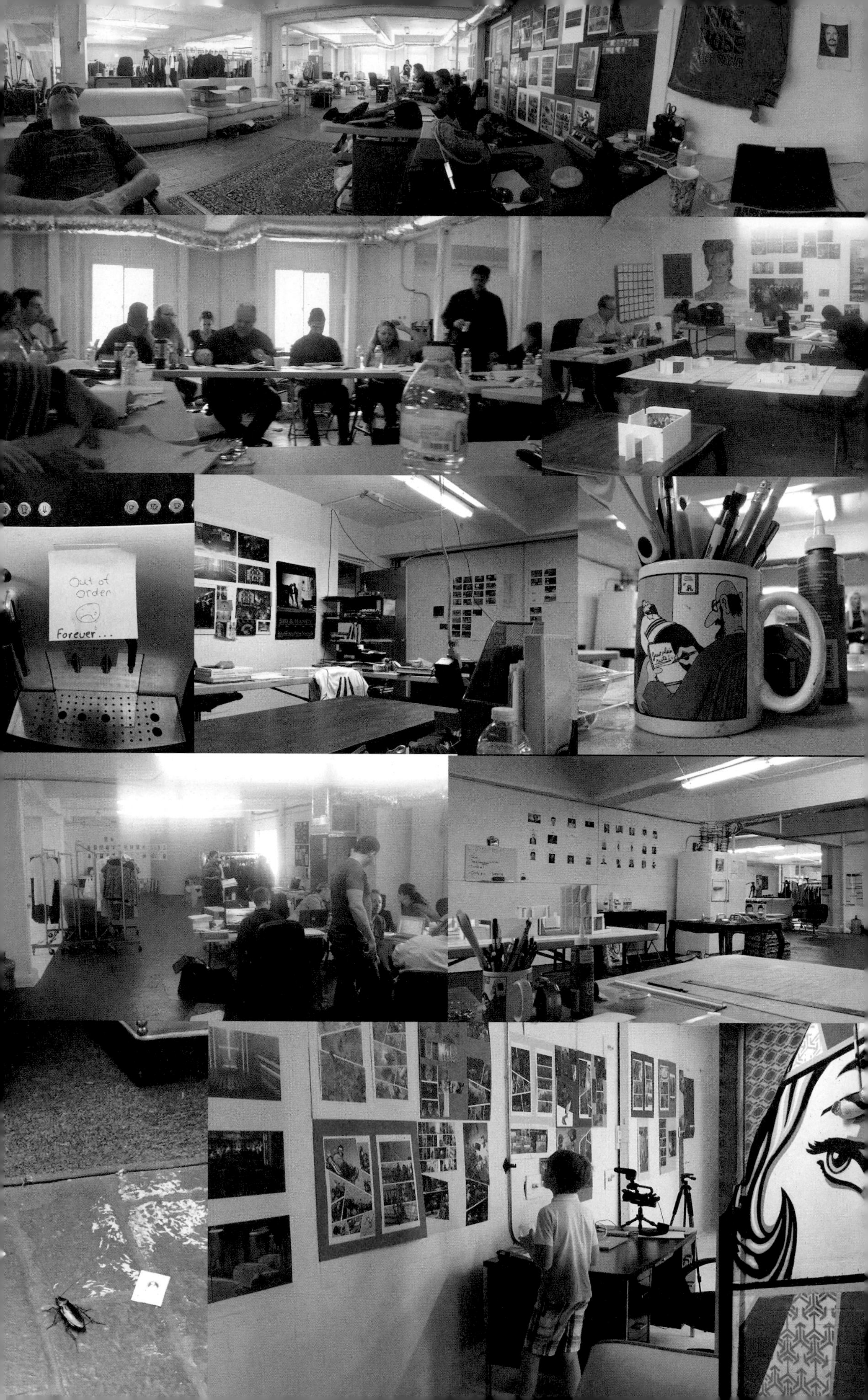
Out of order
Forever...

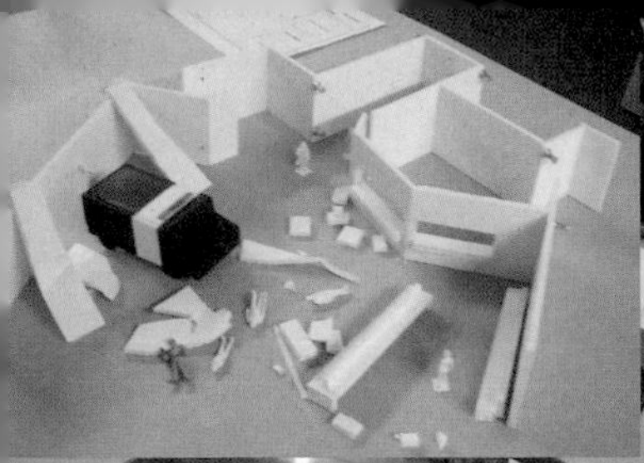
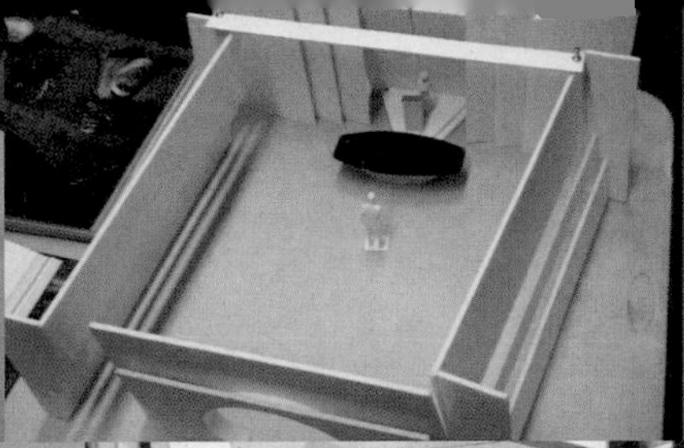
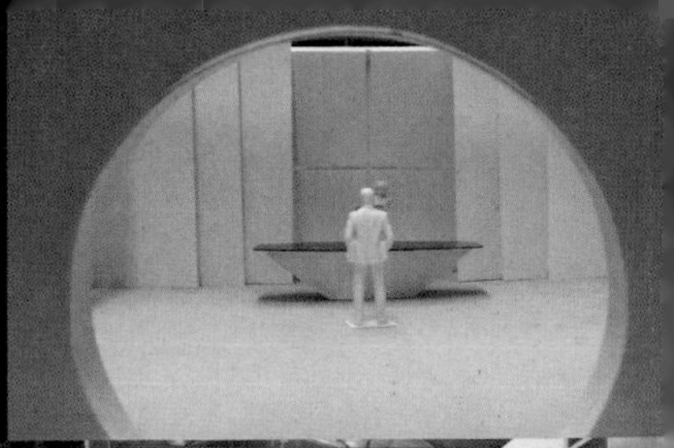
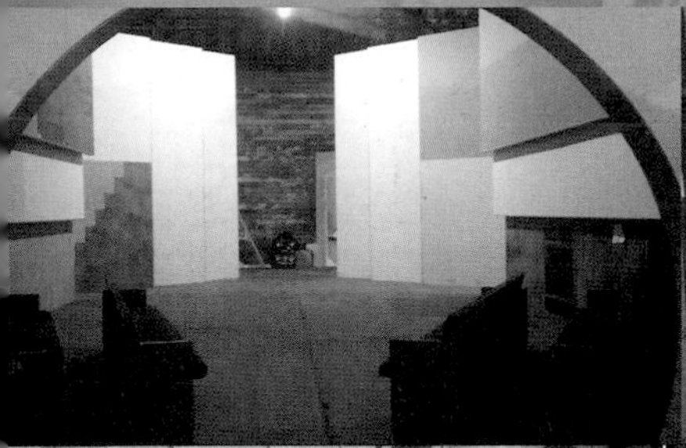
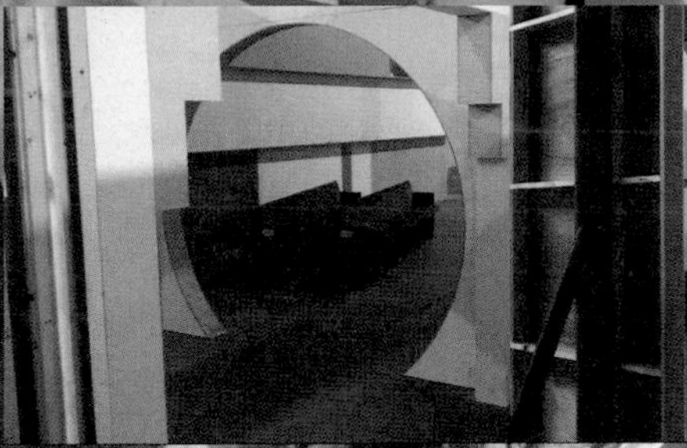
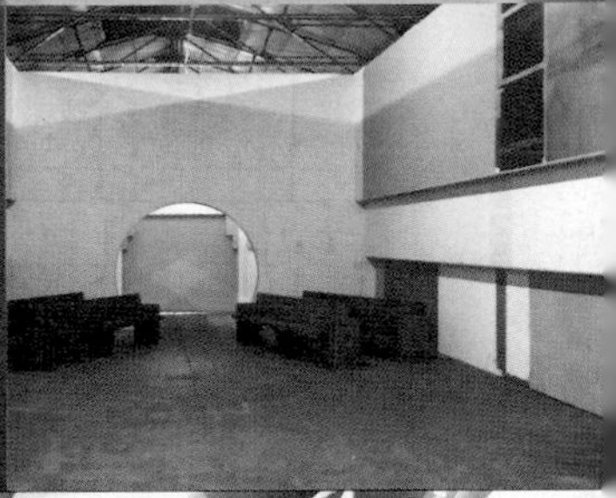
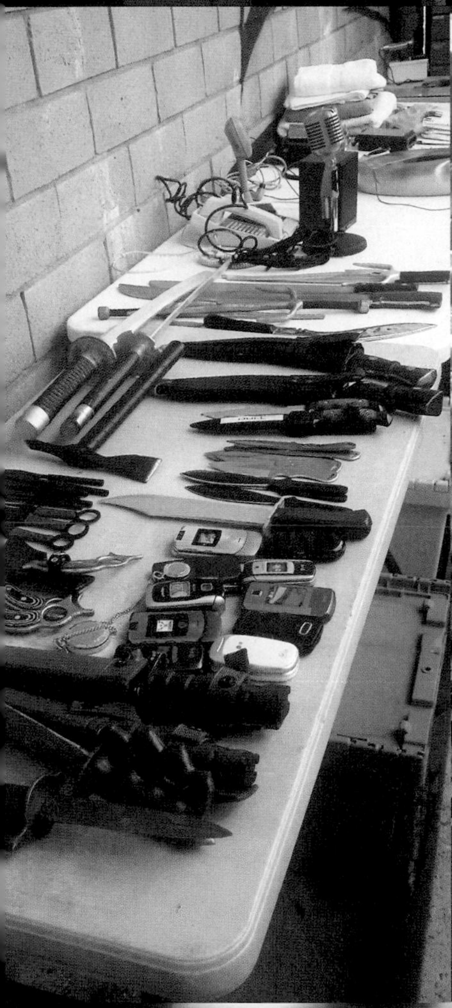
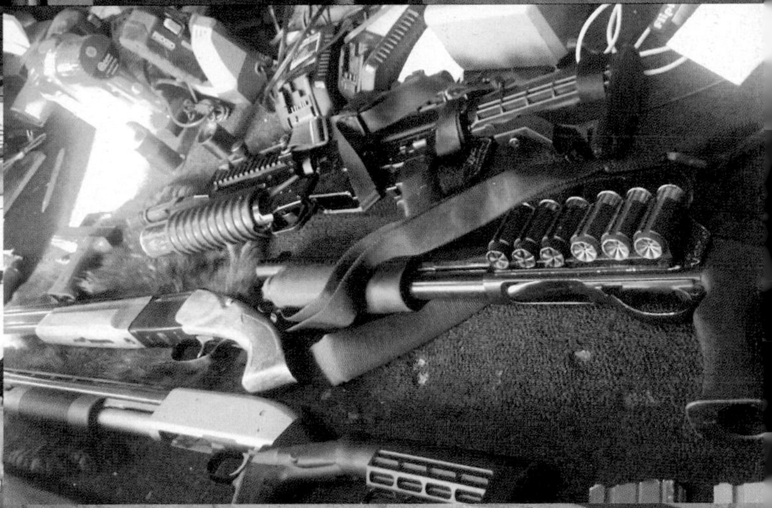
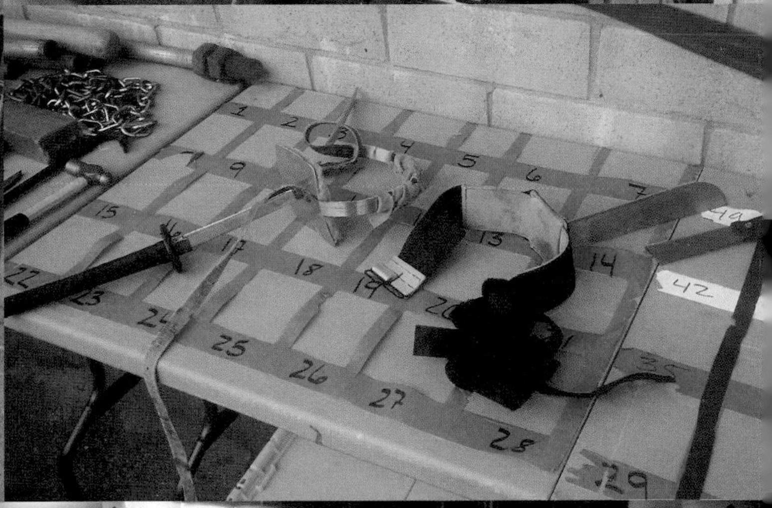
1
2
4
5
6
7
9
15
13
14
18
22
23
24
25
26
27
28
29
42
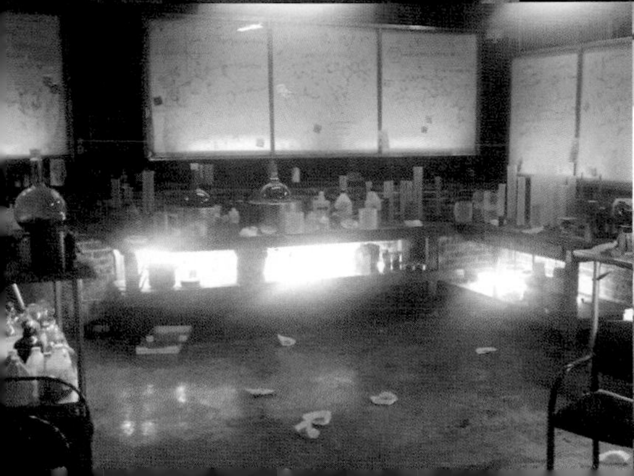
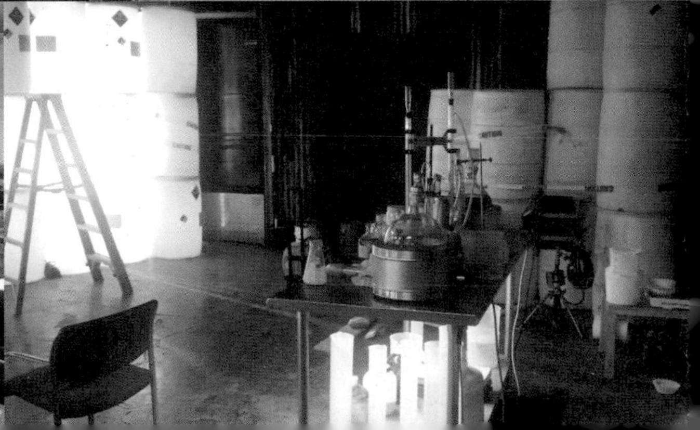

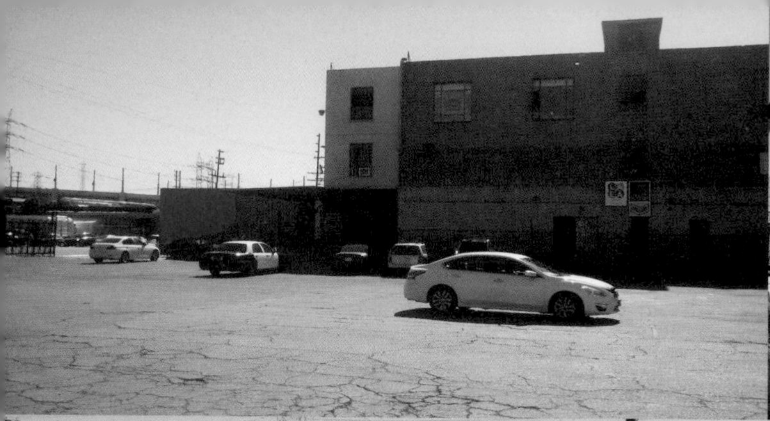

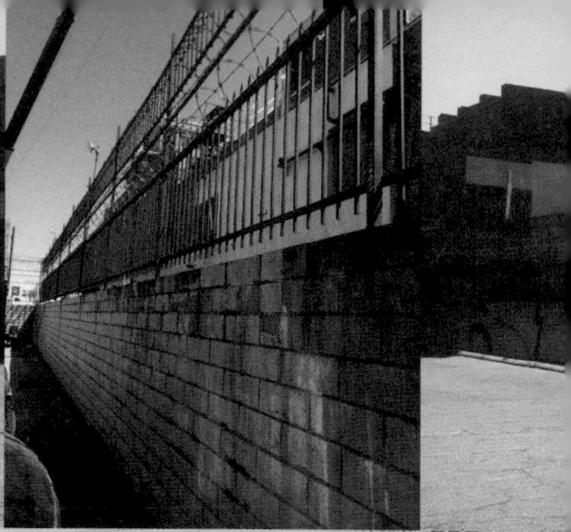

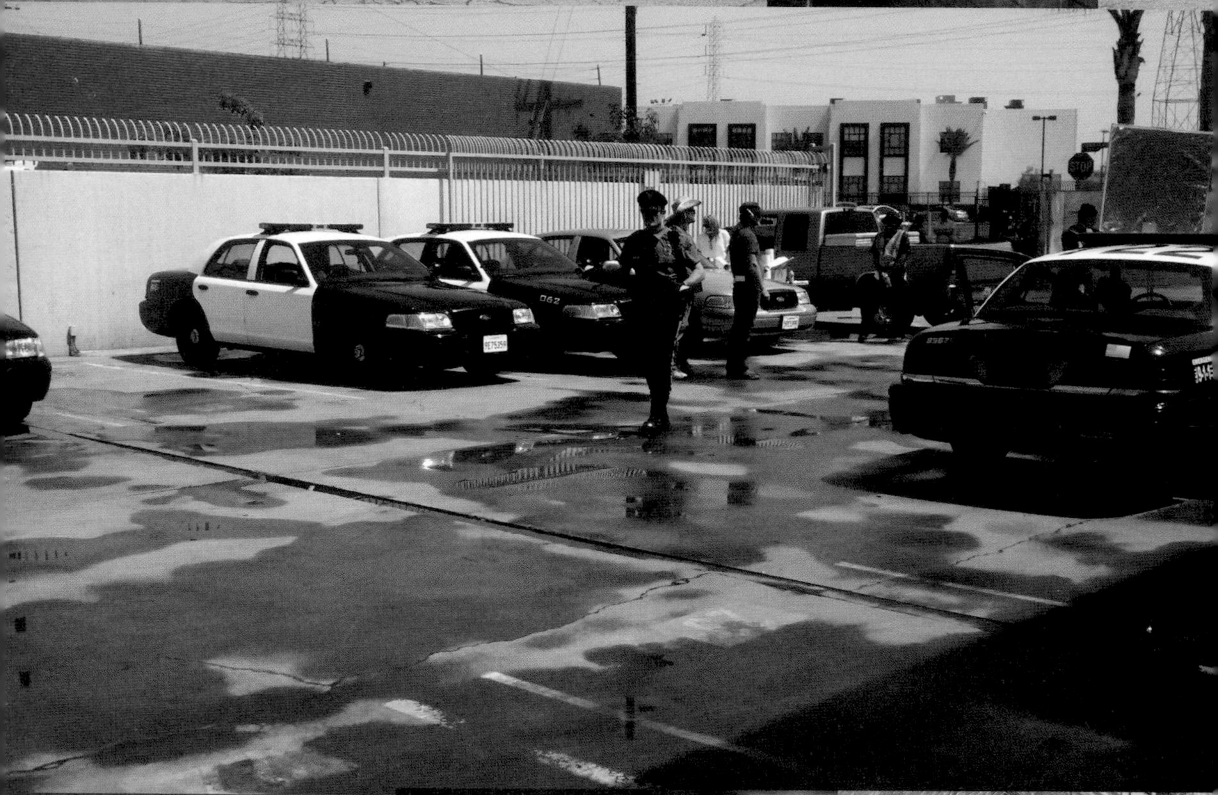
STOP
D62

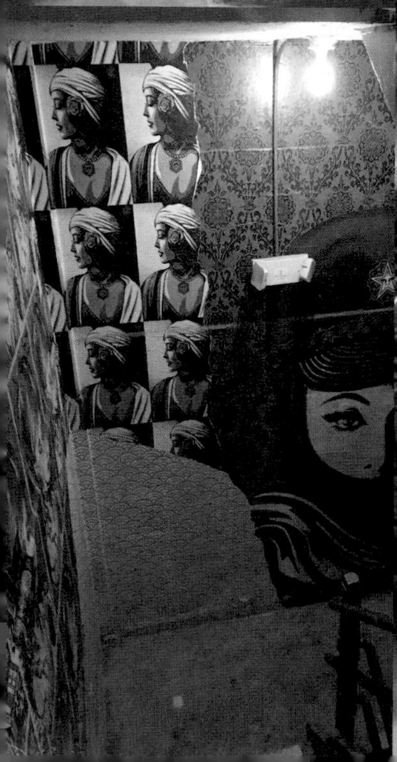

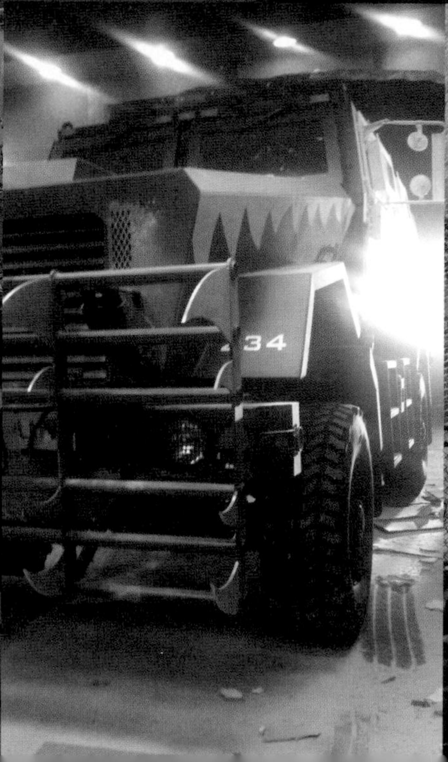
434

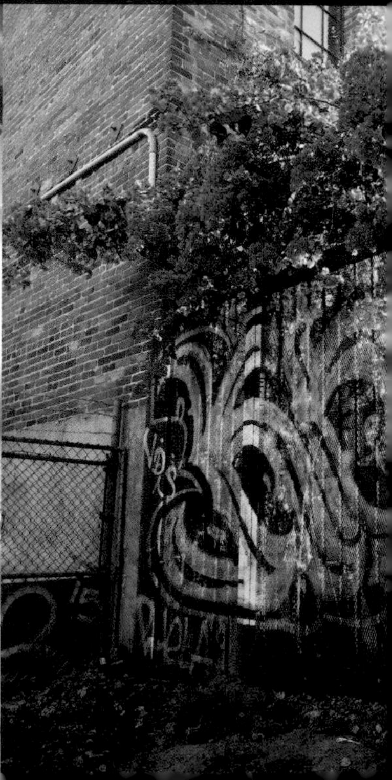

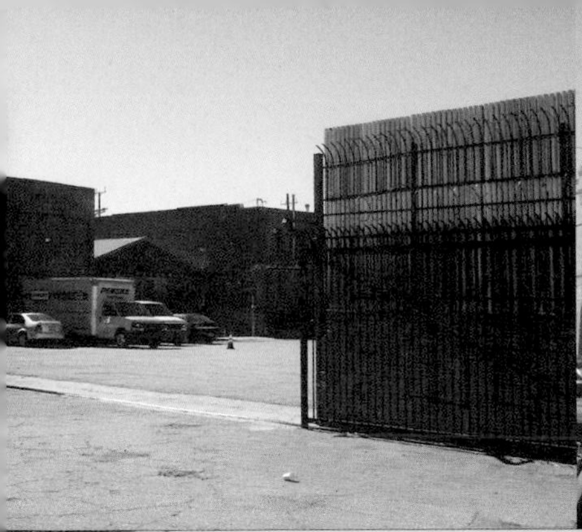
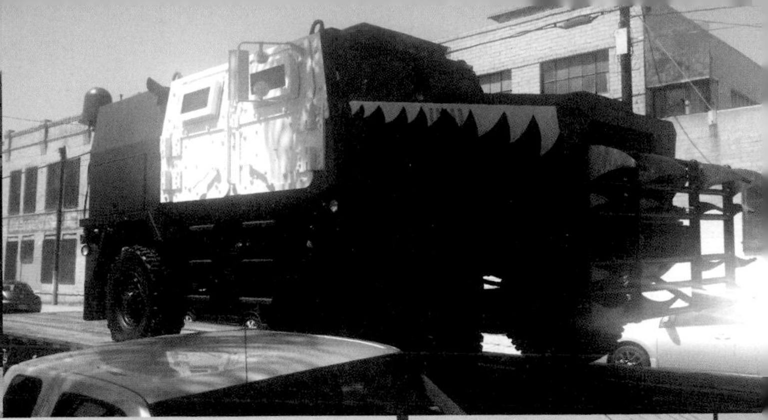
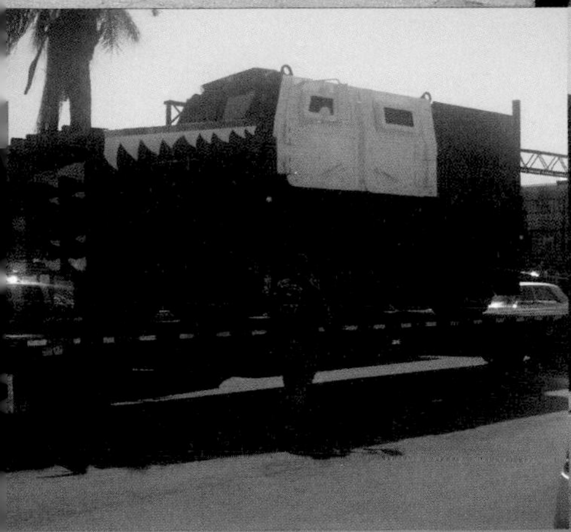
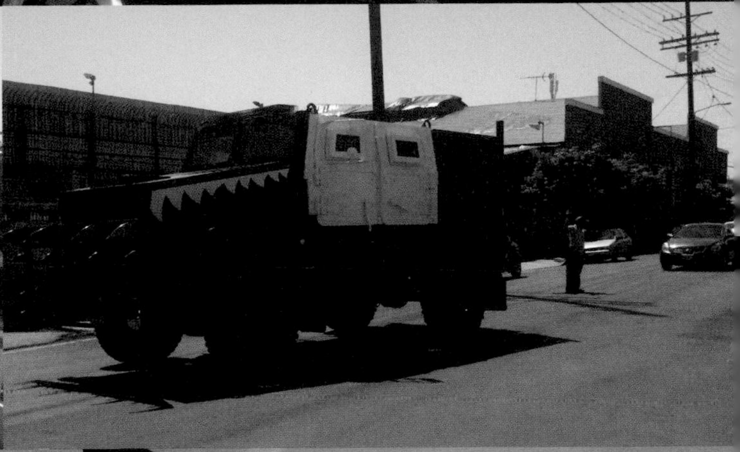
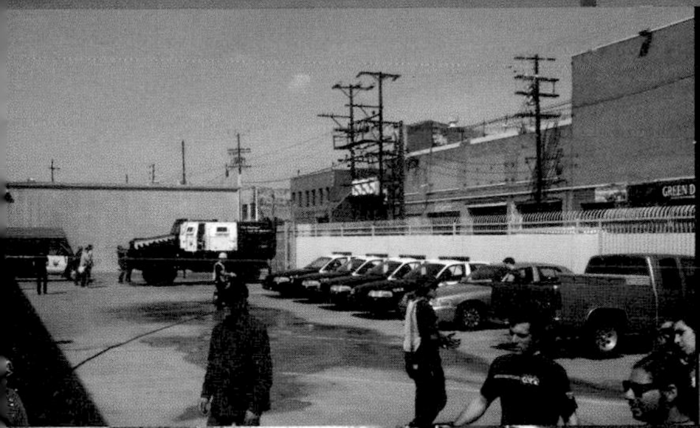
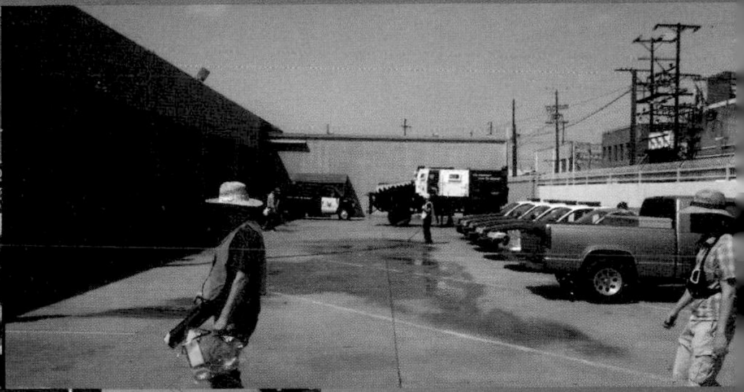
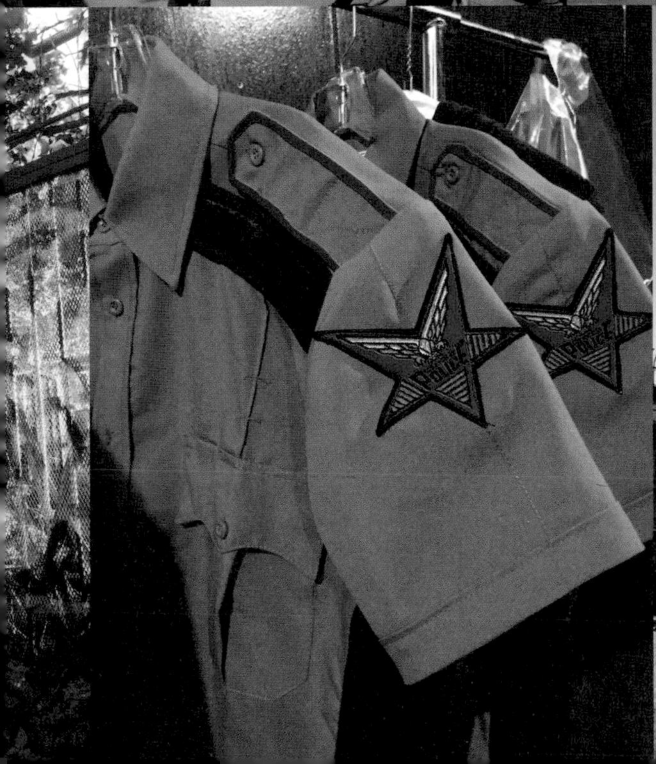
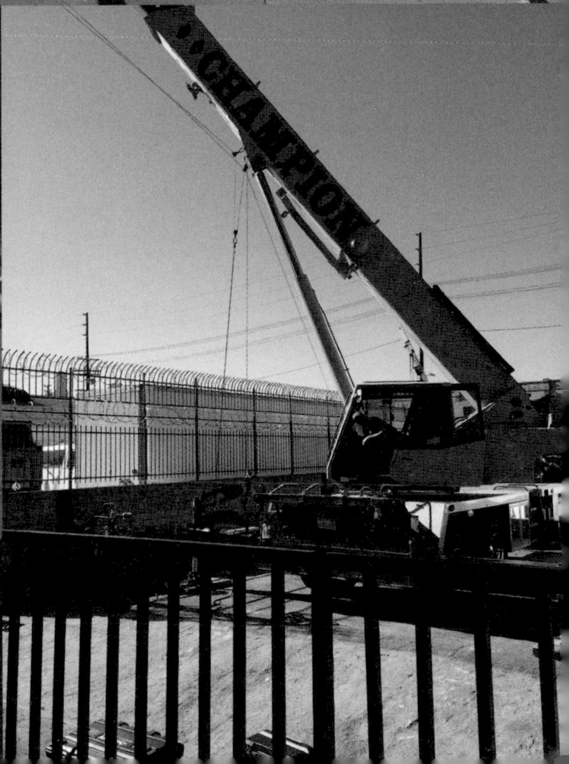
CHAMPION

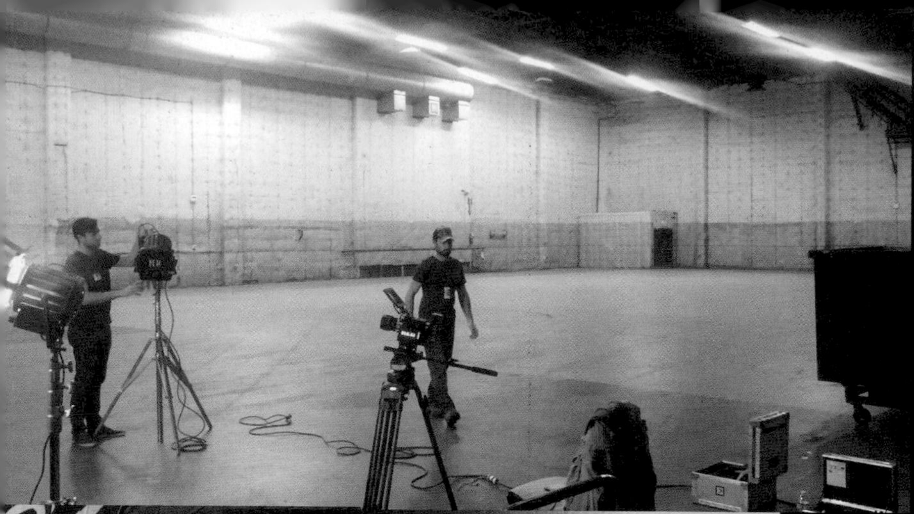

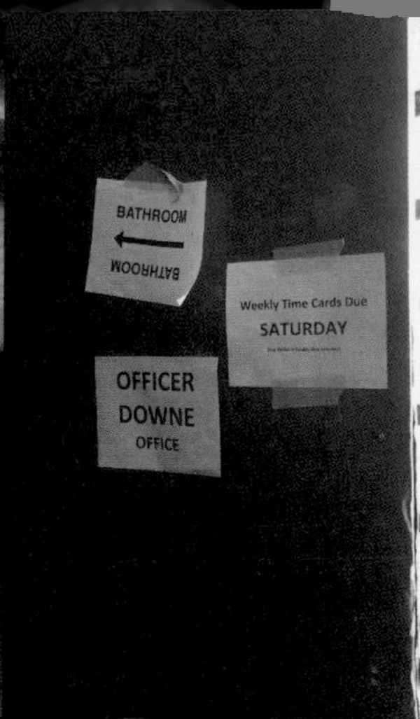
BATHROOM
Weekly Time Cards Due
SATURDAY
OFFICER
DOWNE
OFFICE

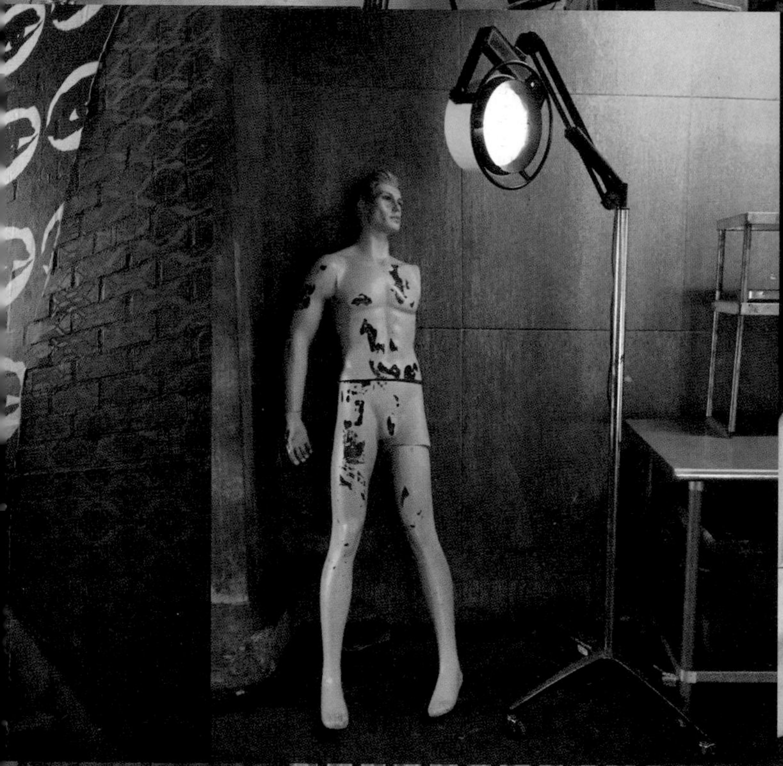

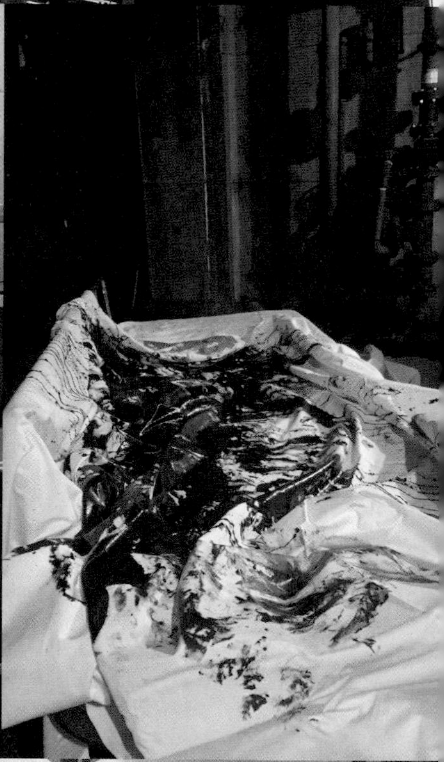

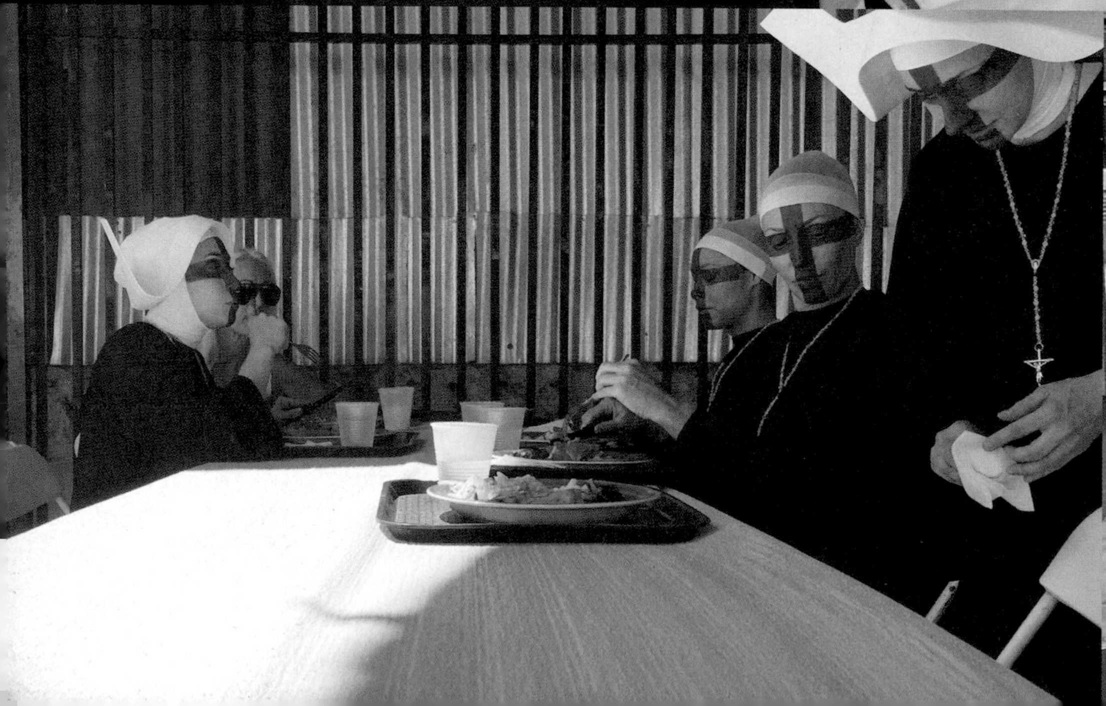

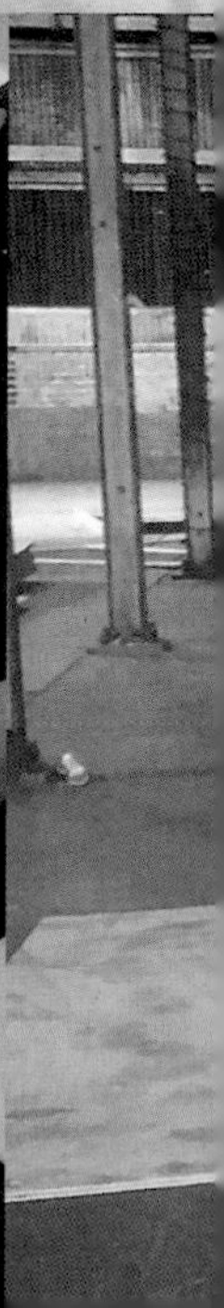

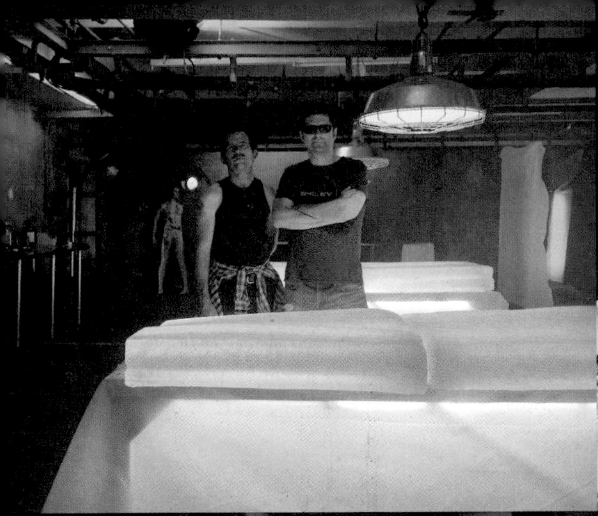
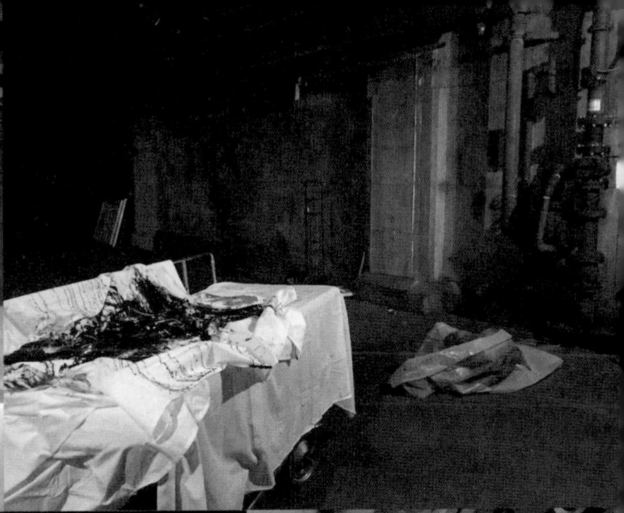
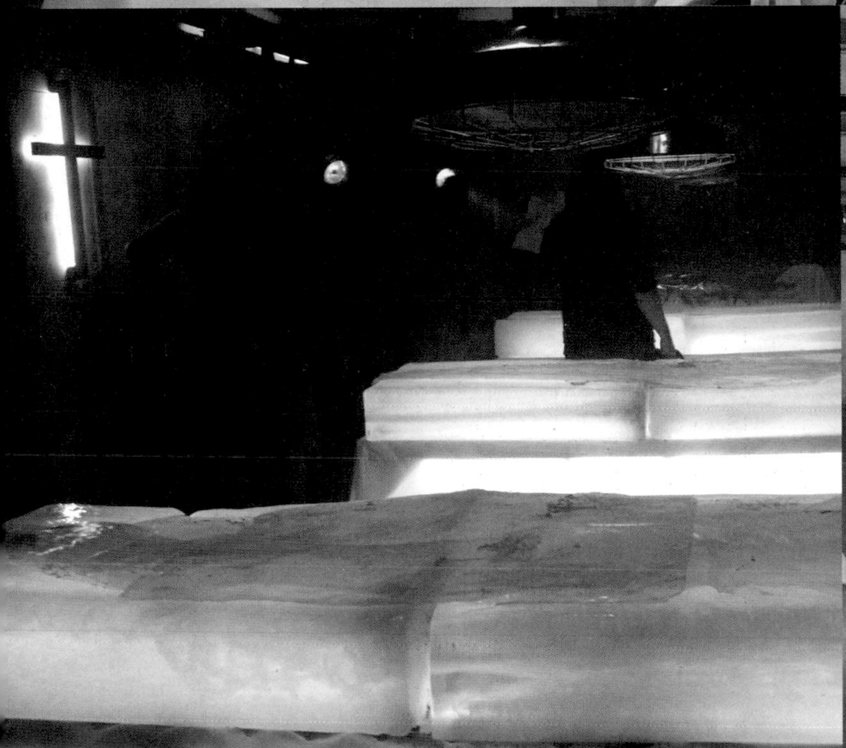
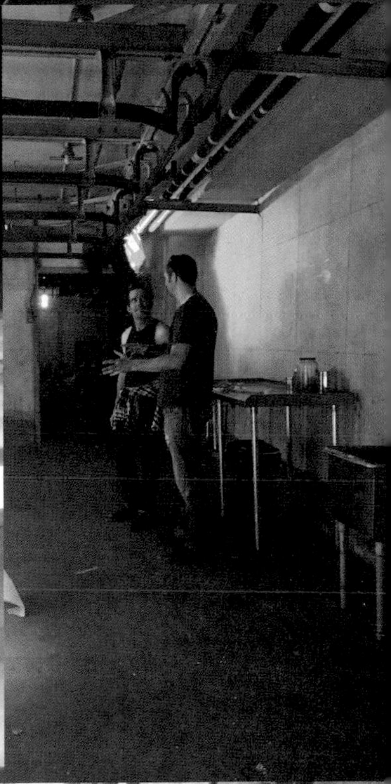
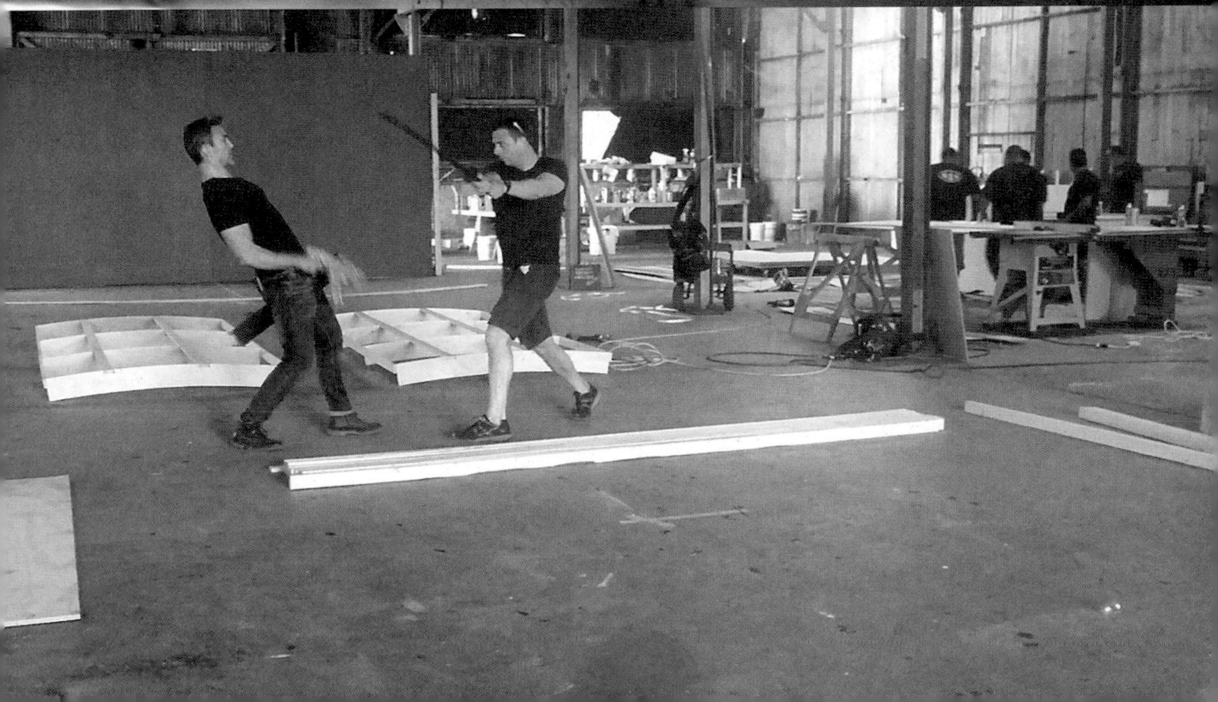

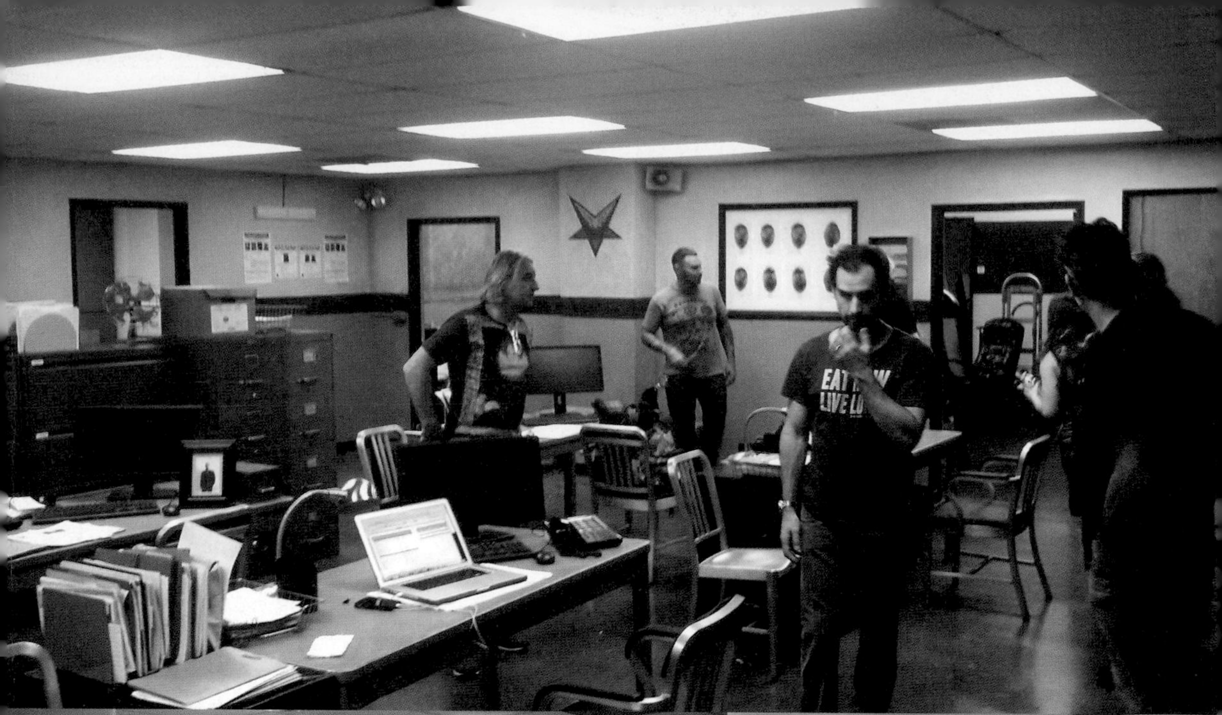

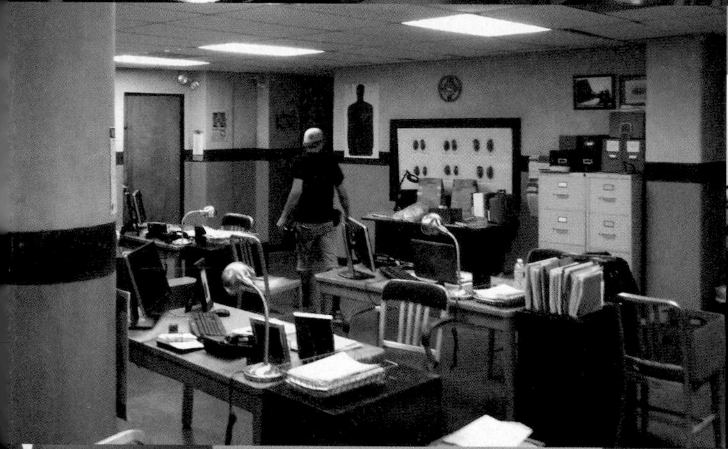

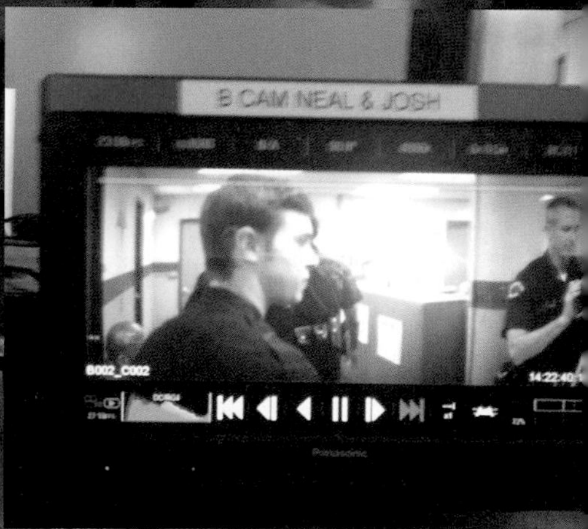
B CAM NEAL & JOSH
B002_C002

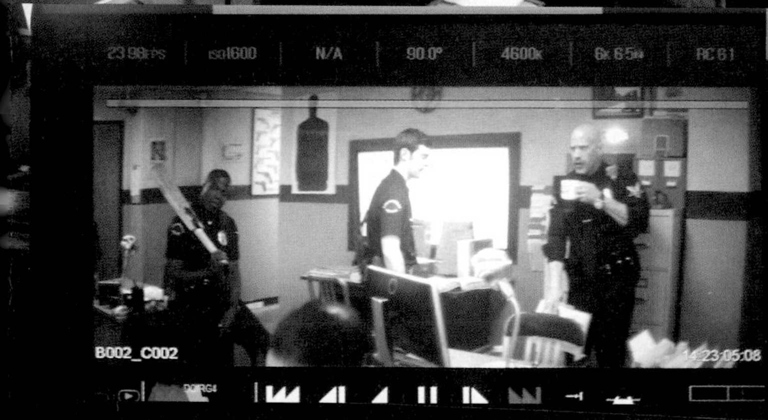
23.98FPS
ISO1600
N/A
90.0°
4600K
B002_C002
14:23:05:08

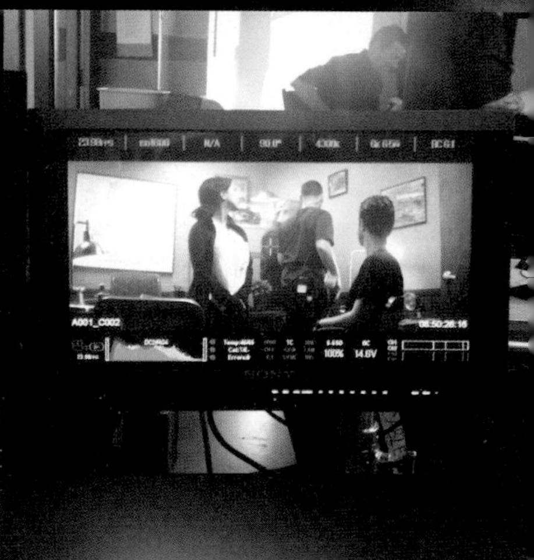
A001_C002

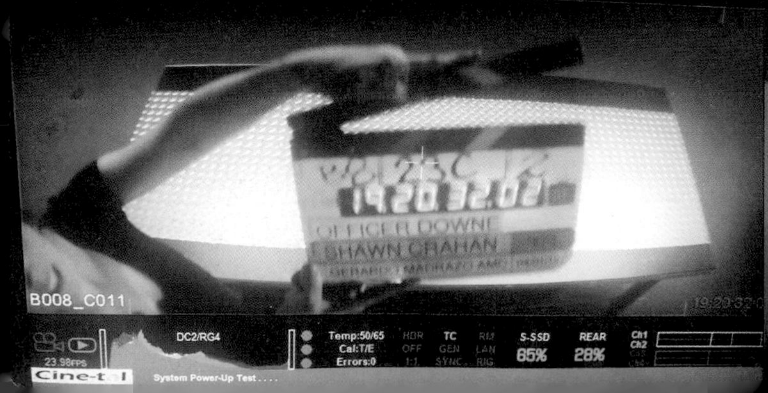
19:20:32:02
OFFICER DOWNE
SHAWN CRAHAN
B008_C011
DC2/RG4
Temp:50/65
Cal:T/E
Errors:0
S-SSD
REAR
85%
28%
Cine-tal
System Power-Up Test ....

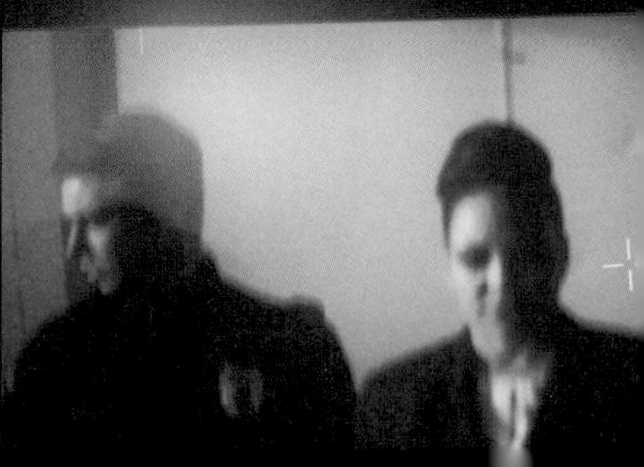

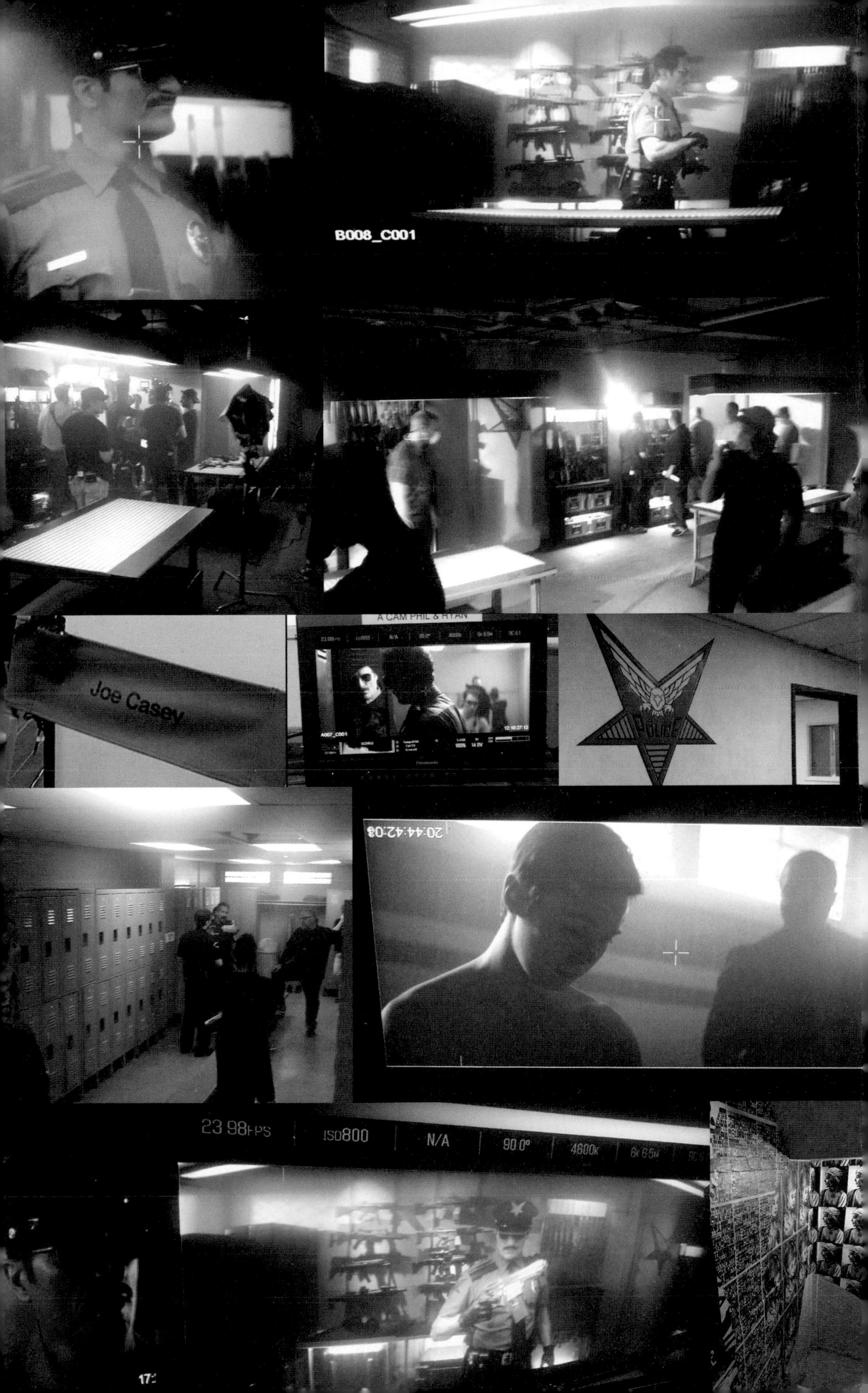
B008_C001
Joe Casey
A CAM PHIL & RYAN
A007_C001
POLICE
23.98FPS
ISO800
N/A
90.0°
4600K

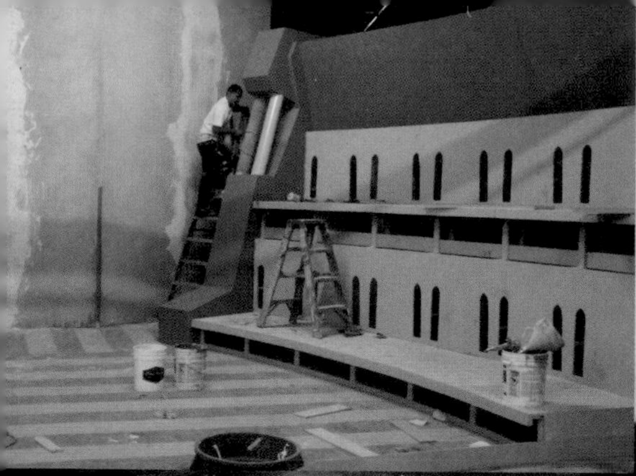

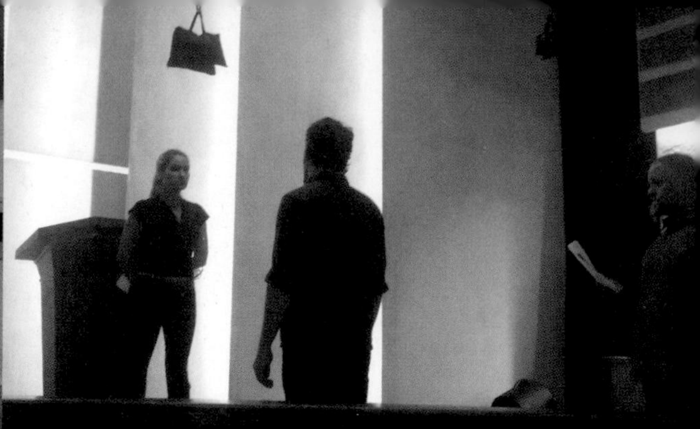

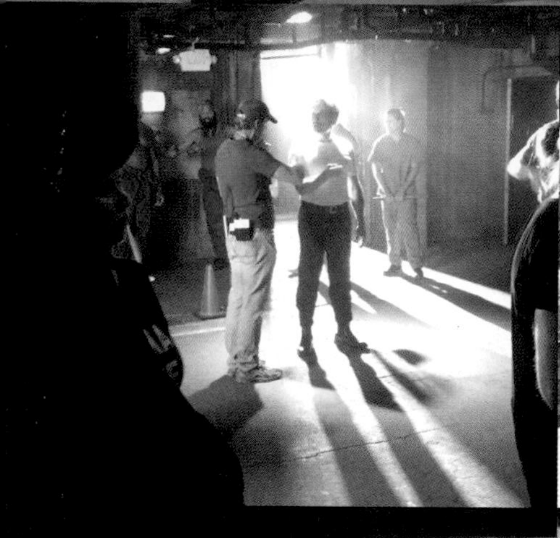

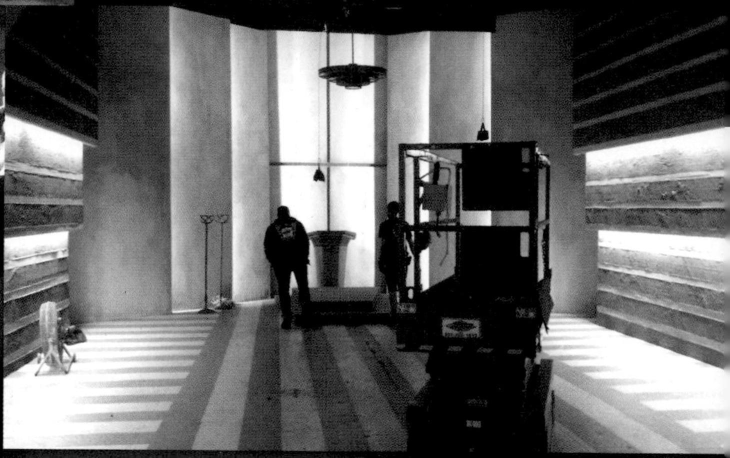

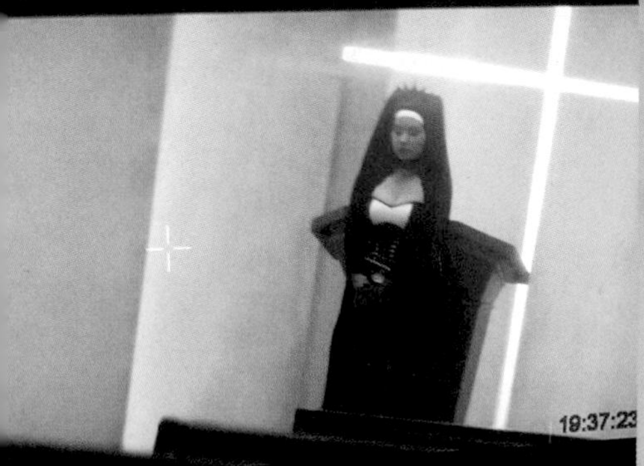
19:37:23

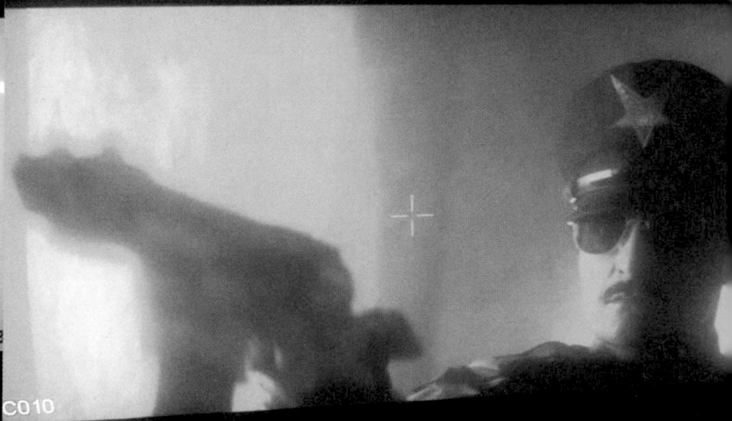
C010

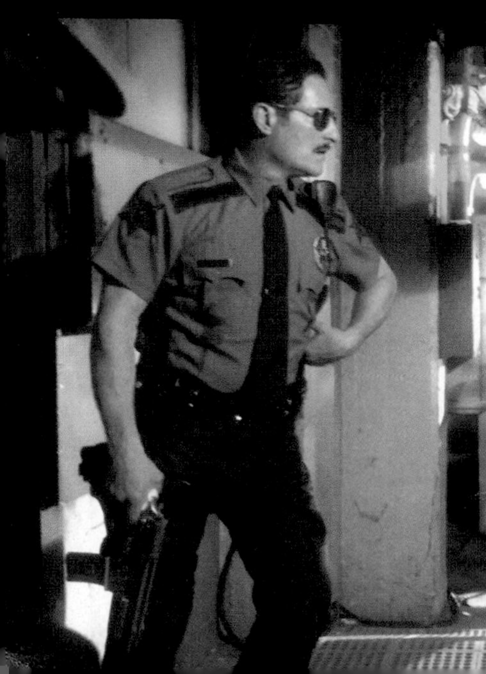

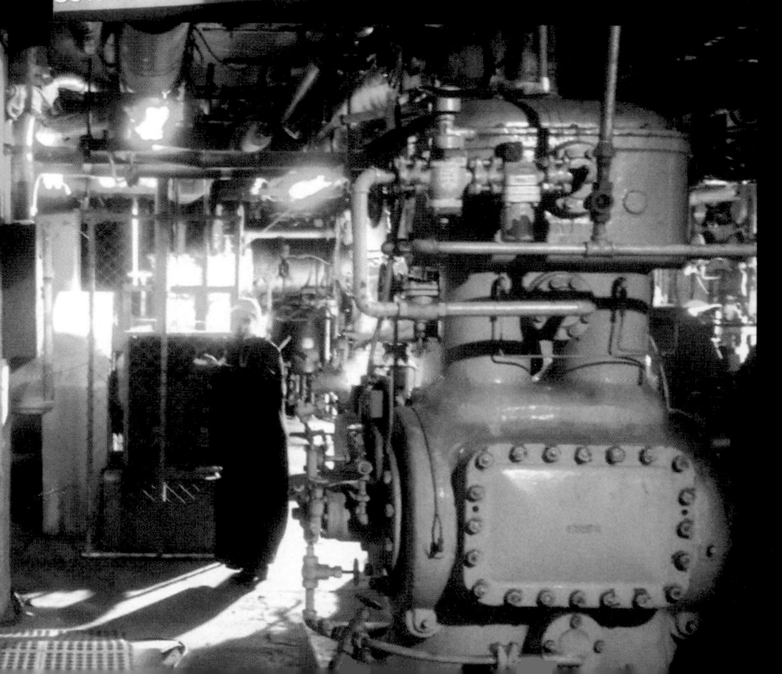

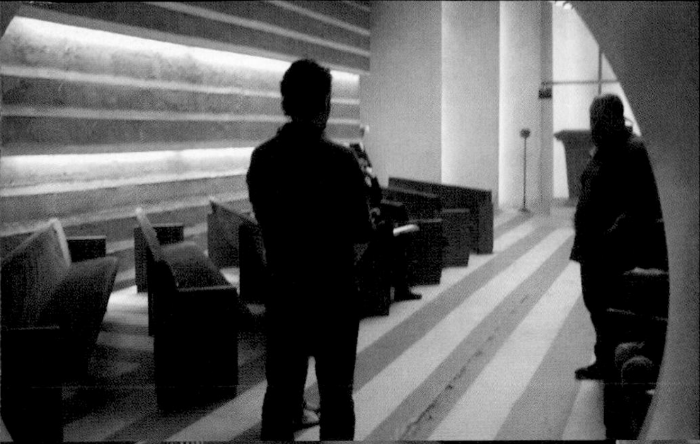
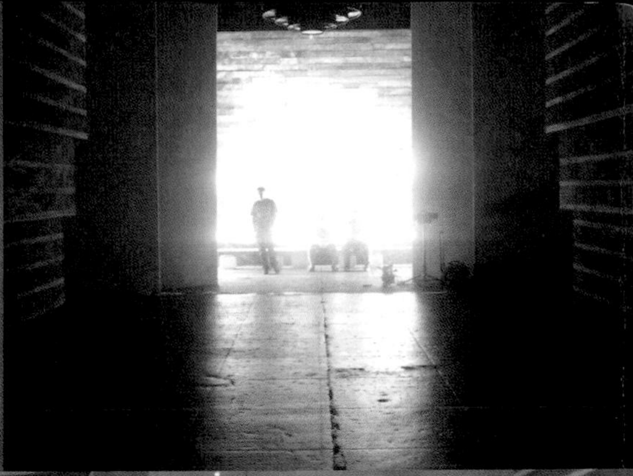
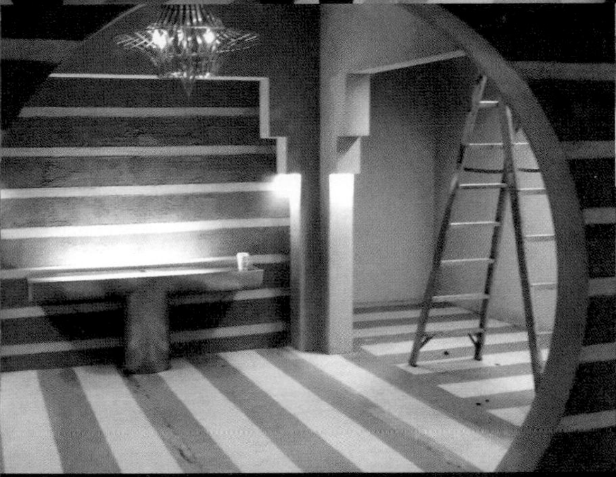
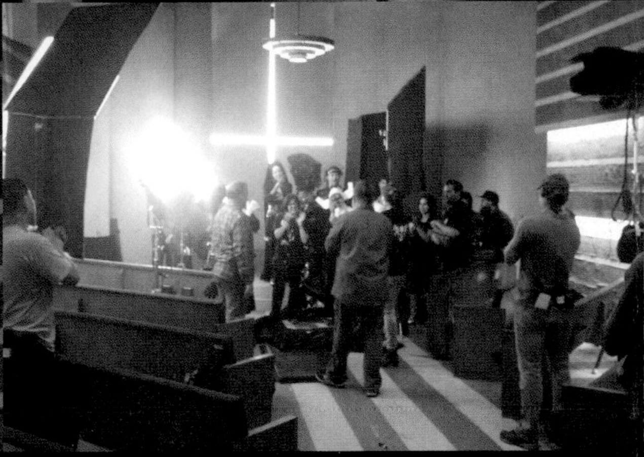
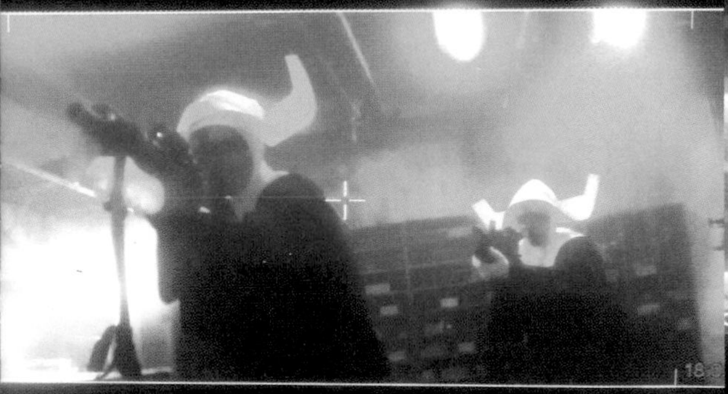
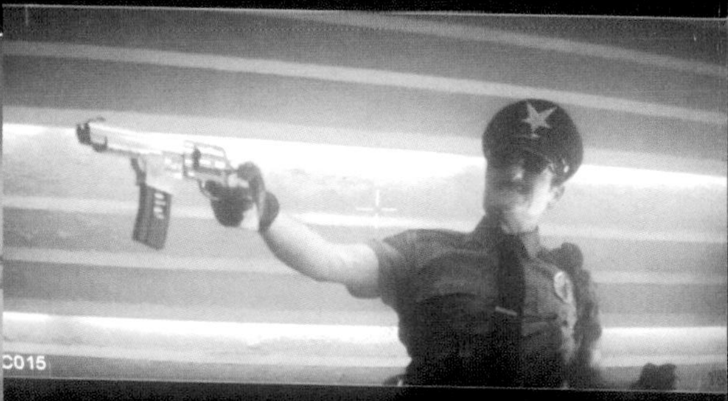
C015
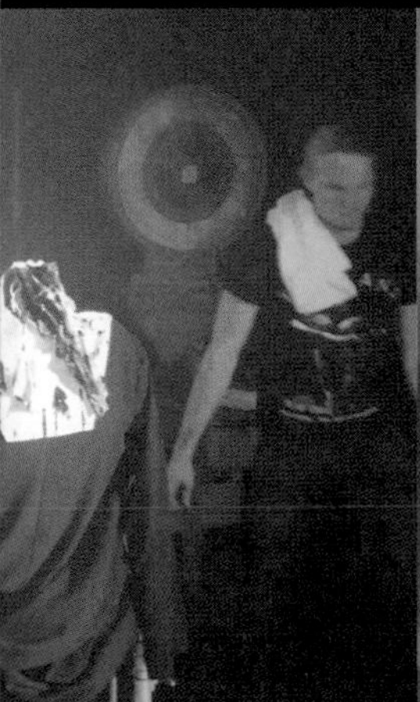
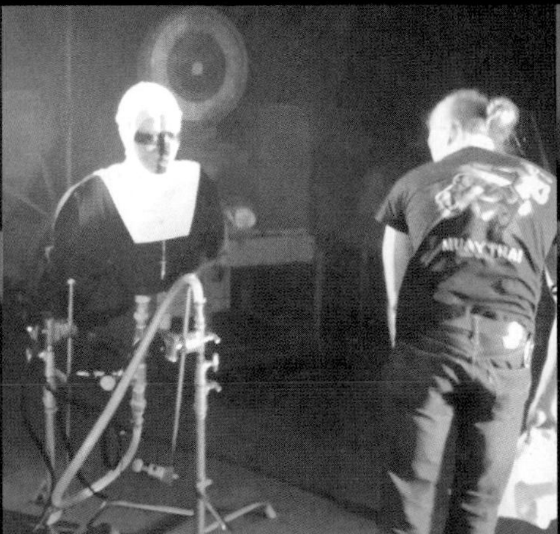
MUAY THAI
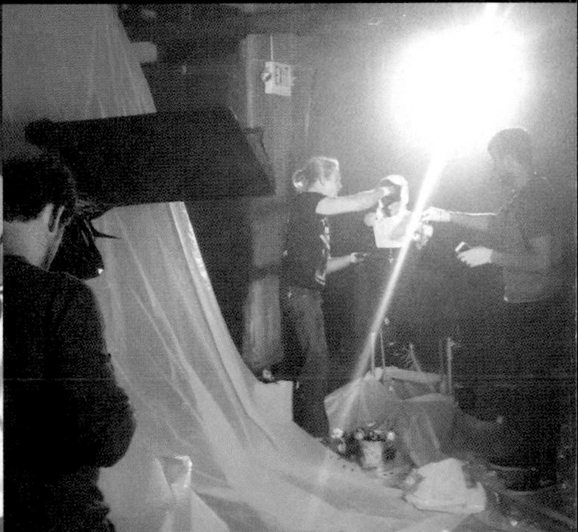

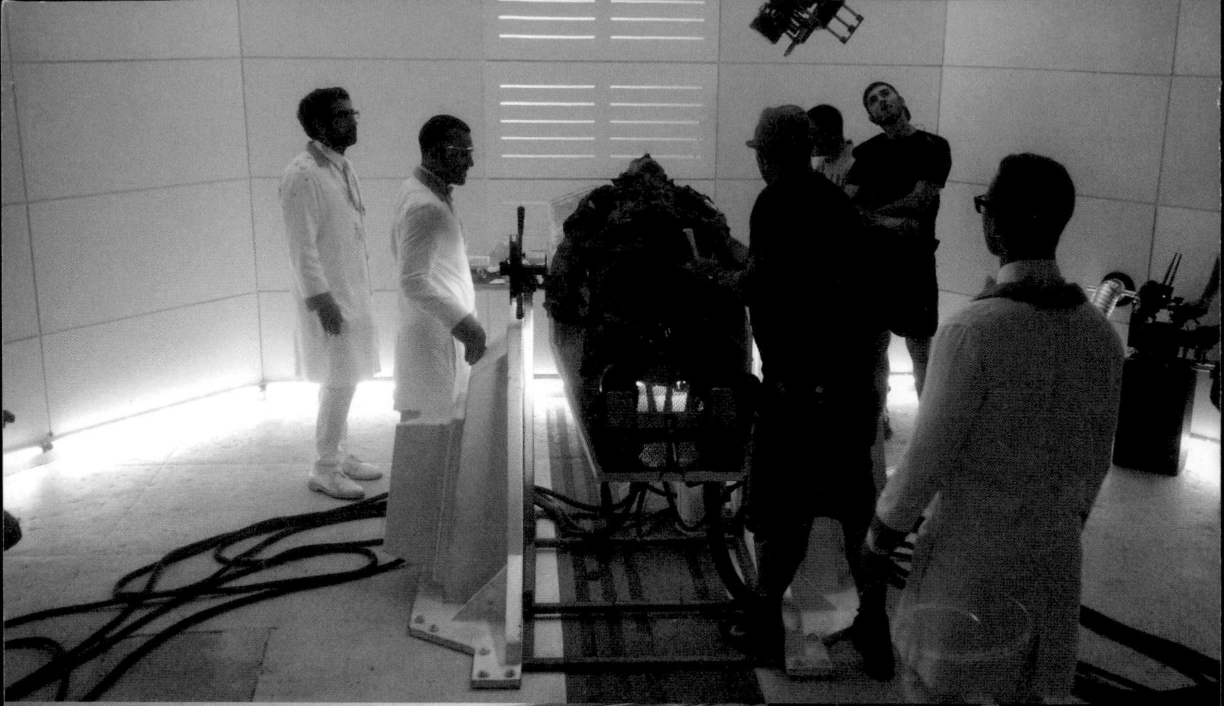

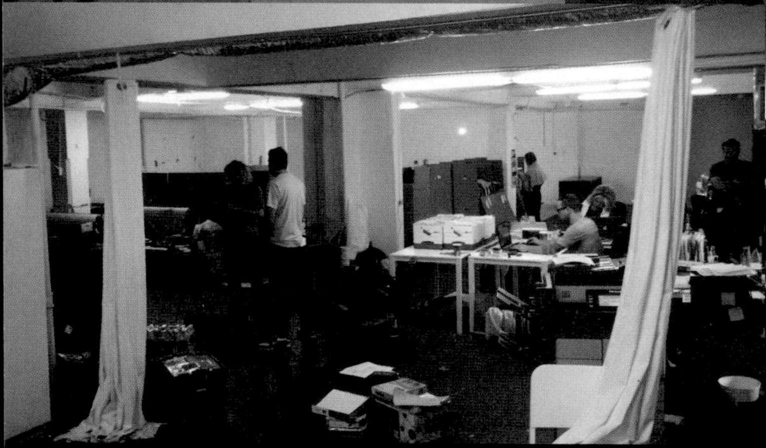

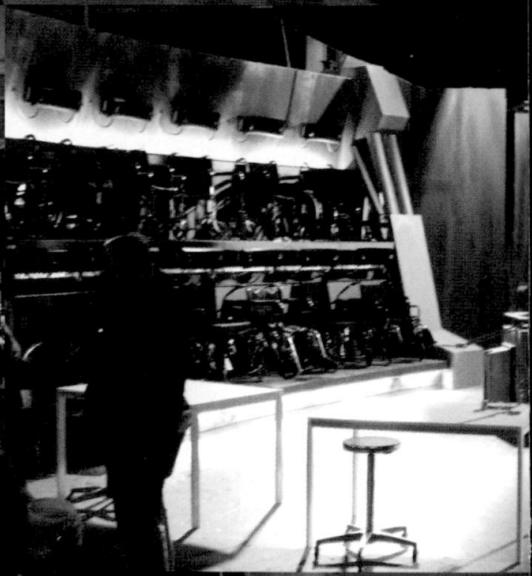

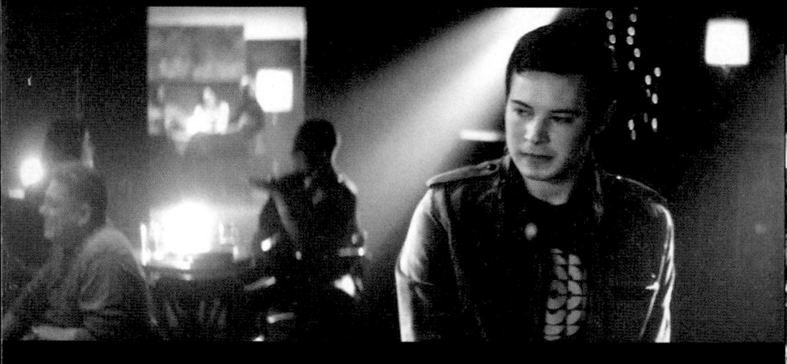

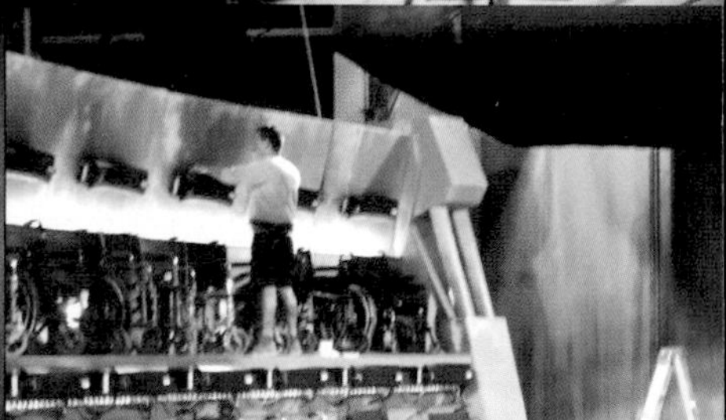

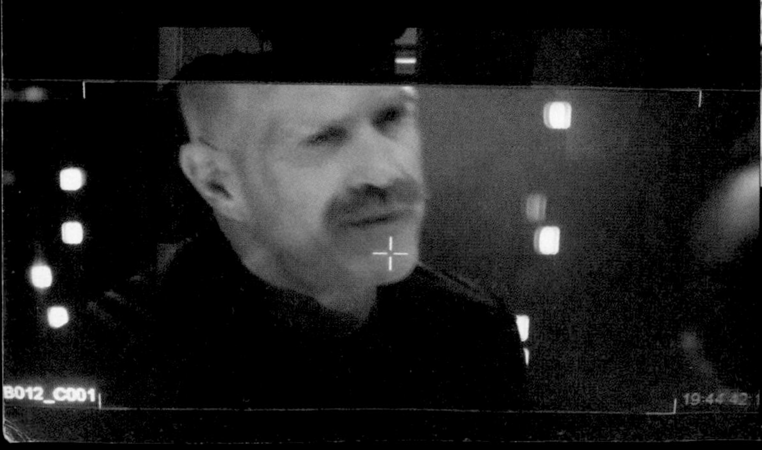
B012_C001
19:44:42

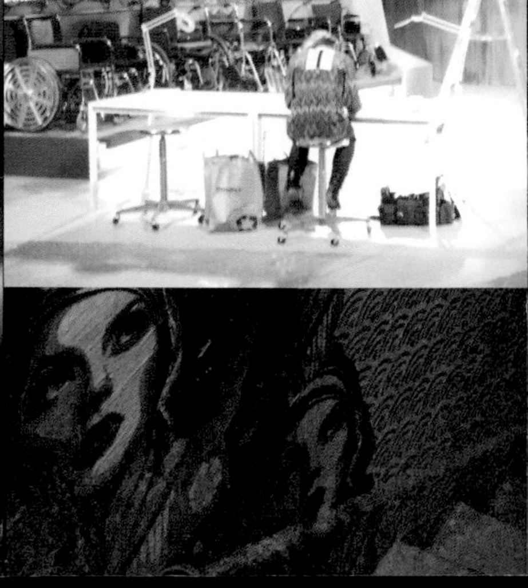

A.074_C007

Temp:46/64  HDR  TC  RM  S-SSD  REAR  Ch1
Cal:T/E  OH  GEN  LAN  73%  75%  Ch2
Errors:0  1:1  SYNC  RIG

DC2/R64

23.98fps

SUB-LEVEL
EAST

OFFICER
DOWNE

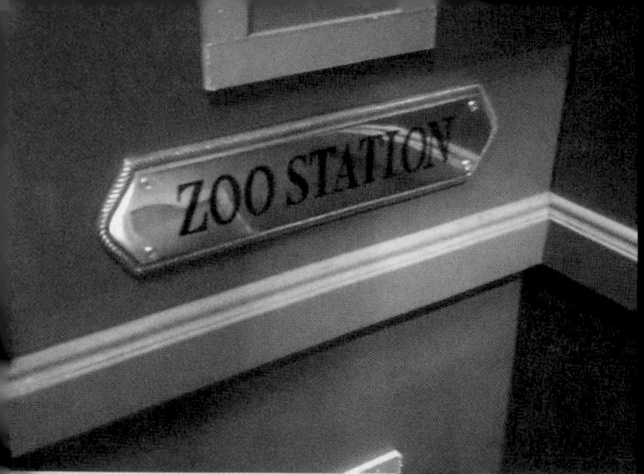
ZOO STATION
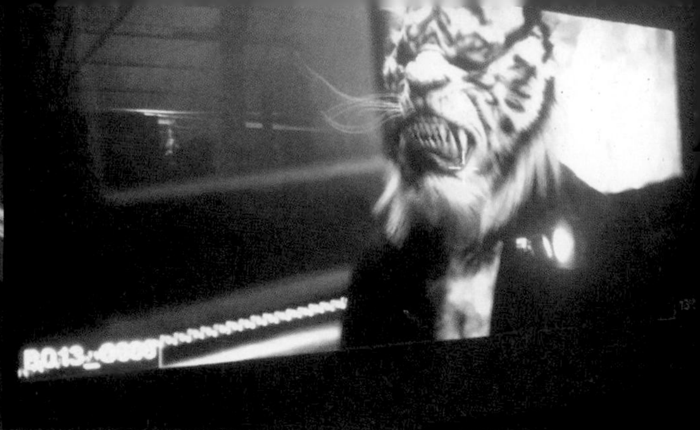
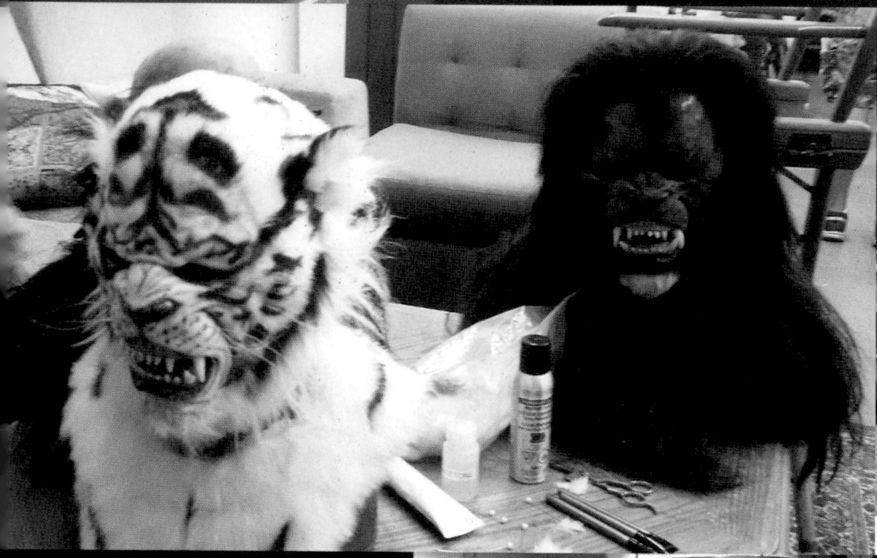
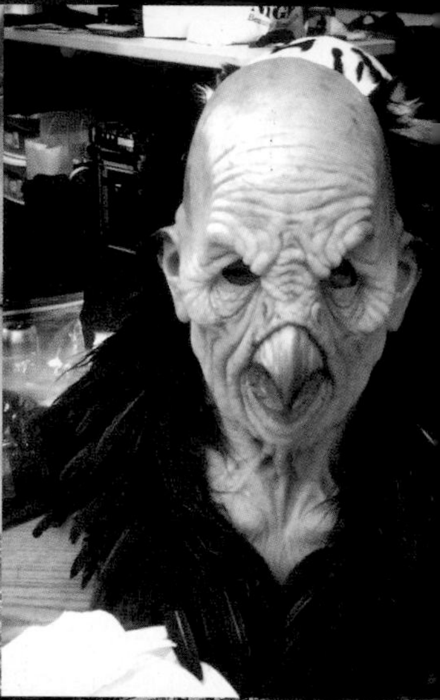
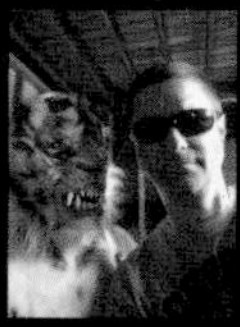
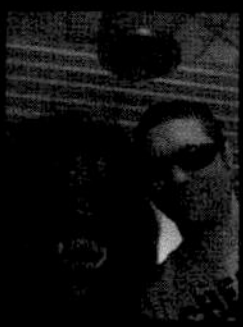
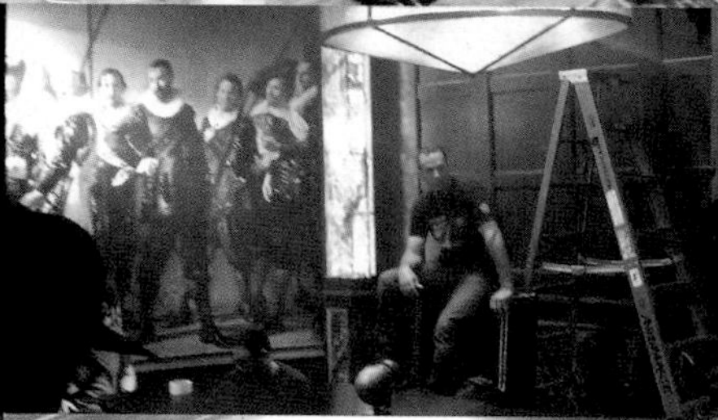
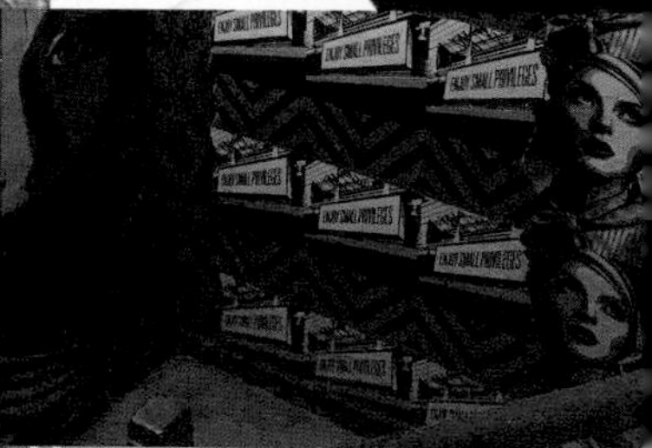
ENJOY SMALL PRIVILEGES
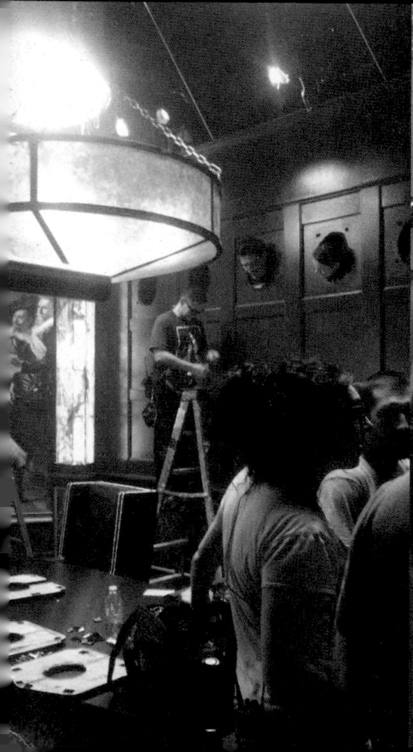
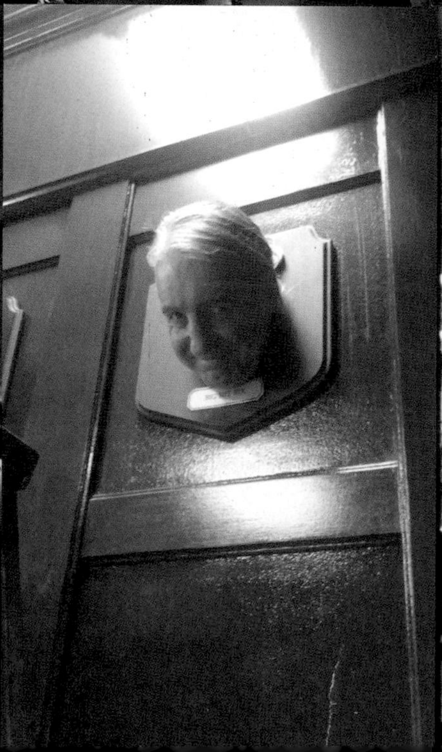
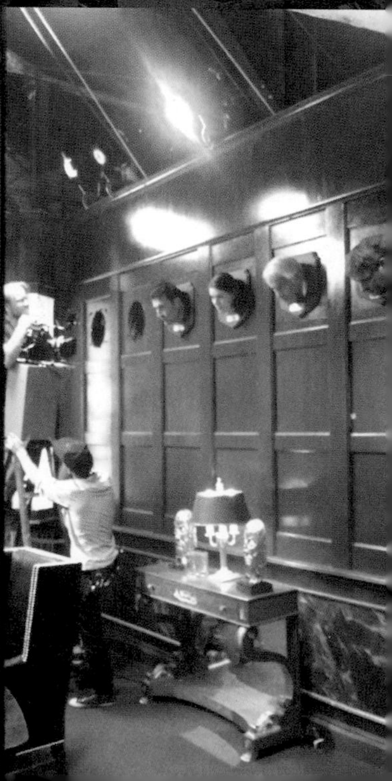

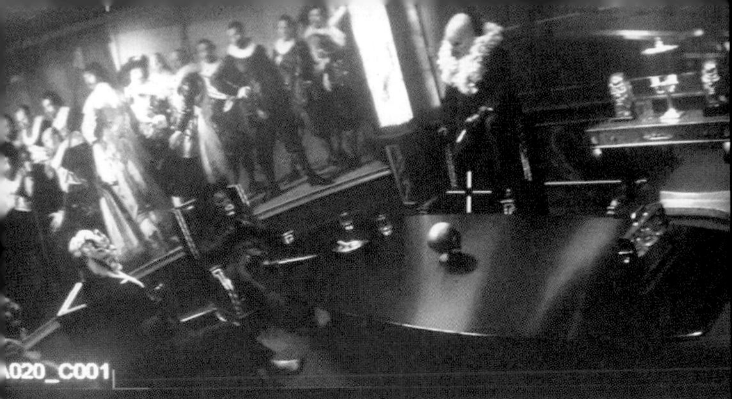
A020_C001
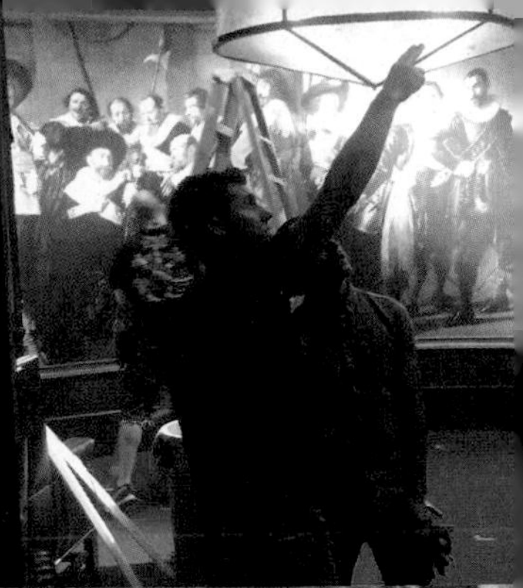
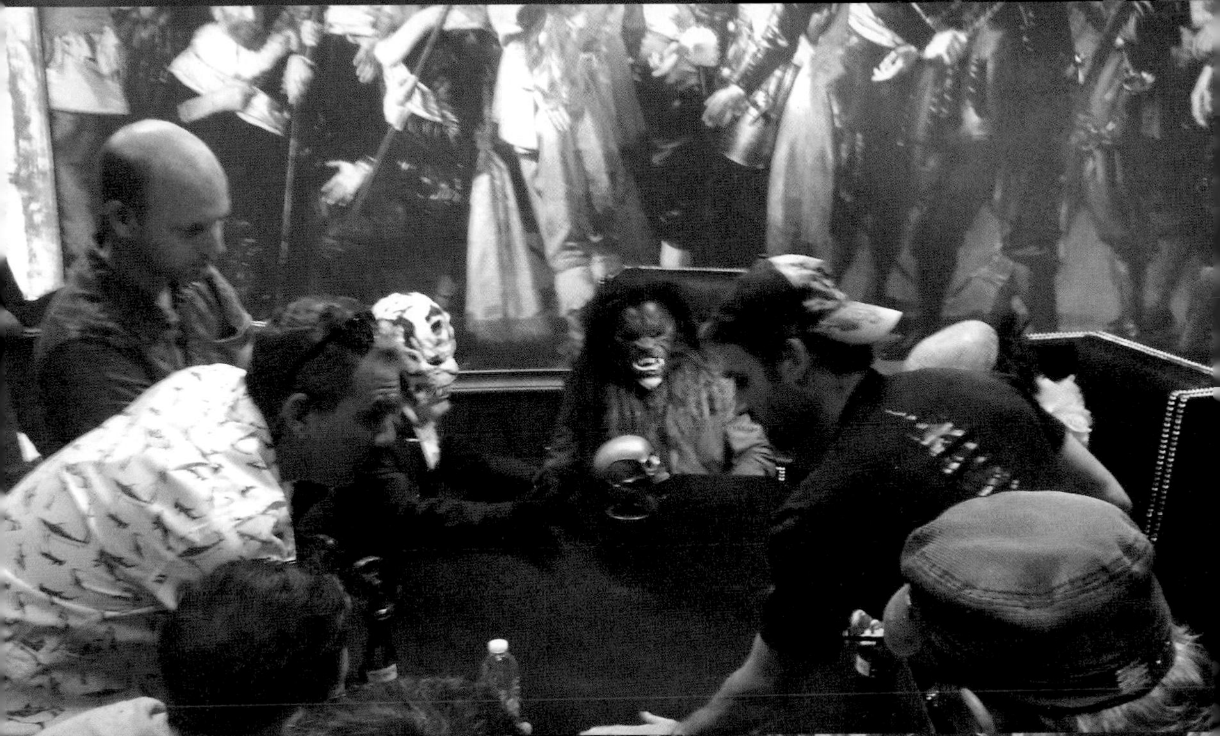
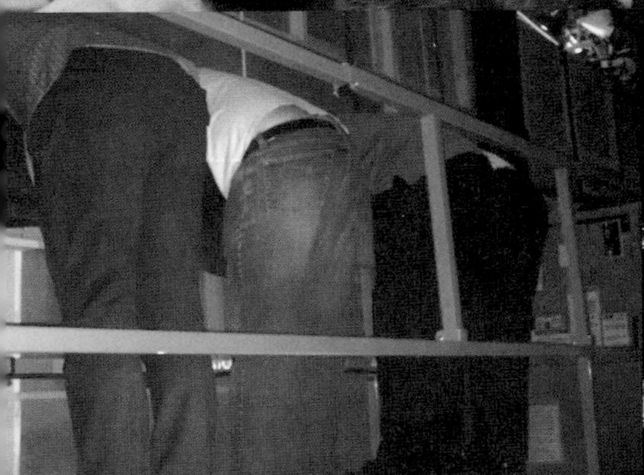
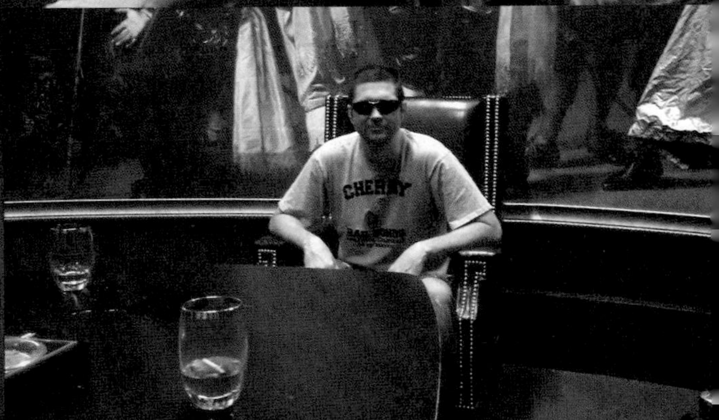
CHERRY
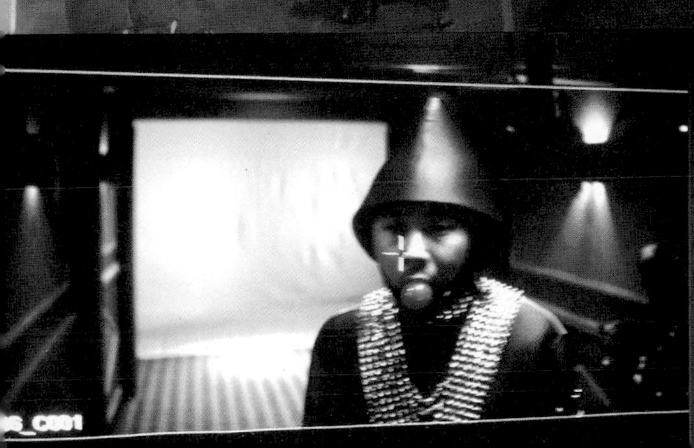
S_C001
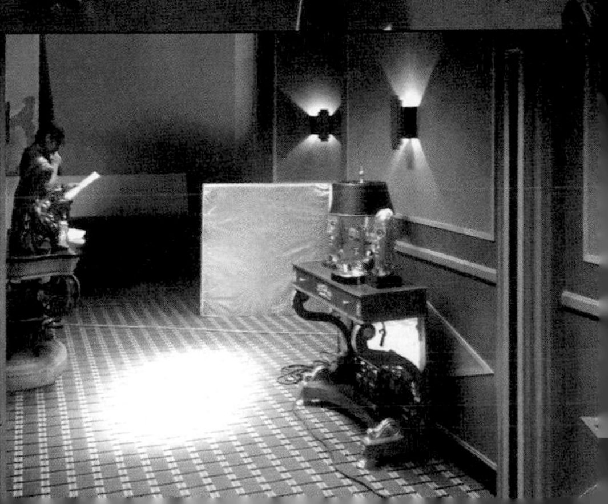

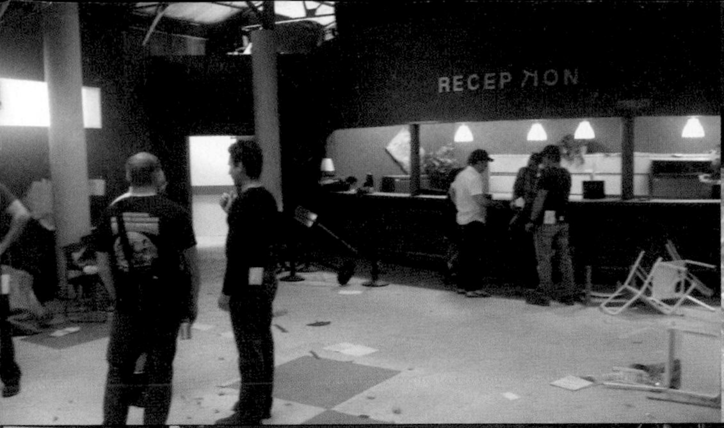

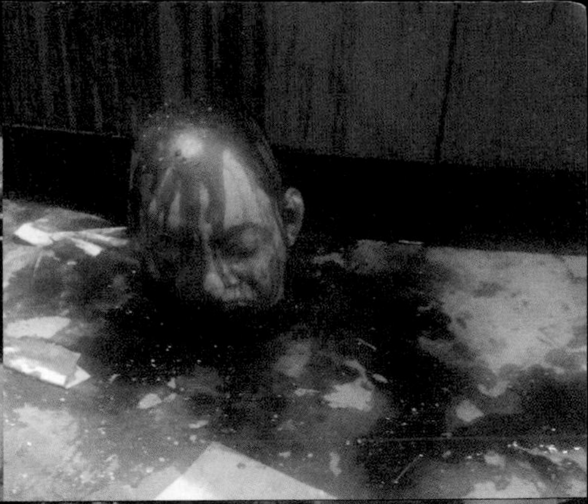

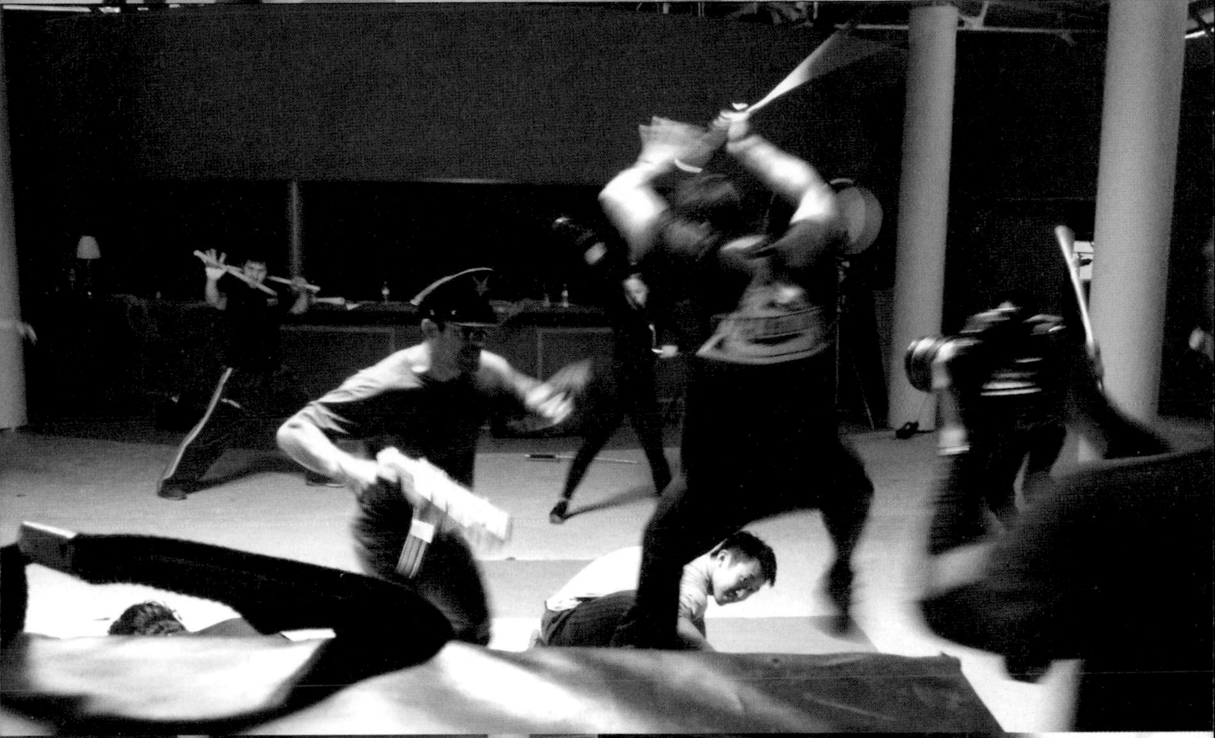

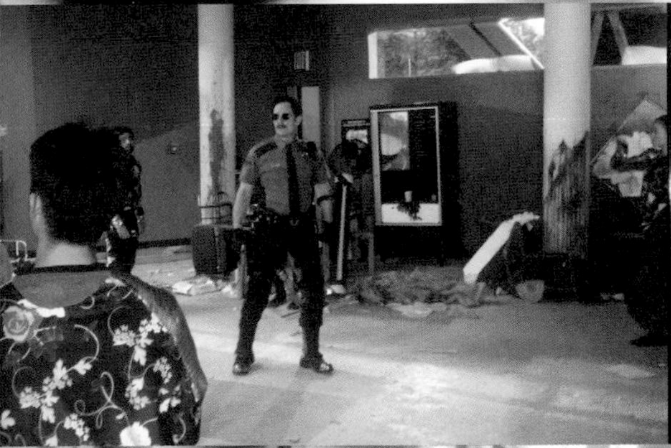

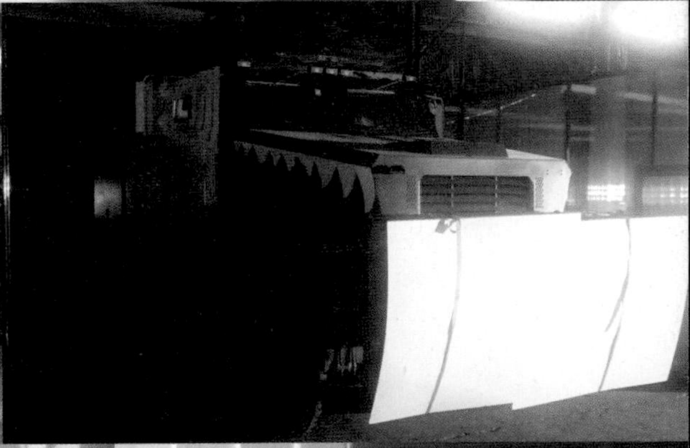

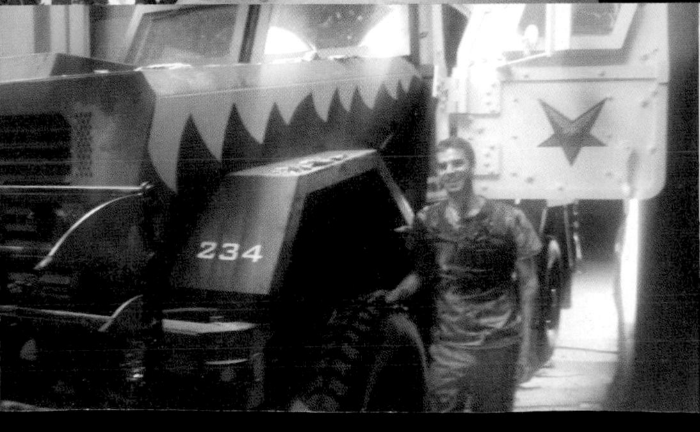
234

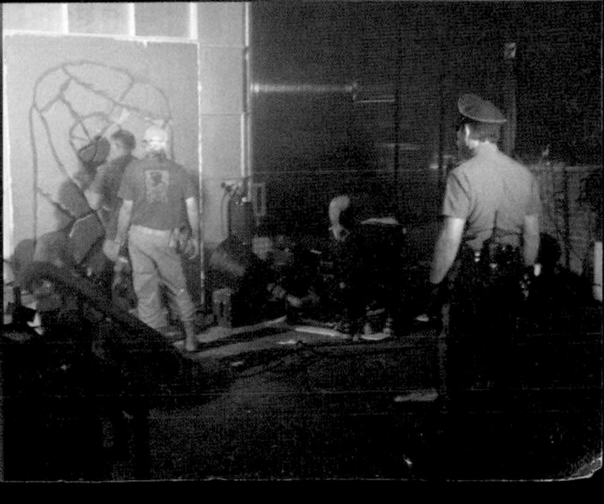

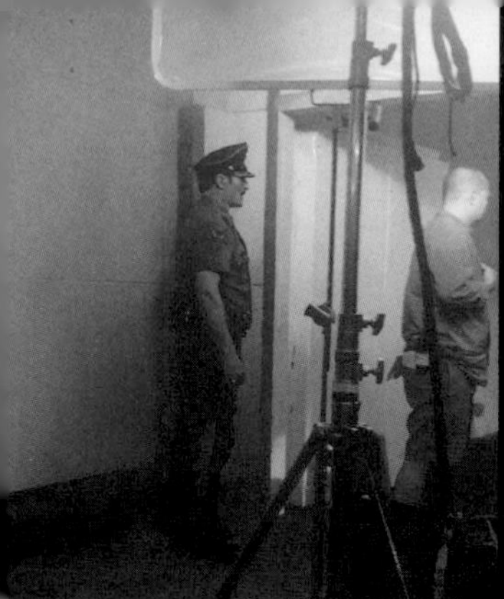
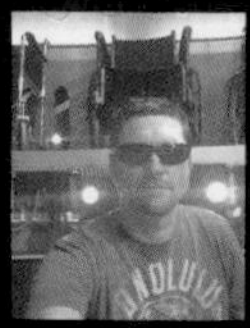
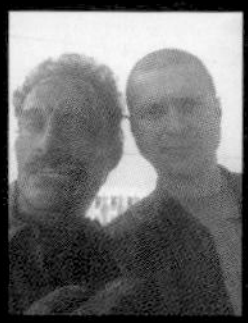
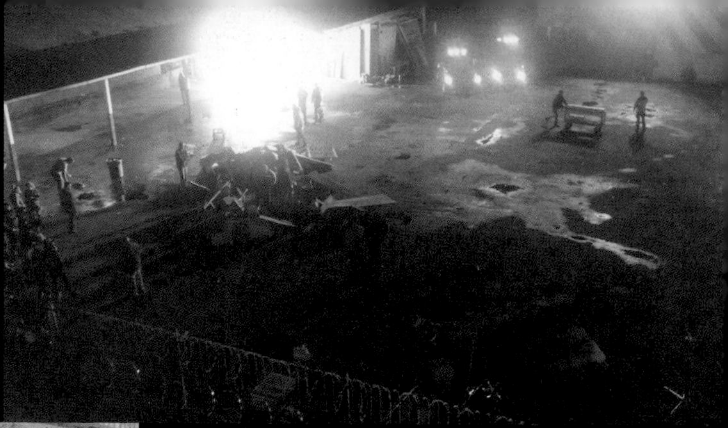
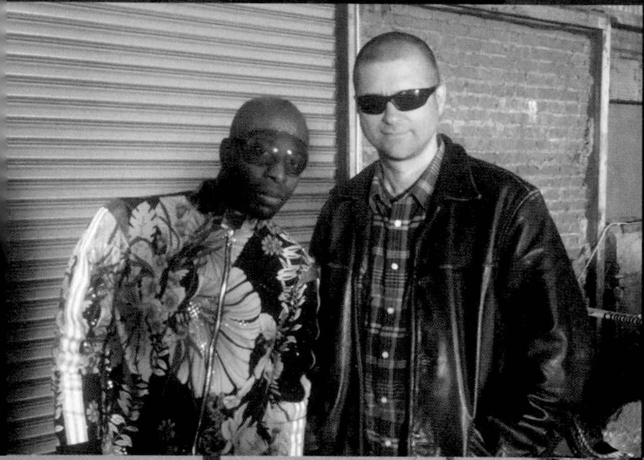
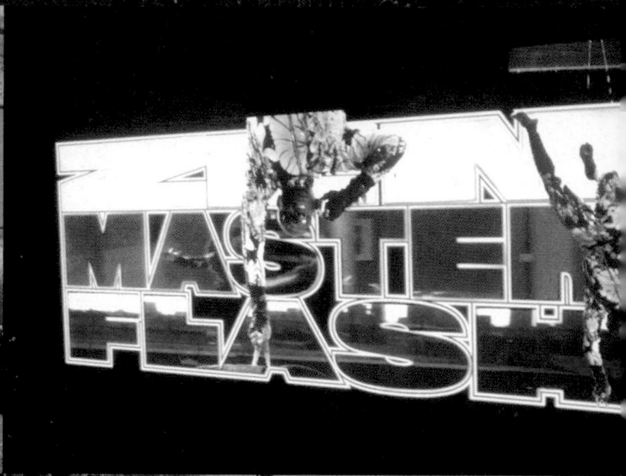
MASTER
FLASH
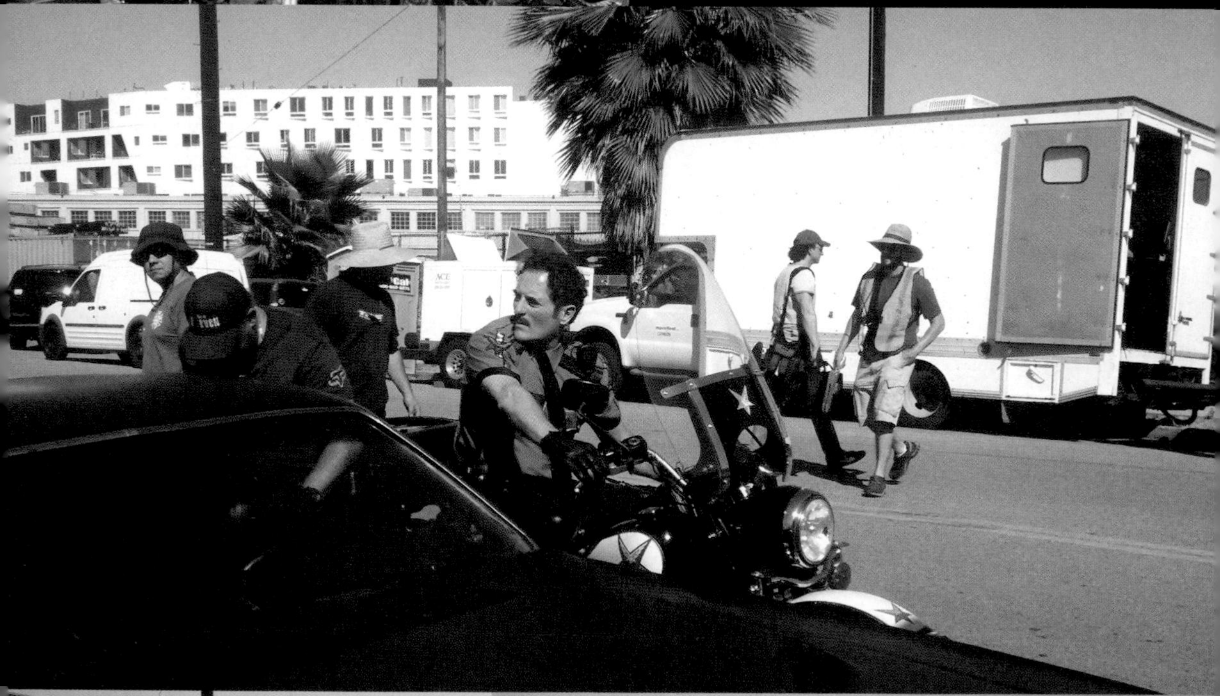
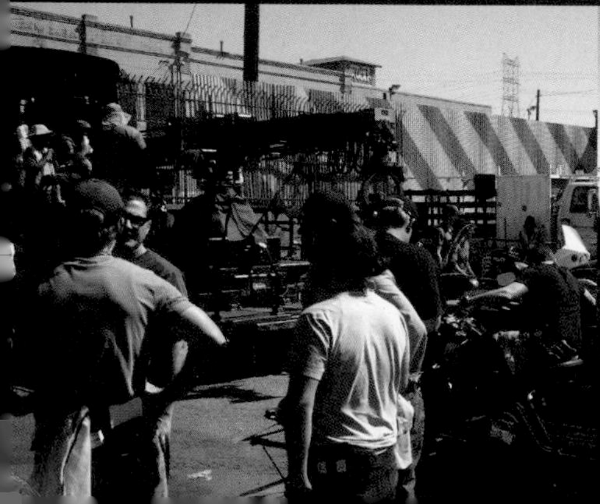
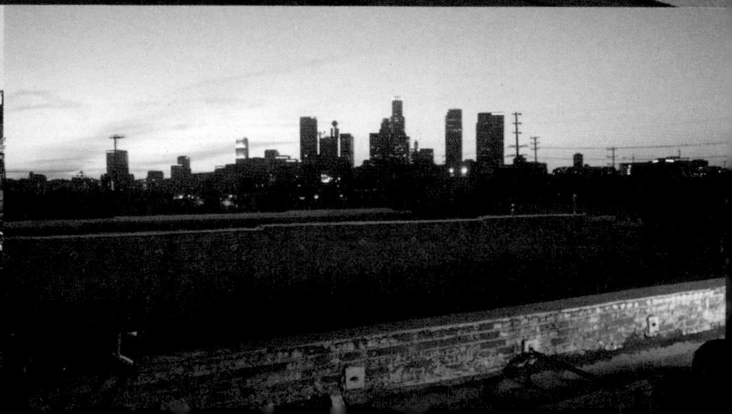

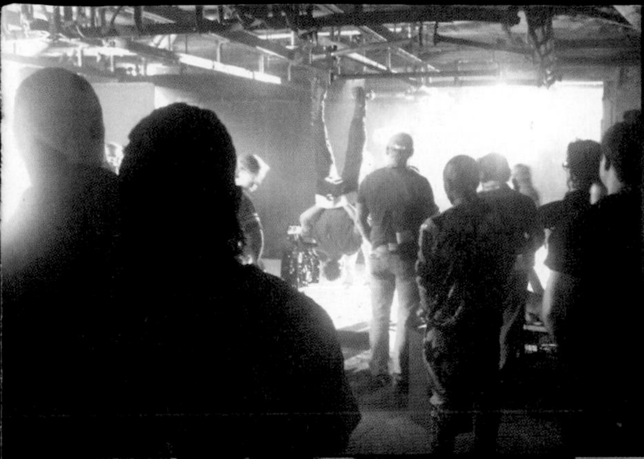

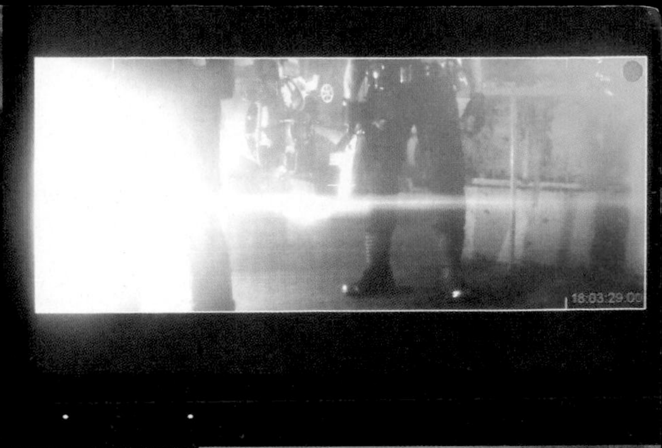
18:03:29:0

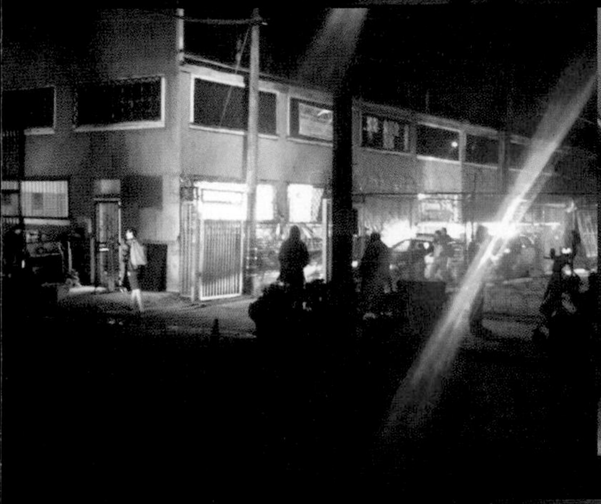

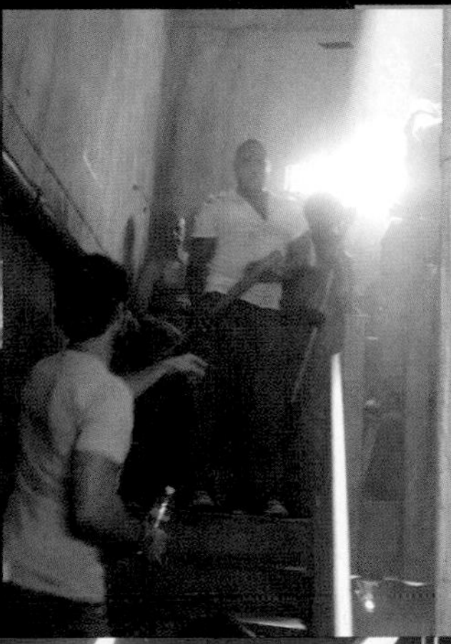

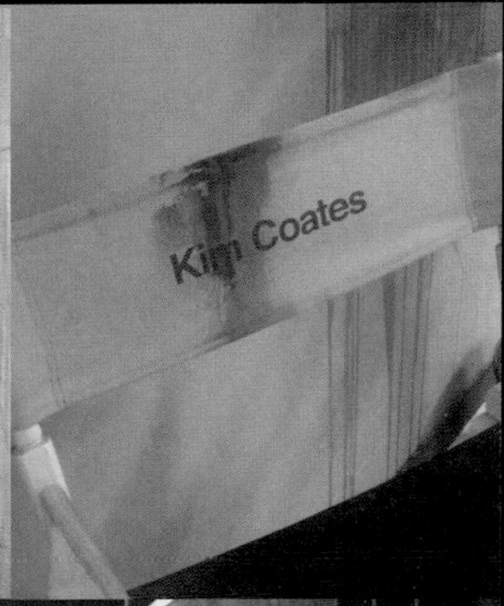
Kim Coates

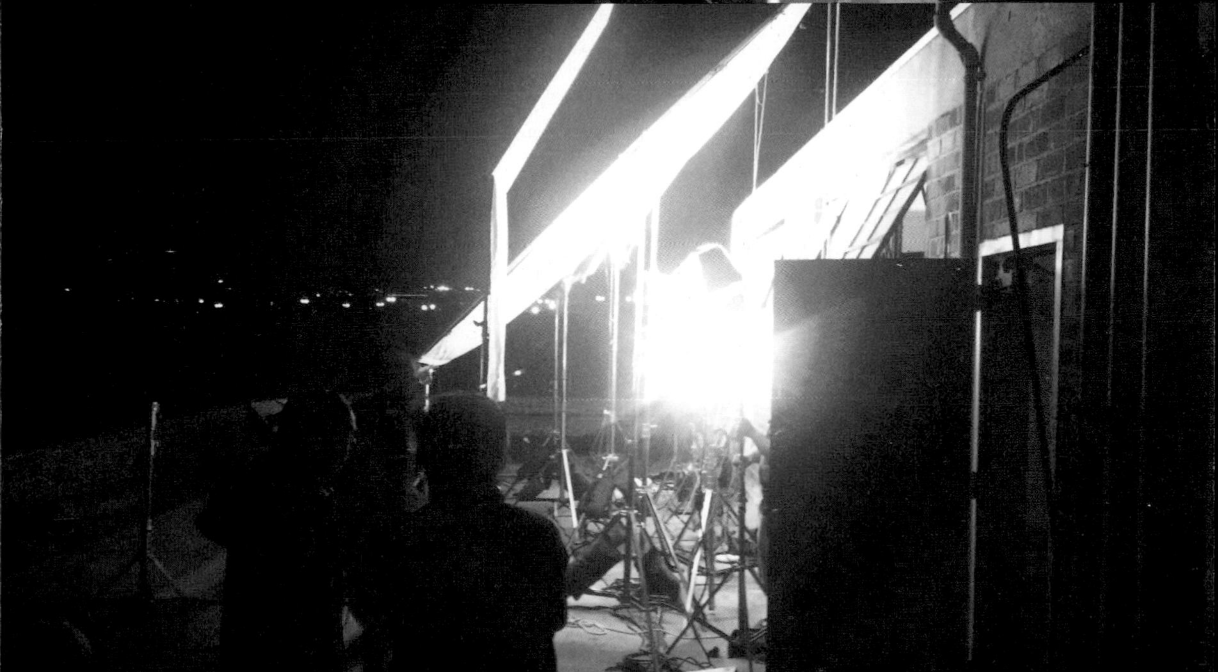

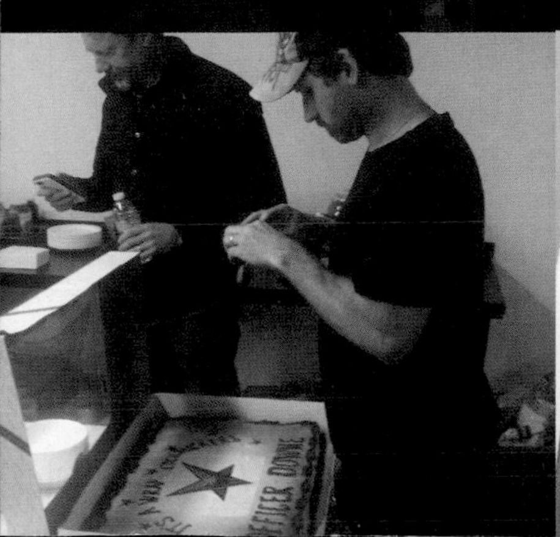

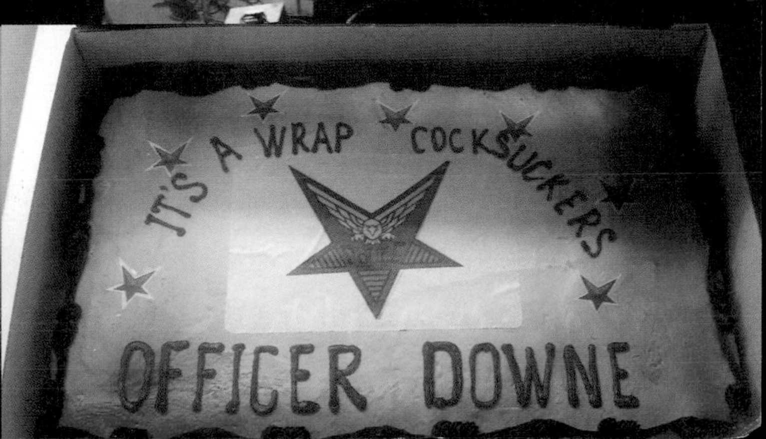
IT'S A WRAP COCKSUCKERS
OFFICER DOWNE

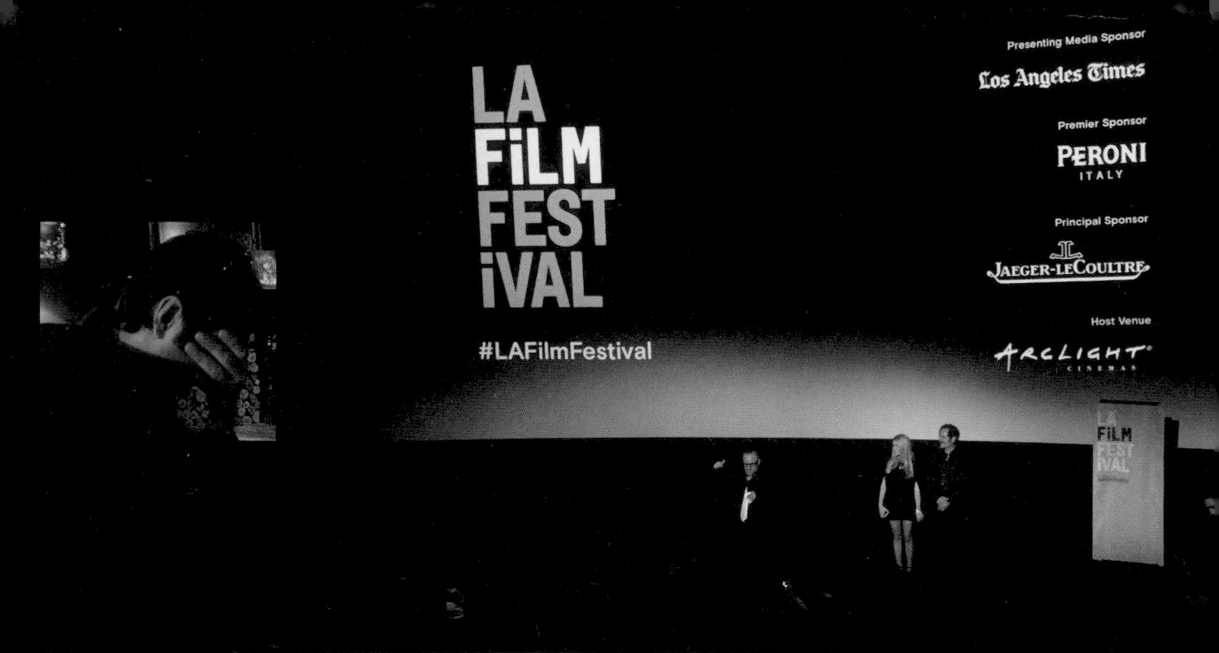
LA
FiLM
FEST
iVAL
#LAFilmFestival
Presenting Media Sponsor
Los Angeles Times
Premier Sponsor
PERONI
ITALY
Principal Sponsor
JAEGER-LECOULTRE
Host Venue
ARCLIGHT
CINEMAS
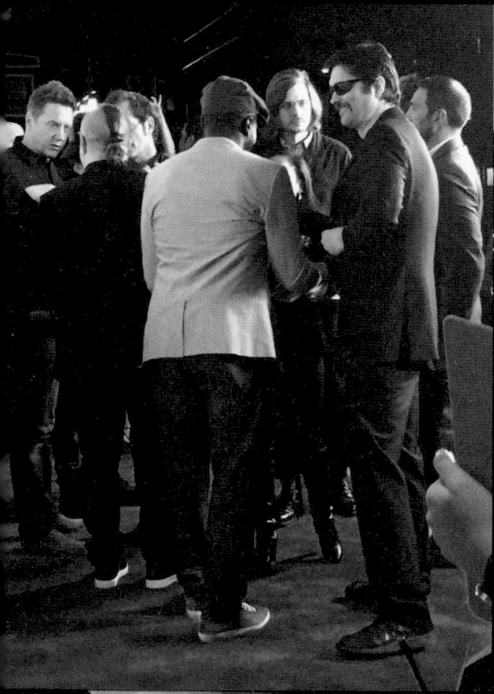
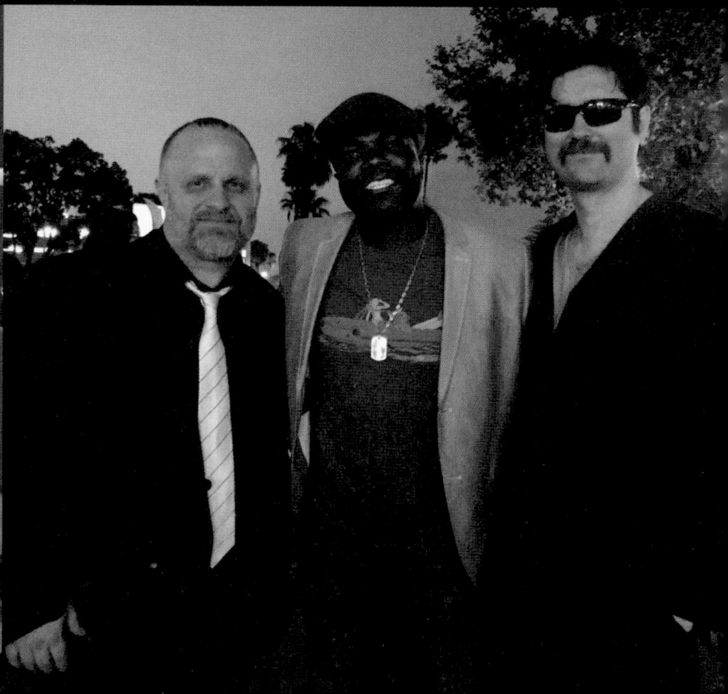
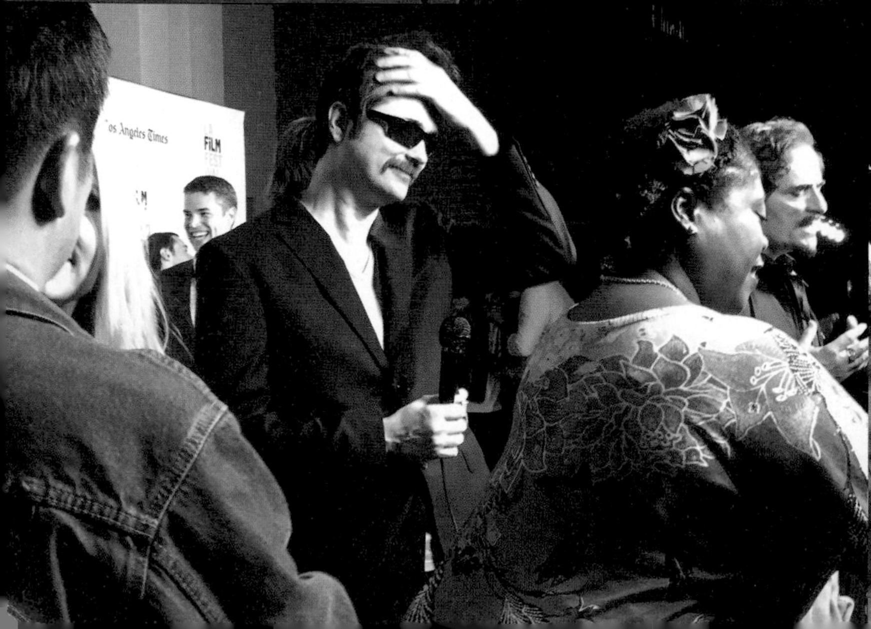
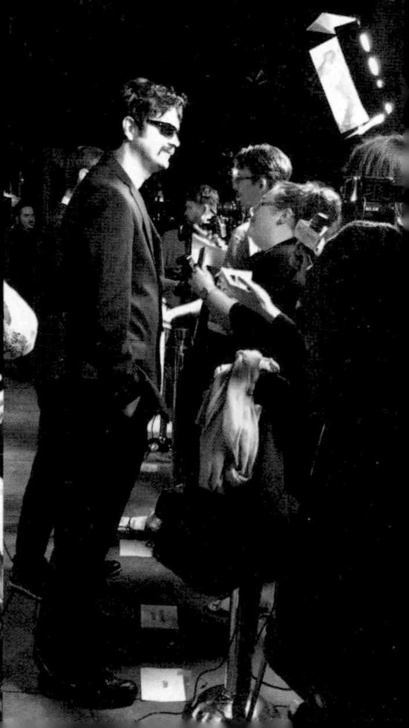

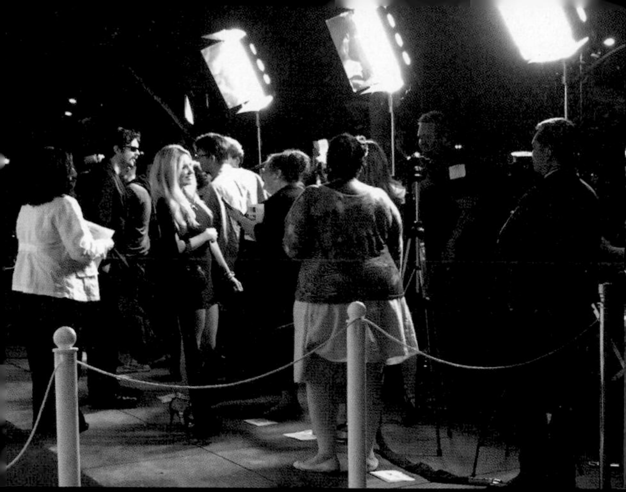

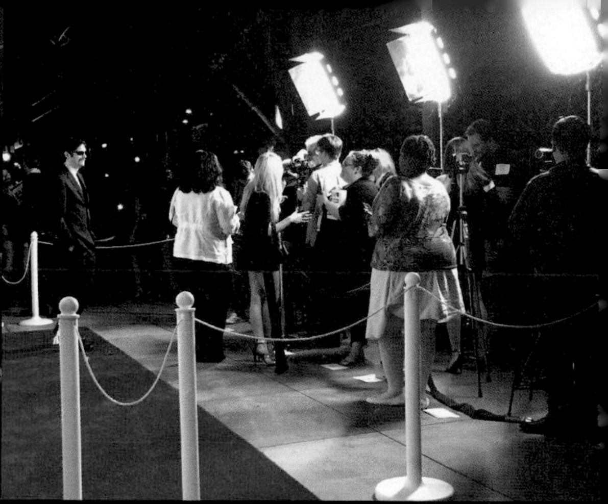

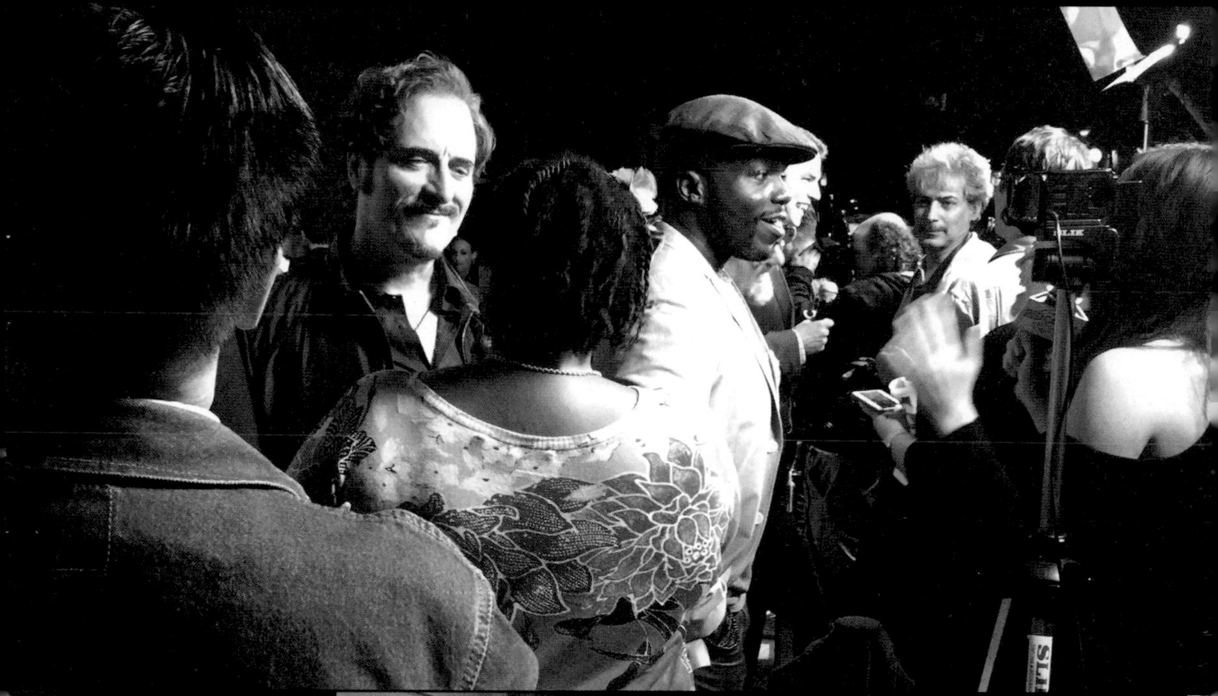

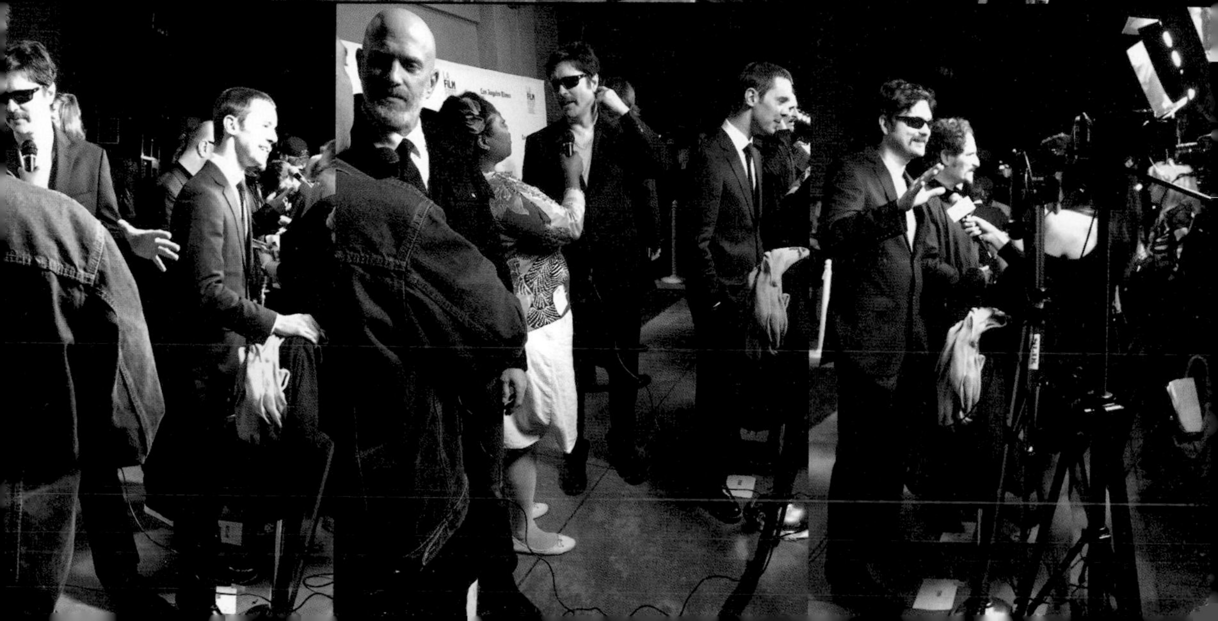

# BIOGRAPHIES

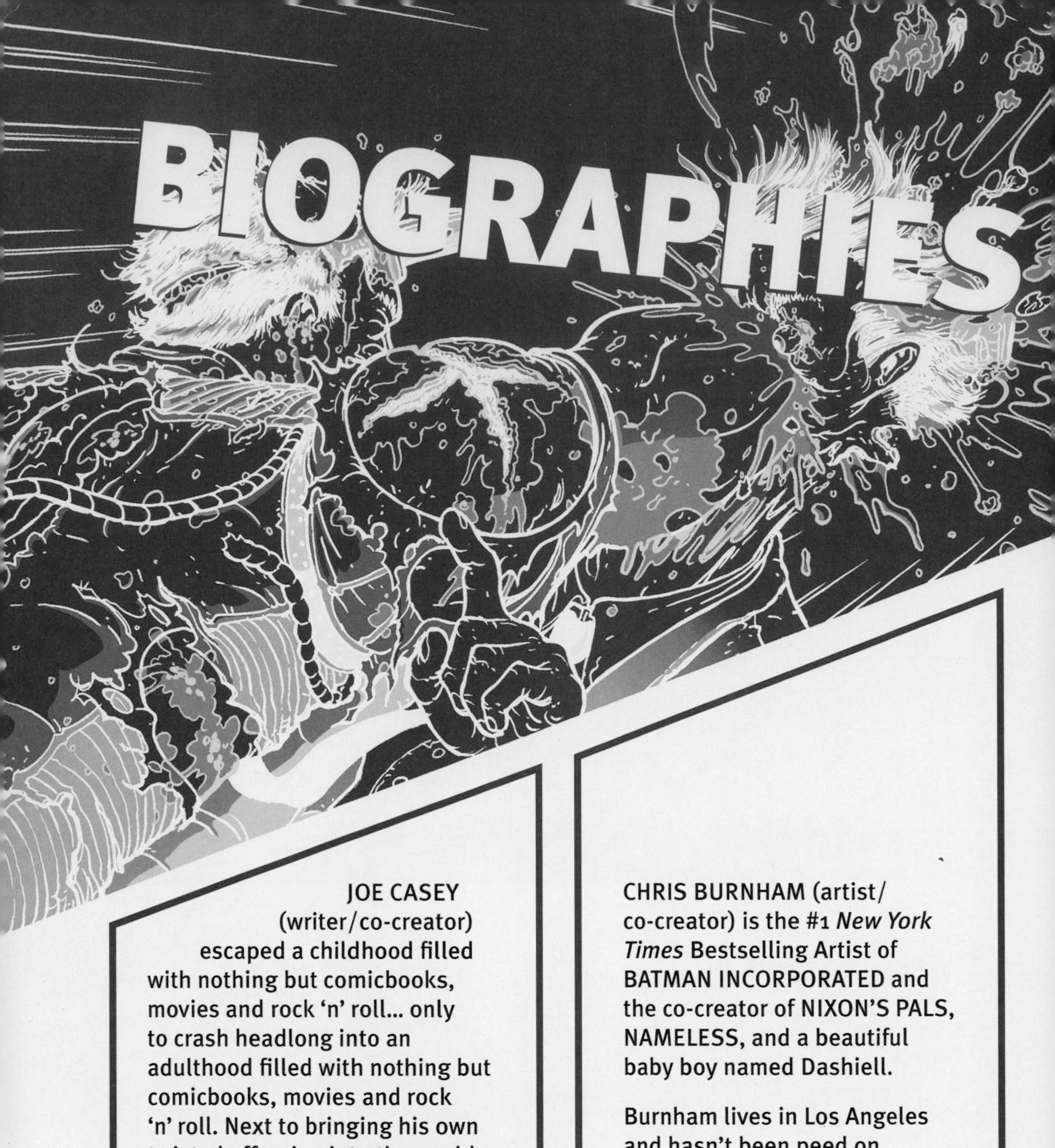

JOE CASEY (writer/co-creator) escaped a childhood filled with nothing but comicbooks, movies and rock 'n' roll... only to crash headlong into an adulthood filled with nothing but comicbooks, movies and rock 'n' roll. Next to bringing his own twisted offspring into the world, finding a way to get paid for his interests is his greatest personal achievement. As a founding partner in Man of Action Entertainment, he also moonlights as a writer/producer in the field of televised entertainment.

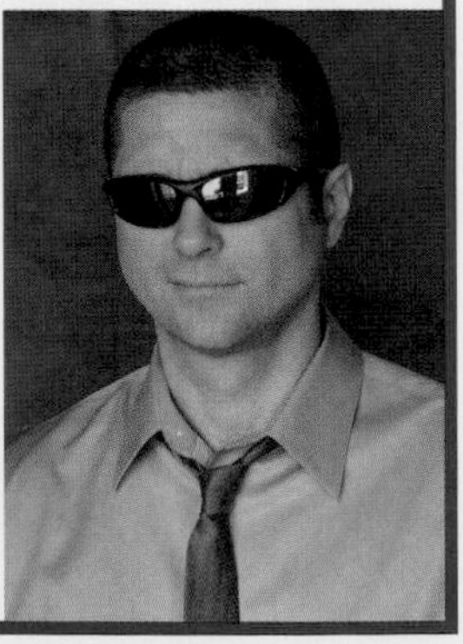

CHRIS BURNHAM (artist/co-creator) is the #1 *New York Times* Bestselling Artist of BATMAN INCORPORATED and the co-creator of NIXON'S PALS, NAMELESS, and a beautiful baby boy named Dashiell.

Burnham lives in Los Angeles and hasn't been peed on in weeks.

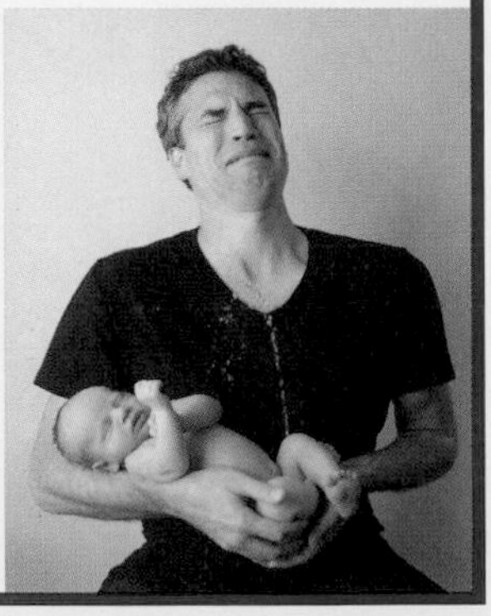

MARC LETZMANN (colorist) is a graphic designer and comicbook colorist who began his career as an assistant to Bill Crabtree. Since then, he has juggled both careers, as well as a variety of other pursuits. His first full-length comicbook coloring work was CHARLATAN BALL. He has also contributed to CODEFLESH and DOC BIZARRE, M.D. He has been referred to as "a smart ass" by Robert Kirkman and once slept on Joe Casey's fold-out sofa bed. He currently lives in San Diego, California.

RUS WOOTON (letters) has been a letterer since 2003, currently hunkered down in Los Angeles. He spends most of his time sitting at his Mac lettering for the likes of Joe Casey... as well as for Image, Marvel and Dark Horse. Drawing and writing keep him sane while Dr Pepper, iTunes and Netflix are largely responsible for keeping him in a state of semi-consciousness. He's available for paid endorsement of the aforementioned products and/or services.

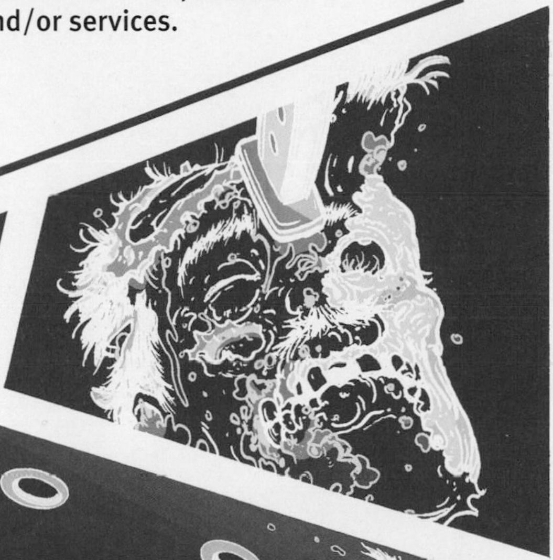

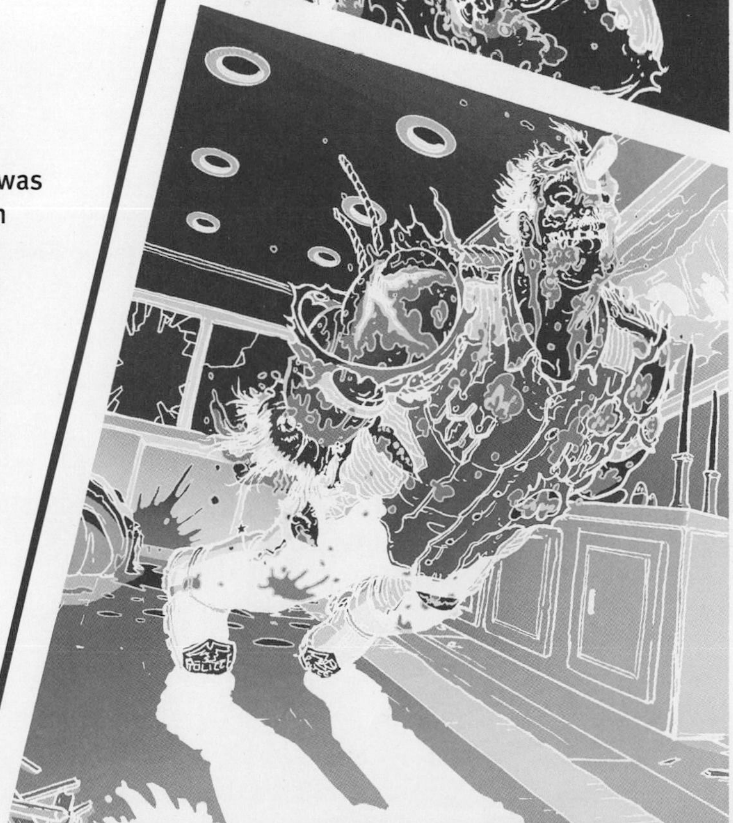

SONIA HARRIS (book and logo design, photography) was conceived in New York, born in London and lives in Los Angeles. She is the graphic designer of many books, websites, ad campaigns, infographics and identities. Comicbook designs include NIXON'S PALS, BUTCHER BAKER THE RIGHTEOUS MAKER and SEX.

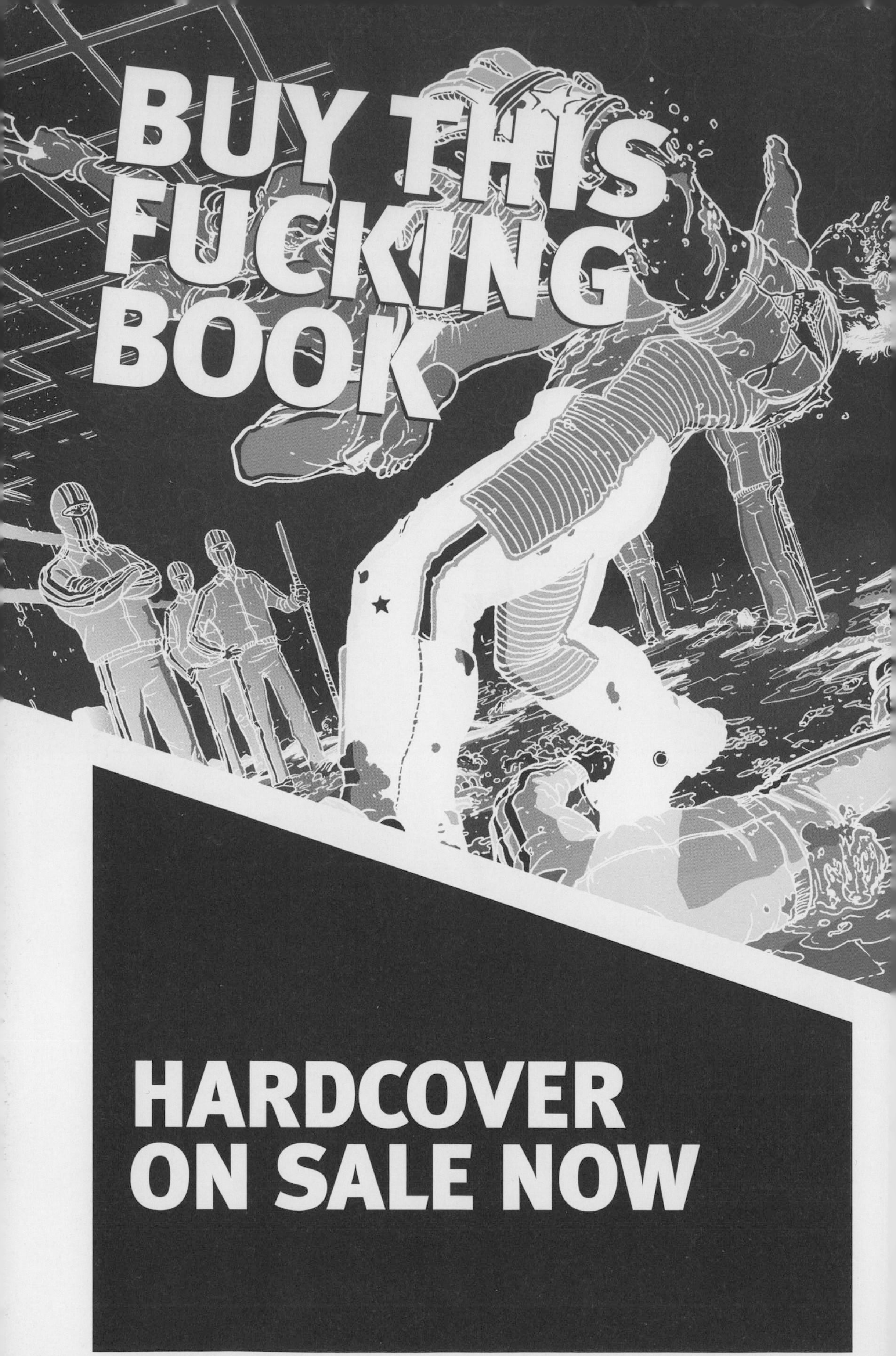
BUY THIS
FUCKING
BOOK

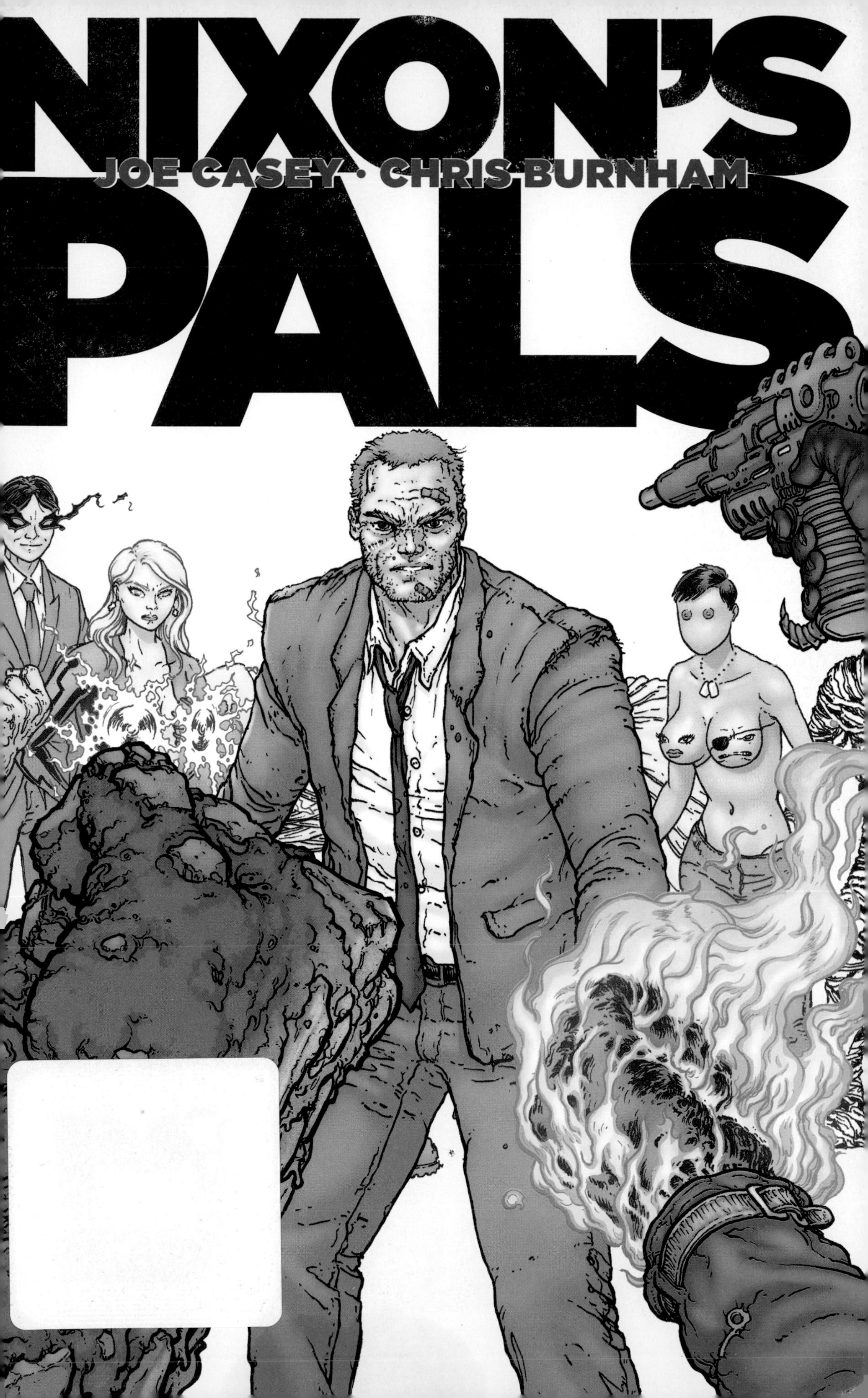
NIXON'S
JOE CASEY · CHRIS BURNHAM
PALS

# BY THE SAME AUTHORS

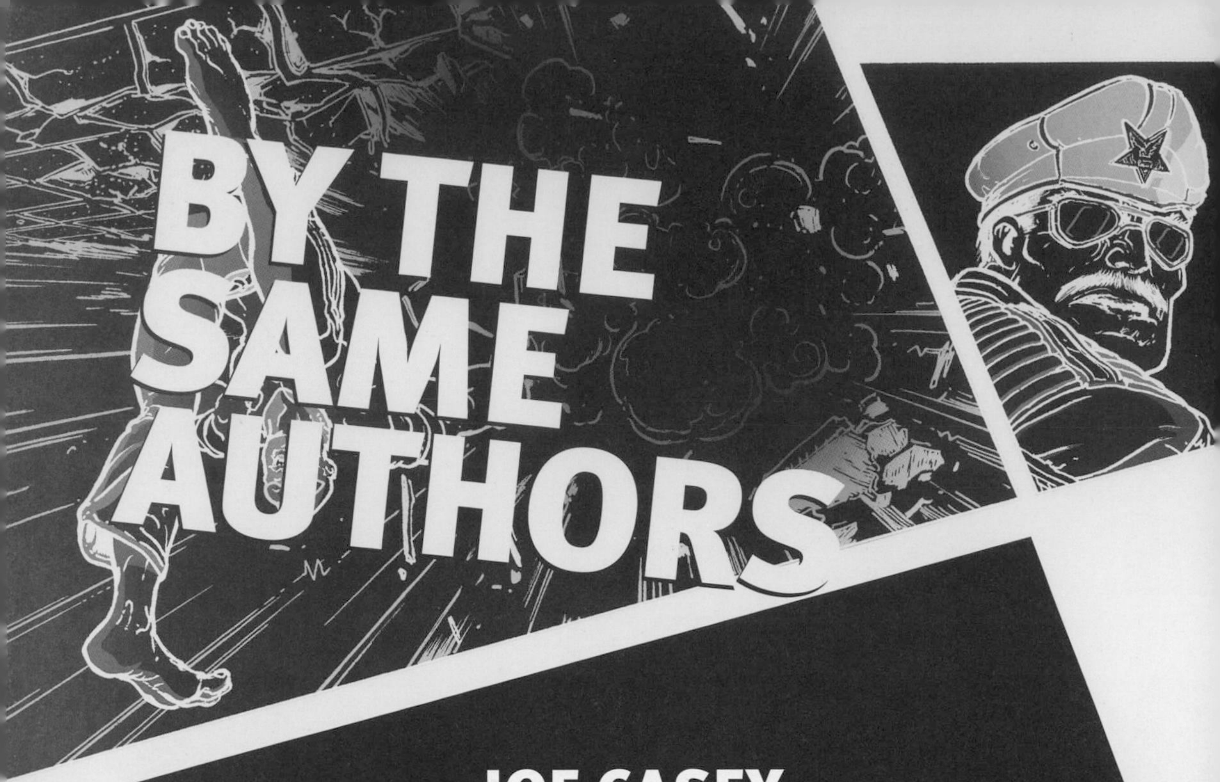

## JOE CASEY

CODEFLESH WITH CHARLIE ADLARD
ROCK BOTTOM WITH CHARLIE ADLARD
KRASH BASTARDS WITH AXEL 13
NIXON'S PALS WITH CHRIS BURNHAM
CHARLATAN BALL WITH ANDY SURIANO
DOC BIZARRE, M.D. WITH ANDY SURIANO
THE MILKMAN MURDERS
WITH STEVE PARKHOUSE
FULL MOON FEVER
WITH CALEB GERARD/DAMIAN COUCEIRO
BUTCHER BAKER THE RIGHTEOUS MAKER
WITH MIKE HUDDLESTON
THE BOUNCE WITH DAVID MESSINA
VALHALLA MAD WITH PAUL MAYBURY
SEX WITH PIOTR KOWALSKI

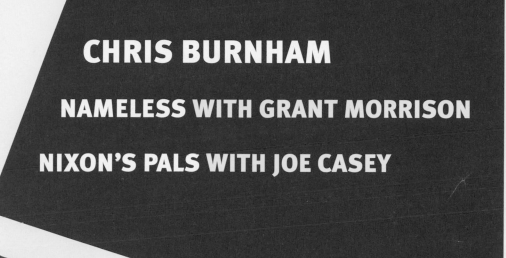

## CHRIS BURNHAM

### NAMELESS WITH GRANT MORRISON

### NIXON'S PALS WITH JOE CASEY

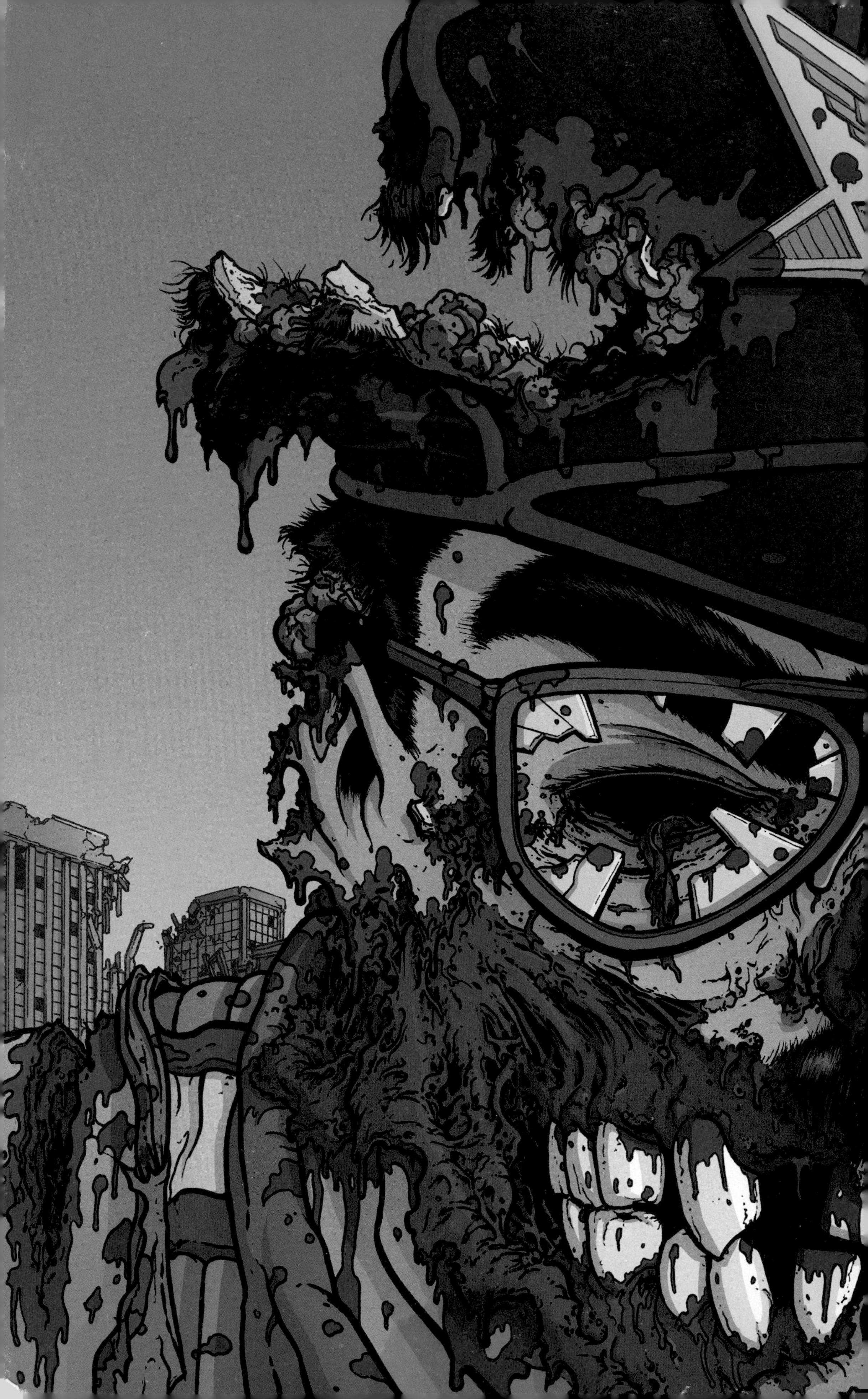